Argyle Gargoyles

A Darkly Humorous Novel
Scott Nolan

ISBN-10: 1481118226
EAN13: 9781481118224

LCCN: 2013900662
CreateSpace Independent Publishing Platform,
North Charleston, SC

Acknowledgments

Thanks to Natasha Fondren from The eBook Artisans and Melanie Hooyenga from Ink Slinger Designs for all of their help in creating this eBook. Thanks also to Jon Nowak and Josh Preston from Oh Boy Records and James Knerr from Bug Music for helping me reprint some great John Prine lyrics, but then again, they're all great.

Aw Heck
Written by John Prine
(c) 1978 BIG EARS MUSIC (ASCAP) and BRUISED ORANGES MUSIC (ASCAP)/both Administered by BUG MUSIC
All Rights Reserved   Used by Permission
Reprinted by Permission of Hal Leonard Corporation

How Lucky Can One Man Get
Written by John Prine
(c) 1979 BIG EARS MUSIC (ASCAP) and BRUISED ORANGES MUSIC (ASCAP)/both Administered by BUG MUSIC
All Rights Reserved   Used by Permission
Reprinted by Permission of Hal Leonard Corporation

Fish And Whistle
Written by John Prine
(c) 1978 BIG EARS MUSIC (ASCAP) and BRUISED ORANGES MUSIC (ASCAP)/both Administered by BUG MUSIC
All Rights Reserved   Used by Permission
Reprinted by Permission of Hal Leonard Corporation

Contents

'Once upon a time' is a bloody bad way to start a story.

"Ho, Citizen! What seems to be the furor?" the cool-headed sloth queried the frantic schoolteacher. They were on the sidewalk, scrutinizing the uproar some three blocks down Main Street. A small crowd had gathered to watch.

"Oh, it's terrible!" she replied to the little Bolivian mammal. She politely nodded to the tall, dark-skinned man who stood silently behind the sloth. He leaned on a staff-like pole which bent horizontally at eye level. It was upon this structure the sloth hung suspended, as sloths do, upside down by his toes.

"Dr. Krumm has unleashed a ferocious land squid on our fair city!" she continued. "I've never seen one so huge. It demolished the children's playground and the school, and now it's tearing the steeple off the West End Chapel." She began to sob. "It's horrible, just, just horrible. We're so helpless. We can't stop it, nobody can stop it!"

Our hero needed to hear no more.

"Do not fear, gentle educational instructor," the sloth soothed in his smooth baritone voice. He unbuttoned his *trenchcoat (which isn't easy to do with your toes, even if you're not hanging upside down), and handed it along with his fedora to Trini, the tall one.*

Indeed, this was no ordinary creature hanging from a pole borne aloft by an unusually tall foreigner. Imagine how the crowd gasped when they saw the purple cape tied to the sloth's neck. Marvel at the schoolteacher's surprise when she saw the letters 'SS' shaved out of the hair on that fuzzy underbelly. Envision, if you can, the way the masses gazed upward, their eyes following the sloth's ascent as he took to the air in one mighty swoop.

"It's a gopher"

"It's an armadillo!"

"It's a mucket!"

While the rest of the crowd puzzled over whatever the hell a mucket was, the schoolteacher realized to whom she'd been speaking.

"Oh my goodness," she said, blinking her eyes behind her cut glass encrusted pussycat bifocals. Tugging excitedly at the chain that hung from them and draped around her neck, the words spurted from her mouth; "It's Super Sloth!"

Yes, it was Super Sloth, the greatest super hero and detective Bolivia had ever known. Acquiring his extraordinary physical capabilities and powers of deductive reasoning by ingesting genetically mutated yareta shrubs, he normally spent his time cracking crime capers and rereading his favorite Mickey Spillane novels. But some months ago (issue 148?), with the help of Mighty Minnow, Super Sloth decoded

Dr. Krumm's technoputer and discovered his scheme for planetary domination. Thus he knew where Krumm would first attack, so here he lay in waiting in the small town of Metzgerville, Minnesota.

"Fret not, oh Good People." Super Sloth hovered above them. "I will save you from this wretched beast!" A battle thought by many to last at least three pages became a quick, one-sided massacre. The land squid, seeing SS's approach, flung the steeple at him. SS caught it and tossed it aside, clear of the ever-growing crowd. It then pointed all eight tentacles in SS's direction, but he dodged and ducked the flinging whips of the crazed creature. Quicker than a Boy Scout, he tied all but one of the squid's legs into a myriad of knots. Gripping the free one, he spun the invertebrate around and around. With a final shrill cry of victory, he flung the huge behemoth into space.

"We're saved!" they cried.

"Super Sloth for President!" they cheered.

"What's a mucket?" they asked.

As the celebration continued, a man in the crowd briskly walked back to his car, got in, and sped away. As Metzgerville got smaller in his rear view mirror, Dr. Krumm gritted his teeth inside his prognathous jaw and vowed, "I'll get you someday, Super Sloth!"

The phone rang. It startled Cliff, who immediately thrust his comic book under a neat stack of newspapers on the coffee table. He was alone in his own house, yet he was in constant fear of being caught reading one. Of course, he knew who was interrupting him. Who else ever calls him? He got that uneasy feeling again, like when he sensed a sneeze coming on in the middle of brushing his teeth.

"Hello, Clifford. How are you, baby?"

"Fine, fine, and yourself?"

"Fine, thank you, dear. It's so nice of you to ask." She actually made that sound sincere. Cliff hated the boring overtones that hung above every conversation he had with his mother. "I'm just calling to see how you are and to make sure you remembered you've been invited to dinner tonight. You are coming, aren't you?" Her tone was like the tip of a knife placed between his ribs.

What's the big deal, he thought. He'd eaten dinner there for the first eighteen years of his life. Why did he have to go through one more?

Sheila felt she had to speak to her son in this manner to command his attention, if nothing else. She sometimes forgot he was no longer a little boy. All Sheila wanted from her marriage to Arthur Dinsdale was money and a baby. She could handle the money neither better nor worse than anyone else who suddenly came upon a comfortable amount of free financial support. As a mother, she was too immature and inexperienced. She didn't care, let alone know, whether or not she was spoiling Cliff. Arthur could plainly see this was exactly what she was doing, but he was Sheila's baby. At her own insistence, she was to be the one to raise Clifford. He was her toy. Arthur had Clifford's half-brother and sister from his first marriage to play with. Cliff would always remember the day when his half-sister Priscilla (he used to call her 'Prissyilla') told him that her mother and his mother were not the same. That knowledge made for a confusing childhood which peaked at the appearance of what was to be Cliff's saving grace. Had he remained the victim of

Sheila's attention, a totally ruined life might've ensued. But like a little child, Sheila discarded her old toy when a new one came along. The new toy was called Elliot. Cliff was abandoned by his own mother and never even gained the attention of his father.

"Yes, I remembered you invited me to dinner, Mother," Cliff tried to copy her sincerity. "It's at seven, right?"

"No, dear, it's at eight," she snapped testily. "I thought you could at least remember a dinner appointment with your own family."

"Okay, Mother, so I forgot. I'll be there. See you at eight o'clock."

"Just one more thing, dear," she managed to slip in before Cliff got away.

"What's that, Mother?" Cliff asked with feigned curiosity. He waited through the pause, dreading the anticipated inquiry.

"What are you going to wear?"

Cliff would rather be pulling shards of glass from under his own fingernails than be putting up with this juvenile bullshit. "I was going to wear the blue suit you gave me last summer," he said.

"Why don't you wear your beige sport coat with the plaid pants I bought you. You haven't worn those yet, have you, Clifford, have you?"

"Mother, nobody wears plaid pants anymore, not even people like us. Besides, they're cut wide. They don't fit."

"Except down your throat," Cliff regretfully neglected to add.

"Well, whatever you wear you'd best look good in it. I've invited the Perrys and Sarah will be with them. I want you to at least talk to her this time."

"Mother, listen. I…"

"Do try to be on time, dear," Sheila stepped on Cliff's interruption. "And oh, Clifford darling?"

"Yes, Mother?" he sighed.

"You look so good in plaid. I'll see you tonight. Mommy loves you, baby." This was followed by the wet, smacking kiss that terminated each of their telephone conversations.

There sat Clifford Dinsdale, phone in hand. He was ready to hang it up. At twenty three his mother still tried to dress him and fix him up with the right kind of girl. That was the sole extent of her interest and attention towards him; appearances.

His father didn't care for him. Cliff represented a personal failure to him. He'd successfully remarried to a younger, more beautiful woman only to have her take over his son and run the family. He would never give the Rockefellers a run for their money, but he did have more than enough of his own. He was passed the age when most men retire, yet every morning he went to his office in town to get away from his wife. Cliff never understood why his father even had an office, because he made all his money through real estate and investments and had no job or business of which to speak. Each day he sat behind his desk in his three piece suit and lit his cigars with flaming one hundred dollar bills. It was an old stunt he really couldn't afford. He'd seen it done in a movie once, never stopping to think they might've used one phony bill whereas he was torching several real ones each week. But that's how he got his kicks and that's the important thing. His desk, drawers and otherwise empty appointment book were full of scrap papers covered with doodles. Each was signed by their creator, who added a 'III' to the end of his name. He knew that annoyed Sheila. She didn't like the idea of being married to a 'III' person. Sometimes he would add 'Esq.'. Once, in a particularly academic mood, he tacked on 'Ph. D.'. None of these titles were befitting of the bored brain that concocted them. He just thought they looked prestigious. Impressive. A Status Symbol.

Certainly, Cliff's house was too large for him alone. It had three and one half 'facilities' as the real estate agent had tactfully quoted. Cliff was presently in need of only one of them but he couldn't decide which one to use. The notion of selling the house, facilities and all, had crossed his mind but it wasn't his to sell. The bill of sale bore his father's signature. It was located an hour away from the Dinsdale Estate. It would've been even further had Sheila complied with Arthur's wishes, which might've put Cliff as far away as Greenland. Buying a house of such undue size was wholly Arthur's contribution. He hoped a large empty house might inspire in Cliff, as it did in himself, loneliness. Perhaps now Cliff would actively seek a friend, marry her and go away forever instead of always showing up for dinner at his mother's command.

As a student in public school, Cliff never attracted a great many friends. He was pleasant to others but he simply preferred to spend his time alone. He never took the time to establish the roots of a relationship with his classmates. His mother, as mothers will, began wondering if it was due to a hormonal imbalance, shades of autism or psychological withdrawal derived from secretly appearing in kiddy porn flicks to support his growing drug habit. She didn't stop to think maybe Cliff liked being alone. As his early school days plodded into high school, the friends Cliff never had time for didn't have time for him. Unaware of this fact, he decided to try crawling out of his proverbial shell when his parents transferred him to a private school.

As could be expected, Cliff didn't make much of himself at Carbleson Academy (named after a noted engineer who developed some popular automotive designs and owned the manufacturing chain of 'Carbleson/Reese Automotive; Manufacturers in Transit', affection-ately known to the boys at the academy as C.R.A.M.I.T.). His grades were decent with a potential of excellence if properly applied, as one of his teachers had put it. Once again, he didn't fit in with any of the crowds. Contrary to what his parents told him, the students at C.A. were exactly the same as those at his old school. Only the parents were different. They were richer.

Upon graduation, he was shuttled off to Breece University. He left his mother with tears in her eyes (that looked sincere), and his father with the relief he was finally getting rid of that mama's boy. Breece U. was where none other than old Carbleson himself received his BS in engineering, although at the time Cliff didn't know that. His father got his way once and insisted he go there.

He enrolled as a business major. The world will always need business majors, his father reasoned. As a rule, he thought, nothing exciting was allowed to happen to business majors. Cliff was an exception to this rule in one respect, and that respect was his roommate, Ignatius Leventhal. His only regret in life was that his name sounded too Jewish, even though that was appropriate. He had a different approach to life, Cliff noticed. Iggy was more aware, more inquisitive. He was also a jerk, but he was one of those jerks who could hold your interest just long enough to forget his foolishness for a while if you had nothing better to do.

Iggy's parents had money, but little of it was needed to get him into Breece U. He got there on a golf scholarship. 'The little nudnik is smart and he can golf, too!' he said of himself. He was a casual whiz kid in computer engineering. But what he really liked to do was to get out in the green grass and knock that little white ball around. His was a natural talent. He'd won dozens of ribbons and trophies and he would tell Cliff about them without bragging but without stopping, either. Out on the course, he truly seemed to be in his element.

He talked the rest of the time, too. Iggy taught Cliff literally all the Yiddish he knew. Cliff was fascinated by words like goya, kurveh, fonfer, knaydl, moichel, etc. He didn't care what they meant. He just liked the way they sounded. That's how he put up with Iggy's incessant *hok a tchynik.* Cliff would ignore what Iggy was talking about and simply pick up the Yiddish phrases that sprinkled his speech. Entire nights would pass in this manner. Cliff would try to study as Iggy rambled on with his putter in his hands, trying to putt the balls into the white plastic cup a few feet away. He usually missed. Besides, if he wasn't talking about his golf he was talking about girls girls girls. Even Cliff knew that anybody who talked so much about girls never talked that much to girls. Poor Iggy suffered the curse of Jewish golfers, never having much success in sinking his short putts.

After four less than successful years at Breece U., enough time to earn a degree although Cliff did not do so, he returned home. His father so enjoyed the four year vacation, he extended it by buying Cliff his own house to go home to.

And so Cliff made his way to the facility of his choice. Had he the time or the nerve, he might've called his mother to ask if she'd be interested in coming over to wipe his ass and change his diaper. "Crude, Cliff. Very crude," he said to himself before closing the door.

2

The saga of the Dinsdale family begins in seventeen seventy six in Trenton, New Jersey. It was the time of the American Revolution and the city was in the hands of the British. Well, not exactly. The British were smart. They got others to die in battle for them. As surely as the French Foreign Legion contained few Frenchmen, the army in Trenton fighting for the King contained few British soldiers. It consisted mainly of German allies, the Hessians, under the command of General Rahl. But after all, it was the British who were at war, so it was only proper that a few Redcoats be there to represent England. Captain Patrick Dinsmore and his handful of men were little more than a special envoy. It was nearing the end of December and they'd be spending a cold Christmas away from home cooped up with a bunch of foreigners, all to represent their country. In an open act of rebellion, Dinsmore staged a party on Christmas night. The Hessians were more disciplined than the Englishmen and wanted no parts of it. This pleased Dinsmore almost as much as the fact he was not under orders of the Hessian general who would outrank him if they were in the same army. As it stood, no one could stop him. Dinsmore and his men took over the only tavern in the small town.

Annie was a maid at the Red Horse Inn. It had always been known as the Smithy Inn, but they regularly changed the name to agree with the presently occupying army to avoid harassment, as was the practice of that day. It was comprised of two stories. Upstairs was the living quarters of the proprietor, Benedict Rosse. Ben was an old misfit, an outcast. Most men his age were on the King's side in this war, but Ben was wise enough to play the rebel. He reluctantly agreed to put the new sign in front of his establishment at the onset of the occupation.

Downstairs was a small bar. It was tucked against a far wall facing the door. On the adjacent wall was a large fireplace, the open hearth big enough for a grown man to step into without stooping. Ladles and pokers hung on either side and a huge cast iron pot could swing in and out of the fire on a pivoting arm. On this same wall was a set of steps which led to a back room where Ben prepared the food he could get or the freshly killed gamebirds and such that patrons brought in themselves.

The rest of the inn was a large room full of round tables and sturdy wooden chairs, the style but not quality of which would be duplicated and sold in furniture galleries two hundred years later. The two remaining walls were mostly windows covered not by curtains but by shutters on the outside. The inn was bare and undecorated. More than anything else, it looked like an Italian restaurant that hadn't opened yet, before they put out the red and white checkered tablecloths and curtains, wine casks and candles.

"It seems these red dogs can't hold their grogs," Ben whispered to Annie as he filled her tray with more fresh tankards of the hot watered down rum. The Redcoats forced them to cater their party, along with some Quaker girls who'd stayed in town.

"Ben, I'm scared. These men are getting out of control. I don't know what I'll do if one of them tries to…"

Ben cut her off sharply. "Now hold together, Annie. If any one of these swine lays a hand on you, he'll have Benedict Rosse to answer to." Annie appreciated the support, but it'd been a long time since anyone called Ben 'Big Ben' like they used to. He was an old man now, no match for even the scrawniest Redcoat.

The party went on. All the Redcoats were there, and a few Hessians actually stole away from their posts to join them. Christmas was not a time for fighting. Even the enemy rebels knew that. Those who didn't come inside were having as much fun in the streets. After weeks of waiting and watching, they were eager for action. There wasn't enough grog to go around, so they broke into the rations where they stored the medicinal whiskey. The locals had left some behind when they went, also. Soon, one of the soldiers was firing drunken volleys of musket balls at anything that moved, passing clouds, trees, loose shutters, and another poor soldier's foot. Fortunately, he was too numb from the cold and the drink to feel anything. He wouldn't feel it or anything else the next morning, either.

"Fetch me some more grog, wench!" a stuporous Patrick Dinsmore bellowed to no one wench in particular. He wiped his chin with his sleeve then slammed his tankard down on the table like a hammer on an anvil. It shattered, leaving only the handle clamped in his dumb, burly fist. He stared at it with glassy eyes, wondering where the rest of the mug was. The crash woke up one of his fellow officers across the table.

"Ere now, Patty! What's all the ruckus fer?" His crude accent was more pronounced than usual.

"Whar's zat pretty maiden fair, I wants a nudder tank a grog." They all sounded more like South Seas pirates than officers in His Majesty's Army. "Wench, more grog!" Dinsmore shouted.

Annie was nearly petrified. The men were too unruly and there was no way she and the other girls could keep up with them. They were short handed while two girls were forced to help a soldier in the corner by the fireplace. His foot was bleeding profusely and no one knew why.

As she headed back towards the bar with her empty mugs, Annie almost walked passed Patrick Dinsmore's table. He reached out and grabbed her by her long skirt. She fell as Dinsmore pulled her towards himself, forcing the tray to fall and shatter at her feet.

"I said fetch me some more grog, bitch!" He ripped a stretch of her skirt as he pulled the struggling Annie closer. Through the hole in her skirt, he caught a glimpse of her thick, naked thigh. Suddenly his thoughts were turned away from drinking.

"Please sir, I beg you don't hurt me. I'm sorry sir. Please let go and I'll fetch a fresh round of drinks just for you! Oh please, you're hurting me!" Annie was horrified of this brute who held her so tightly. Dinsmore didn't realize his own strength, bruising Annie's arm as he eyed her hidden womanly figure. The commotion had arrested the attention of those who were still conscious. They stopped their conversations to observe the scene.

"Please sir, let go!" There was a tear of fear in Annie's eye.

"Lemme get a better look at yer pretty face," Dinsmore slurred as he pulled her lips to his in a sloppy kiss.

"Aye! Dinsy's got 'er now!" his friend cried out. The comment drew cheers and whistles from the rest. They were delighted with the show. The soldier with the bleeding foot ventured to cheer, but the best he could do was moan, so they gave him another drink.

Old Ben could stand no more. He approached the hefty Dinsmore and attempted to loose his one-handed grip on Annie. With his free arm, Dinsmore swatted at the old innkeeper, knocking him into and over a table and three Redcoats. All but those three Redcoats cheered.

But the distraction had been enough. Annie wrenched her arm free and made a mad dash for the door. She escaped the clutches of three or four soldiers before she made it outside. She was running in a frenzy and stumbled off the landing and over the single step that led to the ground. She might have regained her balance had she not run into what she thought at first was another Redcoat. Upon toppling to the ground, even her dazed senses could tell her what she'd run into was probably the only successful snowman those Goddamned drunken bastards had accomplished. Wracked with fear and cold, she lay there motionless, her hands gripping the snow.

Dinsmore would've easily walked through the door had someone not opened it for him. Stepping out onto the landing with two not so innocent bystanders, he caught two soldiers picking Annie up out of the snow. She was not crying. Her eyes were closed fast, her hands still clenching the snow she'd hoped would have held her to the ground and prevented her from being carried away. She was afraid she knew what they were going to do with her.

"That there's mine, lads," Dinsmore proclaimed.

"We found her, go get your own," they said. Dinsmore was not pleased but his mind was too distracted to respond.

"Come on, there's plenty for all of us," suggested a more adventurous participant. One soldier carried Annie while four more followed him through the night to a nearby stable. Once inside (a foul place, Annie had always considered it), the soldier carrying her promptly dropped her, spilling her like a bunch of sticks. He then proceeded to fall straight backwards. The exertion was too much on his drunken frame and he passed out immediately.

"Well now, that just means there's more fer us!" Dinsmore exclaimed. He let out a lascivious laugh and rubbed his cold hands together as he eyed Annie with a consuming desire.

Annie's eyes were still closed and she had no intention of opening them. She shivered with both fright and the cold as her dress was torn from her. She lay there rigid, at first unable to sense how her body warmed the earth beneath her. If numbness can be felt, as pain can be felt, Annie felt numb. She was full of deadened nerves. It was as if her body had already been attacked and those friendly natural defenses that all humans possess were dulling all sensations. Yet she was aware of the first body as its weight pressed her harder to the straw and dirt floor of the musty stables. The pressure made her dizzy. As her head swam around, she realized she wasn't hearing anything. It wasn't as if she couldn't hear, but that there was little sound to hear. She felt like she was far underwater and had to imagine the sounds from above that reached her as muffled grunts.

Her other senses slowed down as the weight shifted on top of her. If she'd opened her eyes, although she dared not do that yet, she was sure she'd see nothing. Annie later thought of her condition during the rape as a blessing. She was somewhat spared the torture of it.

Actually, she was both surprised and ashamed because she didn't feel uncomfortable at all. She was amused, oddly not in a sexual manner but in a way of childlike curiosity. She was not in a horse stable being violated by enemies, she was in her own world alone. Whatever was happening, she couldn't say it frightened her in the way she thought it should.

She soon lost herself. Now all she thought about was the tremendous strain in her groin. A dull ache began to develop where earlier there had been nothing more than the slightest notion of physical presence. Her mind reeled as she tried to wake up and she slipped away in the struggle. Before passing out, she imagined the ground shook with a thundering vibration, rubbing each part of her skin that came in contact with the warm soil. Not knowing if she was still awake, she imagined sharp cracks like so many little explosions, and the rush of many men.

To herself, she appeared to wake up right away. Actually, a few hours had passed, the numbness had been peeled away and throbbing aches sunk deep into her body. The first perception she noticed was in her legs. She knew they were uncovered for they were dreadfully cold. She winced at her effort to close them from their spread eagle position. It took a full ten minutes to bring them side by side, but the bloated feeling between her thighs would not go away.

She sat up in the dim morning light which came in through the cracks in the walls. She found she was naked up to the waist and surprised she was fully clothed otherwise. Her upper body was just as cold as the rest of her, and she recalled she hadn't had the chance to grab her wrap as she ran out of the Red Horse. Her torn garments lay nearby. She swathed them around her as best as she could manage, knocking off the straw that clung to her legs. She looked around from her sitting position. The Redcoat who had carried her inside lay just a few feet away, curled into a harmless fetal position. Finally, she began to hear the commotion outside. The many voices startled her. She backed away when she thought she heard a horse approaching. Her suspicions were confirmed when she watched its shadow and that of its rider pass by on the floor near the open door.

Annie made her way to the back of the stables as fast as she could. She didn't know who was out there but she could hear there were quite a few of them and they apparently didn't know she was among them. One thing she'd learned during this war as towns were taken over first by one army and then the other was to not trust anyone. She knew a horse once kicked several boards loose in the rear wall and she planned to make her silent escape there when she realized something peculiar.

A stable is a building for horses. She was in a stable. There were no horses in this building.

Why were there no horses? Had she the time to gather her wits, Annie would've remembered there were no horses when she first entered the stables last night with the soldiers. No whinnies or gurgles, bucking or clamoring. Had the soldiers not been so drunk or lust-bent, they also might've noticed the absence of their steeds. Annie's aroused curiosity was drawing her back to the open doors and the faraway light that wedged between them.

With shards of cloth that were once a skirt wrapped around her, she shuffled forward. She wasn't paying attention to anything but the door and she stumbled into her unconscious stablemate. He was hardly well rested but jumped right up when most of Annie fell on him instead of over him. She panicked, thinking he would call his compatriots. This fear dissolved when she saw the expression on his face. He wore the look of a man who was terminally deep under water, struggling with no chance of reaching the surface before taking his wet, fatal last breath. It both scared Annie and evoked a certain sympathy for him. She'd been experiencing a similar sensation only hours earlier. But the soldier looked so pitiful and frightened. Annie could not have known why.

Without even acknowledging Annie's presence, he scurried towards the open door and popped through like a frightened animal. What Annie then heard surprised her the most. A man's voice shouted 'There's one, over there!'. Then the Redcoat was apparently thrown against the outside wall. She couldn't tell the soldier had thrown himself against the wall, hoping no one would see him. He was paralyzed with fear, not unlike the animal he'd reminded Annie of earlier.

There were cracks between the vertical boards of the walls wide enough to admit light. The interruption of this light in its particular intervals gave Annie a rough outline of the body that was pressed against it. The Redcoat was clearly crouched down close to the ground. 'Stop, stop I say!' a voice shouted. She could hear and see the Redcoat shuffling in the snow. 'Stop!' the voice repeated. The next sound Annie heard was familiar to her. Close by, a musket discharged. The Redcoat pushed so hard against the wall Annie was sure he'd break through and fall back into the stable. After a few seconds, the wooden boards creaked back into place as the shadow disappeared from the cracks.

The ordeal was followed by a rousing cheer from a nearby group of men. Annie's greatest hope opened up inside of her. She inched towards the door and peeked outside. Minutemen were everywhere. Some stood in groups, others rushed in and out of various buildings.

The American rebels came back! The silly British didn't expect an attack on Christmas night, let alone in Trenton. Annie was so overjoyed she almost cried. As she bowed her head she saw another surprise. Contrary to today's history books which claim not a shot was fired, two more bodies lay stiffened in the snow. Annie didn't recognize the first one as it was face down. The second one was clearly Dinsmore. A patch over the left breast of his coat was, well, redder than the rest. This was accompanied by a dark area of snow that crawled out from under Dinsmore's massive, unmoving chest. Dinsmore and his men must've run out on foot, the Minutemen having stolen their horses to prevent any Hessians or Redcoats from escaping. Annie's eyes were still adjusting to the bright light when she became aware of something lying on the dead soldier's groin. With squinted eyes she recognized what it was. Her relief came out in bursts of hysterical laughter. Dinsmore had literally been caught with his pants down.

Annie's wild, almost insane amusement could not be contained. Her bantering and gibbering soon caught the attention of the nearby Minutemen. They rode over to the joyful noise coming from the stables. Two of them dismounted and entered, muskets cocked and ready. The found Annie dancing around half naked, kicking up straw from the floor. It caught them by surprise but from the condition of Dinsmore's corpse they easily guessed what had transpired.

"Beggin' your pardon, Miss," one spoke, finding it hard to hold his concentration. "They didn't hurt you none, did they now?" He took his hat off in the presence of what was unmistakably a lady and covered his eyes.

"No, no, I'm all right," Annie laughed. She didn't care. Her laughter was soon joined by that of the Minutemen outside when they saw Dinsmore's embarrassing last stand.

The days that followed were ones of rebuilding lives and reassured securities, hoping that the war would not come to the town again. The residents returned, as did some of the soldiers. Annie's brother, Paul, did not return. The Minutemen reoccupied the town and The Red Horse became the Smithy Inn again, much to the delight of one Benedict Rosse. Several bodies were disposed of and a few watchtowers the Hessians had hurriedly constructed were taken down just as quickly.

Since the night in the stables, Annie felt different. She felt a change that was both physical and mental. She knew what had happened to her, even if it was the first time. Or maybe it was the first four times if all the Redcoats got a turn. She had no way of knowing. She hated them for what they did to her, but she would've been happy had it been with anyone else. She'd often wondered what it was like. She had to tell someone, so she told her father. She would've spoken to her friends, but none of them had ever done anything like that before, or had it done to them as was Annie's case. Besides, you were supposed to be a wife before you did those things. She was no wife. She received little help from her father.

The few people who had stayed behind during the Hessian occupation did so because they were Quakers. They were impartial and had no place in the war. Annie was not a Quaker. She stayed so she could take care of her father, Henry, who was too ill to be moved. He'd been on the decline since his wife Hester died long ago. She was his true love and her death was slowly killing him to this very day. Paul's death (to Annie, her brother was just missing; to her melancholy father, he was dead) nearly finished him off, as did Annie's news of her encounter with the soldiers. So it was with great anxiety and caution that Annie broke the news to her infirm father. She'd made sense of her physical condition at last.

"Father?" Annie began softly, sitting down on a stool next to her father's bed.

"Yes, my dearest Annie?" Henry was always too dramatic. His limp arm reached out for Annie's hand both for support and theatrical effect. She placed it back down at his side.

"Father, I have something to tell you," she pressed on slowly.

"Yes, of course, dear," he muffled through his shaggy white mustache.

"It is very important," she stressed.

"You can say anything you wish to me, dear. Remember, I'm your Mother."

"Father," Annie corrected him.

"Huh?"

"You're my Father."

"Yes," Henry agreed, already forgetting his first mistake.

"I'm glad I have you to talk to," she said.

"That's what Mothers are for, child."

"Father..."

"Huh?'

"I have to tell you about, it's..."

"Oh go on, Annie, speak. Just don't mention anything about those British bastards. I hate them, you know. They killed your brother, I know it! And they raped you! I hate them, I say! Hate them, hate them!"

Annie didn't realize her mother, uh, father had enough energy for such a display of emotion. Practically sitting up in bed, he thrashed his arms up and down, pounding the mattress until Annie thought he'd rip the cloth, sending a flurry of feathers and sawdust into the air. He hurled curses at the ugly hoard of humanity that called itself His Majesty's Army. Annie knew her father hated the British. Many people did. She simply didn't realize he was so severe about it. But she did have to admit it made sense. The man had lost one son and one daughter's virginity due to the insolent British. His hampered mind probably blamed them somehow for his Hester's death, too.

"Father, stop that! Father!" Annie got a hold of his flailing arms. "I have something to tell you." At his daughter's continual request, Henry ceased his pillow pounding and laid back like an obedient puppy. She half expected him to whimper. "Father, I'm…"

"Yes, Annie, what was it you wanted to tell me?"

Annie tried to slip around her father's unintentional interruptions. "Do you recall what happened to me that night when I told you our soldiers came back and recaptured the town? Remember I told you all about it?"

Henry's face still wore those sad puppy eyes for a moment until a sudden recollection erased them. They were replaced with the eyes of young fury he'd worn just minutes earlier. He raised his fists but Annie was able to calm him down before he got into his tantrum full tilt again.

"Yes, yes, I remember that," he said somberly. He was out of breath from his second exertion. He stared fixedly ahead, not at Annie but at some point beyond the wall.

"Father," Annie spoke with falsely mustered courage, "I am going to have a child."

"A child," Henry repeated the fact of the matter. His failing memory recalled the birth of a child as a happy occasion. "I'm very happy for you, dear. Very happy indeed."

This time, Annie knew what was happening. She knew her father this well at least, anymore. Conveying an idea to Henry was comparable to kicking a rock from a high cliff down into a sluggish river far below. Annie knew the rock was falling, she'd kicked it. She also knew it hadn't hit the water yet. Oh, what a big rock it was.

"But I didn't know you had a husband Annie." He stared more intently.

"I don't, Father." Her head followed her eye's gaze to the floor.

"But you've never done that sort of thing before, have you?"

"The British, Father. On Christmas night." The rock was seconds away from the water's surface.

"British? Christmas night?" He played with the words "Then it must've been…"

Kersplash!

Henry took a deep, jagged breath. "No! Nooooo!" he wailed. This time Annie could not subdue his outburst. "Such a horrible calamity, how could it have happened? Oh no, it cannot, it mustn't be so!" He regressed into the dramatics of overacting. He beat the bed until he collapsed. Annie left in tears as her father lay in his bed in a quiet, tired agony. She was so sorry to have upset him but she was in no mood to ease his mind.

The weeks and the war went on. Annie and Henry spoke only once more about the baby. Henry did all the talking.

"You'll not be using my name for the child, Annie. Its Father is a Redcoat and I'll not besmirch the Willison name by letting you bestow it upon a child of such vile conception. As far as I want to know, it is a bastard not worthy of my name."

Thus spoke Henry.

Annie viewed her father's speech with all the fierce contempt with which it was wrought. She considered it final in nature, which it very much was. Knowing her father was too stubborn to budge on the issue, if he could remember the issue, she set to work on the new problem. What was to be the child's name?

The first name was easy. Like most young ladies, Annie had always fancied a name for her first child. If it was a boy, she chose Benjamin.

A girl would be Sada. But what of the last name? It had never been a concern. Her child would take the name of her husband, as she would upon their marriage. But there was no marriage and consequently no husband. The closest thing she had was one of several Redcoats lying in a communal grave miles away. All she had to work with was death and memories. She quickly resolved to work on the latter.

She sat alone one night caressing her womb, searching back to that winter night months ago. She wanted a name with some significance, not just any random title. The old gossip mongers were already gawking about her pregnancy without a husband. She dared not use any of her friends' names for fear of incorporating them into an already shameful situation. Many of them weren't even talking to her, anyway, assuming she'd invited her condition on herself willingly. She wished she knew the soldier's names, but of course she was never introduced to them.

"But wait," she thought. "I did hear a name that night." When Dinsmore planted the ugly, slurred kiss on her lips, his friend called out 'Aye, Dinsy's got 'er now!'.

Annie didn't know Dinsy's full name was Dinsmore, but she figured it was a nickname, a shortened version of his real name. Short for what, she didn't know. Dinsworth, Dinsman, Dinington, it was anybody's guess. Upon reflection, she recalled a Major Dinsdale who'd passed through Trenton in the early days of the occupation. He was probably long gone, certainly by Christmas, but who was to know? Perhaps this 'Dinsy' character and the Major were related, perhaps that was his real name. She played with the names. Benjamin Henry Dinsdale. Sada Hester Dinsdale. She thought they sounded nice. 'Dinsy' was the only one whom she was sure had something to do with her present condition. She giggled as she recalled the sight of his half frozen erection lying on his upturned corpse. Scoundrel or not, he was dead now and Annie was sure he wouldn't mind if she borrowed what she thought might be his name. Dinsdale it was.

And so, after only eight months of gestation, Annie gave birth to Benjamin Henry Dinsdale on a hot August night. There was some question in the town about the child's last name. Most of them had fled and didn't know of the Major Dinsdale who'd passed through. Those who'd stayed, the Quakers, remained impartial and said nothing. No one knew the true story but Henry and Annie herself. She didn't even tell Ben from the Smithy Inn. If Henry tried to tell anyone, she needn't worry. He was so sick and senile nobody would've believed him. Not so conveniently, but expectedly, Henry passed away just before Benjamin's first birthday. Annie was happy for him. He was finally with his beloved Hester, and probably Paul also.

Annie raised Benjamin alone. Unlike his eventful conception, he led a boring life. Like his premature birth, he did everything early. He left his schooling at the age of nine to become an apprentice in a smithshop where he learned to be a silversmith. The proprietor was a widower with no children of his own and he took Benjamin on as a favor to Annie whom he thought was widowed like himself. Benjamin was married at eighteen, fathered a son by nineteen, and by the young age of twenty five he was dead. His mother outlived him by many years. She blamed his short life on his premature birth, claiming he wasn't given sufficient time to develop in her womb and consequently never did achieve a healthy, stable state of being.

Benjamin begat Thomas in the year of our Lord seventeen hundred and ninety six. Thomas could barely recall his father, who died of undetermined causes when the boy was only six years old. Like his father, Thomas was left to be raised alone by his mother with Annie's much needed assistance.

Thomas came to own and operate a small farm in southeastern Pennsylvania. He made enough to support his wife and child. His wife insisted they name their baby boy Jeremiah, and the stubborn bitch always got her own way. Thomas was henpecked to death by eighteen thirty five.

After his father's death, Jeremiah ran away from home, which consisted only of his nagging mother, and found his way to New York State. There he learned all about trapping and earned a modest living as a fur trader. He met and married his wife in the same month and that very year she gave birth to their only child, a son. Encouraged by his mother to make a name for himself and avoid the manual labor status Jeremiah enjoyed so much, Samuel went to school in Philadelphia. With much of his father's money and some of his own, Samuel never quite succeeded in becoming a doctor of medicine. Ashamed of his failure, he deserted his wife and son, Nathaniel, and jumped off a bridge to his death in eighteen ninety. Although he simply disappeared and no one was really sure what had happened to him, suicide was the most widely accepted conclusion of his associates.

Samuel ended his life just as his son's was beginning. Nathaniel was fifteen when his father disappeared, old enough to believe the rumor of his father's suicide despite his distraught mother's inability to accept the fact. Many were the occasions she tried to convince him that her Sam was still alive. She wanted Nathaniel to go out into the world, find his father and bring him back to her. It was under these false pretenses that Nathaniel left his home, hopped on a boat in a northern dock city of the Mississippi and flowed southward. It was the quickest means he could think of to get far away from his disjointed life in Philadelphia.

New Orleans would be his final home. In the spirit of interest instilled in him on the trip, he learned to play cards. Poker, to be exact. He saw his first real poker game played by a group of men aboard the *Jour de l' Argent* and when one player won a pot of twenty some-odd dollars, he decided that was how he was going to make his living.

Like most future great gamblers, Nathaniel had to suffer his training regarding tricks of the trade. It was during this time he met Monique, whose father owned a gambling hall in New Orleans. Nathaniel's gambling improved, Monique's father was impressed, and he married her. The marital bliss was brief as Nathaniel enjoyed his executive privileges at his father in law's poker tables more than he enjoyed his new wife. She soon became despondent and strayed while Nathaniel, like most great gamblers, discovered he could be even better by cheating if he played his cards right. Alas, he did not, and the bullet passed over the green expanse of the table, through the cigar case in his breast pocket with the false backing which hid three spare aces before it finally lodged in his chest.

Though he'd ignored Monique, she did not ignore other men. Even she wasn't sure who the father of her unborn child was. She was at least certain it was not Nathaniel. But guessing the true father would be like choosing the winning number on one of her father's roulette wheels. Claiming she needed to leave New Orleans to rest and forget, she went away to have her baby. As soon as baby Jules was old enough to travel, she retraced her deceased husband's trail back up the Mississippi and east to Philadelphia. Nathaniel had told her of his mother's plight back in his early days as a young, struggling gambler when he needed her support.

Monique abandoned Jules at an orphanage. She included a note saying who he was, but nothing about herself or where they were from. She did mention the boy's grandmother might still be in the area. Maybe they would contact her, if she was even still alive. As long as she herself didn't have to take responsibility for Jules, she considered herself done with the matter. She left him there for parts unknown. As it was, Nathaniel's mother was long since dead and the little boy spent his earliest years in and out of foster homes and the orphanage until he thought he was old enough to strike out on his own. He ended up on the farmlands of southeastern Pennsylvania around the turn of the century. He worked on the Linden Dairy Farm. It was not of his own choosing.

Jules managed to strike up a friendship with another young boy his age by the name of Charles Linden. As often as they could, they would scrape together some pennies and go down to Dundee's Store to shoot the works. Sometimes Jules would accompany Charles back to the Linden's house for a dinner they couldn't touch for all the sourballs and jawbreakers laying in their guts.

Some days they weren't lucky at all.

One day they were both broke and nobody would lend them even a single, measly penny, so they sulked all afternoon. By dinner time they were starving but refused to eat out of childish spite. As it got dark, Charles cooked up an eager scheme to make up for the lousy day. He knew all the boring ins and outs of caring for livestock. He was surrounded by it all day long. But he also knew what fun there was to be had at night. It might've been called something different in Jules' day, but today it's called cow tipping. Sometimes confused with the practice of giving gratuities to fat, ugly waitresses, it is an act which, if carried out on a larger scale, might hasten the extinction of many a bovine species and hopefully most of those who practice it.

Cows sleep while standing on all fours thanks to a network of muscles, tendons and ligaments that lock their leg joints in place, giving them a rigidity comparable to most any good coffee table. All night long they sleep in stiff balance upon their four locked limbs. The secret of cow tipping can be found in the vulnerable time it takes for the cow to unlock itself when it wakes up.

"C'mon!" Charles whispered anxiously, trying to convince Jules to join him inside the rail fenced field. It was already dark. Jules glanced back at the lighted farmhouse where Charles' family was doing whatever farming families do at night. "We won't get caught."

"What are we doing?" Jules asked the way an ignorant chicken with its neck on the chopping block might phrase it. Of course, he was over the wooden rail fence...

"You mean, what're *you* doing," Charles thought silently at him.

They made their way across the field to the far fence, cautiously avoiding the dreaded piles of droppings that loomed here and there in their path. The newer ones were detestable clots of rank muck. The older, sun-baked ones were safe. Hard and flat, like dried mud pies, their odor left them long ago and hovered in the air all about the farm. Jules picked one up. It clung dryly to some of the short grass and half of it broke off in his hand. He threw it high into the air as he followed Charles' lead parallel to the fence.

"What do you think you're doing?" Charles whispered, pushing Jules backwards. Up ahead, one of the cows casually went 'phlarnf'.

"I don't know," Jules answered inappropriately sheepishly. Wrong field for that. After all, he didn't know what was going on.

"You'll wake them up, fool! You don't want to wake them up now, that'd ruin everything." They stopped about fifty yards away from the unmoving jam of cows in the corner of the field. "Okay, now look. Here's what you're going to do…"

"What? Wait a minute, I'm not doing anything."

"Will you just listen? C'mon, it'll be fun." Charles explained the finer points of cow tipping to Jules who was both scared and intrigued.

"Oh, I can't do that."

"Sure you can. Go ahead. Pick one out and do what I told you," Charles prodded. Another cow phlarnfed.

"Naw, I can't do it."

"What's the matter, are you chicken?" Charles challenged. Jules wasn't that stupid. Two could play at this game.

"If you're so smart, why don't you do it?"

"I've already done it."

"Sure you have."

"I have. Lots of times."

"Prove it."

"I don't have to prove it. I already told you how to do it. Just squat underneath…"

"Why don't you show me how to do it, then?" Ha!

"I told you, I've already done it." Phlarnf, phlarnf.

Jules chose this moment to walk away. He felt good leaving with a sense of pride. It was a mature gesture for such a young boy.

"Chicken!" Charles called out from behind him. Jules noticed it was the second time he'd called him that. "Chicken!" Charles repeated.

"Knock it off."

"Chicken!"

"I said, knock it off!"

"Chicky chicky chick!" Charles clucked on.

"I'll show you who's chicken," Jules said with the intense sincerity that can only be attained between two boys. It was the same tone behind the 'My Father's better than your Father' scenario. Jules had never gone through that one. He had no idea where his real father even was. "I'll tip all these darn cows." Jules' eyes never left the herd as he briskly strode passed Charles who smiled behind him. Jules didn't notice. Another soft 'phlarnf' forced his thoughts together. He slowed his pace and soon began to see individual animals rather than just the blurry herd in the darkness.

Charles had told him to pick out the largest one he could find. God knows why Jules listened to him. The cows were all still save for an occasionally flicked tail. It was too dark to be sure but he thought some of them had their eyes open. This uncertainty stole away most of his boldness. What if they see me? How can they sleep with their eyes open? He was still trying to figure out how they could sleep while standing up. Rather than face the humiliation, he went on with the task into which his mock courage had snared him.

The closest cow appeared to be the largest. He approached it as Charles seemed to yell, "Hurry, Jules," from what must've been one hundred miles away. His steps brought him within inches of an unnoticed dung pile. Still was the cow as Jules crept no more than ten feet from the beast, facing its flank and hind quarters. He deftly moved alongside of it, making less noise than the flies that dodged its tail which swung like a pendulum. It was a Holstein. Its characteristic black markings stood out against the white background. Inexplicably, Jules wondered if it was black with white spots or white with black spots as he crouched down below the cow, its bulk looming above him like the hull of a ship.

When he had gotten down, all the way down, his back faced the cow and his rounded rump lay poised beneath. His knees were fully bent and his arms were extended, like Superman in flight, to balance his shifted weight.

It was the very cow above him that gave out a soft but belching grunt, not at all like the alleged moo sound it was supposed to make. This sound was crisper and cleaner than the previous phlarnfs. Jules didn't realize his butt was touching the udder of the multi-nippled milkable mammal.

Jules froze in just that squat position, the one used by bears that shit in the woods. That was exactly what was being scared out of him. The poor, sleepy cow thought it was in for a nocturnal milking. It got something quite different. Jules, bent over and trembling below the bovine, could easily imagine being swallowed by this otherwise docile creature. His whole body would ferment in the first two chambers of the four-chambered stomach, only to be regurgitated so the cow could go through the process which gave rise to the saying 'chewing the cud'. Then he'd be digested in the remaining two chambers. Perhaps some bits of his body would survive the ordeal and slither through the intestines only to be scattered in the piles of dung which littered the field. One night, some boys would come out to tip some cows. One would pick up a dried patty and find two of Jules' fingers lodged in the mass as a warning. 'Go back! Go back! These are no ordinary cows, they're man-eaters! While there's still time, go back!'

Jules could stand no more. He got up and started to run. But instead of first sliding out from under his intended target, he stood straight up and unwittingly accomplished his task. Although it took a bit of leverage and force, Jules possessed enough nervous energy to complete the deed. As he sprinted for the fence, the surprised cow heaved, grunted and toppled like a car over a cliff. It didn't even have time to phlarnf before an ominous thud marked its meeting with the ground.

Cows are not dumb animals. They knew someone was in their field the minute Charles and Jules hopped the wooden rail fence. They were simply too innocent to think something like this might happen. Nevertheless, many took offense. Even as Jules ran for the fence, the quickest ones had already unlocked their limbs and were in pursuit. Although he couldn't see it for the darkness, Jules headed in the direction in which he knew the fence lay. But cows are always prepared for encounters such as this. Why, one of their little traps waited between Jules and his fence right now.

He thought he could make out the fence in the darkness. He plotted his steps, preparing to thrust his right foot over, his hands poised on the top rail, his left swinging the rest of his body over without breaking stride when his foot slipped into a freshly laid trap. He slid forward a few inches in the fetid mess, throwing the rest of his body backwards and off balance. His left buttock landed squarely in the soft ooze. The rest of his body followed, the momentum carrying him farther like a toboggan through dirty snow. He stopped on his back, which was covered with cow shit, with his wind knocked out of him. Behind him, he could hear the angry mob of quadrupeds thundering towards him like a set of spotted bowling pins vengefully chasing the ball for a change. He quickly lifted himself up, accidentally placing his left hand into the smeared shit. He convulsively shook his hand in frantic disgust, flinging shitbits all over, one of which he felt sting him coldly on his neck just below the left earlobe.

He froze, disoriented, not knowing which way led to the fence. He spun around until he spotted the lighted farmhouse. Through the open door he could hear Mr. Linden shouting. His fear turned to anger as he sprinted for the farmhouse and Charles' throat, but changed just as suddenly back to fear when he realized the herd was closer than he'd thought. They were silent, intent, furious and they knew exactly where Jules was. He ran on, catching himself before he removed the clump from his neck with his left hand, which would spread more of the vile stuff on him. Desiring to keep at least his right hand clean, he left the neck clump in place, being more concerned about any other traps that might spring upon him at any second. Gagged by the odor that would not go away no matter how fast he ran, his imagination burned with visions of his body being strewn over the field. He wanted to check the smears on his back and sides for fingers and toes, bones and such.

Have you ever seen a cow run? It's quite extraordinary, really. They look so cumbersome, don't they? Sure they do, when they're standing still. But when they move, when all that dead weight picks up speed, they charge like a wave that does not intend to stop when it reaches the shore. But that's not to say they're frightening. Actually, they run like characters in a cartoon. The body stays still, it hardly bobs up and down or side to side. Only the legs move and they seem to do so independently of the rest of the body, as if the body suddenly stopped the legs would go right on running.

Although Jules would see plenty of cows for the rest of his life, he did not get a glimpse of those that now chased him. He did not see the blank stares in their eyes, nor the glazed eyes of the one that stayed behind. What he felt, though, was a terrific surge of speed that came upon him just before he left the field. The fastest cow lowered its head as it charged directly behind Jules and with one fell swoop pitched his ass through the fence. His head broke the top rail, his gut the second and he tripped over the bottom one. When the Lindens came running out of the farmhouse, they found Jules laying unconscious several feet beyond the busted fence. Luckily for him, cows will rarely step over a low partition of any sort. The bottom, intact rail was only eight inches off the ground, but it was enough to keep them contained. Otherwise, they might've milled out and swallowed Jules' body before he could wake up. Then the Lindens would have only found the cows exactly as they found them now, with silly Alfred E. Neuman looks on their faces.

Upon demand, Charles fearfully recounted to his father what he and his friend were really doing out in his pasture. Before Charles had a chance to invent his innocence, Mr. Linden went into a rage. "You get back into that house and stay there, you little son of a bitch!" Mrs. Linden, standing nearby, didn't take the remark too kindly. She remained silent, though, knowing what her husband had meant. She agreed with him.

"But Pa, I…" With that remark, Mr. Linden started Charles' trip with a swat up side the head which sent him six feet closer to the house. Mr. Linden then stepped over Jules' body, paying it no attention except for noticing the dung plastered all over his backside. He was more concerned for his cows. Their Mad smirk was wiped away when Charles ran to the house screaming and holding his head. They looked at their master with ignorant guilt. 'We didn't do anything, did we?' they seemed to ask. One of the older sons picked up a long, broken fence rail, wishing to break it again over Jules' head. Mr. Linden would not have stopped him.

Each time the farmer counted his cows the number didn't come out right. Sadly, he glanced over each one individually until he found the one he was looking for. He strode over to the huge bovine in the front of the herd trying to make its way to the rear. Dung was smeared all over the top of her head and between her eyes.

"Good girl. Good girl." The whole herd breathed easier.

When Jules regained consciousness the next morning, he was plunged into turn of the century Pennsylvania dairy farming. He had bills to pay. He wouldn't start work for two weeks, until his bruises healed. There was a certain cow that didn't have to worry about healing itself anymore. As a result of being tipped, it suffered three multiply fractured ribs and a ruptured spleen. It hemorrhaged all night before dying in the morning. They burned the body and buried the ashes behind the milking shed.

"C'mon, it'll be fun."

Jules' first responsibility was to care for the dozen minus one herd. He did everything but milk them. He wasn't trusted so close to them. They were kept locked safely in the barn at night now. This he did for two years.

That time was a present, that is, from Jules to the farm. He'd killed a prize cow in its prime and his first two year's salary was close enough to replace the monetary value of the animal. He was no longer required to work on the farm, but Mr. Linden was a forgiving man after all. Since he knew the boy had no real home, he'd been letting him live on the farm while he worked off his debt. Now that debt was paid, but Jules still had no place to go. He had been doing a good job at handling his responsibilities. Mr. Linden asked Jules if he'd like to stay on, "at regular pay, of course. But if you're any good, well, we'll see what we can do."

In the months that followed, Jules learned to milk the cows along with other new chores around the farm. Everyone forgot about the cow tipping incident. Everyone except for Jules. Everybody thought he simply turned out to be a good worker and was making up for his past wrongdoings. But his bitterness ran much deeper than that. He didn't know what he was doing that night. It wasn't fair that he'd had taken all the blame. After his two year penalty expired, he intended to stay on the farm only long enough to make some money and move on. He swore he wouldn't leave without chewing out Mr. Linden. More than a year had passed until the seventeen year old Jules felt he had enough, so he approached the boss.

Why did he have to pay for the cow? Wasn't Charles just as guilty? Jules was just a victim of circumstances. Who determined the cow's value, anyway? He probably had some money coming back to him. With these points in mind, he approached Mr. Linden alone in the milking shed one morning as he sat on his short, squat milking stool beside one of the cows.

"Mr. Linden, I've got something to say," Jules started abruptly. Mr. Linden did not turn around. "I don't think I've been treated fairly here," he went on uninterrupted. "As a matter of fact, I think I've been treated improperly. I know I made a mistake a few years ago, but I paid that debt in full, probably more than full for all I know." Mr. Linden had nothing to say. "What gives you the right to treat me like this? I know enough about this farm to run it myself. I know more about it than Charles, your own son! But I don't think I'm going to stand for it anymore, no sir. I'm leaving. I've got enough money now to leave this lousy, two-bit cow shed. Did you hear me? I said I'm leaving, Mr. Linden. Mr. Linden? Mr. Linden?"

Jules inspected Mr. Linden, slumped up against the cow, both hands dangling to the ground. Had the cow moved, Mr. Linden's body might've fallen forward and toppled the empty milk bucket. No one knew how long he'd been there.

In his will, Mr. Linden gave the abused Jules twenty acres of land and three cows. He was to receive this inheritance on his twentieth birthday. It was exactly half of Charles' inheritance, a son in whom Mr. Linden had always been greatly disappointed.

With this incentive, Jules decided to stick around for the extra couple of years. He took his inheritance a few weeks after Charles had taken his own. Realizing there was strength in numbers, the two childhood friends merged and soon became partners in crime. Charles took the crooked path out of bitterness from being gypped out of half his inheritance, Jules simply out of bitterness. He had an imaginary score to settle that the world did not owe.

Charles and Jules were very good together. They found it was easier to steal land than to buy it. They expanded into agriculture and started sabotaging tractors and competitor's crops. More than one family farm went under when Charles' and Jules' scare tactics failed to bring results and they resorted to outright violence. Dogs were shot, silos burned, and many rumors surrounded one farmer's wife's death. Of course, their operation was met with opposition, but it grew so fast in the first years that soon they were too big to reckon with. Their farm grew in acreage every year, swallowing up littler farms including one owned by one of Charles' brothers. Soon they were so big they didn't have to go after other farms illegally. They simply bought them out.

Although the law couldn't touch them, their reputation was well known. Jules courted a lady from out of town and married her. They had a son, Arthur. Jules saw him as a king sees his son as the heir to his kingdom. He wanted Arthur to receive an education. He didn't want an idiot taking over his business.

As soon as he could travel alone, Arthur was shipped off to school. When Jules wasn't tending to his farm he was avoiding his nagging wife. She wanted another child. Jules wanted Arthur to be the sole beneficiary of his life's work. He knew someday his son would thank him.

Arthur hated school. He hated books, he hated classes, he hated teachers and professors and he hated his father for making him go. He only stuck with it as a means of staying away from Jules. He was trapped during the inevitable holidays and summer vacations. The summers were the worst when even after three months he hadn't gotten used to the animal stench in the air. Each year he'd leave again for school on a hot August afternoon and smile many miles away when he couldn't smell the place anymore. Since he was gone most of the time, he never saw the trouble his father and Uncle Charles were having with the authorities. New evidence was cropping up, linking them to numerous incidents of arson, thievery, etc., even though their less than respectable behavior was now on the decline. They were too conspicuous to pull their own tricks and with the police on to them they were having trouble finding men to do their dirty work for them. But their luck had held out. With all the evidence the authorities could put together, there were still enough pieces missing to keep them out of jail. The empire stood.

So it's easy to see why Arthur hated his father so much. The old guy was a regular bastard. Through some fancy legal maneuvers, Arthur obtained ownership of the farm before Jules' death in nineteen fifty one. Charles had died years before, unmarried, no children. Tired of waiting for Jules' demise, Arthur employed the help of a lawyer friend from his college days. They proved Jules to be mentally incompetent, which was easy because Jules was mentally incompetent. He took all the land his father had gained with his tricks and schemes, everything that ever meant anything to the elder Dinsdale, chopped it up into subdivisions and put it up for sale.

Arthur didn't bother to haggle over the prices with the buyers. He never even met them. He handed the whole matter over to a real estate firm. The agents sold the land quickly at good prices, scooped out more than their fair share in commissions and handed the remaining balance over to Arthur. Not that Arthur was so stupid to believe the unsupervised agents were honest or he couldn't have made more money by selling the land himself, he just didn't want to have anything to do with the land. He wasn't selling it for the money. He'd be getting plenty of that in his inheritance which he wasn't able to swindle when he got the farm. To him, the land represented everything his father was, and to get rid of it was to in some small way get rid of his father. It must've worked. Three months after the last deed was signed and all the money was in the bank, Jules died.

Even without trying, Arthur couldn't help making a fair sum from the sales. But it wasn't enough to prepare him for the surprise at the reading when he discovered his father had changed his will. Everything Jules owned at the time of his death was to be liquidated. Arthur had already taken care of that. All proceeds from the sales, all the cash from his private accounts was not going to Arthur but rather to the Agricultural Research and Development Department of Pennsylvania. The money would be used to financially aid farmers across the state. This is not to say Jules hated his son or felt any guilt or remorse for his past actions or that he harbored any bad intentions towards anyone at all. He was just mentally incompetent.

Arthur petitioned the will on this basis.

Jules had changed his will in nineteen forty five, six years before Arthur and company had him tagged legally insane. It was impossible for him to be insane before nineteen fifty one because the state certainly would have found him to be so. Ergo, he was sane when he changed his will in nineteen forty five because he was not allowed to be insane before nineteen fifty one. You cannot be legally insane unless the state says you can be, and no sooner than they pronounce it, either.

Imagine Arthur's embarrassment when everything that was to be his was given away. All he had were the profits from the sales. He was allowed to keep that cash on a technicality because Jules didn't own the land at the time of his death, as specified in his will. Imagine how Arthur felt when he had to buy back a plot of land, one of those he'd sold several months earlier, paying twice the sum he'd gotten for it. He could have moved away but his wife insisted on staying (yes, he'd married somewhere along the line. It's not a particularly romantic tale, certainly not worth going into at length). Imagine how his anger tightened the knots in his stomach ten years later when more real estate companies became interested in the area, undoubtedly for its economic growth potential or some similar, equally as large real estate term. The subdivisions were now selling on an average of nine times their original market value back when Arthur owned them.

Oh Arthur, you are but a fool...

3

I won't be staying down
When the end is over
I'm getting up
When you're laying down
And you bend over
You're sitting up

-Composer unknown

Cliff left the men's room in the Student Union building. He enjoyed walking through the vestibule that separated the facilities from the outside hallway. It was free of the graffiti that polluted the dimly lit spaces on the walls and stalls behind him. "That's just where those dorks belong," he thought as he walked outside and headed for the parking lot.

He had just left his final in Human Physiology. He hadn't done as well in his science electives at Breece and wanted to make up the grade. He always liked the day of an exam, finals or otherwise. At the end of any other class, everybody got up to leave at the same time, saying 'See you later', or worse yet, trying to start a conversation. On exam days, you left when you were finished your exam. Students staggered out one at a time, and Cliff could always finish his test and wait for a spot where nobody else was getting up to leave so he could just drop his paper off at the front desk and walk out alone without all those hassles.

Pulling out of the parking lot for the main road, he saw the empty lane in front of him and the line of cars coming to school from the opposite direction. He chuckled when he thought many of them would go through the same scenario he'd just experienced. Some of the more foolish ones would look at it as a special day in their lives. Cliff was just glad to be getting away from the constantly crowded campus for a while. He was proud to be sensible enough to realize it was just another day.

Much of the land in the area was still being bought up by developers and it was a common sight to see half-built houses springing up in the fields along the otherwise quiet roads. Though construction had slowed down for the winter, Cliff could see how much progress had been made in White Meadow Condominiums since he'd first started watching it last September. Although it was identical to all the others around it, he'd picked out one particular unit he fancied moving into upon its completion.

Driving passed the familiar sign that marked the entrance, he noticed someone had spray painted over the letters 'inium', altering it to White Meadow Condoms.

"Jeez! They've let themselves out of the bathrooms and they're cutting loose everywhere!" Glancing in his rear view mirror, he saw the culprit had defaced the other side, too.

Upon his arrival home, after passing Pleasant Valley Condoms, Sunnydale Condoms and Hidden Bush Condom Complex, Cliff pulled into his driveway and finally realized it was not just another day. Someone was moving into the empty house next door. He stepped out of his Volvo, took one look and said "Shit…"

He watched as movers carried a long green couch into the garage along with other furniture from an Acme Movers truck. Others were rushing back and forth with boxes and chairs. Cliff shivered when he imagined what kind of people they would be. Joe Leisure Suit and his Wife with the Plastic Smile and their three children. She'd go to PTA meetings every night while he puffed on his pipe and talked with Cliff over a white picket fence about how he could never understand why they took The Brady Bunch off the air.

He tried to blot this vision from his mind as he raced to get inside before that Puerto Rican mailman…

"Good Morning, Mr. Dinsdale!"

"Good Morning," Cliff replied defeatedly. His hand was on the door-knob, the key in the lock. He didn't know why, but he disliked the mail-man. Perhaps it was because he knew too much about everybody but nobody knew anything about him. Cliff didn't even know his name. But the mailman knew everybody's name and everything else there was to find out about someone through censoring their mail. He probably previewed Cliff's copies of Esquire and Sports Illustrated before he delivered them.

"I see to it you are getting a new neighbor, yes?" the mailman addressed Cliff in practiced but not perfect English.

"Yes, I see to it I am."

"I know it is more work for just me," the annoyingly cheerful little man joked. "Here, I have mail for you."

"No shit? So that's what mailmen do. I thought they just read other people's mail. I didn't know they delivered it, too." More people would realize what an ass Cliff could be if he actually said anything close to what he was really thinking. As it was, he just thanked the mailman and went inside.

"Have a nice day, Mr. Dinsdale." The mailman parted with a smile and a wave. Cliff wished he'd just go back south of the border or wherever he came from (actually it was Chicago), and also made a mental note to find out why mailmen don't wear name tags.

Cliff went to the kitchen to start his coffee while he sorted through the mail. A letter from the bank, some junk mail, more junk mail, another letter from the bank, the current issue of Esquire (the wrapper never came sealed, so Cliff couldn't tell if it had been read or not, so he was sure it was), and the new issue of Super Sloth (the wrapper always came sealed, so Cliff could tell if it had been read or not, so he was sure it wasn't).

He took the latter, along with his coffee, into the living room and sat in a chair facing the window. Peeling the wrapper off his new comic book, he experienced the usual brief pang of silliness. He felt so stupid reading comic books, but he really liked them. Actually, Super Sloth was the only one he ever read. The others bored him. It wasn't escapism, nor was it an attempt to return to the responsibility-free status of childhood. It was just nice to read a fantasy story that couldn't possibly happen but wouldn't be so horrible if it did.

Why was somebody, anybody, moving in next door? Glancing out the window, he saw the truck had not gone away like he had hoped it would've by now. A neighbor ruined the best feature of Cliff's house; solitude. On one side there was a thick grove of trees separating him from the next house, as well as more trees in the back. In the front was the greatest divider of all, the Delaware River. But all that separated him from the heretofore empty house next door were some well trimmed shrubs and a couple of trees. His nearest neighbor was a Mr. Huston, Hesten, something like that (surely the mailman would know) who lived alone.

From his seat, he watched the moving men crisscross the lawn carrying more furniture inside. He soon noticed a man who wasn't dressed like the others, apparently the new owner. Cliff didn't see him at first because he was walking back and forth with boxes just like the moving men he'd hired to do the job for him. Cliff found his behavior asinine. He knew if he'd paid someone to do a job for him, he wouldn't waste his time helping them. The movers were ignoring the new tenant as he sped by them.

He looked to be somewhere in his thirties. His jeans and denim jacket looked to be somewhere in their thirties, too. Not many holes or frayed ends, just well worn. His jacket was open, displaying a flannel shirt which was all he wore in the unseasonably warm December weather. He was tall and thin, almost emaciated. He dashed across the lawn in lanky trots, leaping from point to point like a little kid looking for skipping stones. His formerly black hair was being invaded by gray strands, giving it the appearance of not having been dusted for a while. It was straight and just long enough to cover his ears. He had a fairly full and surprisingly well kept beard, not the sparse kind that leaves the front of the chin bare and the cheeks visible through scrawny patches. It was also graying slightly like the rest of his hair.

Cliff's attitude sank into one of antipathy. He didn't want a neighbor. Now there would be all those nasty pleasantries, like having to wave to one another and making sure the groundskeeper cuts the grass right up to the property line, or a bit more, just to appear friendly. At least it wasn't Joe Leisure Suit, that much was certain. But then who was it? If this was the husband, Cliff could just imagine what the rest of them looked like. Little kids running around in jeans and beards. His wife probably went on steroids, not wanting to be different.

Later, as Cliff read Super Sloth and the bearded one was talking to the same real estate agent that sold Cliff's house to his father a year ago, the phone rang. Paranoid, Cliff thrust the comic book neatly under a stack of newspapers on the coffee table. It was only his mother (who else ever calls him?) reminding him about dinner that evening. After a thorough nagging he hung it up, went to the bathroom and came back to watch his new neighbor and the agent stroll across the lawn. They stopped at the agent's car parked on the shoulder of the road. It was a company car with 'Ask me about Dunbaker Realty' obnoxiously stenciled on the side. The two men shook hands. The agent hopped in and drove away. The neighbor turned back towards the house and Cliff swore he saw a set of lips buried in the beard form the word 'asshole'. Cliff laughed aloud. Maybe this guy wasn't so bad after all.

No sooner had Cliff retrieved his comic book than another Acme Movers truck pulled up in his neighbor's driveway. It was a smaller version of the one he'd seen earlier. It bore the same logo, only 'Animal Transport Van' was written on the side of the trailer.

"Uh oh, here come the wife and kids."

The neighbor could not contain himself. He watched the truck back in as if he could already see what was inside. He hurried the two men out of the cab. They ignored him as the movers did. One of them unlocked the door while the other tried to get the neighbor's attention long enough for him to sign some delivery papers. After an anxious minute, the neighbor's family did indeed come sprawling out of the van. They were two beautiful Irish Setters. The neighbor was soon covered with the copper colored dogs as they knocked him to the ground. Then one took off over the front lawn while the other got a mouthful of hair when he tried to lick his master's face which tightened up into a look of mock disgust. Cliff watched, waiting for the neighbor to lick back. He also saw the old man, Mr. Hanson or whatever, supervising from his own front lawn, smoking his ever-present pipe.

Cliff was unable to form an opinion either way about this new neighbor of his. There was something in his manner that he couldn't identify, that he didn't usually see in other people. But it didn't concern him enough to keep him away from his comic book while his neighbor and his dogs played on the lawn. Cliff didn't look up again until yet another truck pulled up. This one was totally blank. It was an eighteen wheeler, almost too long to fit out front. Cliff had to walk over to the window to get a better view. The rear door faced away from him, towards the old man's house. Cliff's neighbor rubbed his hands together as the dogs obediently flanked him, like lions aside the steps of a city library. Both Cliff and the old man held an interest from afar.

The driver yanked the trailer door open all the way on the first try, exchanging words with the bearded man whose eyes remained riveted to whatever was in the truck. Still unaware that he was being ignored, the driver prattled on as he slid two long metal planks out of the floor of the trailer. He set one end of each on the ground to form two ramps.

Cliff couldn't see anything that was going on until a minute later when a thick billow of exhaust blew out of the back of the trailer. The neighbor, still silent and anxious, backed up a step with his dogs. Through the smoke, Cliff could not make out the bumper, fender nor passenger side door until the driver backed the rest of the car down the ramp.

It had rusty hub caps and the black convertible top was up. Thanks to a passing breeze, Cliff got a good look at what he didn't know was a sixty eight Ford Mustang that now rolled back on all fours down the ramp. The engine idled weakly, occasionally emitting a deep pop like an ogre's belch. Less exhaust was now spewing out of the corroded tailpipe.

The first part to touch down was not the rear tire but the rear bumper, much to the owner's horror. He ran back around the car at the sound of the scrape. The bumper was already back up off the pavement, but the driver had to stop while the neighbor inspected it with the help of his trusty companions. One of the dogs continued to assist while the other somehow managed to jump high enough to get inside the passenger side window to say hello to the driver. He got it down on all fours and killed the engine. It took him a few seconds to get out while he held off the rambunctious Setter. The owner, rather than calling off his pet, checked out the rest of his Mustang. He saw the antenna was bent halfway down at a right angle. He was blaming the driver, or so it seemed to Cliff who obviously couldn't hear the conversation. The driver was holding up a broken clipboard, a result of the neighbor laying it on the floor of the trailer where the driver ran over it with the Mustang. Cliff watched in interested confusion as each man agreed to cover his own damages.

More papers were signed. The driver then took the truck away, and just as he was out of sight and sound the neighbor noticed one of his tires was slowly but surely going flat, punctured when it ran over the clipboard. He cursed first at the missing driver and then at his hyperactive Setters as they tripped him as he walked across the lawn to his new house. Cliff was laughing hysterically by the time all three had gotten inside.

Later on, Cliff's neighbor was getting around to fixing that flat tire. He'd spent most of his afternoon setting up furniture and hiding boxes of souvenirs he didn't know he still had. He also hooked up his stereo and was listening to some BTO through the propped open door. He was cranking up his old Mustang with a rusty scissor jack when he spotted an old man pretending to be taking a walk. There were no sidewalks, no curbs. The lawns of all the houses just faded into the road out front, over a guard rail and down the tree and bush-lined embankment that dropped into the Delaware.

The neighbor recognized the old man. He'd seen him supervising earlier.

"Hi there!"

Trying to look surprised, the old man took the pipe out of his mouth and returned the greeting. "Hello, how are you?"

Encouraged, the bearded neighbor got up and trotted over. "Hello, I'm Sid Lasvistas. I'm your new neighbor. Glad to meet you." As the two men shook hands, the older one looked at Sid's house.

"Lasvistas, that's Greek, isn't it?"

"Actually, I think it's butchered Armenian. Good guess, though. Lots of people think it sounds Greek." He had that sinking feeling the conversation was faltering already. "Out for a walk, are you?" he asked, wondering why his neighbor kept staring at his new house.

"No, no," he replied distractedly. "I mean yes. Well, I'd like to but there's no place to walk around here. There's all this gorgeous scenery but they never put in sidewalks so you could enjoy it. If I built these places, you could be sure there would be sidewalks, yes sir. I grew up with sidewalks and now I'm old and I don't have any sidewalks." He put his pipe back in his mouth.

"It's a shame, sidewalks would really be nice here. I grew up with sidewalks, too."

The old man was slightly perturbed at the mere comparison of the two men. He was proud of his age and was sure he was a better man than this bearded fellow who reminded him of all those hippies who were running all over the place however long ago. At least he was polite. "You, ah, you play that sort of music often?"

Sid finally realized what he'd been staring at. As usual, he had a plan. "Wait right here," he said and held up one finger to his neighbor. He slipped inside the door and soon the music was replaced by silence.

The old man only meant to act nasty, a little. He didn't mean for Sid to feel like he had to shut down his music. True, he thought it was horrible, but in your own house you do what you like.

"I didn't say that to make you shut it off," the old man said as apologetically as he would allow himself. Inside, Sid couldn't hear. In a few moments, he appeared in the doorway. Head down, hands in pockets, he walked out across the lawn watching where his feet would land before he took his steps. The old man couldn't muster up the apology again. In his reluctance, he found none was necessary. First, he heard the introduction, like a train whistle. He immediately broke out into a grin at the Chattanooga Choo-Choo. Sid whistled the intro that led into the vocals.

"You, ah, you listen to that sort of music often?" he said. Not only was the old man smiling, he was tapping his foot and nodding his head. He didn't think anyone listened to that sort of music anymore, least of all bearded freaks like this guy.

"Now that's better," the old man complimented a satisfied Sid. "Well, I'm on my way, finishing my walk. Doctor says it's good for me, you know." He turned to leave.

"By the way, I'm Sid," Sid called out as his neighbor hopped away to the music.

"Oh, I'm sorry, Sid." He came back to shake hands. "I'm Mr. Hutton. Make that Frank."

"Okay, Frank," Sid tested the name. But Frank was off and walking again, puffing more smoke from his pipe than the aforementioned train leaving the station. Frank seemed to be impressed, but Sid hoped it was with him and not just the music. He was glad he'd saved that old Glenn Miller tape. He really wanted people to like him and he'd usually bend over backwards for them until they did. He didn't even know this Mr. Hutton yet, and for all he knew he might not want to, but at least things were starting out on the right foot.

Leaving the Big Band sound to swing on in the background, Sid returned to his Mustang. Running his finger though the crust of dirt on the hood, he left behind a finger-wide streak of dull red. He walked his fingers like a pair of tiny legs across the hood, trailed by little red footprints. He scaled up the windshield and onto the ragtop. He walked along purposefully to a small rip in the canvas. Pretending not to watch, he stepped into a tear with his index finger and got stuck, like someone who'd found a hole in the ice.

"Help me, help me!" he cried out in a quiet falsetto voice. It was okay, no one was looking. His left hand flew out of his pocket, followed by the rest of his arm, and landed on the roof. Two more fingers scurried over to the imprisoned digit.

"Don't worry, I'll save you!" The high falsetto turned into a rich, bass whisper. Tugging with all his feigned might, he rescued the right hand from almost certain death.

"Oh, my hero," the falsetto returned. The two hands hugged then walked thumb in thumb to the edge of the roof. They jumped in unison and separated in mid air, each landing in its respective pocket in Sid's jeans.

No, he wasn't crazy. A little immature, perhaps, and even more silly, but he was not crazy. He had full possession of his mental faculties at all times. Well, most of the time. Okay, sometimes.

After Chattanooga Choo-Choo, Pennsylvania 6-5000, Sentimental Me and Little Brown Jug, Sid still wasn't finished changing his tire. While trying to decide which was less bald, the flat or the spare, he spotted a tall young man with curly brown hair coming out of the house next door. He was wearing a pair of hideous plaid pants, the kind your mother used to make you wear, with an eyesore of a sport coat and tie.

"So where's the fashion police when you really need them?" Sid thought. Even the clean shaven face of the young man made him cringe. Not enough men realize the importance of facial hair, in his opinion. The barbarians rake their faces each morning with cold steel and lather, not aware of what a blessing it is to have hair sprout out all over their cheeks or chin or any combination thereof. Sid's own beard was only recently regrown. The best thing about a beard is that in order to get one you have to consciously do nothing to stop it.

Cliff saw Sid, too, but pretended not to. He was in his Volvo and gone before Sid got a really good look at him.

"He's a real quiet man." Mr. Hutton came up unexpectedly behind Sid, startling him. He didn't notice his interest had left his gaze in Cliff's direction even after he was out of sight.

"Who do you mean?" Sid didn't know why he was embarrassed.

"Clifford Dinsdale."

"Is that his name?"

"Sure is. The mailman told me so. He said his Father once owned a couple hundred acres of farmland in this county. He's right, too. I used to do business with the man."

"Is that right?"

"Yup," replied Mr. Hutton, puffing on tobacco that smelled to Sid like burning raisins, not altogether unpleasant, though.

"So Clifford is just a poor little rich boy, then," Sid ventured at a factual statement.

"I don't know. Like I said, he's a quiet man. Moved in here about a year ago, I suppose. Hardly ever says a word to me."

"You seem to know a lot about him, though."

"I told you, the mailman told me so," he said as if it satisfied the burden of proof.

"So what else did the mailman tell you?" Sid was quite curious about this Cliff. He felt he knew enough about Mr. Hutton for now.

"Not much else. Besides, that mailman isn't as smart as he thinks he is. You know he reads my mail before he delivers it?"

"No." Sid drew out the word in overly enthusiastic disbelief.

"Yes he does. All my magazines have been gone through before I get them. I haven't read Playboy in years but I still get it because it comes too well sealed for him to get it closed again. They have special tools for that sort of stuff, you know. He knows I'll catch him if he tries to get into it." Mr. Hutton fairly chuckled as he started to walk around the Mustang, eyeing it in the same manner he'd used with Sid's house earlier.

"I can't imagine Mrs. Hutton appreciates that too much."

"Long gone, I'm sorry to say."

Sid didn't want to know if he'd hit a nerve or not. "So you don't like the mailman."

"Oh no, he's a fine young man."

"Oh." Sid no longer felt like he already knew Mr. Hutton anymore.

"Say, what happened to the music?"

"The tape's over, I think. I'll go flip it."

"That's all right. I have to be going anyway," Mr. Hutton said, tamping down his tobacco with the broad head of a roofing nail.

"It's no trouble, really."

"This is a Cougar, isn't it?"

"No, it's a sixty eight Mustang."

"Mercury?"

"Ford."

"Right. Nice car, nice car. Never owned one myself."

Sid noticed the dark gray T-Bird he'd seen in his neighbor's driveway earlier was now missing. "It used to be a great car, back when I got her," Sid began. "This Mother was fast." Mr. Hutton gave Sid a quick stare of fatherly reproach, so Sid watched his mouth. "Zero to sixty in eight seconds flat. Timed it myself."

"If you don't mind my saying, it doesn't look like it'll ever reach sixty again. I guess that means we're safe." Mr. Hutton thought back to the day when he'd hit sixty, nine years ago.

"You're probably right about that," Sid smiled.

"It needs a paint job." Mr. Hutton noticed the car was red, but shades varied from fender to door, door to hood...

"It needed a paint job when I bought it."

"Why's that?"

"It was black back then."

"The top is all the black I see. That and the trunk."

"That's because the trunk is the only part that never got hit."

"Huh?" Mr. Hutton wasn't too confused because he wasn't very interested yet.

"That's the only part that never got hit."

"Uh huh," Mr. Hutton nodded in the affirmative, mustering up a question. "And all the other parts, the fenders and doors and hood, they all got hit?"

"Right."

"Okay, I'll bite. When they got hit you pounded them out and painted them red, right?"

"No, I wouldn't pound them out. I'd just replace the whole piece."

"Because you always wanted a cherry red sixty eight Cougar with a black convertible top."

"Wrong."

"Wrong?"

"Mustang."

"Mercury?"

"Ford."

"Right."

"I like you, Mr. Hutton."

"Call me Frank," said Frank, and they shook hands.

"I like you, Frank. You've got a sequentially logical mind."

Mr. Hutton continued to inspect the Merc, er, Mustang in this new light. The paint mismatched by slight degrees everywhere except the driver's side door and the fender, which matched exactly. Undoubtedly, both were damaged in the same accident. Little rust could be found on the car. A small amount lined one side of the black trunk and even more ate away at the base of the front right fender which had been pounded out, puttied and painted.

"Oh, Sid?"

"Yes, Frank?"

"I thought you said you replaced all the body parts after they got hit."

"That's right."

"Here, take a look at this fender." Mr. Hutton bent down with Sid. He pointed out a barely perceptible bubble. Sid gave it a rap with his knuckles. Expecting a hollow, echoing sound, he got a solid thunk instead. He also hurt his knuckles.

"Damn Germans."

"I don't understand," Mr. Hutton said, a little offended, but Sid didn't notice. A person's nationality was an important thing to Mr. Hutton. At one time in his life, it determined friends and enemies. He could remember a time when all Japanese were enemies, even though precious few had anything to do with dropping bombs in harbors. If you were Irish, you were obviously a drunken slob. There are ethnic jokes about screwing in light bulbs that will always be around. It's an important thing to some people. "I don't understand," he said, scratching his thick, white head of hair. His concerned expression wrinkled his big nose behind which sat the otherwise happy face of an elf. A German elf.

"I can't believe they did this to me. They were so nice, too." Sid shook his head.

"What? Who was so nice?"

"I got this fender dented in a near head-on collision with a German businesswoman."

"And it was her fault?"

"Well…" Sid whined.

"And she didn't help you fix it?"

"No, I didn't say that."

"Well, you didn't say anything," Mr. Hutton complained.

"Sure I did. I said I got this fender bender in a near head-on collision with a German businesswoman. You took it from there."

"Look, just what is it you have against us Germans?" Sid missed the self-inclusive remark from the man who didn't really know squat about Germany.

"I have nothing against the Germans. I don't have anything against anybody based on their nationality or anything like that. If it's worth having something against somebody, I usually find you don't have to go so far as their nationality to find something ugly about them, like the guy who fixed my car."

"So the woman did help you fix it. She did the right thing."

"Who?"

"The German lady."

"Why should she have helped me fix my car?"

"Because she hit you."

"She didn't hit me."

"Then who did?"

"What?"

"Hit you?"

"Nobody hit me. I hit her." Sid acted a little flustered. He was enjoying himself.

"Oh, and do you go around hitting Germans often?" Mr. Hutton accused, on the offensive.

"Listen, there were a lot of them on the damn Autobahn that day."

"So you were on the Autobahn. You didn't say that." It's a rare occasion when people hit it off so well they actually feel comfortable fighting with each other. "I'm just curious, that's all."

"That's okay, Mr. H. I like that."

"You picked a fine spot to have an accident. I hear they drive pretty fast over there. No speed limits."

"I didn't hit anybody on the Autobahn."

"You most certainly did so!" Mr. H. flared up. "You told me so just now. You said there were lots of Germans on the Autobahn that day…"

"And there were lots of Pennsylvanians on the Pennsylvania turnpike that day, too, but I wasn't on the Pennsylvania turnpike, either. You said I was on the Autobahn. I just said there were a lot of Germans on it. It stands to reason, considering its location and all, don't you think? By the way, did you know Clifford Brown died on the Pennsylvania turnpike?"

Mr. H. was silent, wondering what Sid would be doing on the Autobahn in this car, anyway. Oh, right, he wasn't on the Autobahn. And how did he know about an obscure jazz trumpeter who died in the fifties?

"Ha, got you that time. Okay, so maybe I lied a little. I didn't almost have a near head-on collision with a German businesswoman. I did, however, almost have a head-on collision with her car. Thanks to me it was only a fender bender, as opposed to a schnubender, which is only the German word for 'shoelace'."

"Shoelace?"

"Shoelace," Sid confirmed. Mr. H. (what happened to 'Frank'?) was nearing mental incapacitation. "You were almost right. I did have an accident in Germany and it was near the Autobahn. The German businesswoman wasn't in her car when I hit it. It was parked at the curb. She got in after I hit it, though, to get into her glove compartment for a pen and paper to copy down my license number as I sped away and crashed into a windmill." Mr. H. had no trouble keeping his mouth shut. "It was a very nice windmill, only it wasn't used as a windmill anymore. It used to stand alone, they said, but then they built a town around it. By then it was obsolete, a tourist attraction at best. The blades didn't even spin. They were welded in place. It was big, too. I remember how it kept getting bigger and bigger just before I hit it." Sid paused in case Mr. H. had something to say, which he didn't. "It might help to tell you," Sid leaned confidentially closer to his neighbor, "I was a little drunk that day. But it's okay, I don't drink that much anymore." Finally, something made sense. It brought a feeble, humoring smile of comprehension to Mr. H.'s face. "All I learned after that is it's illegal in West Germany to hit a parked German businesswoman's car, or a German businesswoman's parked car for that matter, it's definitely illegal to park abruptly next to windmills, it's illegal to drive drunk and it costs you a hell of a lot more to get your car out of the country when you do those three things than it does to get your car into the country in the first place, which I now realize I never should have done."

"How was the windmill?" Mr. H. was getting a grip on things.

"Oh, fine," said a smiling Sid. "I didn't even scratch it. There was a dirt embankment all around it, so my car churned up a lot of sod which slowed me down. Have you ever seen German dirt, Mr. H.? So dark and rich, so fertile-looking. Not just there but everywhere, all over Europe…"

"Yes, but the fender," Mr. H. cut in.

"Ah yes, the fender. I wasn't too familiar with the language and all I had was one of those courtesy phrase books the airlines had given me. Imagine my surprise when I couldn't find 'How much to fix my fender?' in there," Sid said sarcastically. "They said the damn thing would be so useful, too. I remember some of the stupid things they put in there. 'May I have some more ice?', 'I like my steak well done', 'Where is the rest room?'. I mean, they think all you're going to do is eat and..."

"Right, but what about the fender?"

"I couldn't say 'Will you replace my fender?', but I did pick up a little phrase I knew might be of some help."

"Which was..." Mr. H. hung on expectantly.

"Which was," Sid continued, "'Would you fix me a drink?'. So I pointed to the fender and asked the mechanic in German, 'Would you fix me a drink?' but I kept pointing instead of saying 'drink'."

"Because you couldn't find the right word for 'fender'?"

"You'd think somebody there would know English. Anyway, I suppose I still didn't make myself clear enough. I wanted the fender replaced, and here I find out they just fixed the old one."

"That is what you told them to do."

"Yes, yes, but it's not what I said, it's what I meant that counts."

"Maybe they couldn't find a new fender. It is an American-made car, you know."

"I thought I'd heard something about Ford marketing Mustangs in Germany under a different name. It doesn't matter now, anyway."

"What about the hood?"

"The hood was fine. Not a scratch."

"No, I mean how did the hood get hit so you could replace it with a new red one?"

"That happened in Baltimore. A shoe salesman fell on it."

"Aw come on, somebody fell on it?"

"I guess that does sound a little silly, doesn't it?" Sid surmised.

"Just a bit."

"I think he did so much damage because he hit me after jumping off a five story building. It was really strange, Mr. H. There I was, waiting at a red light, and out of the blue, literally, a shoe salesman fell on my hood. I didn't even know at first that he was a shoe salesman."

"Just, just fell. On your hood." Searching for clarity, Mr. H. was losing it again.

"You got it. Of course, I only have the word of the screaming lady and her husband that he jumped off the roof. I figure he fell a full five stories, because if he'd jumped out of the fifth floor window he'd only have fallen passed the lower four floors, making it a four story jump out of the fifth floor window, right? I mean, where do you start counting? I get confused the same way with pro-lifers. If life starts at conception, doesn't that mean you have to add nine months to figure out how old somebody really is? Anyway, the screaming lady saw the whole thing. I remember she screamed and turned to her husband and said, 'Alfred, look! The shoe salesman just jumped off the roof and landed on that car!'. Alfred didn't believe her. He didn't look like the observant type anyway. The shoe salesman must've been trying to kill himself. He was real sore at me for getting in his way."

"You mean he survived?"

"It was the damnedest thing. I took it all as a good omen. He just bounced off my hood and onto the road. I think he landed on his feet, too. He turned to me- I'll never forget this- he turned to me and said, 'Nice place to park your car, asshole.' I cracked up. Here the guy is trying to do himself in and he's mad at me for having my car at an intersection. He had to put on a show, couldn't down a handful of sleeping pills like everyone else. I was grateful. He'd only dented the hood and bent the air breather and I had no idea how I was going to get my hood replaced without messing up my front fenders. I'd already gotten them red by then."

"Sid," Mr. H. began, then paused, indicating there was some bit of advice to follow. "Why don't you have the whole car painted red?" He expected the bearded one to react as if this was a brand new idea.

"What fun would that be? Sure, I've thought about it, but it was black when I bought it, so I figure it was predestined to be black. Of course if fate or chance come into play, I don't mind altering things a bit. I mean, the parts were already red, right? Oh, I don't know. Why didn't they move that windmill when they built the town? How do you cure the common cold? Why do toilets flush clockwise north of the equator but counterclockwise south? I just don't know, Mr. H.," Sid mused.

"Right." Mr. H. was humoring Sid now. He decided not to ask him what he or his car was doing in Germany, or Baltimore for that matter. He wouldn't even ask why he didn't just buy a red Mustang in the first place. It seemed so, so trivial.

He stopped talking and walked around the car. He was taking it all in silently, like a sponge soaking up a messy spill. He had to admit Sid was one of the more interesting, or at least more curious individuals he had met in the latter half of the twentieth century. He was certainly more interesting than that Cliff fellow, whom Mr. H. did not know at all.

He spotted the custom license plate on the front, the kind found in auto stores which you put your own messages on. In white letters on a black background it read 'S+M'.

Mr. H. wasn't exactly in the swing of things anymore but he did recognize sado-masochism in its abbreviated form. He used his age to his advantage and acted ignorant.

"Say Sid, what does this S+M here stand for?"

"The S you can probably guess."

"You?" Mr. H. hoped.

"Right. Me, Sid."

"And the M?" he asked, knowing full well he wasn't out of the woods yet.

"Maivina."

"Maivina? What's Maivina?"

"No, who's Maivina."

"Okay, who's Maivina?"

"A girl."

"A girl?"

"A girl."

"That's an odd name."

"No, it's a beautiful name. She's a beautiful girl."

Mr. H. was at least relieved to discover it was a girl's name. He'd been afraid it was the car's name, which he was later to find out was Miss Annie Pada. It was a loose play on Mes Ani Pada, the first recorded king of ancient Mesopotamia. Who the hell knew why?

"She's a friend of yours, this Maivina?"

"Was a friend. Mai left me. A complete disconnectomy, no anesthesia." It did bother him a little, still. Nevertheless, he still chuckled to himself. He was sure he'd convinced Mr. H. about the initials. Only he and Mai knew better. "I had made so many plans for us." Sid was thinking back and Mr. H. felt he already knew why Maivina had left him.

They didn't have any plans, he had all the plans made for them. Besides that, he was weird. "She always thought I was a little weird, but I don't think that's why she left me," Sid lied.

"Married?"

Sid brought himself out of distraction. "No, just living together."

"Thought so," Mr. H. passed judgment. "I have a daughter."

Sid was once again sinking his memory into some old mental notes about his Mai. "You do?" He came back with a renewed enthusiasm, not wanting to appear rude.

"Yes I do. She lived with a fella for a while, too, before they finally did get married. I've got a grandson to prove it." Mr. H. was in a constant state of concern for his daughter, Barbara. Having lost the company of his own wife many years ago, he knew what it was like to be a single parent.

"You've got a grandson, huh? How old is he? What does he look like?" Sid turned his full attention towards Mr. H..

"He's going to be four years old." Mr. H. was confounded by Sid's interest because he didn't know him yet. "I think he looks like me, a little."

"I love little kids, they're all so inquisitive," Sid said with a smile. Mr. H. suddenly felt very good, more comfortable with Sid than he had earlier. Not for long. "Three year olds are best. No more diapers and school hasn't gotten a hold on their minds yet."

Sid went back inside the house to flip the tape.

4

"I'll just hop in and take off," Cliff thought as he nervously waddled from his front door to his car. It was an effort of ignorance on his part to avoid the whole 'Hi, I'm your new neighbor' scene as he pretended not to see Sid working on his flat tire. He breathed easier once he was headed down the road. He looked out over the Delaware as he drove, almost glad he was going 'home' for dinner. It delayed his inevitable meeting with Sid. He thought about it with the casual attention that comes with driving until he arrived at the meeting at hand. It started the instant he pulled into the football field-long driveway of The Dinsdale Estate.

The gates marking the entrance had always confused Cliff. They were always open. Why have gates if you never close them? Surely the wrought iron structures were rusted in place. They hinged on either side of the driveway to two stone configurations. On each abutment, a square sign bore 'The Dinsdale Estate' in gold bas-relief lettering. It was pretentious to the point where passersby wondered if the residents were trying to entice St. Peter into a new job. The signs were positioned in such a way that at least one of them could be seen no matter which way a car drove past. At their highest point, the stones were mounted as high as the gates they anchored. They sloped down and off to the sides, describing the arc of the spine of a swaybacked horse.

The lot in front of the house was real cobblestone, as bumpy as all hell. He pulled his Volvo in between two glossy cars. Getting out, he knocked a small dent in the door of the car next to him. He checked his car. Everything was fine.

On his way in, he gazed over the impeccably trimmed evergreen bushes to the shrub artist himself, Rod the Gardener. Arthur sent Rod to Cliff's place once in a while to manicure the lawn and such. Cliff waved because he liked Rod, who politely waved back. The gardener didn't have any feelings for the rich boy one way or the other, although Cliff did occasionally let him sit around, drink some of a six pack Cliff had bought him, and maybe even talk a while instead of working. Rod was one of the few people Cliff cared to be around because he remembered how nice Rod was to him during his adolescence, growing up in this very house. Rod would act kindly when others scorned him, pay attention when others ignored him, but mostly he did these things because he was afraid for his job. He was never in a position to lose it, he simply didn't want to get on his boss' bad side by being anything less than polite to his son. Cliff never did figure that out.

Cliff kept waving longer than Rod who knew he didn't have to be nice anymore. Of all times, this was when Cliff could use a friend, for when he walked into the house he knew he would find none.

He strode up the wide steps, passed the tree trunk-wide pillars that stood like sentinels guarding a secret that nobody cared to find out about. Suspended from the roof over the landing was a lamp on a long, heavy chain. A slight breeze rocked it gently, like a pendulum over his head. The white double doors stood between two decorative pilasters. He stepped aside and rang the door bell like a guest.

Sheila answered the door. Two swings of the lamp above marked the silence before either one spoke.

"Hello, Clifford!" She startled Cliff with her robust greeting. Behind her, several guests peered over like patrons at a zoo to see who had arrived. Sheila pulled Cliff in to give him a formal, game show host hug, the kind reserved for the contestant who lost.

"That's right, Mother, make it look good," he thought as he returned the mock embrace. Sheila closed the door. The other door was a fake, not even functional. It was strictly for show.

"Clifford, you should really wear a heavier coat. It's so cold. It is December, you know."

"Yes, Mother," Cliff simply replied, and they both knew things were getting pretty cold inside, too. "Where are the Christmas decorations?" Sheila normally had them up punctually by the first of the month. She was already over a week late.

"The man hasn't arrived with them yet. Isn't it terrible? I've asked your Father to call, but you know your Father and the holidays," she said as she walked Cliff to the main room to commence with the introductions. They were mostly older couples whom Cliff already knew. Sheila introduced the people she was sure Cliff knew in pairs- 'and you know the Kramers, Clifford'- and those he didn't know as individuals, ladies first- 'These are the Clanerettes, Gloria and Edward'- surely and carefully as per some new etiquette manual she'd seen recently.

He went through the handshake ritual with practiced ease and impressed himself as usual with the way the bullshit pleasantries were exchanged.

"You're looking fine, young man."

"So are you, Mr. Handsteff. You look like you've been practicing your tennis game. Been out on the courts beating my Father again, have you?"

"Ha ha, what a good-natured young man! Ha ha!"

"Ha ha ha!"

"Ha ha!"

"Ha, ahem, and you're looking wonderful this evening, Mrs. Handsteff. That's a lovely dress you're wearing."

"Why thank you, darling. He's such a sweet boy, Sheila."

"Mr. and Mrs. Lindenmuth, how are you both? Surely it's been months since I last saw you. How's the railroad business?"

"Comes and goes, Clifford, comes and goes," Mr. Lindenmuth responded as if asked what he does with his latest mistress.

"Mr. Hammond." Shit, and he was doing so well. "How have you been, sir?" This time it was Cliff who extended his hand first. Mr. Hammond was a long time friend of Cliff's father and even reminded him of the old man. This guy just gave him the willies.

"How's school, Clifford? Your Father tells me you graduated from Breece finally," Mr. Hammond said without releasing the handshake.

"No, I didn't graduate." Cliff gritted his teeth. He knew his father must've told Hammond he didn't earn his degree. "I wanted to come home and go to school here, close to home, you know. I'm doing very well."

"Do you like it as much as Carbleson?" It was common knowledge both Mr. Hammond and Cliff's father both attended Carbleson.

"Carbleson was nice..." The handshake got tighter.

"You've got to try very hard to get anywhere in this world, Clifford. Remember that." He was intimidating the shit out of Cliff. No bull would slow this guy down. At last, he released the handshake.

"Yes, sir, I certainly know that, sir. Hello, Mrs. Hammond. How are you these days?" He remembered too late that for some reason she liked to be addressed as 'Lady Hammond'. In his hasty effort to get away from her husband, Cliff shook her hand with the same vice grip Mr. Hammond had given him. Although he meant her no harm, he was amused by the painfully surprised look she came up with as he gave her arthritis a jolt. It was not as if he'd done it on purpose, but he wasn't sorry, either. Mr. Hammond didn't notice the scene as his snout was buried in his highball. Sheila noticed, though. The atmosphere was cordial, and out of respect for that, Lady Hammond avoided any sensible action. She withdrew her hand in stifled silence, not sure if the boy just didn't know his own strength or what.

"What?" Arthur Dinsdale cocked his ear to his wife's mouth, trying to ignore the din of the other conversations as Sheila relayed the episode to him in hushed tones. "Good, she probably deserved it."

Arthur soon approached his son, or rather the bar at which Cliff was standing.

"Clifford," he said, a one word greeting, not pleased at all.

"Father." The tone echoed.

The old ritual took place again as Arthur Dinsdale gave his son as firm a handshake as his old bones could manage. "Your Mother says you've seen the Hammonds. Knock it off," he said with a glare much sterner than his grip. He let go and picked up a fresh scotch. "Do you need any money?"

Neither was looking at the other now. Arthur stared at his drink as if something was floating in it. Cliff looked at the small crowd rather than at his father.

"No, thanks, everything's fine."

"You're sure now," Arthur reiterated, a demon for clarity.

"Yes, I've got plenty left from last time." This annoyed Cliff to no end. It wasn't because the money was given to maintain the space between them instead of from love and concern. That much was clear. He was annoyed at himself because his lack of ambition put him in a place where he knew he couldn't get by without the free house, the free car and the free money. All of those free things didn't make him feel free at all.

Just before dinner, he saw his half-sister Priscilla and her newest boyfriend, Curt. Curt was in one of the armed forces but Cliff didn't care which one. Priscilla showed him off. She wanted everyone to see how successful she was in her mating habits. Her latest catch was certainly A-1 military with his skull-exposing hair cut and his dress uniform which he wore no doubt to impress somebody, anybody. But the joke was on Curt, because Elliot was also in attendance. Elliot, the youngest Dinsdale, was Cliff's twelve year old little brother. He was enrolled at Plymouth Military Academy. He must've been on holiday break, Cliff thought, otherwise he wouldn't be at home. Elliot was also in full dress uniform. To see him and Curt together was like seeing a before and after advertisement at the recruiter's office.

At the dinner table, the old folks paired off. Sheila and Arthur sat apart at the far away ends. Cliff was seated within earshot of his mother, separated from her by Elliot on his left. On his right sat Sarah Perry, whom he'd been able to avoid until now. He could never get interested in their conversations, which invariably started off with Sarah saying something like, 'So what do you think of the Pope's position on the arms race?'

Really.

Cliff amused himself in other ways while Sarah prattled on across the table with Priscilla like they both actually knew something about Paris fashions. He fielded a few comments that were thrown his way with lackluster responses and only asserted one or two comments of his own, solely to make his mother stop glaring. Her eyes were telling him to be more sociable with Sarah, they weren't seated next to each other by accident, you know. No one seemed to notice how sad his indifference to his own little brother was.

It couldn't be labeled total indifference, though. Cliff was glad that tonight he was sitting next to Elliot, for here was his entertainment for the duration of the meal. All evening long, Elliot had been in, no, he had actually been Curt's shadow. He constantly pestered him over what it was like to be a walking, talking, shooting, sailing, taking orders military man. He followed Curt everywhere except when Priscilla could shoo him away for a few minutes. He was getting on Curt's nerves, as he was having enough trouble making a good impression on Sheila and Arthur. Things were no different at the dinner table.

Since the meal began, Elliot hadn't taken his eyes off Curt, whom fate and Sheila had seated directly across from each other. Elliot had convinced Sheila to order him portions of the same food Curt had ordered. They were offered two choices, beef or seafood. More like a restaurant than a home, it wasn't even a traditional holiday meal. Elliot had been cutting, chewing and swallowing at exactly the same time as his idol. Priscilla caught on to him right away and shot looks at her stepbrother before Curt noticed what was going on. Cliff thought the whole thing was hilarious. He could see Curt was visibly pissed about it. Cliff was even more amused at the control it took for Curt to maintain his composure. He watched him take a long, slow cut from his sirloin and raise it to his mouth silently, infuriated as he watched Elliot follow his every move from start to finish. He paused for a moment and Elliot did the same. It was all Cliff could do to keep from laughing right out loud. Curt noticed Cliff having fun at his expense. Their eyes met for a second. Cliff quickly removed himself from the action by helping Sarah with her crab. She seemed to be having trouble with hers, so he demonstrated with his own how to crack off the front claws and separate the top of the shell from the rest of the body. She gave him a grateful look and a sigh, perhaps mistaking his assistance for a display of affection. Sheila smiled. Priscilla became interested.

Curt pulled a fast one with his fork and tricked Elliot into taking a mouthful of food when he didn't. He almost chuckled with victory over the little brat, attracting Sheila's curiosity. He quickly righted the situation.

"Mrs. Dinsdale, I can't help but admire your son. He looks so regimental in uniform. I'm sure he's going to make a fine officer some day."

Sheila was impressed from the word 'regimental' on. She thanked Curt for the compliment while smiling at her Elliot, reaching out to straighten his collar as if he was incapable of self maintenance. Elliot chewed his mouthful of food. Sheila put her hand on his shoulder where she found a gravy stain on his epaulet.

"How in the world did you get gravy on your shoulder, Elliot Nathaniel Dinsdale?"

"Gff dnt nw ut…"

"Don't speak with your mouth full, young man," she commanded, trying not to attract anyone's attention. "Give me another epaulet." She held out her hand.

Elliot swallowed. "I don't have another one. They never gave me any more."

"How do they expect you to become an officer like Curt if they don't give you spare epaulets? Go change, quickly." Elliot excused himself and reluctantly left the table.

"Even admirals get gravy on their epaulets, Mrs. Dinsdale."

"Kiss ass," Cliff thought to himself.

Eating freely again, feeling immeasurably at ease with the unexpected turn of events, Curt turned to Cliff yet spoke to Sheila. "Priscilla tells me you have another son in the military. Loudon, I believe."

"Yes, actually he's my stepson. He's a technical writer for the Army. I understand it's a very difficult job."

"And exciting, too. They made him the head of a task force to draw up some instructions for the assembly of a nuclear cooling device, or something like that. He told me so in his last letter," Priscilla added.

Cliff barely knew Loudon. He thought being a tech writer sounded like a stupid job. Maybe he got some really tough assignments, like writing instructions on how to load toilet paper rolls in the dispenser so they roll off the bottom, not the top. They could print them on stickers and put them in all the latrines so…

"It's strange you're not serving your country also, Richard," Curt said.

"That's Clifford, dear," Priscilla corrected him, smiling.

"Oh, of course, sorry."

Sarah sank her knife deep into the meat under the crab's shell.

Cliff was numb. He didn't like this sort of attention at all. It wasn't until after Curt took a sip of wine, though, that he thought to imitate him like Elliot.

"So what is it exactly that you do, Clifford?"

"Clifford is a student," Mommy answered for him. Cliff was begin-ning to feel very small.

"Oh, a student," Curt repeated with the same respect he might have reserved to say 'Oh, afterbirth'.

Sarah cut the face off her crab.

"I'm a business major. I just transferred from Breece." Cliff hoped the crew cut wimp would be impressed. He really wasn't.

"Of course, you're working on some type of co-op program. You'd certainly be a fool not to. What company are you with?"

Cliff was stuck. "Uh, none, yet," he dribbled. Why didn't he just lie?

"It's a shame you don't have your degree yet. You don't, am I right?" Curt looked at Cliff for an answer, his eyebrow cocked, his square, vengeful jaw aching to form the words 'How about it, prick?'.

"No, I'm a, no, I'm not, going for it yet. I've been looking into some-thing new."

Sarah stopped scooping the internal organs out of her dinner long enough to listen.

"What?" Curt pressed.

Quick, think quick, Cliff.

"Computers!" The word barely had time to drop out of his brain onto his tongue before he spit it out. His mother looked puzzled.

"You never told us that. Arthur dear," she interrupted her husband at the other end of the table, "Clifford says he's studying computers."

"Really, that's very nice," Arthur responded, too engrossed in a con-versation of his own.

"That's wonderful, dear. We're all so happy for you. Have you decided where you want to study? Surely that little place you're going to now can't have much in the way of computers. Those buildings must be so old, I doubt they even have indoor plumbing!" Curt joined in on Sheila's joke, saving her from being the only one laughing.

"Do tell us, Clifford, where are you going to study now?"

"I've only looked at a few places. There are so many computer schools, I can tell you."

"What branch of computer science are you going to study?"

"Everyone is into computers nowadays. The fields of interest are so, varied. They use computers in, uh, medical fields, and in hospitals…" It's funny how one lie can lead to another. Well, not funny, but, well, you know.

"If there's one thing I've learned in my twenty eight years, I've learned you've got to try very hard to get anywhere in this world, Clifford. Remember that."

Cliff almost choked as he imagined Curt and old man Hammond years from now, leaning on a bar. 'I told him life wasn't easy. I told him you had to try very hard to get anywhere.' 'You did? Hell, that's exactly what I told him! Lemme buy you a drink…'

Cliff was desperate for a distraction. He checked on Sarah, who was having no trouble at all with her dinner. He felt the stares, some real, some imaginary, closing in on him when he was saved for the second time in his life, the first being conception, by the appearance of a freshly changed Elliot. The dinner returned to its previous condition. Sheila soon caught Elliot at his little prank, but by then dessert was nearly over. Cliff dodged too many questions after dinner about his new career moves and made a quick exit, making his 'Happy Holidays' to as few people as possible.

"Be sure to keep us up to date on that computer deal of yours," Sheila said to her son as she walked him to the door. Even she'd caught on to him.

Outside, the December wind had picked up. The lamp was swinging a full foot to either side, casting crazy spider leg shadows that seemed to blow away, just like Cliff. Driving home along the river, he passed a spot not so very far away from where Annie had ultimately started this whole mess.

Sid, had he known Cliff yet, might've been tempted to quote the learned philosopher Ambrose the Penguin to soothe Cliff in his moment of turmoil. As the wise Ambrose once said as his friend floated away, stranded on a loose chunk of ice, "Hey, little buddy, just ride with the tide and go with the floe."

5

Cockroaches.

Las cucarachas. Les battes. If a rose is a rose by any other name, then you could call these buggers anything you wanted and they'd still be disgusting. Sid's new house had them. They were just the little German cockroaches, oddly enough, but still, they were cockroaches. A small population was left over from when the house was left empty for so long before Sid moved in.

Cliff had finished sulking over the dinner party last night. He'd only been there for a few hours but the whole episode replayed itself in his head all night long. When his alarm went off he fixed his bed, swore to his mirror he'd never join any branch of the armed services, brushed his teeth, got showered and dressed, ate breakfast and sat in his living room for four hours with nothing to do. Then he got up to fix some lunch, cleaned up after himself and returned to the living room to continue whatever it was he wasn't doing before. Strangely, it never occurred to him to question why it was called a living room anyway. There was certainly nothing living in his. But there was something alive outside his door, and it was knocking.

"It couldn't be my Mother. Twice in one month? Nah." Cliff wondered if he wanted to get it or not. Why not.

It took just a split second for him to recognize the beard with the man attached to it.

"Hi, I'm Sid. I just moved in next door." Sid flashed a smile and threw out a handshake. Cliff reciprocated. Like a coin deposited in a juke box, there was a lapse of time before Cliff spoke.

"Hello, Sid. It's nice to meet you. I'm, my name is Clifford Dinsdale."

"..."

"Could I come in?"

"Of course. Please come in," Cliff replied in a monotone voice as if he didn't realize he was being an ass. He left the door opened to the crisp air. The stuffy house air ran out to catch a breather. In his hand, Sid held an empty coffee cup.

"I know this is going to sound a little corny," Sid decidedly jumped into the purpose of his visit, as opposed to holding a one sided chat with this avid conversationalist, "but could I borrow, God I feel stupid. Could I borrow a cup of sugar?"

"A cup of sugar?"

"I really do feel stupid. I think I saw a scene like this once on 'Father Knows Best'. It feels like I should be wearing a sweater with patches on the elbows."

Cliff had never even heard of the old series, but he did have a sport coat with patches on the elbows because those who forget history and fashion are doomed to repeatedly dress like idiots. He didn't know what to say. He was unnerved. He wasn't accustomed to visitors, especially unannounced in the middle of the afternoon. Sid looked around the place for that lived-in look he found so comforting. It was nowhere to be found.

"I've got sugar. The kitchen is this way."

"Thanks, this is real nice of you." Sid followed Cliff down the dim hallway, past the dining room. He reached out unseen and wiped a smear from his hand on the vast, unbroken shine of the dining room table as they passed. It sorely needed it. "If I can be picky I'll take some powdered sugar, if you've got any."

"Sure. Powdered sugar." With the astute nature of a well versed librarian easily finding a book in the stacks, Cliff found the container which held the powdered sugar.

"He knows where everything is! This boy needs help," Sid thought, aghast. He stepped forward with his cup like a blind man selling pencils.

"That's not necessary. I'll put it in a covered container for you."

"Oh, okay."

Not allowing a single puff of sugar dust to escape, Cliff neatly measured an even cup, no more, into a round plastic container and snapped on the lid. He even burped it. Not one word was spoken until he was through. "Here you are, one cup of sugar. Powdered sugar." Sid looked at it as if he'd never seen sugar packed like this in his life. "Is your wife baking a cake?" Cliff figured he could at least be pleasant.

Sid, holding the container up and inspecting it, was not looking at Cliff when he answered. "No, cockroaches."

Cliff sputtered and bumped into his sugar reservoir. Before he could close it, a wisp of sugar dust arose. He fanned at it like smoke from a fire.

"You all right?"

"Yeah, yes. I'm all right."

"I was going to ask you for some baking soda, too, but I found some of that," Sid said, then waited for Cliff to ask him what he was going to do with it all. Cliff only leaned on the counter to hold himself up. "Aren't you going to ask me what I plan to do with all that stuff?" Sid was amazed at Cliff's lack of a reaction. Cliff was afraid he was going to tell him he was going to eat the little insects.

"I suppose you're going to tell me whether I ask or not, huh?" Cliff composed himself, stifling the imaginary sensation of little bumps crawling under his skin and in his stomach.

"Probably." He was going to launch into a dissertation on entomological physiology, presenting the prevailing arguments for displacing the cockroach from its present classification in the order Orthoptera into a class by itself, as it were, the name of which was proposed to be the order Dictyoptera. He opted for another angle instead.

"The cockroach is truly a remarkable creature," he began with an authority. "I'm sure you're familiar with the fact that after somebody finally blows us up with their nuclear weapons, we will die but the cockroach will survive. That's what they say, anyway. Most of us find that fact amazing because we compare the circumstances to ourselves and our own susceptibilities, as if they were so precious and sacred because they are a part of the almighty human metabolism. It is for this very same reason we find it incredulous that the cockroach can be obliterated, annihilated, forced at will to cease to exist, sent prematurely to that big city tenement in the sky, all from an externally induced version of one of our most common afflictions." Sid stopped here to allow Cliff to make a guess. Cliff was a little curious, even more frightened, trying to position himself as close as possible to the knife drawer, just in case. Sid was mildly disappointed, but he went on.

When a flower opens to the sun in the morning, it makes a sound. For one brief moment, just as the delicate petals begin to yawn and stretch, a tiny, unmistakable sound is emitted. In the same manner the rose puffs the sound out of its rosy cheeks, the iris cries out softly, and the daffodil yodels aloud, (daffodils are slightly louder than other flowers, you know), in that same way did the word leave Sid's lips.

"Gas…" Sid trailed the word like a Bunsen burner. "Gas kills cockroaches." He smiled widest when he revealed his secret.

Cliff thought it was going to be something more exciting than gas. Everyone gets gas. Why would it kill cockroaches? What do you do, eat lots of sugar and baking soda and break wind on them? Cliff was more at ease now, anyway. The squirmies in his stomach went away. Sid seemed harmless. A few screws loose, but harmless. He stopped leaning towards the drawer.

Observing he now had Cliff's attention and not his fear, Sid went on with the story. "It's an old cure they used to use in New England. It's very effective. All you do is take equal amounts of sugar and baking soda and mix them together. It's best to use powdered sugar because it's easier for them to eat."

"Oh, the cockroaches eat it."

"Right. See, the sugar is just there to lure them in. They like it, I don't know why. The real secret is in the baking soda. They can't help but eat it along with the sugar if you mix it good enough."

"So what, they eat baking soda. Big deal." Cliff still didn't understand.

"The baking soda reaches the stomach where it reacts with the digestive juices. As in any digestive process, a gas is formed. With the baking soda, more gas is produced than normal. Much more, and faster."

"So what happens to the cockroach?" asked Cliff, who had never spoken with such ease about cockroaches before.

"The beauty of it is, cockroaches don't have a diaphragm like you and I do. In other words, they can't burp."

Cliff was more astounded than he would have liked to admit. At least they were talking about something, rather than standing there just thinking of things to say.

"The gas has nowhere to go. It only takes a few seconds for the pressure to build up to the point where the little bugs blow up from the inside out!" Sid felt good. He could see he was breaking the ice and making headway. "I've been using the method for years."

It didn't strike Cliff at the time that if Sid had been using the method for years, that meant he'd been having cockroach problems for years, so how effective could it be? "It's the same basic principle as feeding Alka-Seltzers to sea gulls. Now they can burp, just not quite fast enough. It puts them belly up for a minute, then they're fine."

"That's incredible," Cliff responded. Who knew if he was using the word with its original meaning, indicating he didn't believe a word Sid was saying. Besides, he would never need to use this method because he never expected to have a roach problem, or a sea gull problem for that matter.

"Of course, I give them a sporting chance."

"How is that?"

"I normally leave a Tums or a Di-Gel nearby for them to nibble on afterwards, kind of an after-dinner mint. Not one of them has ever had the sense to take me up on the offer. Guess it just goes to show cockroaches have no survival instincts."

The conversation went on a while longer until Sid had to excuse himself. He was eager to set up his little trap. He told Cliff he'd purchased a special pair of infra-red specs. It wasn't so much because cockroaches would only come out in the dark. That was just a misconception started by people who saw cockroaches running for cover when they turned the lights on before entering a dark room. Their tactile abdominal receptors, or cerci, picked up even the slightest vibration, he explained. Just the same, he wanted to sit still on the floor in the dark, and this would be the first time he'd be able to watch them. Cliff declined the invitation to join him.

"C'mon, it'll be fun."

He didn't want to hurt Sid's feelings, but he didn't want to spend the night watching cockroaches explode in the dark, either. Even someone like Cliff could find something better to do.

Sid left, and once again Cliff was alone. Alone with his comic books and magazines. Alone with more thoughts than he'd had earlier. "What am I doing?" he asked himself out loud in sudden disbelief. "All I want is to be left alone. Now I've got mad cockroach killers in my house." He decided to be more careful in the future. This guy next door certainly did not have both his oars in the water. He was definitely not Cliff's kind of person.

December rolled on like a friendly game of shuffle board. No one was keeping score. Christmas came and went. The only signs of celebration Cliff saw other than the farcical dinner party at The Dinsdale Estate were a few decorations Sid had managed to put up while he was still trying to settle into his house.

On the times he ventured out, (he'd spent two afternoons buying, wrapping and delivering his family's Christmas presents) he'd often see the old man and Sid out front batting the breeze. He could usually slip by unnoticed or with a quick wave that didn't hurt as much as he thought it would. But once, Sid waved him over to join them.

Instantly, Cliff was petrified. My God, there were people over there. He wanted to stay away from people. Being out in the public realm wasn't so bad. The roles were defined. If he was shopping, he was a customer and no one expected any more of him. In school, he was a student and that's all he had to be. At The Dinsdale Estate he was the son, and a trained monkey could be that. But just standing there with no real structure set up, now that was scary. He had to be Cliff. Nowhere else did he have to be Cliff.

"Hey Cliff. How've you been?" Sid asked. "Long time no see."

"I'm fine," he said, trying to remain detached.

"How was your Christmas?"

"Fine," Cliff answered, then looked at the old man whose polite smile clamped the ever-present pipe. Cliff almost couldn't tell if it was smoke coming out of Mr. H.'s mouth or just his breath condensing like everyone else's in the January air, the time of year when winter really starts in Pennsylvania.

"I don't know if you two know each other. Cliff, this is Frank Hutton. Frank, this is Cliff Dinsdale."

"Dinsdale. That's an English name, isn't it?"

"Yes, I believe it is," Cliff said as their gloves shook hands. Mr. H. hid a look of surprise that Cliff wasn't sure of his own nationality or heritage. These young people today just don't know what's important.

Cliff felt odd, rightly so, being introduced to a man he'd practically lived next door to for a year now by the man who'd only known each of them for a month or so.

The pipe Mr. H. smoked was a beautiful one. The style was known as a Rhodesian, comparable to the popular Bulldog only with a squatter bowl and a bent stem. The rounded shank was capped off at the bit with a sterling silver band. The curved saddle bit was shined and polished.

"That's an extremely nice pipe you're smoking." The convincing nature of all Cliff's bullshit pleasantries was packed into that line like an overstuffed suitcase.

"Thank you," Mr. H. acknowledged. Cliff didn't even realize the quickest way to Mr. H.'s good side was through true flattery. He held the pipe up as if to examine it, the idea being to let everyone else see it. You'd think he'd made it himself. "Do you smoke?" Mr. H. asked Cliff with little expectancy.

"No, not me. My Father smokes cigars sometimes, though." Cliff thought he had to salvage the conversation. His problem was he analyzed everything he wanted to say, everything he said, making judgment calls while striving to say the right thing as he'd been taught to do since he was a child. He didn't know how to just talk.

"What kind does he smoke?"

"Some imported label, I'm sure. I think it begins with an 'M'."

"Doesn't this guy know anything?" Mr. H. thought to himself. He had a bone to pick with Cliff, anyway. They'd spent one year as neighbors and not once had Cliff made any friendly attempt to meet him. If Cliff thought he was too good for the likes of everyone else, then screw him.

"Macanudo? Monte Cristo?" Mr. H. threw some brand names into Cliff's brain to see if he'd hit anything. "Montesino, Montoya?"

"I think it's Monte Cristo," Cliff lied, trying not to look like a total fool. Mr. H. would have been more impressed had Cliff told the truth.

"Monte Cristo, those are Cubans. Tough to get. I never thought they were all they're cracked up to be."

"Say Cliff, I'm still new around here. I'm going to go out tonight to hit a few bars, see what's out there. Do you want to come with me?"

"No thanks, Sid. I don't drink much." Cliff thought about the three bottles that were still at the bottom of his refrigerator. They'd still be there next summer when Rod the Gardener started coming around again.

"Hey, neither do I, much. I just like to hang out. Come on, what do you say?"

Cliff couldn't help but wonder why this guy was so interested in him. He'd learned from the mailman that Sid lived alone and hardly ever got any mail but junk mail addressed to Resident or Occupant. Mailmen notice these things. The thought that Sid was gay crawled up Cliff's spine like an eel. "No, I really can't make it tonight. Maybe later. I've got to go now. Bye."

"He doesn't talk much, does he?" Cliff's car was out of sight before Mr. H. spoke.

"I think he's just a little shy," Sid said.

"There's something about him I just don't like, you know what I mean?"

Sid summed it up. "You said it yourself, he's a quiet man."

"At least he's got good taste in pipes."

"Hey, come on, now," Sid began lightheartedly, "I've always complimented you on your pipes and you've never told me I've got good taste. You've never even asked me if I smoke."

"Oh sure, I know what you smoke." Mr. H. chuckled the way older people do when speaking of such things which today are commonplace but in their day was not mentioned by respectable people.

"So I used to smoke joint," Sid admitted, "but I used to roll my own cigarettes, too, once in a while."

"Sure you did," Mr. H. mocked him.

"I did," he insisted, "and I'll bet I even still have some of my old pipes laying around somewhere."

"I tell you, when I was a kid the worst we did was smoke tea leaves. Now that was the big thing to do. We'd all get our own pipes or steal one of our Father's and smoke tea leaves. That or corn silk."

Sid had never heard of the practices. "Why in the hell would you smoke that?"

"I don't know, really," Mr. H. reflected. "I suppose it was pretty much the same thing as tobacco, and no one would sell tobacco to a kid. Not back then, anyhow. Besides, everyone was doing it."

"That's never been enough reason for me to do anything," Sid replied. "My grandma used to say to me, 'If everyone jumped off a bridge, would you jump, too?'."

It's a sure sign people are beginning to feel old when they start reminiscing about their past, when things that were said to them as children start to make sense, when nostalgia becomes more than just a word. It's even rumored that you're not allowed to die peacefully until you figure out the one about having your cake and eating it, too. Mr. H. began to feel old a long time ago. Although he didn't realize it, he felt a sort of affinity with Sid.

"The funny thing about smoking is that I still don't know why I did it. Even nowadays I might pick up a pack of cigarettes but I know I can do without it. I usually end up losing most of the pack or throwing it away. I still can't tell why I like it sometimes, though."

"That's simple," Mr. H. replied to Sid's confusion, "it's all in the smoke." Sid thought that was too obvious to be true. "Really," Mr. H. tried to convince him. Sid had some trouble understanding him because Mr. H. lapsed into his bad habit of trying to hold a pipe in his mouth and speak at the same time. "When you buy your cigarettes you see a hundred different brands on the shelf. You buy a pack of Marlboros because that's all you've ever smoked. Or maybe you buy a different brand once or twice for a change of pace. Same thing with my tobacco or Cliff's Dad's cigars, no matter what letter they start with. It's all just dead leaves, anyhow. We smoke because we like the smoke. The only reason people get hooked is because they hear there's something called nicotine in the tobacco and they're supposed to become addicted to it because a condensed medical journal said they were supposed to do just that."

"Make that a couple hundred thousand medical journals," Sid added.

"Whatever. God forbid they should ever discover what other garbage they put in cigarettes. It's all in the head, Sid. People will listen to the reports that say nicotine is addictive but they'll ignore the ones that prove their two packs a day will kill them with emphysema. They don't want to hear that. At least the nicotine gives them an excuse not to stop." Mr. H. pumped out a beautiful, thick cloud.

It sounded like so much gobbledygook to Sid. He wasn't sure what Mr. H. was trying to say. "But what about you?" he asked.

"My tobacco doesn't have half the chemicals they put into cigarettes. And I don't inhale the smoke. I'm not trying to kill myself. I know, I read all about this stuff somewhere." Mr. H. puckered up and shot out a chain of smoke rings. "Now that's why I smoke. Better than blowing bubbles, eh?"

"There's got to be something else to it, otherwise it wouldn't make a difference if you smoked cigarettes or pipes or whatever."

"Oh, I suppose there is a difference. Cigarettes are more convenient. You smoke what you want then throw it away. I've always preferred a pipe, myself. When I first started, though, I was a bit of a closet smoker."

"Maybe that comes from hiding with your friends and those tea leaves."

"Pipes were for grandfathers or movie actors. I knew if I ever was seen I'd be laughed off my block. As I got older, it became more acceptable for a young man to smoke a pipe. Today it seems everybody thinks it's for grandfathers again, so it's okay because I am one of those grandfathers now. It's all a circle."

Sid used to be sort of a closet smoker. People sometimes thought he was smoking something he didn't want to share with them, which was absolutely correct at times. But they left him alone. On the rare occasions when he did walk around with his pipe, he was surprised that people still left him alone. Nobody ever accused him of being some punk kid trying to act sophisticated or any other misconceptions he thought everybody believed. That's when he started to get away from it.

"You should start smoking again, Sid." Mr. H. blew off another ring.

"Here, let me try that," Sid said, reaching out for Mr. H.'s pipe.

"What?" Mr. H.'s voice crackled like breaking glass. "You want to put your lips on my pipe? That's disgusting, I'd sooner let you use my toothbrush!"

Sid had passed a bowl before. It was no big deal. "Okay, okay, I won't smoke your pipe. But you've got to show me how to do that." He pointed at the disintegrating rings.

"Don't bother, it's too complicated," Mr. H. quickly calmed down and spoke from high on his pedestal. "Just break out some of your old pipes and light up. You can be a closet smoker or you can run out in traffic so everyone can see you. They won't care, you're not hurting anyone. And if you still don't believe people smoke simply because they like the smoke, then I've got a little experiment for you."

Sid liked experiments.

"Light up in a darkened room, so dark that you can't see your hand in front of your face. The idea is to not be able to see the smoke. If you can't watch it, I'll bet you don't enjoy it even a little bit."

Sid caught himself watching Mr. H.'s pipe smoke indirectly while he spoke. "I can do that. I'll just light up and close my eyes."

"Not the same thing," Mr. H. disagreed. "You'll know you can simply open them and you will. Do it in a dark room. Now cigars are a different story. A cigar stinks like hell to everyone except the person smoking it. Their history is more intriguing than anything else about them. Do you know why cigars have a band around them? It's a carry-over from back when the Cuban ladies smoked them. Part of their formal dress included the wearing of white gloves. Dust and oil from the cigar leaf would rub off and turn their fingertips brown, so they used gold rings. They were made of real gold, too. They'd just slip that ring over the cigar. It had to fit snugly, so they always smoked the same size. They'd hold it by the gold ring and keep their gloves clean. Today, a band on a cigar is just a symbol of something they did long ago. It's funny how things people did years back affect the things we do today."

"Yeah," Sid replied. He was interested in more faraway thoughts, like when was the last time he saw a blind person smoking, and where did Cliff go?

Winter break was almost half over when Cliff went to register for his spring classes. This was the late registration period. He knew less people would be there than at the regular time he'd missed on purpose last November. Crowds of procrastinators went early in the morning to grab what courses were still open. It was now late afternoon.

The campus was emptier than usual. Cliff recalled how last semester he'd get out of his last class and duck into a bathroom stall or more often a cubicle in the library and kill fifteen or twenty minutes. After everyone was in their next class or at the cafeteria, he'd come outside to sit on a bench and look at all the people who weren't there. He'd remember the hoards of students who choked up the walkways that formed perfect X's over the courtyards, he'd remember them bumping into each other, dropping their books, laughing, he'd remember reluctantly being one of them just a few minutes earlier. Then he'd look at all the open space, reveling in the fact he could probably walk from one end of the campus to the other and come across no more than a dozen people.

Cliff hated walking in a crowd. He was never sure of what to do. If no one was coming his way, he might look around at something other than his shoes. When someone approached, he turned his gaze away faster than Lot's wife should have from Sodom and Gomorrah. Never make eye contact. There's no reason to look at anyone while they pass you. They might think you're strange.

Once he thought this notion was silly, maybe even paranoid. So as if Lot's wife whispered the salty idea into his ear, he tried looking straight ahead one time, naive fool that he was. He kept looking ahead until someone came along, then backed out and looked away until after they were gone. After numerous trial runs he finally did it. A man was coming his way and he kept on looking. As they drew nearer, Cliff found himself staring the man right in the eyes. The man took notice and looked back, nothing else. 'Oh God, he saw me looking at him.' Cliff felt ashamed for some reason he didn't even pretend to understand. He was embarrassed, and from then on he decided he wasn't paranoid, he was safe.

He walked passed the pond behind Blakely Hall which had become a haven for wild geese and ducks in the warmer months. Cliff didn't even notice they were missing, just as in the warmer months he wouldn't have noticed they were there.

Turning the corner around Blakely, spray painted on the wall in letters so big even Cliff couldn't miss them, someone had written 'Fuck a Duck'. Cliff knew it was proof a person didn't have to grow up before going to college.

In the registration area, several people were milling about in front of a long wall full of computer printout sheets. The many black slashes indicated which courses were already filled. Cliff knew he needn't worry. Business courses were plentiful due to the recent trend in pragmatism exhibited by college students. But these students weren't business people yet. They didn't have to get up early in the morning and go to work. So they scooped up all the late morning and afternoon classes so they wouldn't have to get up early in the morning and go to school, either. A marvelously self defeating training program, really. Cliff knew the early classes would still be open. He wasn't thrilled about getting up for them, but it would only be two or three times a week and there would be fewer people in those classes.

He pulled out a sheet of paper with both courses he wanted to take listed on it. His handwriting was impeccable, perfectly legible. The course numbers were filed in a column on the left, followed by the section numbers and course titles, Accounting II and Principles of Marketing. There were several sections held each day ranging from two to four classes per week. Cliff had worked out five possible combinations in order of preference. Checking the printout sheets, he found his first, third and fourth combinations closed. He chose the second one, keeping him in school from seven A.M. to nine A.M. on Mondays, Wednesdays and Fridays. He'd be getting out when most students would just be getting in. Perfect.

He filled out the proper form following the instructions 'USE BALL POINT PEN PRESS HARD'. He found that phrase comforting. He could always be sure it would be there whenever he filled out a form in duplicate, anytime, anywhere. It was a sure thing in places where he didn't know what to expect next. He stepped into the correct line and, although unnecessary, handed his form to the checkpoint officer to be reviewed for mistakes or conflicts. He proceeded to the terminal.

"My, you're an early riser," the kindly, bespectacled old woman said as she punched the data onto the screen before her.

"Yes," was all Cliff said.

"You know what they say, the early bird catches the worm," she said, undaunted by Cliff's lack of enthusiasm. She absent-mindedly rolled the restraining chain that dangled from her glasses between her fingers as she waited for the screen to respond to her instructions. Cliff's entire collegiate career passed by in electric green letters across the screen. He recalled how he'd been trapped in his lie about computers at the dinner party. He wasn't a very good liar, and he didn't know that being in short supply of such a talent wasn't so bad.

The woman finished with his form and cheerfully sent him to the next terminal where the whole process seemed to repeat itself, minus the geriatric small talk. This time it was a middle aged man in a pin striped suit, black hair slicked back with hair tonic and skin as bland as the color of asparagus when it grows in the shade. His eyes hung like broken windows behind black rimmed glasses. His face was sunken in and the bags under his eyes appeared to be approaching the deep hue of a grape stomper's toes. He said nothing, just ignored his cigarette in the ashtray and processed Cliff's form. The wrinkles of his forehead stood on the ledge of his jutting eyebrows like the ruined executives on the thirteenth floor on Black Friday. But today was Tuesday and the man ushered Cliff on to the next table where his processing was finished. He was free to leave.

Outside, the campus was blissfully still. Strangely, Cliff was disturbed by the mechanical way he'd been whisked through registration. He took a walk around the courtyard but there were several people about, which was several too many. He drove home the usual way, passed the familiar sights that reminded him he was really by himself. Some of the maimed condominium signs were replaced, others scrubbed clean. He passed a few farm lands his father probably once owned. He kept driving until he reached that plot which his father had repurchased, the one on which he lived.

As he pulled into his driveway, Sid was already coming across the lawn with one of his Irish Setters. They were both smiling as usual. Cliff got out of his car and thought, 'How do I get out of this one?', whatever this one was.

"Hey Cliff, what's up?" Sid came around the car to meet him. The dog tried to get into the Volvo but Cliff closed the door just in time.

"Oh, nothing. Your dog sure likes cars, huh?"

"Yeah," Sid chuckled, not quite able to come up with a joke about dog licenses and driver's licenses. "Say, listen. What are you doing tonight?"

"Oh, nothing," Cliff repeated himself. He decided to keep talking to misdirect Sid's attention. "How's your cockroach problem?"

"The cure worked like a charm. Always does. But that's not why I came over. You busy tonight?"

"Ah, no, not really. I haven't fixed my dinner yet." Cliff pointed towards his house, his refuge, so far away.

"Why, is it broken? Hah, but seriously, folks," he continued, "I know you don't like to hang around in bars or watch cockroaches, but that's all I know about you. Tonight, I've got a surprise for you. It's something I've been doing for years. I know you'll like it."

Oh God, he *is* gay.

"What do you say? How about it?"

Cliff usually had a way out of these things. Wherever the person suggested going, he said he simply didn't go to those places. But Sid had outsmarted him. He put him on the spot by not saying where it was he wanted to take him. Why was Sid being so damned friendly, he wanted to know.

No one knows who showed the Egyptians how to build the pyramids. No one knows what they would name a zoo if it was built in Kalamazoo. No one knows what 'vigesimation' means without looking it up in the dictionary. No one knows what 'vigesimation' means even after they've looked it up in the dictionary. No one knows when it's correct to use 'who' or 'whom'. No one knows where George Washington slept, or with who/whom (circle correct choice). No one knows the secret behind the theory of inertia. Things that are in motion try to stay in motion at a constant speed and in a straight line. Things that are stationary try to stay that way, unless of course some force tries to set them in motion. Ergo, therefore, no one, not even the author knows why Cliff said…

"Yeah, sure. Okay."

"Great! Meet me over at my place at seven, all right? Come on, Bump!" he called to the lanky dog who seemed to be best described by the former part of the theory of inertia. Cliff was left standing there with a broken dinner to fix, his mind emptied out like a dry river bed with but one puddle in the middle of it, a puddle which asked simply, "Bump?"

All through dinner, Cliff worried about what might happen. To anyone else it was just another night out. But Cliff rarely spent his nights out, so this wasn't simply another one, it was one of the first in a while. He got so worked up he couldn't finish his macaroni and cheese. He threw the rest out and left the bowl in the sink. He was so upset he didn't even wash it.

As a safeguard against the possibility Sid might be gay, Cliff wore an undershirt, a dress shirt and a sweater over top. He put on a thick pair of corduroys and tied his shoes extra tight with a double knot so they wouldn't come off too easily. Common sense wouldn't say what purpose this would serve, but it made him feel less vulnerable.

The white and yellow colonial house sat next to Cliff's place for over a year unoccupied and he'd never ventured near it. It left him alone and he'd let it be. He never imagined someday he'd be walking up to the front door to meet some closet gay who might rape him, kill him, chop up his body and hide the pieces in the floorboards.

There was still time to go back. He wasn't at the door yet. He could say he was sick or had to go somewhere, or he could've killed himself for not doing either when Sid waved to him from the front window.

"You came!" Sid said from the doorway. He didn't mean to sound so surprised. He was more pleased than anything else. Cliff's heart was slam-dancing against his rib cage. A white furball of a cat slipped passed Sid and out the door.

"Get in here, Goddamnit!"

"Oh, aren't you ready yet?" Cliff almost whimpered.

"Yeah, I'll be ready in a minute, Cliff, as soon as I get this cat inside. Come on in." Sid's bare feet danced on the cold grass as he hopped after the getaway cat.

The slight but not offensive air of a pet shop overcame Cliff as he stepped inside the darkened house. On the opposite wall of the foyer hung a drawing, next to a poster that looked like an old rodeo. It was a plain pen and ink drawing of Albert Einstein, a reproduction of his commonly circulated portrait of the physicist as an old man. The white hair was splayed back, the remnants of a dull gleam was in his eyes, as if doing zero to sixty in a Ferrari but thinking of other things. But what caught anybody's eye who looked at it was a slight alteration. Behind the shaggy, cookie-duster mustache a bright, shit-eating grin flashed across the old thinker's face.

"You like it?" Sid returned with his snowball pussy. He set it down and it ran into the next room. "I did that myself."

"You did? It's uh, very...nice." He sounded as if he was trying to be polite because he spoke out of nervousness. He was intrigued with the drawing, though.

"I got tired of all the photos that made him out to be some old fart who didn't know which way the wind blew. I drew it back when I was more fascinated by the glamour of what a genius he must've been. I didn't know anything about his work, I just heard he had a great mind so I was impressed. I like to think he'd be pleased with me if he could see it."

"Come in and sit down. I'll be right with you." Sid motioned him to the living room where a dog greeted them. More by rote than originality, Cliff greeted the animal.

"Hello, Bump."

"No, no, that's not Bump. Just a minute." Sid then yelled, "Bump!" In a few seconds, the other Irish Setter appeared and both dogs immediately started vying for their master's full attention. Two tails wagged as Sid made the introductions.

"Cliff, I'd like you to meet two (sit, guys!) two of the nicest Irish Setters I know." Pointing from left to right, Sid said, "Meet Bump and Grind."

"Bump and Grind?"

"You got it. You have to shake their paws now."

"You're kidding, right?"

"No, really, they'll be very insulted if you don't."

Cliff wondered what old Albert would make of this. His nervousness was dissipating. "Oh, what the hell." He bent down on one knee and each dog offered a paw. "This is different." Cliff's face was lit up like a Christmas morning child. He shook paws first with Bump, then Grind. It seemed Grind would shake forever if something didn't stop Cliff. Bent down, he found himself a foot and a half away and at eye level with Sid's crotch.

He jumped up and took a step or two or five backwards. The dogs followed him playfully. "H-how do you tell them apar-part?" he asked with standoffish suspicion, glad at least to see no ropes, knives or floorboards around.

Sid couldn't help but show his confusion, if only for a second. "If you promise not to tell anyone, I'll let you in on a secret. I can't tell them apart. I swear they're identical. I just pretend to be able to distinguish one from the other. They don't mind. Both of them will answer whether you call them Bump or Grind. Just please don't tell anybody." Sid smiled in earnest at Cliff which made him feel more at ease. He couldn't remember the last time someone shared a secret with him, anyone who'd ever been so friendly towards him as Sid. They hardly knew each other.

"You stay here and keep the dogs company while I finish getting changed. You're really going to love the surprise I have for you." There was a record spinning on the turntable. The volume was so low Cliff hadn't noticed it when he came in. Sid turned it up as he left the room. The singer sang with an Illinois twang in his voice.

Cliff had never heard the song, which wasn't altogether strange because there were many songs he didn't know. He never tried to cultivate a fascination for music of any kind.

The music played on and so did Bump and Grind. They were hassling Cliff for attention as eagerly as they had with Sid earlier. Their strength surprised him. Cliff petted them and looked around the room. Shelves took up much of the freshly painted wall space where books and odds and bookends were fighting for elbow room. A porcelain Buddha with an opening in the top of its head surrounded by four small hoses that stuck out like tentacles grabbed his attention away from a stack of old road maps, two of which Cliff could see were of New York state. A hard cover copy of Tom Robbin's 'Still Life With Woodpecker' hugged paperbacks of Jack Kerouac's 'On The Road' and 'The Dharma Bums', one on each side like a cowboy with his arms draped around two honky-tonk angels. Other titles showed their faces, like 'The Vengeful Opportunist', 'Bottled Beer and Onions' and 'The Horny Gypsies", which didn't turn out to be about Old World traveling erotica but rather a study of nomadic horned animals by an English anthropologist. More books, mostly technical but mixed with some fiction, shared room with pewter mugs, several ashtrays, a few framed photos of mountains and a girl and what appeared to be some textbooks on medicine or physiology. On the left wall, hanging above an alabaster chess board set up in mid-game was another pen and ink drawing, larger than the first. It was a nude. She was standing, facing off to the left. Her left thigh crossed her front creating a flux of smooth, tastefully hidden curves where her thighs met. With one knee raised and one straight, her legs faded into the white canvas haze surrounding the drawing. Above, the casual slope of her back was lost in the dark, wispy hair that fell well beyond her shoulders. A captured wind blew it around to where it nuzzled her breasts and torso. Her arms were raised, hanging limp over a tree branch just above her head. Her one arm hid the lower half of her face so only her eyes were revealed. They did not intimidate you, they did not penetrate you, they did not look away, they looked *to* you.

Sid came back wearing an old pair of boots, jeans and a sweater. "Beautiful, isn't she?" He caught Cliff's admiring glance. "It couldn't help but turn out so well when you consider what I had to work with. The only thing I had trouble with was concentrating on my work and not her."

"You mean this is real? She posed for you?"

"Sure. Here's a photo of her." Sid handed him one of the small frames from the shelf. What a likeness, Cliff thought. "Her name's Maivina. I call her Mai for short."

"She certainly is beautiful."

"Come on, let's go. I'll drive. I think I know how to get there. You might have to help me out if I get us lost."

Cliff got his first of many good looks at Sid's car. "What kind of car is this?"

Sid laughed. He was surprised neither of his neighbors could recognize it. "It's a Mustang, sixty eight," Sid said like a waiter announcing a bottle of wine. He reached across the front seat and unlocked Cliff's door. He got in amid the flutter of a single dog hair which alighted unnoticed on his jacket.

"So where are we going?"

"It's a surprise. Trust me, you'll like it."

"You're not taking me to some bar, are you?" Cliff asked, dead serious.

"Naw, of course not. I wouldn't do that."

Again, Cliff failed to recognize the music coming out of the speakers that looked old enough to be the originals. They had a way of translating all the electrical impulses from the car into some sort of sound. Each blink of the turn signal made a short crackle over the music. As Sid raced to the next gear speed, a series of clicks from the rotor ran together into a high whine that soon reached a pitch too high to hear until the gears were shifted again. Cliff thought it was like being talked to by Iggy Leventhal, his old roommate at Breece. He ignored the music and just picked up on the static as he did with Iggy's vernacularisms.

He looked around the car. Everything looked old. The dashboard, the little rips in the seat covers, the ashtray that wouldn't close, everything. He checked the odometer which read only thirty four thousand forty four miles. "Is that one hundred or two hundred thousand miles?"

"Hah, I wish it was over two hundred thousand. It's only gone around once. But I plan on seeing Annie go around again someday." Sid explained the origin of Miss Annie Pada as the light up ahead turned from green to yellow. He gunned the engine to try to beat it but the old car just stalled out.

"What the fuck?" The car rolled to a stop like it was supposed to. It was almost like a fail-safe mechanism. Sid had been too far away to make the light, anyway. The first car to go on the opposing light was a police car.

"Either this car likes you or we're just lucky," Cliff said. The policewoman threw a glance in Sid's direction and Sid threw it right back. He tried to start the engine again but she wouldn't turn over.

"Open your door," he ordered Cliff.

"What?" Cliff was confused again.

"Quick, before the light turns," Sid said with his own door already open. Cliff opened his, not knowing what else to do. He thought Sid might've decided he didn't like him anymore and was going to make him walk home. "Now when I say so, slam it shut." Sid began to grind the starter. "Now!" Cliff slammed his extra hard, shaken up by Sid's sudden outburst. The two doors closed almost in unison and the engine started easily in time for the green light. Cliff stared at the car like a spectator searching for mirrors after the magician saws the lady in half.

"So what was that?"

"I don't pretend to know how it works, I just know it does," Sid said. Cliff just started to laugh, no longer ill at ease or even wondering where they were going.

"Hey, sorry if my language offended you." Sid felt the apology was silly but maybe necessary with someone like Cliff.

"What language?"

"Back there, when the car stalled out."

"Yes…" Cliff asked expectantly.

Maybe it wasn't necessary. "When I said 'What the fuck'."

"Oh. So?"

"I just didn't know if that bothered you, that's all."

"No, why should I care?" Cliff said, shaking his head.

"Good, good, I just didn't know. Actually, the word 'Fuck' has a lot to do with where we're going." With that, Sid put Cliff back into a solid state of uneasiness. "Don't you find it strange that no one associates it with reproduction?"

"Reproduction?" Cliff repeated like a high school gym teacher/health ed instructor who lets the unit on human reproduction go until the end and hopes the school year runs out before he has to teach it.

"Yeah," Sid went on. "Nobody ever puts the ideas of fucking and childbirth together. The last thing a person watching a porno movie wants to know is where babies come from. And whenever a baby is born, it's such a sickeningly innocent affair. The whole family gets in on it. Where was the family when Mom was getting it on with Dad? Not in their bedroom with a Minolta, you can bet."

Cliff wished Sid would talk about something else.

"I once learned of a tribe in Russia, or maybe it was Africa? No, I think it was Russia. Anyway, this tribe was so, if you'll pardon the expression, fucked up they thought their women got preggers by looking at the sun at a certain time of day. Can you imagine that? Although it is true the tribe became extinct about a generation after the invention of sunglasses, it's still hard to believe they could be so stupid."

As nervous as he was, Cliff still found himself laughing at Sid's dumb joke.

"Okay, so I lied about the sunglasses," Sid laughed along, "but the rest is true. They were a real tribe." Cliff wondered where Sid amassed all this otherwise useless information. "Take the term, 'Fuck you'. Everybody, almost everybody uses it at one time or another. But what are they saying? They don't even know. What they're practically saying is 'Go screw my wife'," Sid said with the authority of a Lenny Bruce routine.

"Oh, come off it," Cliff responded.

"Really, adultery is what it's all about. Remember in school when they taught you about colonial America and nobody paid attention?"

"Sure I do. It was pretty boring stuff."

"Of course it was. The teachers weren't paid to make it interesting, although you were lucky if you got one that did."

"I never had one of those."

"One form of punishment they had was called the stocks. You know what they are, they're that frame of wood with holes to lock a person's hands and head in place. Sometimes they'd do their feet, too."

"Sure, I've seen those," Cliff said as Sid gunned another yellow light. This time he made it.

"Those stocks were supposed to be a form of public humiliation. They were set up in the town square where everybody could see them. People were free to throw things, tomatoes, mud, rats, anything at those who were locked in the stocks. If it rained, tough. If it snowed, tougher. The criminal had to stay in there for as many days as he'd been sentenced." Cliff already knew this. He did wonder how they went to the bathroom but decided not to ask.

"Now the scandal sheet hadn't been invented yet, so to beef up the town gossip they'd erect signs that told why a particular person was in the stocks. If he was caught stealing, they'd put up a sign that said 'For Stealing'. Blunt, but to the point. If they were caught screwing the wench next door, they were convicted for adultery."

"So they put up a sign that said 'For Adultery'," Cliff surmised.

"No, not quite. Good guess, though. They didn't want a nasty word like that hanging around in public, so instead they used a sign that said 'For Unlawful Carnal Knowledge'. See?"

"That's neat, I never knew that." It actually hit Cliff like some sort of epiphany. Here was a word he'd used and seen in print, a word worming its way into common usage yet still possessing enough shock value so that it never passes by unnoticed, here its etymological history was laid bare by his new neighbor with whom he was sitting in a red sixty eight Mustang pulling into the visitor's lot of St. Elmo's Memorial Hospital.

"Here we fucking are!"

"Are you sick?"

"That's not a fair question. Oh, you're going to love this, Cliff. I'm getting excited already." They drove past a huge anchor, green with corrosion and brownish-red with rust, half sunk into a plot of earth in front of the main building.

"Are we visiting someone?" Cliff was anxious to know. He didn't feel threatened anymore. The hospital was safe. Even the lobby smelled clean.

Sid paused to think. "Yes, I suppose we are visiting someone, sort of," he said as they got on the elevator. They shared it with two nurses and an old man in a robe. They all faced the door as is the custom. Sid spoke, breaking that awkward silence no amount of proverbial elevator music could soothe. "I usually do this by myself. It's nice to have someone else come along."

Cliff felt an odd sense of embarrassment. It wasn't because of what Sid said, but because he'd said anything at all. Elevator silence served a purpose, he believed. Now everyone there was mentally remarking to themselves about something that was none of their business. The two nurses looked at each other and thought, 'Isn't that nice? His friend came with him to visit a loved one'. The old man thought, 'Another sympathy case. Who needs him? Nobody ever visits me. I hope he's too late. Then he'll be sorry...'

The doors opened and the nurses disembarked with the old man who took so long to shuffle through that Sid had to hold the doors from closing in on him. They rode alone to the next floor and got off as five people and a nurse with an empty gurney got on. Cliff left readily, fearing Sid would start talking again in front of the multiplied silence.

"This way," Sid led, following the yellow path which the color-coded directory indicated as the path to the maternity ward. Cliff felt uncomfortable as Sid had to look into each room as they passed, some morbid curiosity drawing him to catch glimpses of the sick people in their beds. Not soon enough for Cliff, a short hallway lined with windows on one side greeted them. Through those windows could be seen over a dozen newborn babies, all cuddled up in the appropriate pink or blue blankets.

"Here we are," Sid whispered. The pieces were starting to fall together for Cliff. He joined Sid in staring at the shriveled prunes of little people.

"Do you do this often?"

"Depends on how I'm feeling."

Cliff absorbed it all for the first time. He wasn't a refined baby-watcher like Sid. Cliff saw babies who didn't care where your eyes looked when you walked passed them, babies who were not self conscious at all about yawning without excusing themselves, babies who didn't have to attend dinner parties. He was feeling envious when Sid said 'Atta girl!' to a little pink bundle whose thumb, after minutes of searching, found a warm mouth to crawl into.

"It's just so awesome to see all this, this new life," Sid prattled on. He smiled to another girl who was learning to flex her hand, hoping she would see him waving back to her.

"They look so fragile," Cliff said, making a standard observation. All the newborns had their names printed on construction paper signs which hung on their bassinets. There was little Robert Sholz, Janice Lawrence, Linda Elaine Kindersol, Karen Carmen, etc. and one little baby boy who had a blank sign in front of him. Apparently, Mom and Dad hadn't decided on a name for him yet. Cliff felt sorry for him. He knew the other kids would pick on him if he didn't have a name. He pointed the blank sign out to Sid who had already seen it.

"Maybe the Father took off," he theorized, "and the Mother is putting him up for adoption because she can't afford him. I could sneak in and take him away and write on that sign, 'That's what you get for unlawful carnal knowledging around'". The idea came out of Sid's head half-baked. He wasn't thinking straight.

"How would you get in?" Cliff treated him seriously.

"I couldn't," Sid said, disappointed. They were both eyeing the anonymous child when a nurse stepped into the nursery. Cliff noticed her wide hips, breeder's hips, hips ideal for baby-riding. She pointed at the baby with no name as if to say, 'This one?'. Cliff started to shake his head but Sid stepped on his foot and nodded in the affirmative. The nurse smiled as she brought the baby up to the window. She pointed with her free hand to a phone that hung on the wall to their left. She had the other end of the line inside. They used this means of communication for security and also to prevent the babies from being exposed to germs and bacteria. Sid picked it up.

"Hi!" the nurse greeted him. It struck Sid as strange to be able to see the person to whom he was speaking on the phone. The baby boy who did not yet know that pink was for girls looked around with closed eyes set in a pink face. "Which one of you is the Father?"

"Well, both of us, sort of," Sid stammered.

"Oh," was all she could say, realizing what Sid meant.

"They haven't, you know, checked it out yet. We're not so sure we want them to. We both know the Mother very well. Intimately, even."

"I'm sure you do," she said, looking over at Cliff for the first time. He couldn't understand why he wanted to laugh. Sid handed him the phone.

"Here, it's for you."

"Hello," he said, addressing the baby, not the nurse, making closed eye contact. He felt an unfamiliar sensation come over him. "Do, do you know how soon they can take a blood test?" Sid was leaning on the glass, shaking off a laugh. "I really want to know my, our son's blood type. I'm O, see, and my friend here is AB negative, and if we could just, who's, which one of us is the, uh…"

Sid smiled like a proud parent. This exceeded anything he had expected. Cliff glanced over at him and found the chutzpah to meet the nurse eye to eye. She was baffled, completely limp except for the baby on her arm and the phone on her shoulder.

Cliff managed to hang up and start walking away before he totally cracked up. He followed the yellow line backwards to the elevator. He staggered with laughter, not giving a sweet fuck about any of the looks he drew from other people. Sid finally caught up to him, laughing just as loudly.

Sadly, there are places where it is just not socially acceptable to laugh out loud. Cemeteries, final exams and hospitals are such places. While the two men quaked, trying to control themselves with little success, a nurse at the reception desk shot them a dirty look as if to say 'Will you please be quiet? There are people trying to be sick around here!'.

Cliff tried to hold it in but that only made it worse. The elevator doors opened and Sid, who was leaning on them, was swallowed in. It was empty except for the same old man in the robe who they had seen earlier. He had nothing better to do all day than to ride the elevator up and down, up and down. Cliff stumbled in and hit the button while laughing right at the old geezer. Before the doors closed, a young lady started to enter but decided to wait for the next one when she saw the scene inside.

No elevator music could hold a candle to the joyful noise. Sid sat on the floor where he'd landed when he fell in. The old man stood in the corner, thin and motionless. He looked at Cliff who was barely able to keep his footing, then at Sid rolling around on the floor with tears in his eyes. Then the old man experienced the same feeling Cliff had earlier. There is no word for it in the English language, although some come close. The old man wanted to grin. He grinned. He looked at Sid's teary eyes. A sound like that of an intravenous tube backing up issued from his wheezy chest. It wouldn't be long now. Another clog, then a gasp let itself out. Two more. Three more. Then he lost count. He opened his mouth wide and laughed, really laughed. One of the secrets of life finally revealed itself to him after eighty four years and three heart operations somewhere between the second and first floors of St. Elmo's Memorial Hospital.

The doors opened like a hole in a barrel of monkeys. The old man was the first to pop, not shuffle, out of the elevator. Sid and Cliff followed and all twenty three people in the lobby stopped what they were doing to look at them. A little girl started to giggle. Her mother silenced her as everyone else acted their age behind their how-dare-they-do-that faces. The old man stepped aside next to a large potted tree and waved to Sid and Cliff. They'd brought themselves down to mild hysteria, but the old man was still in full swing.

From the revolving doors exiting St. Elmo's, Sid waved back to him. Not paying attention to what he was doing, he tripped and got his ankle pinned in the spinning contraption. Cliff was still in the lobby behind him. No one came forward to help. Any ordinary person might have let out a yell loud enough to draw blood from their own teeth. But they say, it ain't funny unless someone gets hurt, and Sid actually started to laugh at himself. He was soon back into an uncontrolled delirium. He lay huddled on the floor, laughing like a hyena, unable to move. Equally as trapped on the other side was a business man trying to force his large frame, his overstuffed briefcase, two ulcers, four-martini dinner and clump of ugly flowers for his sick wife through the doors at all costs. He pushed too hard on them for Cliff to pull Sid free. Cliff finally got the idea through to the man and he backed up grudgingly. He really didn't understand that something might be seriously wrong because Cliff was laughing as he shouted at him through the glass barrier.

Sid and his ankle fell out and Cliff helped him up. One step proved he couldn't exactly walk on it, so he leaned on Cliff who led them to the wide electric doors reserved for wheelchairs only. They departed to the walkway out front without incident amid stares from the gathering crowd in the lobby. Trying to make a fast getaway, Sid let go of Cliff and took a few painful steps on his own. The first two looked good but the third caused him to scream louder than he laughed. He fell off the walkway and would have fallen to the ground if he hadn't caught his balance by grabbing onto the crusty anchor. Cliff rushed over to him but almost tripped himself on a wire hidden in the grass. The wire led to one of the three floodlights that blinded Sid and illuminated the anchor. When Cliff tripped, he tipped the floodlight on its mounting so that it no longer pointed up at the anchor, rather it shined directly into the lobby. The whole front was glass and everyone jumped back and shielded their eyes. Cliff adjusted Sid on his shoulders and looked back at them all. He had to squint from the glare of the light reflecting off the glass. Everything inside was gray-white. The people stood back as if they were watching a rocket launch at close range. At the main desk, the receptionist was screaming and pointing them out to an elderly security guard who looked like an escapee from the geriatrics ward. Since medical bills were so exorbitant, Cliff supposed they took all the patients who couldn't pay and made them serve guard duty to help defray the cost of their treatment. All the guard did was protect himself from the light and the yelling receptionist as Sid and Cliff took off and several people helped a hysterical old man who had fallen into a potted plant.

Cliff only now began to realize what they were doing. The going was slow with Sid's ankle so he took his keys and left him on the curb. He ran ahead until he found where they had parked. Ignoring how weird it felt to be driving someone else's car, he drove around so the passenger side would face the curb when he approached it. Sid was gone when he got there. Instead, two security guards were scanning the parking lot. Cliff stiffened up and drove past slowly, scarcely breathing. He might have frozen up totally had Sid not waved his hand from behind a parked station wagon seven cars ahead on the right. Cliff slowed down even more and reached across the seat to unlock the door. He was almost at a full stop when he reached the station wagon at the same time one of the guards stepped up behind him at his driver's side window and tapped on it. Cliff, looking to the right for Sid, turned around and nearly started to spill his guts when the first thing he saw was the thirty-eight in its holster. The guard motioned Cliff to roll down his window. He complied by rolling it down two inches.

"I'm sorry, isn't this the visitor's lot?" Cliff could hardly believe it himself. That just came right out of his mouth. It sounded good, too.

"Yes sir, it is. You're in the right place. I'm sorry to bother you, but by any chance did you see a two men walking this way? One of them was probably limping."

"No, I'm sorry, I didn't. I just want to find a place to park. Are you sure I'm in the right lot? I could park somewhere else if you want me to."

"No, sir, you're fine right here. This is the visitor's lot. If you see two men fitting the description, would you please notify security at the front desk inside? We would certainly appreciate it."

"I hope nothing's wrong?"

"Well, I would ask that you be careful. There's no cause for alarm, but apparently these two men tried to steal an infant and then they harassed a heart patient. I'm only telling you this for your own safety, sir. You may want to consider coming back at a later time, after we've secured this area."

"Oh my. Thank you, officer. I just might do that."

Sweaty palms jerked the steering wheel through a few turns down the aisles as if looking for a spot to park. Cliff counted three security officers patrolling the lot. Finally, a shadow jumped out on his right. It was Sid with an Albert Einstein grin on his face. He opened the door before Cliff even saw him.

"Okay, easy now," Sid said as he closed the door quietly. Cliff pounced on the gas pedal. Luckily, the old car just lurched forward a bit. "Easy, Cliff, easy!" They were soon on their way out. Sid couldn't help but laugh which, if nothing else, distracted his attention from his throbbing ankle.

"Where the fuck were you?" Cliff quickly sublimated his fear into anger. "Do you know what they think? They think we stole a baby…"

"And knocked out the old man! Isn't it great? I love it!"

"Yeah, great. Just great."

"Cliff, lighten up, man. Hey, I'm starving. Let's see what they have here. I'm buying."

"Are you nuts? We just created a scene in the hospital and you want to get something to eat right next-door? Jesus Christ, you can still see the parking lot from here. What if they come out here looking for us?"

"Then they'd be fools to look here. If you caught someone breaking into your house in the middle of the night and you scared them off, would you go looking for them in your own backyard? C'mon, you'll miss the entrance."

Cliff's better judgment and paranoia didn't stop him from pulling into Thiesmann's Burgers. He went inside for a takeout order and they ate it in the car. He insisted on parking it around back.

"That was a stroke of genius, Cliff, my boy. What blood type? Fabulous." Cliff didn't give in until they were finished with their burgers, toasting the evening with chocolate milkshakes. Sid allowed Cliff to drive home, and by then the friendly natural defenses that were numbing the pain in his ankle were all but worn off. Cliff had to help him into the house, and each step was a cross between a laugh and a moan. Bump and Grind met them at the door, further impeding their progress to the couch with their 'Daddy's-home' carrying on.

"It's all right, guys. I'm okay," Sid answered their lolling tongues.

"We need a bucket to soak that foot of yours," Cliff suggested.

"Yeah, on the back porch, there's a big aluminum one. Fill it with cold water from the kitchen sink. There's ice in the freezer, I think."

Cliff found the bucket amongst all the clutter out back and rinsed it out before he filled it and returned. He spilled some of the water on the carpet.

"Oh God, I'm sorry, Sid," he apologized direly.

"Jeez, don't worry about it." Sid was astonished at Cliff's seriousness. He wished Cliff would loosen up already. "It's only water. Come on, bring that sucker over here and help me get this boot off." Cliff set the bucket down very carefully and proceeded to tug on the boot. Sid immediately responded with the howl of a grizzly bear stubbing its toe.

"It really hurts, huh?"

"Only when you do that. What the hell, try it again." Cliff tried to ease the boot off. Sid just winced in pain. "Again."

"Sid, I think your ankle is already swollen."

"I think you're right," he said as he stuck his foot, boot and all, into the bucket.

"Your boot!"

"It's okay, they're waterproof," Sid said. Cliff just laughed at him. "Why don't you get us a couple of beers in the kitchen?" he asked, not minding at all being waited on in his own house.

"Why don't I?" Cliff agreed and went back into the kitchen. "Do you want a glass?" he called out.

"Of course I don't want a glass."

Cliff returned with two warm beers. "I couldn't find any cold ones." He twisted the cap off his own, awkwardly due to lack of practice, and settled into a comfortable chair near the nude on the wall. Sid took his cap off with his teeth and spit it into the bucket.

"I bet you thought they only did that in the movies," Sid said with one eyebrow raised slightly. "It's tougher to do with these damn twist-off caps. I learned that from a shoe salesman in Baltimore."

They just sat around in Sid's living room for a while, joking about the old man in the elevator, the nurses, a whole mess of stuff. Sid told Cliff about his car and that shoe salesman, and Cliff told Sid about school and his family. Cliff was actually relaxed, so much so that he didn't even realize he wasn't all tensed up like he normally would be in a situation like this. He felt good, sort of, well, normal.

In the course of the conversation, Sid once referred to Cliff as his 'new neighbor'. "You know, you've been living here for quite a few weeks now. There ought to be a word for a new neighbor after he isn't new anymore," Cliff pondered.

"Duh, we're friends, you idiot!"

And that's as sincere as male-bonding gets after only a beer or two.

6

The days that followed were enlightening ones for both Sid and Cliff. In casual conversations that took place exclusively at Sid's house, Cliff talked more about his family and school, although nothing was really in-depth. Obviously, he didn't have much to say. Sid was secretly appalled at Cliff's disjointed, confined life. It was in stark contrast to the things he'd done, places he'd gone and things he'd learned. He told Cliff about himself, consciously avoiding several topics, among which were Mai and what he did for a living. It didn't escape Cliff's attention that Sid was almost always around, but he treated Sid's privacy as personally as he did his own.

Sid taught Cliff the origins of more obscenities, like 'the clap' (which had some loose connections to the French word for 'rabbit hole' that Cliff couldn't quite grasp). He also taught him some palindromes, such as Napoleon's famous line upon his exile to the isle of Elba, 'Able was I ere I saw Elba'. He told Cliff about who shot down the Red Baron, the man who shot Jesse James, and went into great length about Boris Sikorsky, the accepted inventor of the modern day helicopter. He described how the helicopter defies the laws of physics. Sikorsky stumbled upon a loophole because according to those laws, a helicopter should spin itself into the ground rather than fly. "Good thing Sikorsky didn't pay attention to the accepted facts of his day," Sid said.

Cliff was as thoroughly amused by all these things as he was that Sid even knew about them in the first place. But he wasn't astute enough to challenge the trivia even when it was clearly inconsistent. For example, Napoleon was a French emperor. Why was his palindrome in English?

Cliff was particularly drawn to the chessboard with the half-finished game on it, or half-started as Sid saw it. Chess was the only form of recreation ever given any emphasis in Cliff's childhood. Perhaps his parents thought it was more sophisticated than those silly games with cards, balls or sticks everyone else's children were playing.

"Whose move is it?" Cliff gestured to the board one day with a slosh from his glass.

"That's an old game," Sid said, so used to the board being around he hardly noticed it anymore. "It's Polia's move, I'm sure." He opened a narrow drawer in the stand on which the board sat. It was so stuffed with envelopes it jammed and he knocked over a rook trying to force it open.

"Who's Polia?"

"I never met her, but she's a very defensive chess player. Her name is Russian but she lives in Washington State." He pulled out an envelope from the top of the pile. "Here's her last move, B-QR1. That was on May second, nineteen seventy five. I sent out my move, NxP, one week later. That was what, about six years ago. I haven't heard from her since."

"You play by mail?" Cliff had never heard of the relatively common practice.

"Sure. It's great because you're not tied up at the board for hours at a time. It really got big back when Bobby Fisher and Boris Spassky were playing for the world championship in Reykjavik, Iceland." Sid reached way down under the pile and pulled out an old cover from Life magazine.

It showed Bobby Fisher with a crown and a banner across his chest. Progressively smaller concentric circles were drawn on it with the smallest one directly over Fisher's nose. It was a home-made dartboard riddled with holes. "They had a correspondent in Reykjavik transmitting each move by wire to a studio in New York. This funky-looking dude, Shelby something, was on TV with a felt chessboard pinned up to a bulletin board. He would move the pieces according to the instructions from Reykjavik. It was an exact duplication of Spassky's and Fisher's game. I remember watching those matches for days. I rooted for Spassky because I just didn't like Fisher. I really flipped out when Spassky quit. It was a must-win game and at the end of the day, Spassky left his next move in an envelope to be opened the next morning. When he didn't show up, they opened it and found his resignation. I could've killed him. I had my board set up at home just like Shelby's. I could've had Boris out of that jam in five moves. I yelled to Shelby, but he couldn't hear me. Neither could Boris. He never came back. The next week they came out with this perverted cover on Life magazine. I tore up the article but saved this address where you could send in your name and they'd pair you up with someone else to play with by mail. Chess was as in as it gets, what with the championship and all. That's how I got hooked up with Polia. They reported over thirty thousand people responded to the program."

"That is a lot of games going on at once." Cliff was actually humoring Sid this time. He was into the game, but not this into it.

"Yeah, and you're probably looking at the last one."

"I wonder why Polia doesn't write?" Cliff did glance over the board for possible moves.

"She might be dead for all I know," Sid said, leaving out a crucial bit of treachery on his part. Polia was winning the game. Cliff could see she wasn't playing defensively at all. On the contrary, she had Sid pinned down expertly. Cliff knew, as did Sid, that chess is completely a mental game. In a last ditch attempt to shatter his opponent's confidence, Sid had tacked a lame message onto the last move he mailed out:

Dear Polia Somanovich,
NxP.
Fisher won because he's not a commie chickenshit wimp like
    your Spassky.
Your move.
S.L.

"I've got to get home now. Classes start tomorrow morning."

"Whatever you're into, man." Sid shook his head.

"What's that supposed to mean?" He was just curious.

"It means I think it's silly to use your Dad's money to pay some board of educators thousands of dollars to take some courses when all the information you need is in the stacks of any library."

"What, like independent study?"

"No, like independent learning. It's all there, Cliff. Why not cut out the middleman?"

"And I suppose this is the voice of experience?" The words were a little harsh, but Cliff wasn't taking this too seriously. "Have you ever gone to college?"

"I've been kicked out of more colleges than you've ever gone to. By one, as a matter of fact. Half of the courses they make you take have nothing to do with what you're there to study. Does the word 'elective' sound familiar? All it boils down to is more money for them to build more buildings and hire more teachers to teach you more stuff you don't need or want to know. I got the 'broaden your horizons' speech so many times it makes me sick to think about it. I'll broaden my own horizons, thank you very much."

Sid seemed to know too much about nothing of any real value to have this attitude, Cliff thought. He didn't realize how adamant Sid was on the subject. "So if I want to apply for a job, I don't have to show them a diploma, I just need to give them a photocopy of my library card?"

"Save it, Cliff. If you really wanted a degree you'd have one by now. You're not the first joker to use school as a place to hide out from the real world in. Who are you going to school for, anyway?"

Cliff didn't feel at all free to talk anymore about it. He felt more at ease with Sid than anyone he'd ever met before, but this truth was striking too close too soon. His older half-brother was a successful tech writer for the navy. His half-sister was dating a military man and his little brother had delusions of West Point in his head. Cliff had to do something with his life before they got the idea to make him enlist. School was his only way out and he knew he wasn't working very hard at it.

"I'd better get home, anyway." Damn, he was uneasy again. Sid was right, he should have a degree by now. He should have a company job and be out of Daddy's wallet. God knows his days weren't filled with anything more important to do. Sid was right, but where was all this coming from? One minute they were talking about a chess game, then all of the sudden, this started. Why did Sid feel he had to say anything about it? Who asked for his opinion, anyhow?

He made his exit, went home and straight to bed despite the tangle of thoughts in his head. He awoke punctually at five thirty and left in time to contend with the people on the road going out into the real world. As he left, he noticed the light was still on in Sid's living room. Sid had fallen asleep in the same chair Cliff had left him in. Apparently he had some thinking to do, too.

At each red light on the way to school, Cliff checked and rechecked his registration form. Being the nervous type, he was terrified of being one of those people who walks into the wrong classroom on the first day. He was also terrified of walking into the right one because there were people in there, too. People he didn't know were everywhere. He'd forgotten how easy it was to be with another person, to be with Sid. He couldn't recapture that feeling now that he was alone.

He checked his form. BUS 183.01-Principles of Marketing, MWF 7:00-7:50, B121, Staff. Cliff knew if the instructor hadn't been chosen by registration time, it was the practice to list 'Staff' under the column reserved for the instructor's name and you found out who he or she was on the first day. He also read BUS 252.01-Accounting II, MWF 8:00-8:50, L57, Gatlin.

The light turned green, unnoticed by Cliff as he was rechecking to see if Room B121 was still located in Blakely Hall, just in case they moved it. He was ushered through the intersection amid a volley of horns blaring from behind. One continued to sound off well beyond the light.

"Bastards." He was as mad at them as he felt stupid about himself. He could feel them all eyeing his vile Volvo traffic-jammer. He wanted to pull off to the side, to let them all pass by so he could continue on unhampered. Just then, he saw a car up ahead on the shoulder spewing steam from under its hood. The driver, alone, was waving his arms to the convoy of oncoming cars, led by Cliff.

It was Cliff's year for doing things he never thought he'd do before. Once, he was hiding in his house with nothing to do but feel arrogant or bored, and within the last week he'd co-raided a hospital and sort of made a new friend of his neighbor. Just as there was no good reason why he should've passed on this situation a few weeks ago, there was no particular reason why he stopped to help now. Except of course he'd lose those horn blowers behind him. As he pulled over, one of them blew his horn again as he drove by. The stranded motorist must have been confused because he waved to the passing driver as if it was a friend he didn't recognize.

Cliff recalled a story Sid had told of an old lady who thought he was going to mug her when he stopped to fix her disabled car. This was no old lady, though. This was a short, stocky stump of a man, about fifty, wearing a trenchcoat over a tweed jacket. He had a thin beard and mustache. He lumbered over to Cliff like a baby bear learning to ride a unicycle in a Hungarian circus. His brown, unkempt hair spilled out in clumps as he removed his plaid drivers cap and pressed it to his chest.

"My car is hot!" he said with a thick accent and a laugh.

"Yes, I see that," Cliff replied, wondering what he was getting himself into.

"Can you give to me ride, the college, up there?" the Hungarian bear asked.

"That's where I'm going."

"That is good. One moment," he said and returned to his car. He lifted the hood and, through the cloud of steam, removed the air filter. He came back to Cliff's car with the filter in one hand and an overstuffed briefcase in the other. "I paid much money for my car. It will not now be stolen." He smartly held up the filter for Cliff to see.

"I suppose that could happen." Cliff was now sure ignoring others was a very good way to live. But this guy appeared basically harmless, if not too bright. Must be a professor, Cliff thought. They pulled silently back into traffic before he realized he failed to introduce himself.

"Air filter, huh?" he said instead.

"Yes, what a bad luck." His English was deteriorating rather than improving. In the ten minutes before they reached the school, the bear prattled on about his car and Cliff just nodded. The parking lots were nearly empty this time of morning and Cliff quickly grabbed a good spot near Blakely Hall. The bear released his briefcase and gave Cliff a firm handshake. Cliff had hoped they could've avoided that ritual.

"Thank you," he pronounced each letter carefully. "I see you." He was out of the car before Cliff even moved, pedaling away with briefcase and air filter in hand into Blakely Hall. As Cliff watched him walk into the same building he would soon be going into himself, he thought, "What would be the chances…Nah." Cliff just smiled faintly and shook his head. Sid said he'd gotten a good feeling from helping the old lady even though she had hit him with her blue umbrella. Cliff didn't feel a thing except a little amused. He stayed in his car for a few more minutes rechecking his form, repeating the information on both classes over and over to himself in hopes of avoiding the need to check it again between classes.

It was still early but he went in when other cars started to pull into the lot. Registration form in hand, he looked like a new student hoping to find someone giving out maps of the campus. Pretty bad for someone in his second semester here. Actually, it was a breeze compared to Breece. He found his room, checking the number on the door twice, staring directly at it in case it changed when he moved his eyes.

He breathed easier. He liked to be the first one in the room. That way when class was in session, he could think back to when he was the only one there. This usually brought him some much-needed peace of mind with all those strangers around him.

He turned the lights on and took his customary seat in the front row, to the instructor's right. This was a carefully chosen seat. Cliff put much thought and observation into the phenomenon of where professors place their attention. He knew if you sat anywhere in the back, they immediately sensed you were trying to avoid them. They always gaze back there, overlooking the first two rows. It's true. Cliff stayed away from the center, of course. Professors do tend to look straight ahead. Not at first, no, but after a while they stare straight ahead with only occasional sidelong glances to the corners. From his vantage point, Cliff knew he was successfully hiding in plain sight.

He took off his coat awkwardly, still seated, forgetting he normally kept it on to afford a quicker escape at the end of class. Soon enough, other students came in and as is invariably true they went to the seats in the rear. Fools. Cliff chuckled as they walked into the trap. He couldn't see the people now behind him. This was another good thing about his special seat. There was no constant visual reminder they were even in the same room. Why, there were people with whom Cliff had spent an entire semester in the same classroom, and he never even recognized them outside of class because he had never really seen them. He could only see the front row, now consisting of himself and five empty desks followed by a woman in the other corner. He was glad there would be no attention drawn to him for being the only one in the front row. Then he started to worry that attention might be drawn to him and the woman being the only two in the front row. This asinine preoccupation wouldn't be with him long, for it was about to be replaced by the commencement of class marked by a short, fat Hungarian bear pedaling in behind the podium on a unicycle.

Cliff could feel the molecules and atoms which composed every tissue and process of his body begin to separate, the widening spaces between them filling with cold sweat as he spread out in his seat. The bear was prolonging his agony as he failed to notice him yet. His silly-grinned face hadn't noticed a thing except the floor and the plethora of papers he was shuffling through in his briefcase. Coming across the roll call, he placed it on top of the pile of other papers and turned to the blackboard. He picked up the chalk. Cliff should have seen it coming.

Dr. Rikard Staff
Principles of Marketing
BUS183.01 MWF 7:00-7:50
B121

Dr. Staff read down the list until he reached...

"Dinsdale, Clifford?"

"Here," Cliff squeaked from his corner, waiting for the inevitable.

"Oh, strokes of lucks, it is you!" The once hitch hiker turned college professor was overcome by the coincidence.

"Yes, strokes," Cliff mumbled to himself as he felt the eyes, two for each person in the room, staring at the back of his head and wondering who he was and how he knew this strange professor. His face burned hot with the blood that rushed to it as the bear scampered double-time over to him and shook his limp hand, telling everyone in busted English how he never would have made it to class this morning if not for his friend Clifford.

"I am so happy you are here, Clifford." A severe smile contorted his face as he spoke. Dr. Staff forgot about the rest of the roll call and eventually opened the class with a joke about a former student of his who thought he was in the wrong room on the first day. No one quite got the punch line. Cliff wasn't even listening. Class continued with a brief introduction of the course, the text, the syllabus, blah blah blah, and ended early. Before he left, Cliff was greeted once again by Dr. Staff.

"It is not uncustomary, is it not? That you should help me out of my car and you should be my class. It is wonderful."

"Yes, I must be going now," Cliff said and walked away.

"Looks like you've got an A already," a young man joked with him on the way out. Cliff didn't have the inclination to respond. He just walked on dead ahead, feeling unjustly cheated and bitter. What the hell had he done to deserve all this unwanted attention? The thought to skip his last class and just go home crossed his mind, but that inbred sense of responsibility took him not to his car but to room L57, a lecture hall with the capacity to hold over two hundred students. It didn't matter where you sat, the professor would never see you in the crowd. Thank God.

This class was not going to end early like his first one. Midway through, while Cliff was just staring at the door, a young woman, actually she looked more like a girl to him, opened it and walked into the room. She tried to quietly slip into a seat. She pulled out a notebook, dropped her keys, picked them up and started brushing her hair. The professor couldn't pass on this one. There was an example to be set here.

"Name," she asked, interrupting her lecture to log the student's late arrival.

"Who, me?"

"Yes, you." Prof. Gatlin looked over the rim of her glasses the way a parent does when scolding a child.

"I'm Nancy Tristan," she said, realizing some explanation for her tardiness might be in order. "I'm sorry I'm late, Professor Gatlin. It was a real emergency. I had to take my dog to the veterinarian."

"Miss Tristan, what goes on in your personal life is of no interest or consequence to us." Cliff, along with everyone else, paid attention. This might be good. "I am sure that in the future, no similar emergency will interrupt us in the manner you have succeeded in creating in my classroom today. Is that clear?"

There was a brief silence before the response. "Oh, I'm real sure no 'similar emergency' will ever occur in the future," Nancy Tristan said in a sweet, slicing voice. "Rover died."

Prof. Gatlin just looked at her silently for a moment and then proceeded with the lecture. Yet her lack of a response assured everyone she must have felt foolish. They made this mistake because their judgments were based on how they themselves would feel, put in the professor's shoes. But she was too smart and seasoned for this nonsense. She'd heard the sick dog story many times before, and the sick mother story, the sick father story, and once even the sick little monkey story. That one was just odd enough to be true, though.

So what if Nancy Tristan's dog didn't really die? So what if she had a hangover and slept late? Many people thought it was cool the way she stood up for herself.

Nancy would go on to do well in Accounting II, even though she'd be late several more times. But as Prof. Gatlin knew, the great design of things would win out in the end. Call it Fate or Chance, Karma or Christ, whatever you wish. One week after the midterm, her dog (his name was Oliver, not Rover) would indeed die after ingesting half a box of moth balls in a closet Nancy would unthinkingly leave open before going out to party with her friends.

But that's not to say the vet excuse is not a good one. It will get you by most of the time. The outcome in this particular case was purely coincidental. No connection existed between what Nancy said and what happened in the end. It just worked out that way. Really.

Cliff had no idea what was going to happen to him by midterms, or at any point in time before or beyond. But at least he was thinking about it, thanks to Sid. Cliff was beginning to realize he was wasting, no, killing his time in school. He had no real goals to achieve. They were all achieved for him. All he had to do was put up with it.

Later in the afternoon, after finishing his reading assignments from his first day's classes, he went over to see Sid. His Mustang wasn't in the driveway but he knocked anyway. Only Bump and Grind responded behind the locked door.

He hoped Sid wasn't still mad, or still whatever he was last night. He went back home, not really feeling disappointed because he didn't have anything in particular to say. He didn't want to relay the day's events, he wanted to forget them. He piddled around the house, reread a previously hidden comic book twice and checked his freezer. He had a yen for goulash over rice but lacked the ingredients. Living alone, he knew he had to either develop his culinary skills or be doomed to survive on take-out food and meals that came in cardboard boxes and hermetically sealed boilable pouches. He made fettucini with clam sauce instead, and just before he was done eating he heard Sid's car rumble in next door. He hurriedly hand-washed the dishes and headed over to see him.

"So where were you all day long?" was Cliff's greeting.

"Come on in." They sat down in front of an old movie on TV. The stereo, as usual, was playing low in the background. "I had some running around to do. I checked out that poor excuse for a library at your school." He gestured to a small stack of books on the floor that Bump (or was it Grind?) was sniffing.

Cliff hoped they weren't going to get into this one again. "I haven't seen it yet myself."

"Uh huh." Sid wasn't interested in the small talk. He seemed agitated, farther away than usual. The movie neither of them was watching ended and was followed by a hygiene commercial. "Oh God, not another one of these," Sid whined, making a face at the screen.

It was a commercial for the famed champion of feminine hygiene, Dr. Anna Runn. She was a Canadian gynecologist whose entire academic and professional record was documented in the first half of the advertisement. The second half showed several busy professional women endorsing Dr. Runn and her revolutionary new designs in feminine protection. The ending was the tackiest in Madison Avenue history. A woman hopped into a taxi on a busy city street, rolled down the window, smiled and said, 'I've got to go, I'm on the run!' The sponsor only meant for it to be taken as a cliché, but even the American general public wasn't so stupid as to overlook its implications. Neither was Sid.

"That does it, I'm getting into advertising. If they can make money with garbage like that, so can I." Cliff thought Sid was just kidding around. He was serious. "How's this? Two guys playing a macho game of tennis. The camera zooms in for close-ups to show off their sweaty, competitive American spirit. The camera backs off to show one guy missing a relatively easy shot."

"Darn it, Butch, what's wrong? That was an easy one." Sid was doing the voices of both players.

"You know, Max," the other player responds, crossing his legs.

"You don't mean, Jock Itch?" (echo echo).

"Yeah, I've got the rot. I just can't concentrate on anything anymore. My job is suffering, my family is suffering, even my tennis game is going downhill."

Cliff laughed. He needed this.

"Have you ever tried Rot-Gone, Butch?"

"Rot-Gone? No, what's Rot-Gone?"

"It's the wonderful new anti-fungal spray that simply eliminates the irritation many active men suffer from jock itch." The camera cuts to Butch in the steamy locker room of the country club. He's wrapped in a towel with his lean, hairy chest, tan and golden, reflected in the mirror (bathroom mirrors are never fogged up in commercials). The camera shoots over his shoulder to a can of Rot-Gone. He removes the cap and just as he goes to remove the towel, they switch to a split screen image of the fungus under a microscope. The Tinea cruris was active on the before side but motionless on the after side. Switch scenes to the next day out on the courts. Butch drives Max back to the line and charges the net to put one away. Game, set, match, Butch. He trots to the side where a voluptuous redhead hands him a towel and a scotch.

"I see you took my advice," Max says, down on one knee, beaten. The woman hands Butch a canister which he holds up to the camera.

"Yes, Rot-Gone sure worked for me, Why not try some, for your active lifestyle!"

Sid even had himself laughing by the time he was finished. "Ah, I tell you," he was getting his breath back, "I must've gotten into the wrong business." That statement sparked a question Cliff had only thought of before in passing.

"What business did you get into, Sid?"

"The usual," Sid hedged. "I do a little bit of everything. I'm what you call a jack of all trades but master of none." Cliff thought that was a catchy phrase, but it still didn't tell him what Sid did for a living. Cliff knew it was possible he didn't do anything. That would describe his own life, and he was doing just fine with a house, a car, even a small investment portfolio. To make the silence that followed brief, Sid decided to give Cliff a little schtick, to throw him off a bit. "I've done all sorts of things. I used to work on cars though I was never any good at it. I worked in a steel mill, loading docks, all that. I did some time as a stone mason's apprentice. I stayed with that for three years, the longest I ever held a job. I used to run a produce stand years back in the Italian markets in Baltimore. I also worked for a landscaper in New York. That's how I learned to appreciate rainy days." He hoped this last line would change the subject.

"What?" Cliff asked. Sid was relieved.

"Rainy days are a landscaper's holiday. You can't do a thing outside when it's raining. You can't dig, can't cut, you certainly can't lay seed, it would just wash away. We all used to sit around playing cards each night praying to God to either win the next hand or make it rain the next day. As a matter of fact, I recall I lost that job because God answered my prayers, sort of."

"You won the next hand?"

"No, no, I woke up early one morning before my alarm went off. I hate that when it happens. Anyway, sure enough, it was raining. It was still dark out, but from where I lay in my bed, I could hear it hitting the side of the house and I saw the water running down the window pane. I smiled and thanked the Big Guy and went back to bed. I must've slept until about noon. When I got up, I thought it was still raining but it looked like the sun was out. Here what had happened was the guys I shared the house with had hooked up the garden hose with a spray nozzle they had stolen from work. They had taped it to the fence and pointed it up to my bedroom window on the second floor. The boss fired me for not showing up."

"You don't sound too disappointed."

"I'm not. It was a bloody bad job. And those guys were assholes, anyway."

Sid went to the kitchen for a beer. As he passed the stereo, Cliff asked, "But what are you doing now?"

Sid stopped. "Listening to *music*." He said 'music' as if it was a holy word. He turned up the volume as the record spun on the turntable.

The song went into a chorus that had something to do with Jesus and blowing up your TV. Alone in the living room for a moment, Cliff wondered why Sid listened to this stuff. Sid came back with a beer.

"This town is dead. I can't find a decent hangout anywhere. I think I'm going to try over the bridge into New Jersey tonight."

"You don't know anything about living around here, do you?" Cliff shook his head.

"What do you mean?" Cliff had his attention. "I know you don't know where to go."

"Yeah, but I know where not to go. You're talking about going to Jersey, for crying out loud."

"Yeah, it's just over the bridge, over the Delaware out there."

"But that's Jersey," Cliff repeated as if the name alone was reason enough to stay away. "I guess what you don't know won't hurt you."

This was different. Sid could tell that Cliff was actually trying to be funny, and a little sarcastic. He hadn't seen this side of Cliff before. It was really intriguing, and a little amusing in an odd way.

"You don't know what it's like over there, Sid. There's a rivalry going on between us and them. All they do is tell Pennsy jokes. The first thing they'll ask you when they find out where you're from is how many Pennsies it takes to screw in a light bulb."

Sid was delighted to see Cliff's shrouded life hadn't cramped his style too much. He'd rarely seen him so relaxed, acting so much like himself. This situation about the rivalry between the states wasn't totally made up, either. Cliff went on to tell Sid the oldest Jersey joke he knew, about the lower bridge into Trenton, not even named for the road which crosses over it. It has a message on it, spanning most of its length in illuminated letters tall enough to be seen from the banks of the river and more importantly from the freeway bridge, which, ironically, is a toll bridge. It reads 'Trenton Makes, the World Takes'. It was erected many years ago, probably by the Trenton Chamber of Commerce as a sign of metropolitan pride in its business and industry. People from Pennsylvania often lampooned it, preferring to say 'Trenton Uses What the World Refuses'.

"You've got to know that if you're going to live on this side of the bridge, Sid." Cliff went on some more when he saw Sid's positive response, about Jersey being the toxic waste capital of the world and things like that. It wasn't much, but it was a start, Sid thought.

Cliff's stories were interrupted by a knock at the door. Sid uttered a falsely formal 'Excuse me' and answered it. Cliff could not see but was as sure who it was as old Albert E. on the wall facing the door. Cliff could smell Mr. H.'s pipe tobacco preceding him.

"Maybe just for a minute," Mr. H. conceded to Sid's invitation to come inside, "but I want to be home in case Barbara stops by with Billy."

"Tell them to come over here. I haven't even met them yet. Come on in, I'll get you a beer."

"I really can't stay that long," Mr. H. explained, walking inside the foyer. "Here's that book you wanted to borrow."

"Great, thank you. I'll have it back to you in no time."

"No hurry," Mr. H. said, coming into the living room. "Hello, Cliff, I didn't know you were here. I'm not interrupting anything, am I?" He directed the question to both of them. Cliff couldn't help but notice Mr. H. was decidedly more friendly than the first time they had met.

"No, no, of course not," Sid told him, leafing through the book. "Take a seat." He headed to the kitchen engrossed in some pictures. Mr. H. just stood there until Sid caught himself. "I'm sorry, say, Cliff, would you mind letting Mr. H. sit in your chair? He likes that one because it faces away from my 'dirty drawing'."

"Of course," Cliff complied readily. He slid over to the couch.

"Thank you, Cliff. It's a nice drawing but frankly," he made sure Sid was in the kitchen, "I find it a little embarrassing, don't you?"

"I don't think so," Cliff answered slowly, seizing the opportunity to scrutinize the drawing longer than was necessary. Sid came back and handed Mr. H. a beer.

"I really shouldn't."

"I was just telling Sid about Jersey people," Cliff told Mr. H..

"Oh, that." Sid noticed Mr. H. knew exactly what Cliff was talking about. There might be some credibility to this after all. "Did you tell him about the lower bridge?"

"Just before you came in." Cliff smiled and looked at Sid. "See?"

"It's a good thing to know about," Mr. H. puffed.

"I'm going to have to get back into this," Sid said, his nose buried back into the book on pipes that Mr. H. had loaned him.

"It wouldn't hurt," Mr. H. said. Cliff couldn't believe he was hearing this. He voiced the majority opinion that smoking was horrible for you and dangerous to your health.

"Horsefeathers!" Mr. H. scowled at the comment. "You've got to look passed the surgeon general's warning. Who cares what he's determined? What do you expect from a Navy man?"

"I think he ought to have his stupid beard shaved off," Sid commented. "He's giving smoking a bad name."

Cliff didn't know a thing about the surgeon general's military career or his facial hair preference. He was out of his element, so he bowed out as Sid and Mr. H. went on about the merits of smoking. Cliff at least agreed there had to be something to it for so many people to overlook the health risks in order to pursue the habit. He had never smoked himself, and he remembered a picture of an autopsied lung from an emphysema patient in his Human Physiology textbook. Apparently he never saw the picture of the atrophied liver, as he excused himself to the kitchen to get a warm beer.

"Well I for one am going out tonight. Any takers?" Sid asked as he took the spinning record off the turntable. "What do you say, Mr. H., do you want to come with me?"

"You've got to be kidding," Mr. H. joked. Cliff came back from the kitchen, beer in hand.

"How about you, Cliff? Do you want to come with me? We can go make fun of the Jerseys. Besides, I think you drank all my beer."

"I'm sorry," Cliff said, stopping in mid-chug.

"I'm just pulling your leg, you idiot." He patted Cliff on the arm. "That's what it's there for. So, do you want to come with me?"

Sid was too good for his old excuse. God forbid, honesty might do the trick. "I never go out to bars much, Sid. I don't think I'd be comfortable." He knew he sounded stupid but he wanted to be truthful.

Sid was sympathetic. "Okay, far be it from me to take you out against your will. I understand."

Mr. H. heard a car go by. The sound jolted his memory and he recalled his daughter. "Uh oh," he said, setting down his untouched beer, "I'd better be going now. Barbara might be here soon."

"Did she say she was stopping by today?" Sid asked.

"Well, no, not for sure. But she might be coming by anyway. I've got to get home or I'll miss her. Thanks for the beer. See you, fellas." He let himself out. Sid felt sorry for what he thought was a lonely man. He watched Mr. H. pass by his front window against the darkening sky. Cliff missed the whole scene.

"I'll be going now, too, Sid." Sid conceded to going out alone again. He walked Cliff to the door and smiled when he said 'Good night' to Albert. "Maybe next time." Cliff said as he walked out.

"Thanks, Cliff. See you later."

Now, when he first walked into a bar, Sid never liked it right away. It normally took him a few drinks to tell if he could put up with the crowd, how long it would take to clear them out if he didn't, the length of the bar, the mixologist behind it, etc.. Chances are, if he didn't mind the place after a few drinks, he minded it even less after a few more.

Sid enjoyed trying to get used to bars, but he could be picky. That night he tried to get used to Joe's bar, Larry's bar, Peter, Paul and Mary's bar, Jack's bar, Jill's bar, and uselessly a dairy bar. He criss-crossed the Delaware over rickety old bridges and would try to remember to tell Cliff that yes, they do still light up the 'Trenton Uses What the World Refuses' sign on the lower bridge at night.

He could not recall how he'd gotten back to his driveway. His tongue tasted like the back of a dog's leg. He flopped out of the Mustang and fell while trying to close the door. It had been a long time since he was this drunk. He had sworn off overdoing it, but all that driving had made him thirsty. He recalled how he used to laugh uncontrollably when he used to get this drunk all the time. What do you know, he still did. Laugh uncontrollably, that is. With his hand over his mouth, he just made it inside the door and hit the light switch before he cracked up and fell down again. He stopped suddenly, uncertain whether or not he'd closed his car door or not. It was the same uncertainty he felt when he got up in the middle of the night to pee ('piss' wasn't so much vulgar as it was simply an ugly word to him) and returned to bed, unable to remember whether or not he flushed.

He made it into the doorway of the living room before he fell down again. It was well past the middle of the night. He got up and went to pee. He was in there a while because he flushed three times for peace of mind.

He returned to his lucky doorway where he had fallen down earlier and fell down. He might have pissed or peed himself laughing had he not just gone to the bathroom. He got up when he wondered if he had flushed. He knocked down a stack of books in the process, trying to step over Bump or Grind. While trying to restack them, he came across the book Mr. H. had loaned to him. He hugged it and stepped over the other books without falling until he reached the couch. He finally turned a lamp on after a few minutes of trying to read the book by the light out in the foyer. When he did, he realized the book was upside down. He then dropped it, picked it back up, but it was still upside down. A firm believer in chance and statistics, he dropped it again on purpose and picked it up. It was right side up this time.

The book mostly covered the history of pipes and tobacco. It showed many color photographs of pipe styles long out of fashion, many only found in collections. There were Turkish chibouks with stems so long the clay bowls rested on the ground at the smoker's feet; Calumets, or American Indian peace pipes, heavily adorned with beads and feathers. Sid recalled he used to own a small imitation calumet that was actually a hash pipe. It seemed like such a silly idea now; The Calabash, constructed from a gourd and fitted with a meerschaum cup, more commonly referred to as a Sherlock Holmes pipe; Something he was more familiar with, the Arghile, which unfortunately isn't pronounced anything like it's spelled; There was one particularly nice Bavarian pipe with an elaborately lathed and stained wooden stem that pointed down to the smoker's chest, then up and forward to hold a porcelain bowl of an inverted teardrop design. A forest scene, done in Wedgwood, seemed to melt into the bowl, capped off with a sterling silver lid and chain. The once white meerschaums were well smoked, as evidenced by their honey brown color, brought on by the juices extracted from the tobacco. Meerschaum is easily carved, and the one shown in the book was a finely detailed Bacchus, the Greek god of wine. His jubilant face surrounded by a wreath of grapevine was as golden as the original polished amber bit.

Among the more modern briar styles, Sid spotted one that reminded him of one of his old pipes. It was true what he'd told Mr. H.. He used to smoke some tobacco. He wondered if he still had any of his old pipes lying around somewhere.

The longer he stayed down, the harder it was for him to get back up. But he managed and made it upstairs to a spare room where he hid some old boxes with the intention of unpacking them someday. The only light he had came from a sixty watt bulb in the hallway ceiling fixture. This was one of several rooms in the big house that he didn't use much, and he never did put even a lamp in there. He started with the boxes that were lined against the wall and in that light from the hallway. They were crammed full of old junk. One box was completely filled with stolen ashtrays from dozens of hotels. There were old clothes, a bent fender from his old motorcycle, which was all he could salvage after the crash, sheet music, the complete Playboy from Miss March '71 through Miss September '77 and piles of eight track tapes, all snapped and in need of splicing.

He shuffled through some more boxes looking for his pipes. They had to be here somewhere. He opened a closet to find it full of clothes, which he couldn't remember putting on hangers. He pushed them aside and found himself being stared at by a guitar case. It was the tomb of his first acoustic guitar. He didn't really want to play it again. He could see it plainly though the lid was closed. Not every boy gets a Martin as his first guitar, but that's what his Grandma bought him on his twelfth birthday. It was not because she knew anything about them, she simply went into the music store and asked for the best. Sure, she had to go back home for more money but when she left the second time, she left with a Martin. She wanted her Sidney to be the next Eddy Arnold. Oh Grandma, what has your grandson gone and done?

Sid bent down and undid the clasps. He didn't feel like laughing now. He lifted the lid slowly, like a gangster going for his Tommy gun before a hit. Before he even got it opened far enough to see the Martin, the pent up air inside flowed out. The smell of the blue felt lining and the oil and polish of the wood combined to turn his thoughts back to the first time he opened it. He always did like that smell…

"Gee Grandma, this is neat!" Little Sidney Lasvistas jumped to hug his Grandma Carol. There was no birthday party, just Sidney, Grandma Carol and Ed, the widower from next door.

"He likes it!" Grandma Carol smiled back at Ed.

"Boy, I sure do!"

Ed smiled approvingly then said in a fatherly tone, "Now if you practice real hard with that there guitar, Sidney, why maybe someday you'll be as famous as Carl Perkins."

"You mean Eddy Arnold," Grandma Carol corrected him.

Sidney took his guitar out of its case and started strumming and dancing around with it all over the living room. Grandma Carol laughed until she recalled how much she'd paid for it and told her grandson to be careful. Ed calmed her down and told her to let the boy have his fun. He felt just like he was Sidney's father. The boy deserved one after what had happened. Ed was still on the police force full time then. He was the first one to reach the car…

Shirley Lasvistas and her mother, Carol, were in the kitchen preparing a spaghetti supper for Ned, Shirley's husband. Carol was proud of her son-in-law. He was a good husband to her Shirley and a good provider, too. He was kind enough to offer her a home when her husband, Hoyt, died five years ago. Carol wished Hoyt could be with them to witness the birth of their first grandchild whom Shirley was now carrying at full term.

"Ned is going to love this. He can eat spaghetti until it comes out his ears," Shirley said, checking the huge, boiling pot.

"I'll set the table. Ned will be home soon." Carol left the kitchen with her arms loaded with dinner plates. When she reached the table she heard Shirley gasp, followed by a moan that got cut off. It was her birthing pains, Carol knew. The doctor said there might be complications. She spilled the plates onto the table and ran back to the kitchen. Shirley was at the stove, half bent over, one hand gripping her womb and the other balancing herself on the stovetop. She was straightening up.

"Take it easy, child," Carol told her. Before she could reach her, Shirley doubled over spastically, grabbing onto the pot handle. With an involuntary flex of her muscles, she pulled the boiling pot off the burner.

Screams and steam hit Carol in the face as she leaped forward. Shirley was down on one knee, leaning rigid against the stove. The water had spilled over her right arm and shoulder but mostly down her back. The noodles stuck to her pinkening skin like hot whip lashes. Steamy mist rose from the water, which was spreading out all over the floor.

Carol was too horrified to scream as Shirley's own screams were deafening her. She kept her wits about her as she whisked the noodles from

Shirley's back as she screamed louder and louder and clutched her womb. Carol grabbed some dishrags, ran cold water over them and wrapped them around her daughter's scalded flesh. Ned had pulled into the driveway and heard his wife's screams even before he killed the engine. He busted into the kitchen.

"It hurts it hurts!"

"I know honey I know now it's going to be all right," Carol tried to soothe her.

"Oh my God, it's the baby. What happened?" Ned was taken back when he saw his wife. "The baby, the hospital, we have to get her to the hospital quick," he babbled as they helped her, wrapped in rags and arms, out the door and into the back seat of the car.

Ned shot out of the driveway and through the red light at the end of the block, weaving in and out of traffic. Sebastian Lake Hospital was only five miles away.

Carol was in the front seat leaning over to the back where Shirley lay quietly sobbing. The highway widened into four lanes and Ned sped back and forth, blaring his horn. A green light up ahead turned first yellow then red. He gripped the wheel tighter. Shirley let loose an agonizing wail that made Ned turn around to her.

"Honey you're going to be all right!"

The car never reached the red light. It did, however, stop.

When Ned turned around he jerked the wheel and so the car into the opposing lane. The driver's side of the car hit the driver's side of the pickup truck. It happened just outside the coffee shop where Officer Ed Walleski was finishing his afternoon break. He turned to see the white pickup just before it rolled over after demolishing half the Plymouth. He rushed over to the truck before he realized what was left of the Plymouth looked familiar. He recruited some bystanders to extricate a young lady from the pickup while he went around and looked through what used to be the rear window of the car. His suspicions were confirmed when he saw Carol splayed over the seat. The smell of gasoline was overpowering and he feared both the car and the truck were going to blow. He climbed onto the trunk and pulled Carol, unconscious, out from between the collapsed roof and buckled front seat. He could see a fine red line trickling down her scalp through her thin, graying hair. Two others pulled her the rest of the way out and Ed went around front while his partner was still calling for assistance on the radio. With the help of a truck driver, Ed pried up the hood and roof which partially covered the front seat. The trucker doubled over and gagged.

"Oh Ned, Ned…" Ed shook.

"Shirley!" He knew she was expecting soon. He was talking to her just the other day. But where was she? He ran around to the passenger side screaming, "There's somebody else in there!"

"Ed, get away, it's going to blow any second!"

"She's in here somewhere, I tell you. It's Shirley, she's pregnant. She's in here, I know it." Only two men came forward to help as an ambulance arrived at the scene.

Ed was halfway in the rear window. The back seat was mostly covered by the front. With the gas fumes making him dizzy, he pushed up on the front seat which would only give a little. He pushed harder and a single stream of blood ran down the blue vinyl seat covering from the driver's side. Ed didn't want to see again what was left of his friend Ned. He pushed harder and again more blood spilled down. He saw a rag. He pushed so hard and grunted so harshly the other men thought he was hurt now, too. He got the seat back far enough to expose Shirley. "She's here!" Two of the men started lifting her out and a third joined in, all being especially careful of her protruding womb. They saw her swollen skin under the rags as they loaded her limp body onto a waiting cart. Carol briefly regained consciousness, long enough to see her daughter being put into the ambulance before she blacked out again and was loaded into an ambulance of her own. Both vehicles finished the intended trip to the hospital as rescue workers hosed down the gasoline and pried the third body out of the front seat. Ed relayed some information to his partner and went to the emergency ward.

He practically lived at the hospital for the next two days, during which time Carol came around. Though too weak to speak, she did recognize Ed. He was at least sure she could hear him when she started to cry as he told her Shirley had given birth to a healthy baby boy. Carol cried longer and harder two weeks later when Ed also told her Ned was dead and Shirley died the day after the delivery.

A few years later, Ed's wife passed away. Childless, he retired and bought the house next door to the old Lasvistas place where only Carol and her grandson Sidney now lived. Keeping an eye on the boy and Carol was the best way he could think of to spend his retirement. It was a small suburb, and even though it had been years since the accident, somebody would always be dropping by with food, clothes and such every now and then. Ed helped out with his pension and Carol received survivor's benefits from her late husband's policy, so ends were met with some to spare. Little Sidney kept growing up, and when people saw him they saw a miracle, a little boy who was fortunate to be alive. He grew up and learned to play that guitar better than the first day he'd gotten it. But he didn't become the next Eddy Arnold...

Sid threw the lid back. The startling blue felt outlined the blonde Martin guitar like a corpse in a funky casket. He ran one finger over the pick guard, scratched and nicked by thousands of repeated chords. The pale wood it protected was cleaned and polished. He took better care of that guitar than he did of himself, that was for sure. He passed the same finger over each of the five minus one strings, releasing the shallow hum of an instrument long out of tune. He recognized the macramé shoulder strap some girl had made for him. He tried unsuccessfully once more to rub out a cigarette burn on the neck between the fifth and sixth frets that someone once used as an ashtray.

Rather than look at it anymore, he closed the lid and clasps and stood it up against the back wall of the closet. The hanging clothes hid it from view. He opened the box upon which it had rested. The rising dust provoked a sneeze which provoked more dust to rise. Through watery eyes and the dim light behind him, he tossed aside some souvenir copies of Licks and Riffs, a music magazine, that undoubtedly contained some reviews. Among some books, papers, one roach clip, guitar picks, a broken bong and a rolled-up one hundred dollar bill which he pocketed, he found a square cedar box. Inside were three of his briar pipes, two freehands and a Prince style. He pulled out one of the freehands, remembering it as one of his old favorites. The bowl was too big inside to smoke anything but tobacco. Also in the box were some pipe cleaners, new and used, a cleaning tool, three empty packs of matches and a crumpled piece of newspaper. He unraveled it to find a plastic bag still half filled with tobacco. He opened it and took a whiff of the sweet leaves. He held it up to the light and read the label; Palindar Reef. It was way too dried out to smoke but Sid was in no condition to distinguish good from bad. He spilled more on the floor than he got in the pipe. He packed it down and hunted for matches, finding only the three empty packs. He did find a few packs he had scarfed from the bar in his leather vest.

He thought of how much he must look like Mr. H. with the loaded pipe in his mouth. He recalled the brief conversation they'd had, when Mr. H. suggested smoking in the dark so you couldn't see the smoke. 'Light up in a darkened room,' he'd said. With only that and curiosity sloshing about in his mind, Sid rolled all the way into the closet and closed the door. He pulled some clothes down from their hangers and stuffed them against the bottom of the door to block the hallway light from sneaking under it. He sat cross-legged with his back against the door. He had kept the pipe clenched between his teeth the whole time. Striking a match, he held it up to find the top of the bowl, which had been bumped to one side. As he straightened it, he dropped the match. It extinguished itself on his left pant leg. He went to strike another one but lost his grip on the pack and effectively flung it against the wall, a foot and a half away in the darkness. He broke a few pretzels in his pocket looking for another pack. He struck another match and proceeded to draw with the flame held above the half-filled bowl. A second match was needed to light the rest of the bowl. The tobacco glowed red-orange on top, the flame jumping higher with the rising smoke oozing up from the pipe. In the matchlight, Sid couldn't tell the sweet coils of tobacco smoke from the smoldering newspaper smoke from the fallen match to his right.

Mr. H. was right, after all. Sid really wasn't enjoying this even a little bit. He'd just started and the little closet was choked with smoke, and the dry tobacco was burning too hot, biting his tongue. This unpleasant sensation, coupled with the gagging attempts to breathe, convinced him to abort the experiment. He could not see but rather he imagined he felt the smoke wrap around him as he reached up for the doorknob. He was cut short by a coughing fit and dropped his pipe, spilling the hot embers. He was having no luck with the doorknob from his awkward sitting position. He kept coughing and banging his head against the door, sobering himself up quickly in the process. He finally got up to his knees and turned around. He gave the knob a sharp twist and the door fell open under his weight. The light from the hallway rushed in as quickly as the smoke poured out. Sid landed on his back with his legs still in the closet. His bleary, teared eyes watched the smoke rise and splash all over the ceiling and consume the whole room. The smoke was soaked into his throat and eyes, making the hallway light a burning beacon. Still on his back, he rubbed his eyes for a few moments and reopened them, only to find a new light coming from within the closet. He looked down at his legs to see the box of magazines and ashtrays burst into flames. He slid himself out on his elbows, butt and kicking feet, ignoring his singed jeans as he watched the fire spread to the clothes on the floor and the hanging garments as well.

He got up, ran to the window and yelled something that was supposed to sound like 'Fire!' but came out of his mouth as a coughing, wheezing sound that only started with the letter 'F'. He didn't see the fire engines he wanted to see lined up in his front yard. He dodged back into the closet and reached for his Martin, but the fire lunged at the side of his face like a rabid Doberman. He grabbed some clothes off their hangers with which to beat the fire out, succeeding in only fanning the flames higher. Dazed and desperate, he started hauling the rest of his junk into the hallway away from the blaze. He'd only moved a dozen boxes when he was almost overcome by the thick smoke.

He glanced at the fire roaring out of the closet before he ran down the hallway to the steps, stumbled down the first one, caught himself and took them one at a time until he jumped over the last four and out the door. The air hit him cold and clean as he ran to Cliff's house, never breaking stride. He banged and banged on the door until a frightened Cliff turned on the light and opened it just a crack. "Sid, what happened to you?" Cliff stared wide-eyed at his beard.

"My house," he panted, "fire. Fire! Call somebody."

"Your house? Is on fire?" This was no time to verify the obvious. He got on the phone to the fire department immediately, reading the number from the emergency list he kept nearby. He had to shout to make himself heard over Sid, who was standing next to him, catching his breath.

"Come on, we've got to get over there quick! Hey, I didn't know you slept in the nude."

Cliff followed Sid out the door after grabbing only a pair of pants and a robe. He ran barefoot through the frosty grass, trying to close his robe over his bare chest. Luckily, he didn't step in any of the glass on Sid's front lawn that had been blown out of the upstairs window because of the intense heat building up behind it. Flames were clawing out and up from the hole where the window had been like a mouse-eye view of a hungry cat's paw reaching into its happy home. Sid screamed from the doorway, "Get in here and help me haul this stuff out!" By the time he reached the door, Cliff had to back up to make room for Sid. He was carrying out the huge framed drawing of Maivina. "I'm taking this over to your house. I don't want it getting busted."

Cliff was then alone in the house. It was terribly peaceful in contrast to the fury of action he knew was spreading above him. Only a fine mist of smoke mingled with the air. Cliff struggled with Albert, unable to get him off his hook. "Never mind that, help me get my records," Sid said as he ran back in. Cliff never realized how much LP's could weigh. They stacked half the collection on the coffee table and carried them out to the bushes by Cliff's place. They went back in for the stereo and the rest of the records. Sid stuffed things into his pockets, running from room to room, while Cliff grabbed the first speaker. Sid followed him out with the turntable and tuner, ripping the cord out of the tuner as he ran because he forgot to unplug it. He handed them both to Cliff and ran back in for the tape deck, the other speaker, more records, running from room to room for anything else he could carry.

The fire engines had arrived. Sid stepped out, dumped his load and tried to return for more but one of the firemen held him back.

"I've got to get back in there!" Sid shouted at him.

"Sid, over here," Cliff called out. Bump and Grind were with him.

"Where's my cat, Goddamnit?"

Cliff pointed up the tree to a white fluff resting on a low branch. Sid was relieved but there was so much more he wanted to retrieve. The firemen already had two hoses trained on the upstairs windows. Sid tried to get back in and would have succeeded if another fireman hadn't stepped in to assist the first in restraining him. They dragged him away, screaming and kicking, dropping all kinds of things all over the lawn.

The sound of more sirens got closer and closer and another engine arrived. Soon, more water would be sent special delivery into the upstairs windows. Sid and Cliff were back near the trucks on the shoulder of the road. Mr. H. came running over as speechless as everyone else at the sight. The front door was wide open and Einstein seemed to shake with laughter in his crooked frame. His eyes were bright and wide. Three firemen carried a dripping hose towards the front door. When they were only a few steps away they jumped back as three flaming support beams punched down through the ceiling, obstructing the doorway. Einstein was all lit up now with the light reflecting off the glass covering his likeness. The flames stepped out and waved to everybody as the firemen broke through the living room window. They weren't in time with the hose, though, and Einstein was laughing out loud before being engulfed.

Sid knelt down and put an arm each around Bump and Grind, his head held up, staring as he hoped the fire would start to subside. He was oblivious to the flashing red lights of the engines and the volunteer's cars, the loud hum of the compressors pumping water through the hoses and into the house, the mob of men in long coats and red hats competently containing everything and somehow bringing a semblance of order to the atmosphere. He didn't see the handful of other neighbors lined along the street and even across the river, the shining chrome dials, meters and gauges on the trucks. He didn't notice the fireman who approached Cliff, stomping back and forth in his bare feet in the cold grass. "I'm afraid there's going to be extensive water damage to the house, sir. And damage from the fire, of course," he said, mistaking him for the owner. The way he was dressed, he certainly looked like he was rushed out of his house in the middle of the night.

"There's your man," Cliff pointed and Sid looked up at them with hollow eyes and a burned hole in the side of his beard the size of a small orange.

As the fire was already being stifled to a smoldering calm, the Fire Captain asked Sid a series of questions in an attempt to ascertain the cause of the fire. Sid avoided the issue and contemplated asking the firemen to call a hook and ladder truck to rescue his cat out of the tree. He'd once heard firemen did stuff like that. But on second thought, he decided to let the cat come down when it was good and ready to, Goddamnit.

The Captain could get no real information out of Sid. "At any rate, Mr. Lasvistas, we can't let you go back in until we determine the extent of the damage."

"You don't tell me when I can go back into my own house, pal," Sid said, drawing astonished looks from those around him, "but I will stay out only because you seem to know what you're talking about. You did one hell of a job putting it out. Thank you." The Captain didn't know if he wanted to acknowledge Sid's gratitude of turn the hoses on him.

"Do you have a place where you can stay the rest of the night, Mr. Lasvistas?" he asked.

Sid turned from his house. His gaze passed over Mr. H. who said, "Barbara came over late, she's in my spare room with Billy." Sid's eyes rested on Cliff.

"Do I have a place to stay tonight, Mr. Dinsdale?" He asked, showing a knowing look that might have been mistaken for arrogance by someone who knew less about Sid.

"Of course you do, Sid. But the dogs sleep on the floor."

"Whadaya mean? You've got two great big couches in your living room, one for me and…"

"And one for me. You're going to tell me exactly what happened. Your beer is probably all warmer than usual now," Cliff said, looking at the house. "I really hate warm beer, you know that?"

It was after five thirty in the morning before the last fire engine pulled away. Only a handful of firemen would stay around to do the post-catastrophe work. The first rays of sunrise were bouncing off the Atlantic Ocean and feebly illuminating the skies over New Jersey. The inspectors would come later in the morning, and until then Sid's house was off limits.

Cliff went upstairs to collect some blankets and pillows while Sid arranged his salvaged goods in the corner room downstairs.

"Do you mind if I set up my stereo?"

"No, go ahead." Bump and Grind were exploring their new home, sniffing out the stale air that had been hovering in corners for months undisturbed. Cliff allowed the dogs in the house only because Sid kept them scrupulously clean.

Sid only now noticed the cord was missing from his tuner. It wasn't such a horrible thing in comparison to the other events of the evening. He plugged the speakers directly into the turntable and put on an album. He slumped back on the couch where Cliff found him, listening to some Jimmy Buffett.

"Here, take these," he said, dropping one of the pillows and a blanket on his lap.

"Thanks," Sid whispered, not bothering to open his eyes or clear his throat. Cliff placed the rest on the other couch, his makeshift bed for the morning. Still dressed in his jeans and a robe, and also a warm pair of socks, he went into his kitchen for two cold beers.

"You know, they still light up that bridge you were telling me about." Sid sat up to receive the bottle.

"That's wonderful. You look like shit, Sid," Cliff interjected matter of factly. "I don't suppose you've seen your, um, your…" Cliff couldn't say it. He just rubbed his hand over his own cheek.

"My what?"

"Your face is, uh, you haven't seen a mirror around here, have you?"

With that, Sid tried to hurry into the hall and instinctively found the downstairs bathroom. He was out of Cliff's sight with the light shining on the drawing of Maivina in the hallway opposite the bathroom.

"Aw heck," Sid whined. His lousy evening just got worse. He remained quiet for a few moments before he turned off the light and came back to his couch. "I'm too tired to do anything about it now," he said, patting the hole in his beard, feeling its size, and inspecting it manually. It didn't hurt until now that he'd seen it. "I'll take care of it tomorrow."

"It is tomorrow." Cliff pointed to the clock which read five thirty seven. He was glad he didn't have class this morning.

"How could I be so stupid?" Sid said to no one in particular. With his eyes closed, he chugged down half his beer and set it down on the coffee table. He fell back with his arms limp at his sides, his legs bent askew to avoid crushing into the table which was much too close for comfort. Cliff was anxious to hear about the evening and he waited for Sid to go on with his story. He didn't.

"So? What happened?"

Sid remained quiet, unmoving.

"Sid, what happened tonight? Sid? Sid!"

Disappointed but knowing it could wait until later, Cliff walked over and covered Sid with the blanket. He tried to get a closer look at his mauled beard but Sid's breath drove him away. He moved the coffee table and Sid's legs automatically fell into a much more comfortable-looking position. He then went into the hallway and brought out the drawing. He propped it against the chair where Sid would see it when he woke up.

He lay down, reached up behind himself and turned out the light. There was still a soft glow from the display on the front of the turntable, and it was getting light outside. Cliff watched it get lighter until the album side wound down and finished. In the silence he lay there with his eyes open until he realized the music had stopped and found it strange how he'd gotten lost in the sound of it and Sid's breathing. He'd been hearing a lot of music lately, as would anyone who hung out with Sid. He always had something playing. Of all he'd heard, one song came to Cliff's mind before he fell asleep. It was by one of Sid's favorites, another one by that John Prine guy;

> *I could be as happy as a sardine in a can*
> *Long as I got my woman*
> *I could run stark naked and live in an old oak tree*
> *Just as long as she's with me*
> *My woman*

Cliff surprised himself when he had no trouble recalling the lyrics.

> *I could get the electric chair for a phony rap*
> *Long as she's sittin' in my lap*
> *My woman*

That line always raised a smile, even if it was only playing in his head.

> *They could torture me and stretch me like a rubber band*
> *Long as I got my woman*
> *I could jump off a cliff and never have no fear*
> *Just as long as she is near*
> *My woman*

Cliff fell asleep looking at Maivina.

7

The sun rose, and all was relatively quiet that morning. After all, it was winter, meaning there were no blooming flowers outside. The dawn light trotted over Cliff's eyelids, daring him to remain asleep. The sun lost the confrontation as Cliff slept straight through until noon when he was awakened by an unfamiliar sound. It was a staccato whisking sound, like windshield wipers over sandpaper. Whatever it was, it came from the bathroom. Cliff assumed it was Sid, who was not on the other couch where he'd left him. The blanket hung to the floor, the coffee table was pushed farther towards the middle of the room and one of the pillows had inexplicably made it all the way to the hall.

He hopped into his jeans, hoping he could remember the dream he had last night. "That is you in there, right? Sid?" he asked, standing in the hallway.

"No, it's Sweeney Todd," Sid answered from behind the closed door.

"Sweeney what?"

"You lead a sheltered life, my boy," Sid said as he opened the door. What Cliff had heard was Sid sharpening his straight blade razor. He had grabbed it, along with plenty of other things, last night before the firemen arrived. Two strops, laid back to back, hung from the inside doorknob. The first, a belt of vinyl weaved mesh, did the rough sharpening. The second, made of leather, honed the already keen edge to an even higher degree of perfection. This was achieved by laying the blade flat on its side and gliding it up and down the strop, always trailing the razor's edge behind. Normally a few strokes on each strop was sufficient, but Sid threw in some extra repetitions. He had an important shave ahead of him.

"What in the world is that thing?" Cliff noticed the straight blade as Sid applied more lather to his cheeks with his shaving brush.

"You don't expect me to walk around with half a beard, do, you? It's a razor."

"It doesn't look like my razor."

"That's because you use one of those sissy safety razors," he said in a macho, jock-itch commercial voice. "This, this is a man's razor."

"What are you going to do with it?" Cliff kept in the tradition of asking stupid questions and getting the same sort of answers. Sid stood there before the mirror. He raised the razor, holding it between his thumb and his middle and index fingers. His ring finger rested on the grip and his little finger wrapped around the built-in sheath. It was made of ivory and shaped long and curved, like a femur or ulna, or even half a mandible.

"Watch." Sid placed the razor against the bare flesh of his upper cheek and started chopping down into the lather with quick, short thrusts. Before Cliff's fingernails dug all the way into his palms, it was all over. "See? No blood, no chunks of skin floating in the sink." Sid turned a clean cheek to show Cliff while he wiped off the razor for the next pass.

"How come you didn't cut yourself? That thing is dangerous."

"Of course it is, it's sharp. It's supposed to be." Sid held the razor up like Mr. H. might hold up a pipe. Cliff took a step back. "It can't hurt you if you know how to use it. Hey, I borrowed some of your shaving cream. I hope you don't mind."

"No, that's okay." Cliff kept his eyes on the razor, afraid it might jump out at him. Someone knocked on the front door. Cliff gladly got away from the bathroom to answer it.

"Is Mr. Lasvistas here?" It was one of the firemen from last night. "The marshal says it's okay for him to go inside his house now."

"Tell the marshal he'll be right over if he doesn't kill himself in my bathroom first," Cliff told him and closed the door on the bewildered fireman.

Curious, Sid went back to where Sid's neck was under the knife, so to speak, the shining steel separating hair from skin. Cliff moaned and grabbed his own neck.

"Cliff, it's safe I tell you." He laughed at Cliff's anxiety. "No matter how sharp it is, it can't cut you if you keep it perfectly straight at all times," he spoke as he shaved. "It will only cut skin if you pull it on an angle, like a guillotine." He stopped to rinse the razor in the sink, now cluttered with cloudy water and clumps of hair.

"You're crazy."

"Cliff, watch me." Sid pulled the blade down the other side. Soon the hair was gone, revealing a second smooth cheek. "Now do you see any blood?"

"No, but you're still crazy. You could kill yourself with that thing."

"No, I couldn't. It's a straight blade razor. It's been around a hell of a lot longer than what you use." Cliff watched for a few minutes more as Sid carefully evened out his sideburns and explained, as if Cliff cared, how we got this term from an American Civil War officer named Ambrose Burnside. Sid reshaped the rough spots and ran fresh water with which to rinse his face. Dripping wet, he turned to Cliff to show off his new goatee. "Well, what do you think?"

"I think you're nuts," Cliff replied, still looking at the opened razor.

"It was primarily designed for barbers to use on their customers, not on themselves. Say, hold still, you've got a little stubble there this morning." Sid shook the razor at Cliff.

"Jeez! Get that thing away from me!" Cliff took off for the kitchen. "It's okay to go back into your house now. The guy was just here," he yelled from a safe distance.

Cliff had put on old clothes for the expedition. Sid was still wearing yesterday's clothes. "Want a pretzel?" he asked, spilling the crumbs out of his vest pocket as they walked across Sid's front lawn. Two men stood in his doorway. One was frail and preppy-looking, the other an immensely obese man in a pair of white overalls, twisted onto his girth like a garbage bag. Underneath his immaculate uniform, he wore a suit like the first man. His ruddy complexion contrasted his white hard hat. Both men carried clipboards jammed with papers.

"Who are you?" The fat one directed the question sternly at Sid and Cliff as they approached.

"I'm Mr. Lasvistas," Sid replied, twisting the 'Mr.' sarcastically. "I own this house," he told the rotund, presumptuous man who nevertheless appeared to be in charge.

"Lasvistas, Lasvistas," he mumbled, reviewing his papers. "According to my information, this is the Schrieber household. It would be against regulations to permit you to enter. You cannot go inside."

"Where did they get this guy?" Sid asked Cliff.

"I am Deputy Fire Marshal Marshall Marshmallow and I am in charge of the investigation of the Schrieber's house."

"Marshmallow, huh? You should've been here last night. We could've…"

"I know, I know, you could have roasted me!" Deputy Fire Marshal Marshall Marshmallow interrupted, suddenly exasperated. "You do not know how many times I've had to put up with that joke. I'm sick of it, I tell you, sick sick sick! I was in therapy for three years. I thought I was finally over it. You do not know what it's been like for me all these years. I swear I never saw it coming." Marshmallow twitched and jiggled, not meeting anyone's eyes as he spoke. "The first time somebody said it was the first time I realized my name might hamper my career. Oh, I could have done anything I wanted," Marshmallow began to sob, "but I always wanted to be a fireman! I used to make my sister Marcia light little fires so I could put them out with the garden hose. I never knew, I never…"

The preppy assistant consoled Deputy Fire Marshal Marshall Marshmallow as he totally broke down, heaving with massive sobs. "Go ahead in, Mr. Schrieber," he said.

"No!" Marshmallow collected his senses in one syllable. "I may be vulnerable, but once you pull that one joke on me, you're disarmed. You played your trump card too early, Lasvistas. Nothing you say can hurt me now. I am Deputy Fire Marshal Marshall Marshmallow and I don't care who knows it! You're not getting inside this house alive. You neither," he snapped at Cliff and blocked the doorway with his bulk.

"If you'll just check your records again," Cliff reasoned.

"Oh no you don't, I'm too quick for that one. You could have switched my papers or slipped in a falsified document while I was breaking down. How stupid do you think I am?"

"I think you're so stupid," Sid began.

"Sir?" Marshmallow's assistant called, trapped inside the house behind his corpulent chief, "I don't believe this is the Schrieber's house."

"What?"

"Look here, sir." Marshmallow had to step out of the doorway to turn around. "We completed the preliminaries on the Johnson, Fieldcrest and Hammond residences," he indicated on one of his many forms, "and we left the Schrieber residence for Deputy Wallace to complete so we could finish the rest of our appointments before the three o'clock meeting."

"Oh, yes. So who's after Schrieber?"

Shuffling through a second section of deputy fire marshal forms, he found the correct list. "Lasvistas," he answered slowly.

Marshmallow composed himself under Sid's glare. Sid really felt like laughing out loud but figured this was a better way to humiliate him.

"Mr. Lasvistas," Marshmallow began the prepared speech which he had written himself, "fire can be a dangerous element. If gone unchecked it can cause extensive grief, damage and deep personal loss. I am here to inform you that such an incident occurred last night at your house…"

"I'm not paying for this, am I?" Sid said as he and Cliff left Marshmallow and his fireside chat out front and entered the house. The smoke-tainted air outside in no way compared to the acrid, musty smell inside. They stooped under the beam that crossed diagonally in their path. Inside the foyer, light from the upstairs window illuminated them through the missing ceiling. Scattered all over were lengths of burnt wood, their surfaces black and cracked like dark, eroded soil. Sid stood in the center, looking up to the second floor like a child marveling at the moon. Among the debris, Cliff found a piece of broken glass, part of the pane that once protected the now lost portrait of the smiling

Einstein. The heat had been so intense it melted the sharp edges so smooth that Cliff could run his finger along them without even scratching his skin.

He tossed the shard down and joined Sid in the living room. Aside from some water damage, there was more dishevelment evident from the trampling firemen than from the fire itself. Perhaps the only significant loss occurred when one of the firemen (or more likely Marshmallow) knocked over the stand on which the Somanovich/Lasvistas chess tournament had been stagnating. That too, along with the house, could be rebuilt.

The kitchen and Sid's bedroom were virtually untouched, except again for minimal water damage. An empty spare room downstairs had two charred joists jutting halfway into the room from a gaping crack in the ceiling. It was flooded with nearly two inches of water.

"Sid? Are you in there, Sid?" Sid was in the spare room with Cliff and the two firemen who were cleaning up the water. It was Mr. H. calling from the front door. "Hey Sid, who is this guy?"

"Coming." He cut through the living room and fought through the foyer. Once outside, he found Deputy Fire Marshal Marshall Marshmallow physically restraining Mr. H. from entering the house. "That's my neighbor, Marshmallow. Let him in, now."

"Let him in? Let him in?" Marshmallow was in a frenzy. "Look at that. It's on fire! He's not going anywhere near this house, not while I'm in charge. Quick, Crennley," he turned to his assistant, "get me a glass of water, I think we can put it out," he ordered as he tried to knock the pipe out of Mr. H.'s mouth.

"You fool, what do you think you're doing?" Mr. H. started hitting back.

"Shove off, Marshmallow," Sid said, "or I'll shuffle your appointment papers again."

"Aha! I knew it all along! You don't scare me, you, you, you had better stop that, hey! Stop that!" Sid grabbed Marshmallow's clipboard full of papers, holding it at arm's length away from the leaping white blob like a bully stealing an egghead's textbook.

"Would you do the honors, Mr. H.?"

"Do what?"

"Your lighter," Sid whispered. "Our friend here is a bit of a pyrophobiac, if you know what I mean." Sid waved the papers.

"Oh yes, I think I do, yes." Mr. H. was now on Sid's wavelength. Sid held Marshmallow at bay while Mr. H. passed his lighter under the loose pages.

"Aaaiiihgh!!" Marshmallow screamed. Sid undid the clipboard and flung the flaming pages on the front lawn.

"Crennley, help me, there are dry leaves down there, this whole place could go!" He sloshed onto the ground, rolling his body like a steamroller over the burning papers. Crennley ran around him in circles, kicking leaves out of the way, forming a moat of non-combustible grass to contain the supposed inferno to a specified area. Even to the untrained eye, these men were obviously professionals.

"That ought to keep those idiots busy for a while," Sid said to Mr. H. as they entered the ruined house. "What do you think?" he asked after helping Mr. H. passed the obstacles in the foyer.

"I think the rest of the house had better not look like this," he said, looking up to the second story. "Sid, it's pretty bad. These joists are shot. They'll have to be replaced before you can rebuild on them. That's all I can see so far." Mr. H. spoke with the authority that comes with thirty years of running your own construction company. It was not merely by chance that he used a roofing nail as a pipe tamper. "You still have a lot of supports left, though. That's good." They walked up the steps but were stopped at the landing near the top. What little remained of Sid's stuff sat in soggy, sagging boxes before them. Five more steps led to a black, impassable end.

"Sorry, you can't get up there yet, Mr. Lasvistas," one of the firemen said from the foyer below. "We grabbed all we could find and put it on that landing. We figure the fire started somewhere in that empty room towards the side of the house," he pointed out.

"You'll have to rebuild that whole section." Mr. H. peered through the burnt vertical studs into the gutted room. The ceiling was gone, exposing the underside of the rafters. "Looks like a roof job is in order, too."

"You haven't seen the downstairs yet."

"Don't worry about the water damage, Sid. That's the least of your troubles."

"I mean the room downstairs below this one," Sid said, trailing Mr. H. back down the steps after quickly inspecting the boxes alone.

"Nothing else, huh?" he hoped, asking the fireman.

"Nothing," he answered. "I'm sorry."

"I'm sorry too." They all joined Cliff and the others in the spare room.

"They went straight through." Mr. H. was fascinated by the two beams dangling their scorched lengths midway between the water-logged floor and the split ceiling. As if on cue, no sooner had Mr. H. finished his sentence than one of the beams jarred itself loose and fell the remaining distance to the floor. The first two feet snapped off on impact. The rest remained suspended just off the floor while the burned, splintered piece smacked against the far wall before coming to rest in a puddle.

"I think you'd do best to get out of this house for a while, Mr. Lasvistas. In the meantime, I know it would be a good idea for all of us to get out of this room right now," the fireman said.

"Listen, Sid," Mr. H. said as they all walked single file through the living room, "if you need a place to stay for a few days, until you can find something else, you could stay with me for as long as it takes."

"Thanks, Mr. H. but I've got all my stuff over at Cliff's place. If he can put up with me for a day or two, I guess I'll check into a hotel or something." Cliff walked on ahead, pretending not to hear.

In the foyer, Mr. H. said he'd call around for some estimates on repairs. "Your insurance should cover most of it. I still know a lot of people in the business. I'm sure I can find somebody to help you."

"Talk about having friends in the right places. I'll bet you do have some strings you could pull. Thank you," he said over his shoulder as they walked out. Mr. H. patted him on the back.

"No problem, Sid."

"So!" It was the dreaded deputy with his assistant. Marshmallow was straightening his tie while Crennley picked bits of leaves out of his boss's hair under his hard hat. The firemen, knowing all too well who he was, ignored him.

"We'll be leaving for now, Mr. Lasvistas. If you have any questions, you'll have to direct them to Marshalmallow here."

"That's Marshmallow!" the deputy shouted at the departing fire fighters.

"Yes sir," they said, and one of them whispered to Sid, "He hates that."

"Thanks, guys."

"Well, Mr. Lasvistas."

"Please, call me Sid."

Marshmallow ignored the comment. "I normally issue a copy of the inspector's report at this point, but you and your friend seemed to have burned it." He turned an evil eye on all of them. "We still have a duplicate copy but we won't give it to you. We need it for the records. I'll see if I can have a copy made and sent to you within the next few weeks," he said in a snide manner.

Sid just shook his head. "See you later, Marshalmallow." They all left, smiling and smirking.

"That's Marsh-mallow, Marshmallow, Deputy Fire Marshal Marshall Marshmallow. You got that? Marshmallow!"

Cliff told Sid he could take as much time as he wanted to find another place to stay. One week later, they moved Sid's bed and belongings into a spare room upstairs. Sid didn't care for the second floor, but Cliff's room was one of the two downstairs. It was more private this way for both of them. Bump and Grind spent most of their time either in Cliff's fenced backyard or roaming over Sid's unused property. It was solely Sid's responsibility to clean up after his two hairy best friends.

Nearly a month went by. Sid wasn't looking for any rooms or apartments and Cliff didn't mind. They were getting along great. Cliff was still in school, and once Sid got up early to go with him. He went with the idea of sitting back and watching girls go by or maybe checking out the library again while Cliff went to his classes. It was the first and last time he went with him, though. As early as it was, the library wasn't even opened yet and there was nobody, let alone any luscious coeds to drool over, anywhere on the campus until later in the morning. Sid didn't mind killing time, but not at seven in the AM.

Cliff's only real responsibility, his schoolwork, took up little of his time. He was doing well in the Hungarian bear's class and had unwillingly become the teacher's pet. Professor Staff constantly praised his excellent work, peeing off the others who rarely opened their textbooks. He was leading the pack in his accounting class which was still huge despite the fact that a handful of students dropped out each of the first few weeks of the semester, finding the material too difficult or time-consuming. Cliff didn't see anything that was so hard about it.

Sid, when he wasn't out looking for the Great American Bar, spent his time going over his house with private contractors and renovators who Mr. H. had gotten for him. They finalized on a very special deal. Mr. H. contacted Ben Crosley, the man he'd sold most of his business to seven years ago. Mr. H. and Ben were friends from way back and this was perhaps only the third time they'd seen each other since Mr. H.'s retirement. Ben came out to inspect the house with Dwight Winters, a young man whom Mr. H. had hired on for general labor two years before he left. Dwight was now a senior employee. Although Ben certainly wouldn't be losing any money, the old friends struck up a deal to reconstruct the house at a minimum above cost. Between them they knew all the suppliers in the area and where to get the best materials and prices. It was almost a whole new crew, though, since Mr. H. had run the operation. Ben assured him they were all good workers, most of them, anyway, and joked that Dwight was just as lazy a supervisor as both of them had been in their early days. They already had other jobs lined up, so it would be a while before they could put a big enough crew on Sid's house, but the job was nonetheless scheduled to begin in April, three weeks away.

As a sort of a thank-you to Cliff, Sid talked him into going to a new bar he'd found. Cliff went reluctantly. He was glad it was at least on their side of the Delaware. It turned out to be a suburban cowboy dive called the Crazy Ass Saloon. It was one of those places that switched over to a western theme to cash in on the country music craze that would be around for longer than anyone would have guessed then. Everyone there wore cowboy hats and the girls wore polished snakeskin boots and bandanas around their necks. Sid thought it looked kind of sexy. There were shirts with shoulder patches and huge brass and silver belt buckles, and logos with horses and bulls and lassos everywhere, all looking kind of out of place in eastern Pennsylvania. The only thing it had in common with so many other bars in the area was that everyone was trying to get laid. Cowboy style, of course.

"You've got to be kidding me," Cliff said, looking around him.

"It's such a joke, isn't it?" Sid was skeptical too, but amused. Some guy walked by with a phony, saddle sore limp. "This place is crawling with guys who haven't worn a cowboy suit since their sixth birthday party." Cliff self-consciously adjusted the cowboy hat Sid had bought him. Sid already had an authentic one of his own.

"I don't know why I let you talk me into this," Cliff said, shaking his head at his own reflection in a mirror on the wall.

"You're just jealous because my hat's prettier than yours. Maybe I should've gotten you a corduroy one to match your jacket."

"They probably make them," Cliff said as they sat down at a table near the crowded dance floor. Ignoring the line dancing, he watched as a waitress who looked like the loser in a Dale Evans look-alike contest approached them.

"Can I git y'all somethin'?" She smiled. Cliff smiled, too. It was all that he could do to keep from laughing in her face.

Sid felt like having some fun. "What's that thar fer?" he said with a better drawl than the waitress, referring to the whip which lay coiled against her hip. She was used to this sort of treatment.

"It's fer th' unruly characters what come in heah."

"Oh Lordy, you must be talkin' 'bout me. I'm as unruly as they come, yes ma'am," Sid said. Cliff just looked at him as if to say, 'Just stop it already, will you?'

"What'll it be?" she asked again.

"I'll have two fingers of three cents plain," Sid said, confusing everybody as he leaned back and pulled his hat down to his eyebrows. "A shot of whiskey," he clarified when she just looked at him. She then looked at Cliff who just said "Uh, beer. One of those." He pointed at one of the promotional banners on the wall nearby.

"Yeah, bring me one of those, too," Sid added.

They overheard some people at the bar betting shots that nobody could come up with the name of the character Clint Eastwood played in his spaghetti westerns.

"I hate trick questions," Sid said to himself.

"So how much is two bits?" Cliff asked. A sign above the bar announced the price of a shave and a haircut at that price.

"Twenty-five cents."

"Then why doesn't it say twenty five cents?"

"You're forgetting where you are, Cliff. This here's a genuine slice of the Old West, yup. Back then it was two bits." He went on to explain how

American currency was affected in pre-colonial times by the peso, which was the prototype for the dollar. The peso was divided up into eight realos, or 'bits'. Each realo was worth twelve and a half 'cents', so two bits equaled twenty-five cents. That system was still in effect in the cowboy days.

Cliff asked him what he planned on doing with all the useless crap in his head. Before he could answer, the waitress arrived with their drinks. She set them down on the baize-covered table, turned and walked away.

"I guess we're running a tab," Cliff surmised.

Sid thought that was pretty knowledgeable for someone who didn't get out much. He threw the shot down his throat without a wince. Before he set the empty glass down, something caught his eye. At the far end of the bar was a small section of a severed tree branch, the wood finished and mounted into a stand for decoration. Frozen taxidermally in mid slither around the limb was a stuffed snake. "A bull snake," Sid identified it. "I used to have a bull snake."

"A snake? As a pet?" Cliff made a face as he raised his beer glass.

"Dildo was a good pet," Sid said defensively. Cliff blew the head off his beer and onto the table.

"You named your pet snake 'Dildo'?" he blurted out loud enough for the group at the next table to hear. One of the girls cracked up.

"I knew I'd get you with that one," Sid said as Cliff sopped up the mess with a napkin.

"Whatever made you think of that, I wonder."

"Actually, Mai thought it up. I'll have to tell you about her sometime."

"Now that's a story I'd really like to hear, but somewhere else. Let me finish my beer and let's get out of here." Sid conceded to the idea of leaving early. When they got up to leave, Sid paid the bill and winked at the waitress before she found her two bit tip. It was still early when they got home, so Sid went back out for a six-pack while Cliff reheated some leftover chili.

"Quick, put the radio on," Sid said before he was even in the door, a six-pack in each hand.

"What's up?" Cliff asked from the kitchen.

"It's time for Mickey!" No, Sid was not making a reference to any three-fingered rodent from the largest peninsula in the continental US. He was talking about Mickey the Flying Boss Jock, better known as just Flyin' Mickey when headlines announced his arrest back in the summer of sixty six. The popular disc jockey from WBJB in Trident, NY was connected to a drug smuggling operation when his private twin-engine plane was confiscated during a raid by police in Texas. Although no personal involvement beyond the use of his allegedly stolen plane was ever proven, he still spent some time in jail and several more on unofficial probation before he suffered a nervous breakdown.

After recuperating clandestinely in Florida for two years, he returned to the airwaves via public radio with a once-a-week program. It was an immediate cult success. It was syndicated from coast to coast within the first two years. Mickey played some of the old hits from his days as a fast-talking boss jock back in the sixties, but what was really important to him were the tunes that came out during his absence from the airwaves. His enthusiasm due to that absence shined through, and although he had tuned down his style a bit, he still reminded people of a time when all the hip DJs had stupid names like Jivin' Peter and Cool Joe. A little nostalgia goes a long way in radio, apparently.

Now, there's a literary term that describes words that are meant to sound like the action they describe. Bow-wow describes the sound a dog makes, (although Spanish dogs go Wow-wow, look it up). Pistols go Bang, breaking storm windows go Crash and cows go Phlarnf, at least sometimes they do. And for some reason, so many slightly brain-damaged people consciously say the word Achoo when they sneeze. That literary term was the title of the first song Mickey played that night. The song was a funny look at greedy music promoters who know absolutely nothing more than the fact that they can make a buck off of other people's talent. It wasn't the first time nor the last that somebody bit the hand that supposedly feeds them, but it was a good shot.

"Who is this guy, anyway?" Cliff recognized the voice singing the first song on Mickey's show.

"Not too shabby for an ex-mailman, huh?" Sid was listening more to the music than to Cliff.

"Okay, but what's his name again?"

Sid started going off on one of his favorites, but Cliff stopped him.

"John who? Oh yeah, I remember, the guy you only listen to always. You gotta start listening to other people's music, Sid." Cliff sort of meant it.

"He's probably one of the few people this universe has known who can translate the world around him to others like this, man," Sid said in a slightly biting tone that Cliff missed.

"He must have lost his grip, because I've never heard of him, except through you."

"Just because you've never heard of him doesn't mean he doesn't know what he's talking about."

"Enough people would stand up and take notice if he was really that good. He'd get a Grammy or something," Cliff said, picking through his chili. "It's as simple as that. I've never heard of him."

"Is that all you can say? Awards? Public recognition?" Sid responded. Cliff was unknowingly banging on an open nerve. "Plenty of people have never heard of you or me. Does that mean we have nothing to say?"

"I never said I had anything to say."

"I'll drink to that!" He was mad now. He was discovering something about Cliff for the first time here. Cliff could be an unstable person in the simplest situations, like being around strangers, although this was a common affliction that he was beginning to overcome. But when it came down to voicing opinions and arguing points of view, he was unshakable. Stubborn, even. Cliff had his own opinions and no one could change them, and that was that. He was his own self-contained organism, unalterable by external means. Cliff changed when Cliff wanted to change, no matter if the time was right or not. All a person could do was to put ideas into his head. The idea couldn't change him until he thought about it so much that it became his own idea. People's opinions of him could send him into a panic at the drop of a hat, but when it came to matters that didn't directly concern him, he could be such an immovable putz.

Cliff just shrugged, unmoved.

"This man is a fucking genius. Listen to what he's singing about. He's talking about how he's been conned and bullshitted by promoters and agents, man. That's a part of his life he's telling you about, Goddamnit." Sid pointed a rigid finger at the stereo for emphasis. The cat appeared out of nowhere and jumped into his lap.

"What do I care about some singer who I've never heard of telling me about his problems with managers or producers or whatever? I don't plan on ever meeting one, let alone doing business with one. I mean, I like the way he's telling it and all, I like the tune and the words, but I don't care about it. It's not relevant to me."

"Well I hope you don't mind if the rest of us find it important," Sid fired at Cliff, who remained calm.

"Of course I don't mind," said Cliff. He was only now noticing just how seriously Sid was taking the discussion. "Why should you have to agree with what I think of it? After all, it's only a song."

"Only a song, just like that, huh? I suppose you could come up with a song right now while you're sitting there, you make it sound so easy. 'Well I finished all my dinner and the dish is in the sink/ and Sid is such a moron, doesn't matter what he thinks…'"

"Sid, what's the matter with you? It's a good song, okay?"

"Oh please. Don't patronize me."

Cliff was utterly confused at Sid's overreaction. He felt he should get away from him.

"I'm going to take the trash out," Cliff said slowly as he started to rise.

"Never mind, I'll get it." Sid was out of the room before Cliff sat back down. He was alone with the music for the next half hour. He thought about what kind of person he was getting hooked up with in Sid. They'd always gotten along so well before, now they were fighting over who knows what. He finished his beer, sat back with the empty bottle and listened to the music. He recognized none of the songs although they did sound old to him.

Sid walked back in and apologized to Cliff without even looking at him. It didn't impress Cliff, who wasn't looking for one. They sat in silence and things didn't loosen up until Cliff reviewed the connotations of naming a snake 'Dildo'. Sid finally smiled again and opened Cliff another beer.

"I really have to go to bed. I've got class in the morning."

"I used to love to stay up late on school nights when I was a kid," Sid reminisced. "If you don't want to, you know you don't have to go to school tomorrow."

"Did you eat all the chili?" Cliff asked without looking back as he entered the kitchen.

So passed the night. Cliff nearly fell asleep in his chili, and the last song Sid could recall hearing before crashing was 'Fat Man in the Bathtub'. That was around four AM. Four hours later, a sunshine crowbar pried at Cliff's eyelids. He opened his eyes to the light without first turning his head. He hated when he did that. The stab of light burned a hole clear through his head. Blinded, he stumbled up and kicked over the near empty pot of chili on the floor that Sid had eaten from. He felt his way to the radio. Mickey's show had ended three hours earlier while he'd slept. It was syndicated on public radio which had to play a diversity of music to please everyone so everyone would send donations to keep them on the air. At least that's the way it's supposed to work. That's why Mickey's show was followed by baroque harpsichord music that Cliff wanted desperately to stop.

He fumbled with the radio and turned it off. His eyesight was slowly returning. He would have thrown some spilled chili at Sid had he been on the couch. He'd gone upstairs at the first sign of sunrise. He'd slipped away from the dawn's early light that invaded the living room to the sanctity of his dark bedroom.

Cliff went to the kitchen, gave Bump and Grind fresh water and returned with a rag to clean up before he noticed the time. He had slept through his first class. It struck him that he was cognizant last night that he had school in the morning but he hadn't really thought about it. The circumstance just sat in his skull like stagnant water. Even the shock of sunlight didn't disturb is thick, algae-covered surface. Only when he looked at the clock did he think, 'Oh, I slept through my first class.'.

He sat down on his couch in the sun which was beginning to feel warm and pleasing. This reminded him of when Sid first started staying here, when they both slept in the living room for the first few nights. He glanced through the sheer curtains of his living room window and saw no truant officer with a pair of Dobermans waiting for him on his front lawn. The Hungarian bear was not balancing himself on a unicycle in a phone booth, dialing to tell him he knew he'd skipped with no good reason and was no longer his favorite student. Professor Gatlin wasn't even calling to see if his dog was ill. No one gave a damn that Cliff missed his classes that morning, including Cliff. His only regret was not waking up earlier to watch the minutes pass by on the clock, knowing there was a delicious difference between what he was doing and what he should've been doing. After all, he had never skipped a class before in his life.

By the time he cleaned up the living room and fixed breakfast (Sid only grunted when Cliff knocked on his door and offered to make him something), he decided he had started the day off well. He felt so good he knew he could even survive a visit with his parents, had he been inclined to do so. But soon, as always, he ran out of things to do and it was not even noontime. Sid was still sleeping and the house was quiet.

Cliff felt bad for the millions of other people who couldn't shirk their responsibilities that day, too. Whether it entered his head or he found the idea floating in Bump and Grind's water dish, he left a note for Sid and packed the Setters into his Volvo and drove them to Tammerlane Park. He took them for a walk the way Sid always did, without leashes. It was late March and the sun shone crystal clear in the cloudless sky, and the air was warm enough to afford Cliff only a light jacket. For such hyperactive dogs, Bump and Grind were obedient to Cliff's voice unless they found something under a pile of leaves or a bench that completely encapsulated their attention. A jogger was reduced to a fit of giggles as the dogs chased her down the paved running path. They slowed her down until she stopped, and even then they continued to chase her like she was a parked car. She was trying to pet both of them when Cliff finally caught up. He apologized and called them off. The girl laughed and said they were adorable before she turned and ran away. Cliff was almost as out of breath as the dogs seemed to be as he watched her body bounce away in her bright pink outfit before she disappeared beyond a grove of trees. He somehow couldn't help thinking it was all a trick Sid had taught them. 'Now only stop the gorgeous girls who are running alone,' he could hear him instructing the loyal beasts.

He shuttled them back into the car after making sure each did what dogs do on the grass so they wouldn't do it on his back seat. He took the long way home and found himself driving passed St. Elmo's Hospital. He smiled. He drove on a block or two further and pulled into Thiesmann's Burgers for a late lunch. Thiesmann's was fast becoming their favorite place when Cliff didn't feel like cooking. They were going there more and more often recently. The kid behind the counter didn't recognize Cliff by himself until he added two plain burger patties (no pickles, no onions, no ketchup, mustard nor bun) to his regular order. Sid and Cliff were the only ones to ever place such an order, and Bump and Grind appreciated it, although Cliff told them they'd have to wait until they got home to show it. Maybe Sid didn't mind hamburger grease all over his car seats, but Cliff certainly did.

The three of them busted in the front door, the dogs leaping at the bag held high in Cliff's hands. He took them out to the back porch and placed a juicy burger at each end as simultaneously as possible, lest one of them gobble up both meals.

Cliff was surprised to find it was already almost three o'clock. Time had never spread its wings and flown for him before. He was not as surprised to find his note to Sid untouched. He'd slept all the while. His car hadn't been moved from the shoulder of the road out front. Cliff stopped asking him why he never pulled it into the driveway, as his answer was always because he simply liked it out there.

Cliff grabbed his burger, left Sid's on the counter and sat down in the living room. He flipped through a stack of magazines Sid was always buying and came across the Playboy. He had just found the hidden bunny on the cover and gotten through the table of contents, memorizing the page numbers of the pictorials so he could go directly from one to the next when someone knocked on the door. Only a hint of the old trepidation that used to swarm over him like a cold rain was there when he opened it.

Cliff was hit with a smile, the kind that comes at you off a campaign poster from the face of the defeated politician the day after the election.

"Hey Cliffy!" Iggy said in a way that had not changed since he and Cliff shared a room back in their days at Breece. "It's me, Iggy," he shouted as if he thought Cliff didn't remember him. Oh Iggy, who could forget you?

"Iggy," Cliff stated. "Hi," he followed in the same monotone.

"I was afraid you wouldn't be here. I called your parents and they told me where you were staying. I've been calling since noon but nobody answered."

"Well, I wouldn't have answered if I'd been home and I knew it was you calling," Cliff felt like saying. Aw, what the heck. That's exactly what he did say.

The comment silenced Iggy for a moment, which is no little feat in itself. Cliff eased the moment when he brought up a laugh inspired by the look on Iggy's face. Iggy soon joined in, a little uncertain of the free manner of wit and speech his friend had apparently acquired during their separation.

"This is some place you've got here, Cliffy. I love the Tudor design. Did you know somebody has a beat up old car parked in front of your house? It looks like they pulled it out of the river and left it there to dry," Iggy said with a laugh, pointing at Sid's Mustang.

"Looks like it's just broken down." Cliff decided then to not mention Sid.

"So how are you?" Iggy sat himself down on a couch and began with renewed enthusiasm. "What have you been doing since you left Breece? You should have seen the guy who replaced you in your old room. He was this big, fat hairy guy who sweated a lot. He had this wiry beard that looked like it started somewhere up his left nostril. I just had to get my own room. I couldn't take it." His voice expired in another laugh. Cliff noticed the conspicuous lack of Yiddish in his speech. When asked about it, Iggy responded that Yiddish wasn't hip anymore. Cliff just sighed inside.

"So how's the golf game?" Cliff knew how to talk to Iggy, or rather how to let Iggy talk.

"That's why I'm down here. There's a celebrity pro/am tournament at the Ginger Glade Country Club. It's up north near the Poconos, but I thought I'd come down to see you. We got here two days early because of a foul up in the scheduling. You'll never guess who I'm paired up with on the tour, Cliffy. I'm playing with Jack Ringley," Iggy said with pride.

"Who?" Cliff asked with feigned interest.

"Don't you watch TV? Jack Ringley, he's the star of that new sitcom on Monday nights, 'Pass the Butler'."

"Oh yeah, that show," Cliff said with no presence of mind. "Can I get you anything to drink, Iggy?"

"Thanks, whatever you've got is fine." Cliff went to the kitchen and Iggy turned on the stereo. The volume was set too high from Cliff fumbling with it that morning. It blasted out until Iggy figured out how to turn it back down. "Sorry about that. Hey, this is nice, very nice," he shouted to Cliff who returned with two bottles of beer. Cliff expected to find Iggy admiring the stereo. Instead, his eyes were glued to Mai's drawing. "She's beautiful," he said, staring. "I wish I was playing with her tomorrow," He said as he nudged Cliff, almost spilling the beers out of his hands.

"Here you go."

"Cliffy, do you think I could get a glass with this?" he said with an are-you-kidding gesture in his voice. Cliff came back with the glass this time to find Iggy sitting on the couch again, dividing his attention between drooling over the drawing on the wall and skimming through the Playboy he'd picked up, loosing Cliff's page.

"Yes indeed, you're living quite well." He handed the bottle to Cliff to be poured. He did not look up from the turning pages. "I went out with a girl who looked just like her." He stopped to point out a photo to Cliff, who was intentionally pouring his beer straight down the middle of the glass, filling it more with foam than beer.

"I've got to teach you how to pour beer someday, Cliffy," he said before taking a mouthful of foam. He stared at the same page while Cliff sat down on the other couch. "Mm yes, couldn't forget a pair like that." Cliff suddenly felt like he was in a psychiatrist's waiting room with a patient who definitely had to go in first. Iggy found the center-fold. He was in the middle of that classically awkward position, turning his head sideways to better see the centerfold while at the same time rotating the magazine to hold one end up while the other end unfurled when Sid came downstairs. He first looked at Cliff with just-opened beady eyes, (Cliff just smiled appropriately sheepishly), then at his stereo, (tuned to a talk show about livestock mutilations in the Midwest), and then at some asshole who was reading his magazines. Iggy quickly noticed Sid standing on the bottom step, wearing only a pair of jeans and an annoyed look. His full, dark goatee was a stark contrast to his skinny, white, hairless chest. He stood there with one hand on the railing, the other on his hip, staring at Iggy who shot a perplexed glance over at Cliff.

"Are you two…I'm interrupting something, aren't I?" Cliff was suppressing a smile. He could see Sid was doing the same thing with more success.

"Iggy, Sid. Sid, Iggy."

"I don't understand. I mean the drawing and…this and…"

"Hi," Sid said in a sultry voice.

"You never seemed, I mean you never tried," Iggy stopped again. "I roomed alone with you for two semesters." He said it as if he'd just discovered he'd caught a disease. "I'd better be going now."

His face was flushed. He jumped off the couch and quickly hid his erection, care of Miss March, with his glass. He was in such a hurry to leave he forgot his coat. Sid never took his eyes off him. Iggy never let Sid out of his sight, either. Cliff got up too late to walk him to the door. "I'll be seeing you, Clifford. Nice to, nice meeting you," he stammered to Sid.

"Likewise, I'm sure," Sid eyed him closely.

Iggy spilled half his beer in his crotch on his way out before murmuring 'bunch of faygelehs' as he closed the door on his own frightened escape.

"That was fun, we'll have to do it again sometime, Cliffy," Sid said as he went back upstairs to get dressed.

"Thank you. Thank you so very, very much," Cliff called up to him after he stopped laughing.

Mary had a little lamb whose fleece was white as snow, and everywhere that Mary went the damn thing followed her. Evidently, this would not be the case with Cliff and Iggy anymore.

8

Father forgive us for what we must do
You forgive us, we'll forgive you
We'll forgive each other till we both turn blue
Then we'll whistle and go fishing in Heaven

'Fish and Whistle' by John Prine

Cliff skipped school the rest of the week and felt even better about it because he did it on purpose. Sid went over his house almost every day, with or without the contractors, covering the details of the renovation. Mr. H. was usually there, and Sid finally got to meet his daughter Barbara and her son, Billy.

Cliff was subject to a minor anxiety attack, enough to hasten his return to classes the following week. Having never skipped before, the emotion he experienced Monday morning in the parking lot was a new one. He decided some excuse was in order, so he would tell Professor Staff that he'd been sick. But he didn't know if he should come right out and say it or wait to be asked. What if Professor Staff didn't believe him? Oh God, what if he wanted a doctor's note?

Uncertainty settled on the beige Volvo in front of Blakely Hall that morning. It was almost strong enough to make Cliff turn back and skip again. But because of that sense of responsibility in him, he knew the longer he stayed away the harder it would be to return. So he mustered up some kind of courage and went inside. He sat in the empty room for twenty minutes until people started coming in. Soon, class began as it always had before. Halfway through, Professor Staff referred to some sheets he'd handed out during Cliff's absence. He pulled out some extra copies and handed them in his simple, cheerful way to Cliff.

"Here, Clifford, these you will need."

He was returning to the lesson when Cliff, still tense and expecting the equivalent to the Spanish Inquisition, blurted out, "I had a cold."

Professor Staff, only slightly puzzled, consoled him. "I hope you are feeling much better sooner," he stopped to say before he went on. Cliff didn't feel right until the class was over and he was out of the room. He'd worried so much over creating an alibi and kicked himself for saying something as stupid as 'I had a cold'. He felt like such a jerk. He wasn't even asked. He never understood how easy it could be, that he was concerned about something that no one else even noticed. His next class went much smoother. Professor Gatlin had stopped calling the roll weeks ago, and someone he didn't even know offered to bring in a photocopy of the notes he'd missed.

He planned to tell Sid about what a strange morning he thought he'd had when he got home, if he was awake yet. He was distracted when he passed the new condos but couldn't recall which one of the complexes had attracted so much of his attention last fall.

Driving on, he got a kick out of the sign in front of the Bunning Rod and Gun Club. The mad graffiti artist had struck again. Normally this would upset him, but this time he thought the rearranged letters on the sign were amusing:

GNU CONTROL
Gnus don't kill people,
people kill people.
Speak your peace about
gnu control in our society
on Thurs. March 29 at 7:30.

The graffiti artist was getting bolder now, displaying his, or her, handiwork in the populated business district. The sign in front of the gun club, though, didn't compare with the one in front of the Ladies Auxiliary #709 building. Like the other, it was the type of rented sign where the letters hung on rods and were removable and interchangeable, like on an old movie marquee.

SEWING CLASSES
Crewel, embroidery, both
machine and by hand.
Register by Sunday, March 26.
Bring a friend!

It had been switched around to read:

SCREWING CLASSES
Both machine and by hand.
Register by Monday, March 26.
Bring a friend!

This one was stupid, not even mildly amusing. It amazed Cliff, though, that the signs were just sitting there without anyone changing them back. How could people miss what was right under their noses?

When he got home, Sid was not only up but he was on his own lawn with Ben and two of his crew. They were surveying the yard and appeared to be marking something off with stakes and strings. One ran the full length of Sid's property out near the road. They were working on a second line that ran perpendicular to the first and all the way up to the front door.

"Hey Cliff!" Sid yelled over as the Volvo came to rest in the driveway.

"What's all that for? I thought they weren't supposed to start working on your house until April."

"They're not working on the house yet. They're working on the yard."

"Why?"

"It's a surprise. Hey, listen, do you still have any course catalogs from the college laying around?"

"I don't know, I might. If I don't, I'm sure there's some up at the campus. What do you want with one of those?"

"This surveying these guys are doing," Sid said, pointing to the men and their equipment, "it's pretty interesting. The closest I ever got to this was when I almost ran over some workers while they were measuring off an intersection for a new traffic light. There's a lot of mathematics in it, mostly geometry and algebra as far as I can tell. I thought it might be worth looking into."

"Oh yeah, 'Fun with Math'. Fascinating, Sid. Why don't you just look it up in the library?" Cliff made fun of him.

"I'm just looking into the options, that's all." Sid realized he was being inconsistent. "I want to know what's available, that's all."

"Whatever you're into, man," Cliff mimicked him.

"Exactly. That's why you're going to school, right?"

Cliff ignored the comment. Sid mistook his sudden silence for hitting a nerve. He hated to see someone of Cliff's caliber wasting his time with business courses. He'd seen Cliff zip through his work at home as if it was second nature to him, yet he never got excited over a historic marketing campaign or balancing the books for a hypothetical megacorporation. He knew Cliff would be hell on wheels if he'd only sink his brains into something that interested him, something that could grab his attention and hold it for a sustained length of time. That's why he didn't feel guilty about never passing up the chance to make Cliff take a look at what he was doing with himself. Cliff was more of a project than a friend. It didn't matter to Sid if he had a right to treat him like that or not. Cliff was either too ignorant or easy-going to notice.

They went inside Cliff's house where all he could find was a listing of the spring semester classes already in session. "What do you say we take a run up there to see what they've got? I'll drive," Sid suggested.

"Don't you think they'll miss your assistance?" Cliff was enjoying picking on Sid.

"Actually," Sid said in a confidential tone, "if I ask one more question, I think that Ben guy is going to hit me." They walked outside towards the Mustang. Mr. H. had come out and was speaking to Ben.

"Hi Sid, Cliff. Where are you fellas off to?"

"We're taking a run up to the college. We'll be back later. So long." They hopped in and took off. Mr. H. waved back as they drove past.

"Nice kids," he remarked.

"If you ask me, that Sid asks too many questions," Ben cut in.

"Yes," Mr. H. chuckled, "but he doesn't ask too many stupid questions."

"He comes across pretty smart, no doubt about that," Ben had to agree.

"So what were you saying this was all for again?" Mr. H. gestured at the stakes and strings.

"He asked us to put in a sidewalk out front here and up to his front door. He said something about a curb, too. It's a little strange, if you ask me."

"A sidewalk," Mr. H. repeated. He kind of liked the idea. "But his insurance won't cover this job. He'll have to pay out of his pocket."

"His insurance won't cover his house either, apparently," Ben informed Mr. H. "He asked me not to say anything about it to anyone, but frankly it's got me more than a little worried. He wrote me two checks as a deposit to start these jobs. They add up to twenty three thousand dollars. They're personal checks, Frank. Drawn on a personal account, they are. I told him I didn't need so much down but he insisted I take them. He never mentioned insurance once. It's none of my business, you know, but how well do you know this guy, Frank? You know he owns this place outright? How does a guy like him get the money to buy a house and then a couple of months later slap down that kind of dough to fix it up?"

"Twenty three thousand?"

"What are you going to do with all that money?" Cliff asked Sid as they wound down the road. He was referring to an old glass Skippy peanut butter jar, super chunky, in the glove box. The door of the compartment kept falling open with each bump, revealing the jar full of coins and bills.

"I keep that out of force of habit more than anything else. I used to keep spare change in there to pay for tolls when I was traveling. Now

I don't travel so much so the change just keeps adding up. I suppose when I get too much money in there it'll be time for a road trip."

Cliff grappled with the logic of it as he leafed through an issue of Licks and Riffs which lay on the seat. The cover story was about Stupid Rooster, a heavy metal guitarist who had just gone solo after the breakup of his band, G-String, and was recently in a plane crash. He had survived but lost his left leg in the accident. He was now returning to touring, and his big gimmick was finishing his show by ripping off his prosthesis and throwing it into the crowd. L+R had the first exclusive interview with him, as well as uncovering the scam of people selling counterfeit Rooster prostheses to unsuspecting collectors. There were also features called 'Hell's Well in Devil Music; A Survey of Occult Rock' about the persistent trend of groups turning to satanic themes as a ploy to sell more records. 'It's Nineteen Eighty One; Do You Know Where Your Kid Is?' a profile of a musician who dropped out of sight in the middle of his growing popularity. Also included was a look at the newest form of rock proliferation; Music Videos.

"Not many people know much about that guy." Sid nodded to the magazine.

"Who?"

"Stupid Rooster. Everybody thinks he just jumped into the scene after G-String and made it big. He goes way back into the early seventies. He came out with a progressive punk sound that was too far ahead of its time to be popular, I think. You should hear some of his early stuff. It sounds like a cross between The Sex Pistols and Don Ho."

"Don Who?"

"No, Don Ho. It's a real shame, the accident and all. Did you know Stupid was the first person to put a whammy bar on a ukulele?"

Sid went on to explain the mechanics of the whammy bar. Cliff still didn't understand what Sid was talking about when he started going 'boING boING boING' in a desperate attempt to describe the effect of the whammy bar on guitar sounds, or ukulele sounds for that matter.

"It's a shame you never heard Stupid's first album. I looked for it, but I think it got burned up in the fire. It's irreplaceable."

"That's a tough break," Cliff said, knowing what Sid's record collection meant to him. "What was it called?"

"Puke Uke."

"School's up ahead on the left, Sid."

Sid found a spot in the crowded parking lot out by Wilke Hall. Cliff had never before been in it. He was a business major. Wilke Hall was the art major's building.

"Sid, administration is this way," Cliff said, pointing back towards Blakely Hall. Sid was already out of the car and walking around the side of Wilke. On the way in, he'd noticed a mural painted there. He had seen it before from far away and wanted to check it out. Wilke sat alone, apart from the main campus, and the mural faced in that direction on purpose, Sid thought. 'Hey, look at us, we're up here!', Sid figured the art majors were trying to say. That's how he would have done it, too.

Sid walked around the rectangular building and stood before the painting. It was an old style collage, full of bright but fading colors, abstracts, lack of any defined form. Each scene poured into the others around it, coherently if that's how you were inclined to see it.

Many scenes, full of symbolic meanings which existed solely in their creator's heads, people who had long since left the school, stretched from the front to the back of the building, canvassing the full length and height of the wall. A huge face peered over a mountain top, while the sun set in the background. Plants with long, spiked leaves of Cannabis sativa rode the orange and yellow rays and lay in piles at the foot of the mountain. A woman with long, dark, snake-like hair ate a piece of pie, the top crust of which was a circular American flag. Her piece contained the field of blue with its fifty stars, a dozen or so of which were dripping and falling into a night time scene of a wolf ignoring the moon and howling at the stars. Its hackles were raised and it was poised to pounce, yet it was most soothing, awe-filled. Sid didn't just see it, he watched for what it would do next. Beside it was the Empire State Building, complete with the biplanes and King Kong. But here, a single biplane clutched the pinnacle of the building with one wing while the other took swipes at the little gorillas which buzzed through the air around it. Leaving the scene at the bottom was a gorilla with a bent arm, trailing flame and smoke as he pummeled towards the unseen pavement far below. Stuffed in the lower right corner was a black and white sketch of a naked man. He was partially saved from total exposure by a guitar that he carried but did not play. Above him was an obscure scene of King Neptune (or was it Poseidon?) using his trident to impede his body from being sucked down a drain at the bottom of an emptying sea. Several mushroom clouds appeared throughout the mural to remind everyone that someday we may not have any more walls to paint on, and an old lady helped a boy scout to cross an intersection, stopping traffic with her raised umbrella, in a scene that narrowly squeezed over the whole top border.

It was definitely college-level work, but duh, that's why it was on a college campus building. Sid could tell it was old, not only from its conglomeration of different styles and contents but also from signs of restoration. Some of the colors were fading and had obviously been painted over more than once. The red stripes in the woman's pie matched about as well as the Mustang's hood matched the two rear fenders.

Cliff leaned on one of those fenders. He did not opt to join Sid. Instead, he looked around and noted the difference between the cars around him now and those that surrounded his Volvo when he was parked in front of Blakely Hall. Most of those cars were clean and undented, fitted with chrome that had never known the meaning of rust. They were of a smart, contemporary style and many could be seen in current automobile advertisements. Cliff didn't stop to think they were probably owned by the parents of the students who borrowed them for lack of a car of their own. Not every kid's parents buy them a new car, and if they do it's usually after graduation.

Cliff now found himself in a den of dinosaurs. Although the school was not known for its creative curriculum, there were many cars in front of Wilke, most of them made in the early seventies. The most popular import car by far had to be the hoards of Volkswagens, some so old they still had the original rail bumpers. Cliff counted eight old VW buses and one Chevy van with marigolds painted on its sides. There were also a lot of Chevelles, Novas and, of course, Mustangs. Fresh oil stained the asphalt under almost every engine. Sid's car fit right in with them.

A young man with wavy hair that did not look good long walked out of Wilke. He wore dark glasses and a jawline beard. He lit a cigarette as he stepped over a rusted muffler and tailpipe that had been tossed aside. He looked at Cliff, who forgot he was staring.

"How's it goin'?" the stranger said through his cigarette. Without waiting for an answer he hopped into an old Gremlin. The car was presumably white under a coat of grime. He put on an old railroad engineer's hat he'd picked up off the front seat. The engine cranked a few times before starting and it wasn't until the stranger was pulling away that Cliff noticed a pair of rotting sneakers tied to the roof rack.

"Let's check in here," Sid said. He was coming around the building and heading for the front door.

"Sid, hey Sid," Cliff called, reluctantly moving himself towards Wilke Hall. He caught up with Sid inside the lobby. If he was going to be inside this hall, he wasn't going to be in it alone.

Although Wilke was older and slightly altered in design from the other buildings, it still had the characteristically huge lobby. It was open all the way up to the ceiling, four stories high. Where translucent skylights illuminated the other hall's lobbies, stained glass served the purpose in here. Where other lobbies were conspicuously bare, like echo caverns, here was a display of the student's creative images. A perpetually changing gallery of artwork filled the open space. Sid and Cliff passed through it slowly on their way to the secretaries at the other end.

Sid wandered through a series of busts, the first few of which were in pseudo-style of ancient Roman figures. These were followed by equally as boring noble profiles of American historical figures. Cliff passed over some drawings that didn't interest him, and Sid found him poring over some pieces of hand-blown glass.

"How do they do that?" Cliff mused. Sid had seen it done but didn't know enough about it to explain.

"Can I help you with something?" One of the secretaries asked as they looked at some macramé wall decorations displayed near her desk.

"Yes, how much?" Sid pointed at a particular wall hanging. The secretary laughed, only because Sid's response was different and unexpected.

"They're not for sale, but you're welcome to take a course in macramé and learn how to do it yourself."

"Then I'll need a course catalog." Sid surprised her. She didn't know that's what he was there for in the first place. "Can you please tell me where I might find one?"

"Oh, you'll have to get that over at administration." She started to direct them back towards Blakely Hall when the other secretary interrupted her.

"Wait a minute, Carol. I have a spare one here. They can have it." She handed it to Carol who handed it to Cliff.

"Why, thank you." Cliff was intrigued by their casual manner. He was also surprised at how natural his voice just sounded, not at all stifled and tense like when he first came in.

"Yes, thanks, Carol," Sid said, "and thank you, too, Ms. A. Shandler," he said, reading the nameplate on her desk.

"It's Ann, and you're welcome."

After that little transaction, they split up again and roamed about in the collection of donated art which in some places was packed so tightly it cluttered the area. One glance could never take it all in. Sid went straight to the center of the menagerie of stuff where stood a twelve-foot high tree made entirely from sheets of aluminum. Like everything else, a name tag was affixed to it, identifying the artist and the year it was donated. He marveled at the precision with which every leaf was cut out and the way the trunk was worked over to appear like real bark. Cliff wondered over what seemed to him to be paintings of pre-colonial dog kennels by Dutch surrealists, or anything else equally as obscure.

His neck stiff from staring, Cliff lowered his gaze and faced a sculpture in the far corner of the lobby. He walked around the maze of other displays without once removing his eyes until he stood directly before it. What was this obsession with nudes that he was getting into? He hadn't ever really looked at art before, and while these nudes weren't so much a turn-on for him, they weren't a turn-off, either. This one was almost life-size, mounted on a pedestal. It was of a woman, not a young girl, down on one knee. With arms at her sides, her shoulders were thrown back and her head only slightly raised, as if looking at Cliff's shins. The smooth hair lay close to her head and trailed into the curve of her back. The clay was dark and dusty, as hard and cold as cast iron.

"Will you look at that," Sid said, not so much as a question but a plea. Cliff was so engrossed he did not notice Sid had walked up behind him.

Finally, here was something they both liked. Sid thought everything was in perfect proportion, and although the pose could be viewed as suggestive with the coy, swan-like tilt of the head and breasts thrust forward, when taken in as a whole, yes, it exuded sexuality, but not in any way crudely.

Cliff saw it in much the same light although he would disagree about the proportions of the body. He looked at the nameplate which read simply 'A Self Portrait: Eliza Brickham, 1970'. Scanning up, his eyes stopped once again on the thighs. He felt they were oversized, bigger than life. He could imagine Eliza standing in front of the pliant mound of clay, recreating herself in a frozen, preservable form. She would age, certainly she had since she did this work, but the portrait would always be the same. He could imagine her not just feeling herself, the way the flesh and sinew hung on the bones, the way the bones behaved when moved, but also practicing the freedom to display herself as she saw herself. He could see her studying the nearly finished form, her leg raised with her foot resting on the pedestal, both hands running alternately over her molded thighs then over her flesh ones. Moist clay smears in a dry paste on her skin from hip to knee, rubbing from the sculpture to her hands, hands to thigh, back to the sculpture. Her true thighs flex and loosen, they can be squeezed and they return to shape under their own power. She is distraught because the clay thighs of her likeness don't behave the same. She applies more and more material, as if they will become real, as if too much is really not enough. Finally, it is complete. The thighs are bigger than her own, but they are still not too big, not too big to Eliza, their creator. They look just fine, just real to her.

After all, how much of the artist is in the art?

Three weeks passed and Cliff hadn't missed another class. He was back to his old ways. Returning home one day, he found Sid was off and running on unusually early errands. Having the house to himself but no energy with which to do anything, he sat down and did nothing in order to amuse himself. It was a trick Sid had been showing him. Too many people have bought the theory that in order to be amused, one has to be doing something. There are extremists in the group who carry the issue so far as to feel uncomfortable at doing nothing. 'If God wanted us to always be doing something, He wouldn't have invented nothing,' as Sid was prone to put it. Cliff had never been of this belief. He'd belonged to the group who were indifferent to the stagnation of the mind and body, unwilling to change for good, bad or worse. All along, Sid had been showing an unsuspecting Cliff how to enjoy the passage of time. How many times had Cliff looked at his watch in the past few weeks or months, only to find time was rushing by now that he had a choice of something or nothing to occupy all those minutes and hours and days he would never admit he used to subconsciously count?

Plunked down on the couch, he thought. He hadn't mentioned anything to his parents about Sid moving in and easily rationalized that they never asked about it. He could never have second-guessed their reaction. He whittled away the morning by imagining making love to Maivina if her reproduction in Sid's drawing was even close to true.

What effect is Sid having on me, he thought to himself. He knew he was not the same person he was a few months ago. That may be true of a lot of people, but Cliff was just realizing it about himself. It's easy to see change in others, but it takes a special sort of open-mindedness to see the same thing in yourself. Cliff was slowly picking up on it. He knew he'd gone from a hateful hermit through circumstances which brought a veritable stranger, his two dogs, one cat, a stereo, records and ex-lover suspended in two dimensions in black and white into his house, his retreat, the one place he could always go to get away from it all. What made him bring in all that he was avoiding, and why didn't he mind it?

Sid even had him thinking about school. He never found it challenging, and he never found it interesting, either. If he was this good at it without even trying, what might he be like at something he actually found stimulating, something he really wanted to do? But what? If it were up to him, he wouldn't be in school at all. It was not because he was lazy, he was just not motivated. He was now closer than ever before to getting his business degree and he still didn't know what he wanted to be when he grew up. And what would he do with a degree? Probably continue with graduate school. He'd been going to school all this time for somebody else because of what they might do or think of him if he didn't go. He had to look good by comparison. Everyone else in his family was at least doing something, and he knew if he wasn't, they would make his life a living hell. They never said they would, but Cliff knew his car and his house and his bank account weren't exactly free after all. He didn't want to sound like a crybaby. He had more in the way of material things than anybody he would have known if he knew anybody. But they'd rip up his checkbook, impound his car and kick him out if he said he was tired of it all and wanted to do something less than what was expected of him, he was sure. Why else would his mother have been excited about him switching to studying computer science? She was excited, until she realized it was all a scam. Beyond all this was a fundamental difference between Cliff and Sid. If Sid were in this position, he'd drop out. He did say he had dropped out of school. Maybe his reasons were similar to these. There's always a simple way out, right? Cliff decided that morning to give some serious consideration to continuing with school, but to start doing it for himself and just see what happens.

And what's with this beer thing? He'd jumped on that bandwagon too easily. Before he met Sid, he had been sloppy drunk only once, as many times as he'd been with a girl. Because the two events occurred simultaneously, he never knew if he or she had a good time. It was unlikely. It was the one time he knew of that Iggy actually 'made a hole in one' and it turned out she had a friend for Cliff who came back to the dorm room with them. What a wasted evening.

All that passing of time made Cliff thirsty. In a similar frame of mind as a smoker thinking about quitting, he went to the kitchen for a beer. He caught sight of his profile in the hallway mirror. It's not possible to get a beer gut in such a short time, is it? He closely re-examined himself, his stomach already sucked in. He watched with unpleasant fascination as he let it all hang out. He tightened his belt which only made his excess poundage leap farther over his waistline. Refusing to believe such a change could come about without his noticing it, he went into the bathroom and looked again. It was true, his stomach was more plentiful than before. He only momentarily imagined he had Eliza Brickham thighs before he looked at his face. The curls in his light brown hair were loosening up, a sign he'd have to get them done again soon. He looked as healthy as ever. His eyes were only slightly bloodshot. He was more than surprised he had forgotten to shave that morning. He didn't really need to shave every morning, his beard didn't grow that fast. He always shaved on Monday, Wednesday and Friday mornings, between his shower and breakfast. But that's right, he was running late this morning. He had grabbed a quick shower and only had time for a slice of cake he'd baked to Sid's delight before he ran out the door. He thought he would have realized it if his morning routine was upset so. All the same, he didn't look too unkempt. The silvery stubble scarcely showed.

He remembered the morning Sid's house burned down, when Sid was threatening his safety with that God-awful razor. He remembered the easy way it caught the light as it slid down his throat, sending Cliff into near convulsions simply by watching. Not that he was all that fond of convulsions, but curiosity, the same thing that killed the cat, prompted him to open the medicine cabinet where, of course, was a dead cat. No, really, the straight blade razor was there. Concealed in its own little case it was, like the fangs in a snake's mouth.

Maybe he should have closed the cabinet. Maybe he should have run for his life. The ghost of Sweeney Todd smiled as Cliff reached for the razor. The grin was wiped from the demon barber's face when the telephone began to ring. Perhaps saved by the bell, Cliff was soon talking to Sid on the other end.

"Cliff, listen, you've got to come down here and get me."

"What's the matter? Where are you?"

"I'm at the Franklin Mall. Bring your Volvo up here, I'm going to need a ride. We're on the far corner, near Third and Green. I've got to get back. Hurry up, okay?" That's all he said.

Not knowing what else he could do, Cliff hopped in his Volvo and took off for the mall. The late afternoon traffic held him up, so when he finally arrived, the tow truck was just pulling the Gran Torino off Sid's Mustang.

With shoppers-turned-spectators rubbernecking everywhere, Cliff pulled his car in behind one of the police cars. One of them tried to send Cliff back before Sid came forward and cleared things up. Nevertheless, Cliff had to move his car, so he made Sid get in with him and he backed up to a parking space.

"What in the world is this?"

"There's a spot, over there," Sid pointed, out of breath. "I don't know for sure what happened, I didn't see it. They said this guy in the Gran Torino came ripping through the empty lot over here. He popped the curb and rolled over that little green TR7. They're still looking for the owner. It didn't have its parking brake on, so it figures that it became a sort of portable ramp, right? They both rolled across the aisle to my car.

The only reason the TR7 didn't reach my car was because the Gran Torino rolled its two right tires up one side and down the other. By the time it came down, both cars were next to mine. The Torino's front tire landed right on the end of my trunk."

"Did it hit anything else?"

Sid was smiling. "The bumper ripped the plastic window out of the ragtop, that's all."

"So all it hit was the trunk, right?" Cliff rechecked.

"Just the trunk," Sid affirmed.

"Just the black trunk, right?"

"Uh huh. I think I might have to get it replaced..."

"With a red one!"

"A cherry red sixty eight Mustang with a black confuckingvertible top! Wahoo!"

Cliff still didn't think he would ever understand the logic behind Sid's fascination with Mustangs, or even the more obvious question, like why he didn't just get it all painted at once. He saw no sense in waiting to replace each part as it got hit, but sense was no longer part of the equation. The deed was done and it had happened Sid's way.

The Mustang, which once laid low under the weight of the Gran Torino, remained in its place with the mangled trunk popped wide open.

"You're lucky, Mr. Lasvistas. That sports car took the brunt of the impact. I hate to think what would've happened to your car had it not been there," the officer said.

Sid was too excited to care about what might have happened. All he knew was he was getting a new trunk. He didn't want to appear too excited, though, fearing they all might think him loony. What kind of person gets excited when their car gets hit? He knew another shoe salesman would never jump out of a building and land on his car again, but he never imagined an event such as this would ever take place, either. It was the perfect accident.

With the black Gran Torino out of the way, they got a better look at the massively caved-in trunk. Miraculously, the only other damage aside from the plastic window and the trunk was a busted tag light and several scratches and dents on the driver's side fender. They would be touched up when the new trunk was installed. There were no gas fumes or any other indications the tank had ruptured. A strong scent of gin, however, reeked from a broken bottle the driver had pitched after the crash. He was now in the back of a patrol car.

They traded some small talk with one of the officers until another one approached their small group.

"Mr. Lasvistas?"

"Yes," Sid answered politely.

"Mr. Spruance has agreed to pay for the damages to your car," the officer said in an official monotone. Sid looked over at the man called Spruance but couldn't get a good look at him. His face was turned away, hidden by the cage in the patrol car.

"He's drunk. He'd probably agree to anything just to get you off his back."

The officer continued. "You are responsible for acquiring an estimate for the repairs."

"Where do I have to go for that?"

"You can take it anywhere you like." The officer then handed Sid a small card. "This is Mr. Spruance's home phone number and address. When you receive your estimate, you are to call him at once and give him the amount. He will be responsible for making the payments and he can request a copy of the estimate."

"That's all there is to it?"

"That's all, sir."

"Hey, that's simple, Sid."

Sid was a little confused. Was this Spruance supposed to be around when he called, or wouldn't he more likely be in jail or at least a rehab somewhere? Sid knew he would get his own car fixed, that was no problem. But he didn't want to hang around with all these cops to ask more questions. He didn't like all this attention from them. Luckily enough, the owners of the TR7 arrived, loaded down with shopping bags that they dropped when they ran over to the scene, ranting and raving about their demolished car. The police were calming them down and explaining the situation to them now. One of the cops gave Sid a length of rope with which to tie down his trunk. With Cliff following behind him, he drove his Mustang home.

Mr. H. and Ben came over to further inspect the damage when they pulled up. Sid had to tell the story of the freak accident again. Already getting tired of repeating it, he went inside, leaving them to pass it on to the other workers who were straying over to see what had happened. Cliff stayed and told the story two more times before he went in and joined Sid. He found him alone in the living room, beer in hand, standing at the window and looking passed the small group at his soon to be all red car.

"I always wanted a red Mustang, Cliff. It's funny, you know?" He stared out the window as he talked. "I always went for the unusual, the different things. The Mustang was a very popular car back then. Almost everyone had one, and God knows, most of them were red. But I had to get it. It was just so damn classy." Cliff never before saw someone so attached to an old car. "I liked it when I bought it black. It was different. I didn't see too many others like it. Everybody I knew said it looked too black. What a stupid thing to say, huh? Of course it looked too black. But it looked just fine to me."

"When the sixty eights started to disappear, my car wasn't uncommon because it was black anymore but because it was an old Mustang. The design of the newer ones was changing every year, but I always thought the sixty eight looked the best."

"So why didn't you just get it painted red, Sid?"

Sid thought for a minute. "The first time I got hit was in seventy five. They had to replace a door and a fender. Some asshole in a Monte Carlo ran a red light. They put the new body pieces on and they happened to be red. I didn't care if nobody else liked it. I liked it and it was my car, so I kept it that way. I got hit again soon after that. Another Monte Carlo. God how I hate Monte Carlos. I had the other front fender replaced and painted red. I just kept it up after that. I don't know why I never got the whole thing done at once. I guess I thought my way was more interesting."

All in good time, Sid's good time, he called around to a few shops and it was over a full week until he dropped it off at Al's Auto Body. He did it against both Cliff's and Mr. H.'s advice. They felt he should have gotten Spruance to pay the estimate before the work started. But Sid was too eager by then to get his car back and only called Spruance one time at their insistence.

"Hello, Mr. Spruance? This is Sid Lasvistas, the guy with the Mustang," he said into the phone, looking at Cliff and Mr. H., both in eager attendance. "Oh, okay," Sid said, then was silent.

"What? What is it?"

"Mrs. Spruance, I guess. She's going to bring him to the phone." After a short pause Sid said, "When will he be back?" Mr. H. stomped away in disgust. "Could you tell me when would be a good time to call him? All right, thank you."

"The hell he's not there. I don't like being jerked around like this," Mr. H. prowled around like a caged lion. "This asshole is going to pay." It was the first time either Sid or Cliff had heard Mr. H. curse, or even seen him angry. They guessed he was serious.

"Let me call him back on Thursday. Let's give him a chance," Sid reasoned.

"He doesn't deserve a chance. I'm going to call the police right now," Mr. H. said as he made a grab for the phone.

"Now hold on there, buckaroo." Sid sensed the need for some levity. "This is my problem and I'll take care of it. Okay?" he said with his hand keeping the receiver in its cradle. Luckily, he didn't say 'Okay, Dad?' sarcastically like he wanted to. Mr. H. would have whaled off on him at that.

"I never thought you'd turn out to be the kind to let himself get steamrolled by scum like this, Sid."

"Nobody's fooling me. I said I'd handle it, didn't I?" He really didn't want to pee Mr. H. off. "I just want to do it my way, all right?"

"I still think you ought to call the police," Mr. H. said in a less harsh tone.

"Maybe I will," Sid said, reaching out to grip his neighbor's arm, "but not now."

"You really should call them." Mr. H. walked away with averted eyes. Sixty nine years of stubbornness wasn't going to melt away in one conversation. "They'd know what to do, you know," he said from the other side of the room.

"I already know what to do. Cliff, can you take me out to the township building tomorrow?"

"Yeah, sure."

"Okay, I want to get a copy of the accident report. I want to see how much I can find out about this Spruance putz." Mr. H. was pleased to see Sid directing some hostility in the right direction. Cliff wondered what he had up his sleeve.

After classes the next day, Cliff and Sid picked up the report. Normally, a five dollar fee was charged for the service. When Sid explained the situation to the clerk, he gave him a copy for free and wished him luck in nailing Spruance. Cliff then dropped Sid off at the college library where he spent the rest of the afternoon poring over the Pennsylvania Consolidated Statutes, title seventy-five, 'Vehicles', to do what the bear did when it went over the mountain, to see what he could see. When Cliff brought him home late that afternoon, Sid had a not so small stack of photocopies which he spread all over the coffee table. He had another few pages of handwritten notes full of scribbles and cross outs and circled passages. Cliff thought it all looked rather crude and disorganized, which was coincidentally the same feeling Sid was beginning to get about the laws concerning motor vehicle accidents. Cliff found form E-2, the accident report, among the jungle of papers that were now spreading to the floor.

On the first page, all drivers were reduced to a few lines each, (name address, etc.). The Gran Torino was specified as vehicle number one, the TR7 as number two, and Sid's Mustang as number three. These numbers were used throughout the report. The word 'car' did not exist here. Not official enough. Cliff noticed in box number thirty four, Spruance's insurance company was listed as 'none'. Great, just great. He checked Sid's insurance company. It was also listed as 'none'.

"Hey, you don't have any insurance!"

"Hey, I don't believe in it," Sid muttered, not paying much attention to the comment yet.

"What the hell is that supposed to mean?"

Sid took a deep breath. "It means I refuse to pay some joker a thousand bucks a year for the sacred privilege of driving a car in the Commonwealth of Pennsylvania. I'd lose thousands of dollars over the years and when I needed it, the insurance company would just give me their 'We only provide partial coverage in your type of accident' scam. They'd pay for a quarter of my damages then jack my rates up to the sky for being a high risk. No thank you, I'll take the money I'd be sending them and cover my own costs."

"But they can take your license away now, can't they? That's against the law."

"That's only because it makes sense. As far as I can tell," Sid pulled out one of the many photocopied statutes, "the only thing they can do to me is refuse to renew my license when I reapply, as long as I don't get picked up again." That wasn't exactly correct, but it could make sense, Cliff thought. "That gives me time to think and time for you to read this while I read that." Sid swapped the report for the statute which Cliff found more confusing than amusing. He stopped reading at the third repetition of the phrase 'ensuing damages inflicted on the first party by the second party'. Sid quickly finished with the report and handed it back to Cliff. He then immersed himself back into the work at hand. Cliff could plainly see the do-it-yourself determination on

Sid's lowered face. Sid didn't trust his affairs with anyone. If he was in a tight spot, he would get out of it himself. He didn't want anyone's help. That's not to say at times he didn't need it.

Cliff left him alone and scanned through form E-2 again. The first page continued with a concise description of the principle and intersecting roads, both boxes filled with the term 'parking lot'. Boxes fifty two through fifty five outlined illumination, weather, road surface conditions and type of traffic control device at the scene. The second page got into the meat of it, the accident itself. At the top left was a drawing that looked like a third grader's rendition of the event. Rectangle number one was on top of rectangle number two and slightly overlapped at the edges with rectangle number three. An arrow indicated the motion of rectangle number one through the nearby parking lot and over the curb before coming to rest on the other two rectangles. The diagram was accompanied by a narrative description which outlined Spruance's outrageous driving habits with unbiased clarity. Along the right side of the page in a column that ran from top to bottom, all the cars were identified by numerical code as one of eighteen types of vehicles. Box sixty two revealed a birds-eye outline of a car divided into seven numbered sectors. Each car was assigned a sector as the initial point of impact. Vehicle number three was indicated with sector zero six, rear of the vehicle. Vehicle number one was marked with a separate code, zero eight, undercarriage. Cliff wondered if they had an all encompassing code, the only possible one to assign to the demolished TR7.

Cliff could sense no immediate beauty in the report, but he was drawn in by how the accident, which had nothing to do with desks, offices and pencil pushers, could be reduced down by those very means to eighty one efficient little boxes. It wasn't the next best thing to being there, but who wanted that? It was fantastically functional, almost but not quite to a fault, in his opinion. Obituaries try to achieve the same effect, without the benefit of diagrams. They list a person's age at death, where they were born, then they go back and cover all the stuff in between those events. Perhaps obituary writers could learn something from the Department of Motor Vehicles, Cliff thought. They could print up forms in the newspaper, replacing make and model with the stiff's name and nationality. They could still list weather conditions and the time of day of death, and replace the insurance company with the name of the church the dearly departed attended. Then there would be a lot of 'none's listed in that box. A diagram could be drawn with stick figures of the body's final resting position in relationship to tables and chairs, doors, buildings, telephones or even cars around it. A composite of the body could be divided into, say, a dozen sectors so the part(s) damaged in the process of death could be readily identified. If there was more than one death involved, they could be rendered anonymous by giving them numbers. Victim number one, victim number Whoa! Where the hell was this all coming from?

Sid called Spruance's number on Thursday afternoon to find, surprise, he still wasn't there. Cliff argued the advantages of going to the police.

"Your car has been in the shop for a week now and you're not even sure the estimate is correct. How can you let this idiot get away with this?" On a lighter note, Cliff added, "And if you think I'm being a pain in the ass, just you wait until Mr. H. gets a hold of you."

"Don't tell him a thing," Sid warned. "I like Mr. H., but he'd have me burn Spruance at the stake if he knew what was going on." Cliff badgered Sid some more, mostly for fun. Sid was getting sick of the subject and suggested a diversion.

"I'm going to watch them rebuild the house. You want to join me?"

It had become Sid's habit, and recently Cliff's also, to kill time by watching the workers reconstruct the house. It was a slow show but a good way to pass a few hours. Spring was rushing in like gangbusters, pulling the grass out of the ground and unfurling the leaves on the trees. Flocks of birds could often be seen vigorously working their wings as they flew by high overhead, as if someone had just released them from their cages.

They sat in Sid's customary corner at the base of the towering oak by the side of the road, well out of the way. It was the same spot from which they'd watched the house burn weeks ago. Sid sat with his back to the trunk. Cliff lay on his side, propped up by an elbow as he handed Sid a beer. He took another for himself and saved the rest for later.

They usually had to use their imaginations as most of the pounding and sawing went on inside. They didn't mind. They were content just sipping their beers, watching the overalled workers with their tool belts carrying planks through the front door and leaving before the afternoon sun began to set behind the house, blinding the view. Today they were enjoying the grand opening of the roof. A charred section as big as a quarter of the full expanse had to be ripped out and replaced. Soon it would be a window through which they could view the action.

"I remember reading once about a soldier in the Civil War or something," Sid said. "He'd been shot in the stomach but he lived. The doctor bandaged him up and when he took the bandages off, instead of closing up, the wound had healed around the edges, leaving a tunnel ripped out by the bullet straight through to the guy's stomach. The doctor got famous from his reports on observing digestion first-hand and pioneered the foundation for further research."

"Yeah, right." Cliff had forgotten learning about the same thing in Human Physiology last semester.

"That does sound a bit far fetched, doesn't it?"

"Uh, yeah, just a little. What's it got to do with anything, anyway?"

"Well, with the roof being opened up and all, it kind of reminded me of it, that's all."

Throughout the course of the conversation, Cliff kept bugging Sid to tell him how the fire started. Sid only said it was an accident, his own fault, although he promised to tell him the whole story some day. Before he could ask any more questions, Sid ran off to get a tape player. While he was gone, Ben pulled up in his pickup.

"Where's your friend?" he asked.

"He took off for a minute. He should be right back, though." Cliff handed Ben a beer. Just as he started drinking it, Sid returned.

"It's not enough I pay this guy so much money to fix my house, he's got to drink my beer, too," Sid said with a sarcasm that Ben was already comfortable with.

"If you were such a nice guy you'd be buying a round for my crew, too."

"You're not as smart as you look, Chief. That's exactly what I've been doing, when you're not around, of course." Ben stopped drinking and opened his eyes wide, and Cliff tried not to look at the unusual sight of the tangle of hair growing out of his ears. "Oh, they're real nice about it, too. They wouldn't take it at first because they said you're a slave driver and you'd have their asses on a platter if you caught them. So I just told them I'm the guy paying the bills and I made them take it."

Nobody but Cliff noticed the half empty bottle being thrown from someone in Sid's backyard high through the air and into his own back-yard, into some bushes, as per Sid's instructions and permission. Sid had told them they could do that when they saw Ben coming, if they wanted. Sid cleaned up the bottles almost every night, making their trash can look like it belonged behind the Budweiser Research and Development building. "I thought you'd have it figured out by now, someone as smart as you," Sid teased.

"Why you little son of a bitch," Ben started laughing. "I had no idea!"

They shared some more small talk and Sid asked too many questions about joists and headers that Cliff didn't understand. Ben told him to stop asking so many stupid questions, to leave him alone to do the job himself. Before he even asked about the sidewalk, Ben pointed out the furrow dug out between the tree and the road.

"We'll start pouring maybe next week, if the weather holds. We have to dig out the row to the front door, too. I still don't have enough people to put on this job yet. We have to wait for the permit on the streetlamp, anyway. Frank says he knows an electrician who owes him a favor."

Mr. H., who'd come out of retirement to help supervise this job, stuck his head out the front door. "Hey Ben, where did you get these morons? You'd better get in here before we have to get a real crew in here to straighten out the mess they're making. They couldn't rebuild a dollhouse, let alone this place." The last part of his sentence was nearly obliterated by banging hammers and buzzing saws, all going at once on purpose to drown him out.

Ben shook his head and laughed. "You know, this job is the best thing that ever happened to that old fart." He turned to go inside. Crossing the lawn, bellowing loud enough to be heard over the racket from all the tools, he said, "Hey, anybody got a beer for me?" It wasn't a question, either. All the tools stopped at once.

"It doesn't seem to be hurting him any either, does it?" Cliff remarked.

"Yeah," Sid agreed. "Say, listen, the auto shop called while I was next door. My car is almost ready."

"So soon? Good. I was getting tired of doing all the driving. Especially to dives like the one we went to last night."

"That was a classy place," Sid said.

"The Purple Worm Bar and Grill was definitely not a classy place, Sid."

"Oh, I thought you were talking about Hanover's."

"No, no, that place was okay. I liked the ribs."

"Anyway, I'll need a ride in an hour or so."

"And that's the last one?"

"Promise."

"Maybe we can stop by Spruance's house and see if he got back yet."

"Yeah, maybe."

"Hey Sid, I was wondering. You've got to pay on this renovation and the car and all, you know if you need any money…"

"Haven't I been paying every time we go out? It makes me feel better since you won't take any rent from me."

"Sid, I don't need it. If you…"

Sid cut him off. "And neither do I. Thanks just the same, though."

And that was that.

A white van passed the house then doubled back and parked. Cliff thought it might just be somebody from the crew.

"Are you expecting company?" Sid asked. Cliff surmised Sid would have recognized it had it been one of the crew.

If Helen of Troy's face could launch a thousand ships (not necessarily a compliment; they could have been just trying to get away from her), then the face of the girl who got out of the van could draw two thousand armadillos out of their burrows and cause them to spontaneously change their gray armor shells into rapturous pastel colors as they took flight and spelled her name in rainbows across the sky. Her body could bring them back for a second look.

"Hi Sid!"

"Suzi!" The dirty trench that was soon to be a sidewalk held Suzi back from running up and hugging Sid. Her high heels and sheer white summer dress were not made for moto-crossing. Those wild armadillos couldn't drag Sid away as he deftly cleared the trench with one leap of his long, spindly legs. As they were putting that hug together, three people got out of the van with a bunch of photography equipment. Two of them viewed Sid's house perplexedly while the third, who appeared to be in charge because he dumped all his equipment on the other two, approached Sid and Suzi's embrace. He was a tall, skinny man, like Sid. He had long, straight brown hair which he wore with bangs in front. A thin, wispy mustache arched over his mouth and joined in an equally as thin goatee that outlined his small chin. He wore a dark sport coat over a beige turtleneck, and what looked like a very heavy medallion was suspended about his neck on a gold chain.

And people thought Cliff was out of fashion.

"Sid, this is John. He's the photographer from the magazine I was telling you about. John, this is my friend, Sid." While Suzi made the introductions, Cliff, as well as the workers far behind him, checked out the gorgeous blonde at Sid's side.

"John, how are we supposed to shoot here?" one of the photographers whined.

"Don't worry about it, Philip," John said. "What's the story here, love?" he said to Suzi. "I thought we were going to shoot the layout here?"

Before Suzi could speak, Sid said, "I had a slight problem here, John. The house is under construction. Just a little fire, don't you know. I realize I should have called you but I had no way of, uh, I didn't know you were coming now."

"I wish you would have. We spent a lot of time getting here. I sounded like a great location." John turned around to look at the Delaware River rolling behind them.

"Wait a minute, I've got an idea. Let me see what I can do." Sid excused himself and jumped back to the other side of the trench. "Cliff, this is Suzi, John, Philip, that's, that's Philip's friend," Sid introduced them hurriedly before he pulled Cliff back behind the tree, out of view. "Cliff, you've got to go along with this," he blurted out.

"Go along with what? Who are these people?"

"Listen, I met Suzi a couple of weeks ago. She was singing at this bar in Trenton, see? I bought her a drink and we started talking. She's real nice, Cliff. Honest. She said some guys from Orifice magazine were there taking some pictures of her because they were thinking of using her in one of their upcoming photo essays."

"Yeah?"

"Really. So I told her, half joking, understand, if they needed a place to shoot some more pictures they could use my house. I didn't think she would take me seriously. I was just, you know, coming on to her."

"You must have given her your address, though."

"Yes, I suppose I did," Sid tried to recall.

"I guess they want to take those pictures now."

"That's the whole idea. And they can't exactly use my place now, can they?"

"Let me straighten up the living room," Cliff said as he led them all into his house.

"Uh, that's okay. I don't think we'll need it." John cringed at the plain decor.

"There's some empty rooms upstairs you might be able to use," Sid suggested.

"That sounds better. Philip, Denise, check it out, would you?"

"Can I get you something to eat?" Cliff asked. Suzi giggled.

"No, no thanks, man," John answered, looking at Sid, wondering how these two guys ever got hooked up with each other.

"You can, you can get changed, in that bathroom if you want to, uh, Miss Suzi," Cliff stammered.

"That's okay, Cliff. I don't need one of those." Suzi slipped the white summer dress over her head to reveal a pair of sheer lace panties, a smile, and more beautiful flesh than Cliff knew could ever exist on one body. Suzi laughed at his uncontrollable stare.

"Nice," John said of the drawing of Maivina that hung on the far wall. "Where did you get it?" He walked up to it for a closer look.

"I drew it," Sid said, trying to make no big deal out of it.

"You did this? Man, it's beautiful." He took a step back. Suzi stepped in between him and Mai and struck up vaguely the same pose. It was enough to start John up. He raised his medallion up to his eye like a camera and pretended to shoot her poses from all different angles.

"Do they do this sort of thing often?" Cliff asked quietly. If he trusted anyone's judgment on this one, it was Sid's.

"Orifice isn't one of the richest magazines in print," Sid answered. "I saw one pictorial they shot in a used car lot in the middle of the night. They'll use any background they can make interesting, and the cheaper the better. They did some crazy things in a Volkswagen on that lot…" Sid stopped talking when John turned to him.

"Would you mind if we used your drawing in one of the sessions?" he asked, prompting Suzi to pout just a little.

"That's flattering, but I wish you wouldn't. It's kind of personal."

"All right, I understand. Do you have any more like it?"

"Afraid not."

"It really is a nice piece of work."

"Thank you."

"Oh John, come up here and see what you think," Denise called down. Cliff couldn't help but watch Suzi trot up the steps in nothing but high heels and lace. John followed.

"Etgay an ipgray, Iffclay," Sid whispered.

"Huh?"

They all gathered in an empty room upstairs. Philip and Denise had hung yellowish cellophane over all the windows of the empty room, frosting the white light into a pleasant shade of amber. John was setting up the first of two tripods while Philip took readings from his light meter.

"What's he doing?" Cliff asked as Philip aimed his meter at the wall.

"He's measuring the intensity of the reflected light so they can set the aperture commensurate with the shutter speed to achieve a correct exposure, or something like that," Sid said.

"Oh." Cliff's attention was redirected when Suzi walked out from behind a blind where Denise had been applying make up to her.

The cellophane softened the light as it formed a distorted shadow of the window lattice that stretched across the wall. The straight lines of shadows curved when they reached Suzi's body, wrapping around her neck, waist and thighs, seeming to pin her to the wall. This effect was lost when she started to roll freely from side to side even before John manned his cameras. The shadow from her body lay in exaggerated arcs to her left, opposite the window where they molded into the corner and continued on the next wall.

After a few more checks, the cameras started clicking in a staccato rhythm. Suzi stood with her back to the wall with one heel on the floor, the other raised, pressed flat as if standing on the wall. She folded her arms over her head and her hands ran through the long strands of blonde hair that fell about her shoulders.

"We need wind," John said from his position behind the second camera. The first one was spent and Philip was reloading it with fresh film. They went through three fast rolls in this fashion before John asked, "Do you have a fan around here?"

"Cliff? Cliff, John wants to know if you have a fan." Sid bumped Cliff to attention.

"Uh, no, no fans. Central air conditioning..."

"What's the matter with him? Hasn't he ever seen a girl before?" Denise asked. Cliff didn't even hear her.

"I don't know if he's ever seen one like her." Suzi continued to pose, eyes closed, oblivious to anyone else in the room.

The phone rang. "Don't worry, Cliff. I'll get it." Sid went downstairs.

"You can pitch the lace now, Suzi. Just do it slowly. I want to get a few shots of it." Cliff actually moaned as Suzi wiggled more than slid out of the panties that were no longer riding high on her hips. She began to roll faster.

"Take that cellophane down, Philip." Philip complied. Sid returned after the white light entered the room, bleaching out everything but Suzi in a bright haze.

"Hey, that looks better than with the paper on the windows, don't you think?"

"Wha?"

Seeing it had come to the point where Cliff had trouble pronouncing full words, Sid was glad to pull him away. "Come on, my car's ready. I'm getting the old crate back today, remember?"

"Now? Wait, it can't be ready now."

"Now. Let these guys, and ladies, do their work."

"But…"

"Now." Cliff stretched back as long as he could to watch Suzi as Sid led him away. "I'm going out, I'll be back in a little while. I'm taking Cliff with me."

"Thank you," John paused to say.

"Be still my beating groin." Cliff was out of it.

"Cliff, come on, this is embarrassing. Take it easy, will you?"

"Don't you think we ought to hang around, Sid? I mean, you hardly know them. They might steal something."

"If they do, it'll just be something of yours. It's your house."

As they got into Cliff's Volvo, he said, "They might use your drawing of Maivina. John was real disappointed when you wouldn't let him use it." Although this was enough to slow Sid down, they were soon on their way to Al's Auto Body with Cliff rationalizing all the way.

"It looks great, really great," Sid said, eyeing his Mustang the same way Cliff had drooled over Suzi. He stood behind it, amazed at the now smooth expanse of the trunk. The paint even matched the touched-up fender.

"We had one hell of a time matching up that paint there. You know you got about three different shades of red on this car, don't you?"

"You did a great job. It looks fantastic."

"Glad ya like it, sir." It was Al himself to whom Sid spoke. "Now if you'll just step into my office, I got a fully itemized bill for you in there somewhere."

Chewing on an unlit cigar, Al led the way into his office, which looked like nothing more than a large converted rest room. He scooped up Sid's bill and handed it to him.

"This is four hundred dollars more than the original estimate!"

"Now sir, I never said that estimate was guaranteed. You got yourself one old automobile out there. Parts are hard to come by for it. You're lucky..."

"Save it, asshole." Sid unfortunately knew there wasn't much he could do about it now.

"You're in my place a business, pal. Nobody talks..." When Al went to poke his finger into Sid's chest, Sid grabbed the hand and must have put some weird Vulcan death grip on it, because Al dropped the slimy cigar out of his mouth and just froze there in pain. Excruciating pain, in fact.

"Now you listen to me, asshole. I'm not going to do anything more than make you shit yourself here because I can afford to buy and sell people like you." With his one free hand, Sid pulled out his wallet. He deftly maneuvered it with three fingers, pulled out enough hundred dollar bills, dropped them on the floor next to the cigar and tossed Al back into his chair. He grabbed his keys from among those hanging on little hooks on the wall and left.

"So how much was it?" Cliff asked, waiting outside the garage door.

"Too much," Sid said as he rolled up his receipt. He cooled down a little when he got behind the wheel of his car. "She missed me, I can tell." He caressed the ripped vinyl seats.

"And Suzi misses me. Let's go back."

"Not so fast, I'm still a little peed." He looked back towards the office. Al did not come out. "Maybe this would be a good time to go see Spruance. What do you think?"

"I think I ought to see if everything is all right at home."

Rather than try to persuade Cliff, Sid gave in. "Just don't get in anybody's way, okay?"

"You got it."

They parted ways at the body shop, Cliff looking for another type of body and Sid looking for Spruance. The repair bill was greater than he'd expected. He had no trouble paying for it, that wasn't the point anyway. He had a feeling this Spruance was bad news. It simply wasn't right, paying for his own damages. Spruance was making no moves. It was time Sid made his.

He located the address from the accident report, which did match the one on the card the cop had given him. It was in a residential area that didn't look like the worst part of town, just not far from it. A black Gran Torino, fully repaired, sat in the driveway. Sid pulled up behind it.

On the barren front yard, an occasional patch of grass cropped up through the dirt and garbage. The stump of a once immense tree stuck out near the sidewalk where its roots had lifted and split a five foot section of concrete. Sid followed the slate walkway to the front door. White paint was flaking off the house everywhere. The walls were brushed bare of all paint behind two scrawny shrubs that marked off the front door. It was evident they would rock back and forth in a good wind, scraping the walls clean with their branches. A rusty bicycle with only one wheel lay in Sid's path. He kicked it out of the way where it landed on a section of the fallen gutter. He knocked again. "Hello in there?" It wasn't until the third try that a little girl answered. She had the cutest face despite the dirt and grime smeared on it. Her long brown hair lay stiff and uncombed, matted close to her scalp. All she wore was a tattered pair of jeans. Both she and a strong waft of incense greeted Sid. She looked at him the way little girls do, with puckered lips and eyes that looked up from a downturned face.

"Is your Daddy home?" he asked in a sympathetic voice, shocked at how anyone could treat a little girl like this. He had come expecting a confrontation, and the sight of her just knocked the wind out of his sails. From what he'd seen so far, this guy wouldn't be able to give him anything towards the repairs. But he did have enough to fix his own car, didn't he?

"Mommy!" the girl suddenly spoke. It was more a cry for help than a call for attention.

"I told you honey, tell whoever it is to go away." Sid heard the mother's voice come from the darkness of the inner room.

"Excuse me, darling." Sid eased the little one out of the way and started down the long entrance hall. He could just see the living room with its dark curtains drawn. The incense got stronger as he approached. He pulled out his repair receipt and said, "I'm Sid Lasvistas, I've got some business to take care of with..." Sid's footsteps, voice, heart, spleen, eyebrows and knuckles stopped. Growing toenails froze in their tracks. His goatee grew not. There was no exchange of oxygen and carbon dioxide in the alveoli of his lungs as his breath was taken away. Osmosis trickled to nil in the cells of his body. His eyes, locked in their sockets, saw the small living room dimly lit by a single candle and the red glow of the incense sticks. A dull gleam came from a long aquarium centered against the far wall. It sat on a table rather than a stand, covered with a velvet cloth which hung to the floor. Above the tank on an otherwise bare wall hung a large disc, hanging like a picture. On it was painted the crude outline of a black fish with one red eye. Above it was a broken arrow, and below were four triangles arranged so as to describe the shape of one large triangle. Each of the four was a different color; white, black, blue, and the center one red.

Hidden fluorescent bulbs illuminated the fish tank. The light looked eerie on the red gravel, the only ornamentation in the tank other than the fish themselves. Sid had seen them before. He used to keep some as pets. In the tank were several dozen or so black mollies. They were easy to identify, with their dull black sheen on a body void of any other markings. Unlike other fish that swim in schools, each mollie took its own private course, ignorant of the people in the room.

The furniture had been pushed aside to make room for the nine robed men and women who knelt on the floor facing the aquarium. Sid squinted, as his eyes had not yet adjusted to the darkness. He was stunned at how silly they all looked. One of them stood in front of the tank, the leader, Sid assumed. He wore a small helmet with several plumes sticking out of the top, color coded to match their emblem. It must have been of some obscure importance because he took it off as soon as Sid entered the room. Sid didn't know whether to laugh or apologize for barging in until he saw the knife, the silver platter and the mollie laying on it, flipping its tail. Mollies are such little fish, and the knife was so big. What were they going to do, sacrifice it to the Great Mollie God? Sid honestly wanted to laugh. This was too weird, too stupid even for him. He didn't get the chance to laugh or apologize as the leader rushed him, aided by the followers. The leader was a big man, and he picked Sid up off the floor before he bounced him like a rag doll off the wall.

Before Sid could speak, or breathe for that matter, all the members of this strange sect fenced him in.

"What do you want?" One of them growled, apparently trying to mask his real voice.

"What are we going to do? He saw us," another man whispered to his fellow followers.

"I say we make sure he doesn't say anything," a woman's voice spoke craftily.

Had he been the type, Sid might have envisioned having his tongue cut out with that knife. He got his wind back and realized he might be in some sort of a jam here. "Look, wait a minute, I just want to talk,

I want to talk to Mr. Spruance." Sid hated having to be polite after being bounced off a wall.

"This is the guy with the Mustang that Steve hit at the mall," said the young woman who just chased the little girl outside. All Sid could gather was that Spruance wasn't there. He was more immediately concerned with who these fish followers were and what they were going to do with him. The woman closed the front door. Another one pulled him to his feet.

"Hey, I don't care what you people are doing, I just wanted..." He was cut short when someone took him down with a shot to the ribs. Several others were checking out the repair bill he had dropped.

"You got ripped off, man. This guy really took you for a ride," a not too intelligent sounding voice laughed. Sid couldn't make out any of their faces.

A pair of hands picked him back up. "And what do you think you're doing with this? You don't expect Steve to pay for this, do you? Is that why you brought it over here, so you could shove it in his face? Is that it, tough guy?" The man's face was inches away from Sid's.

"Uh, breath mint?"

Uh oh, bad move. The man braced his hands against the wall to either side of Sid and rammed his head into Sid's forehead. The blow snapped his neck and threw his head back into the wall against which he slid down to his former position, dazed and barely conscious. It took three of them to pull the big guy away before he did more damage.

"Easy, Jake! We can't kill the guy." Sid would have been put somewhat at ease had he been able to make out all those words, but it was difficult with that buzzing in his head.

"We gotta make sure he doesn't say nothin'."

"Wait until I get that little Cindy for letting him in."

"First things first. What are we going to do with him? He's already seen too much."

"No he hasn't. He doesn't know anything about us. He didn't see anything."

"He's seen our ceremony."

"And our crest."

"He's seen our toothpaste?"

"This is serious, you shithead," the leader said, pointing to the coat of arms on the wall.

"I'll make sure he doesn't say anything." Jake picked Sid up. No one could stop him. "You're not going to say anything, are you, boy? Are you? You're gonna keep that wise ass mouth of yours shut, isn't that right?"

Sid stared incomprehensibly with glazed eyes and drool coming out of the side of his mouth.

"You, a little more to the right. That's it, a little more. Does anyone have a spare tool belt for Suzi?" John asked the construction workers. They were all crowded on the side of Sid's house. Philip and Denise were setting up the equipment and all six workers were ripping off their tool belts and offering them to Suzi who wore only a bathrobe as she stood next to John. Cliff had just pulled up and joined Ben off to the side.

"Having fun, Ben?"

"Oh, hiya Cliff," Ben said. "Your photographer friend here asked if he could use my boys in a layout. That's what he called it."

"Oh yeah?"

"Yeah, Dwight was in earshot and threatened to quit there on the spot if I said no. Well, he was just kidding, y'know. He told the rest of the guys and they all said the same thing, only I don't think they were fooling around. So here we are."

A temporary scaffold was set up with four workers on the suspended board and the other two on the ground. They all helped Suzi up to the board. She took off her robe and they all went crazy. She wore white lace panties, garters and fish net stockings.

"Here Suzi, let me help you with that." All four men up top offered to help her on with a tool belt.

"Okay men, can you all look at the camera please? Guys? The camera, it's over here. Yo!" John pleaded with the workers who were only paying attention to Suzi. She didn't mind at all. One man next to her, the rugged-looking type who appeared like he ought to be in a cigarette ad, put his arm around Suzi's bare waist, above the tool belt.

John got off two rolls but couldn't capture the feeling he was looking for. "Come on, Suzi, concentrate."

"I can't, John."

"Why the hell not?"

"I'm getting horny."

"All right, that's it, everybody down. Come on come on, down down down. I want some shots of Suzi alone," John commanded. "I said everybody, and I mean everybody!" He stepped forward to usher the men away. "Everybody back behind the cameras." They were herded back next to the bushes and trees that separated Sid and Cliff's houses. Suzi stayed on the platform, giggling at some of the comments they made to her. John tried to silence them with a stare, then turned his attention to Suzi and spoke with her privately for nearly ten minutes.

He emphasized everything with hand gestures, and Suzi nodded in agreement to whatever it was he said to her.

Soon the session was rolling again. Suzi was slow to get back into the posing mood. The crew more or less backed off, except for one guy who took off his cap and threw it. "Here Suzi, catch!" She caught it and put it on, coming back to life. John shot a look back at the man and wanted to kick the whole lot of them out. Realizing there wasn't even a little chance of that ever happening, he turned back to his camera. He couldn't deny the effect it had on Suzi, though. She was posing and dancing back and forth along the platform. She started doing a burlesque routine with lots of slinky shakes and sultry pouts towards the crew.

"The camera, love, look at the camera."

Cliff was enjoying the show and Ben was remembering what it was like to be young again. Cliff's attention was diverted when he heard Sid's Mustang screech to a halt out front with one wheel up on his front lawn. Cliff peered around a bush and called to him.

"Sid, over here. Sid?"

Even from a distance, Sid didn't look so good. He stomped across the lawn, ignoring Cliff's hail, holding a rag up to his mouth.

"Sid? Hey Sid, what's wrong?" Not many things could drag him away from his Suzi, but he followed after Sid into the house and found him in the downstairs bathroom. Sid was bent over the sink, his arched back heaving with gulps of breaths between rinses. "Sid, what happened, tell me." Cliff really got worried when he saw the bloodied water running down the drain. Sid answered by looking up at him with a blackened eye, a puffed cheek above a battered fat lip and a centered bruise on his forehead.

"Who did this to you? Did Spruance do this?" Sid didn't say a word, he just continued ridding his mouth of the blood that wouldn't stop gushing out of it. "He's going to pay for this, he's going to pay!" Cliff worked himself up into a frenzy. "I knew I should have gone with you, Sid, I'm sorry, oh, he's going to pay..."

There was a knock at the front door. Cliff had left it open. It was Mr. H.. Barbara and Billy came running up behind.

"What happened, where's Sid?" They'd heard his car pull up and were wondering why half of it was parked up on the lawn.

"Sid, what happened to you?" Mr. H. came in wincing when he saw Sid's bruises.

"I'll get some ice." Barbara headed straight for the kitchen. Sid was muttering something in a low growl through swollen lips and a fresh towel. He sat down on the end of the couch.

"Let me get a closer look, Sid." Mr. H. made him lower the towel. Billy cringed.

"Spruance," Cliff said.

"Spruance?" Mr. H. snapped. "Spruance did this? That's it, I'm calling the police."

"Gno!" Sid finally spoke although it was obviously painful for him to do so.

"Sid, I'm calling the police, this is it."

"Gno!" Sid yelled louder than before. The pain showed in his face. He got up and held the phone down in its cradle. The two men stared at each other. "Peas, gno," Sid said quietly, sternly.

Barbara returned with some ice wrapped in a dish towel. "Stop fighting, you two. Sid, get back on that couch." Cliff was amazed at the effect she had on a room. In seconds, she had him back on the couch, trying to decide whether to put the ice on his lip, cheek, eye, or on that curious welt in the middle of his forehead. "I'm going to get some more ice." She got up from her crouched position next to Sid. "And don't you touch that phone, Daddy."

"I'm not touching no phone," Mr. H. grumbled.

"Come help Mommy in the kitchen," Barbara said, leading her toddler son out of the room.

"So that's your daughter," Cliff said. He'd only met her once before, from afar.

"Pain in my butt, sometimes," Mr. H. said. She quickly returned with some more towels. Billy followed carrying a tray of ice. While Barbara fixed some more ice packs, Billy looked first at his Grandpa then at Cliff. He smiled and Cliff smiled back before Billy set down his ice tray and plodded over to his Grandpa.

"You should have seen the other guy, Billy Willy," Mr. H. said with his arms wrapped around the little boy.

Sid moaned a little. He'd be lying if he denied enjoying the pampering he was getting. Barbara exchanged a bloodied towel for a fresh one. "Looks like you've been playing with the big boys, huh?" She hated violence and was just trying to keep things light. Sid tried to smile, although no one could see it. "Do you two know what's going on outside, on your side yard?"

"Oh that. That's, uh, that's art." Cliff suddenly felt like he'd just been caught playing with himself.

"Yeah. Art. That's what I thought."

The next day, late in the afternoon, Barbara, Sid, Billy and Cliff were out by the tree watching the house go back up. Sid was repeating the story of yesterday to Barbara.

"At least it was a fair fight," Barbara said sarcastically.

"Yeah, real fair." Sid gingerly rubbed his hand over the bruise on his forehead.

"Good thing you're not a Cyclops or you'd be blind, too," Cliff added. Somebody's stupid humor was rubbing off on him. It drew a that-was-dumb look from Barbara, but she laughed anyway.

"So what are you going to do about it?" she asked Sid.

"I'll think of something." Sid's speech was only slightly slurred today. His face still looked like something even Goddamnit wouldn't drag in.

"Regardless of how strange they are, they still owe you a lot of money for your car. You can even bring them up on assault charges now. You should go to the police, Sid," Barbara advised.

"You've been talking to your Dad too much, Barbara. Besides, they'd just twist it around to illegal entry on my part."

"You were just trying to collect the money they owe you. Who are the cops going to believe, you or a bunch of goons who pray to fish?" Cliff pointed out.

"And I suppose they'll show up in their robes so I don't look like I'm off my rocker, huh? No, whatever they're doing, they're keeping it a secret. The cops will start thinking I'm the nut if I come up with a story like that. How can I prove it?"

"But Spruance was drunk when he hit you. Can't you hold that against him?"

"Drunk driving is a summary offense. That's not even a misde-meanor. If Spruance refuses to pay, I take him to court. I pay the court fees. I get them back when Spruance pays up. That is, if he shows up in court. If he doesn't, his application is refused the next time he goes to renew his license." Sid had done his homework.

"And…" Cliff asked.

"And that's it. Think about it next time you pay your car insurance premium. Part of that money goes to pick up the slack for people like Spruance." Sid was peed at the situation and also at the fact it hurt his lips too much to smoke. He had started doing homerolls again. Of course, he didn't want to smoke, or curse, with little Billy around anyway.

"You could put up a lien against his property," Barbara suggested.

"This guy's such a bunghole, I'd probably have to take a number and wait in line to do something like that. Besides, like I said, I'll bet he hasn't got much property that's paid off."

"There's got to be something you can do."

"I said I'd think of something."

"I still think the police could help you. They would know what your options are."

"I already know my options."

"It couldn't hurt," Barbara said.

"Did you know most small children live under the illusion that they're actually dogs? Here Billy, go fetch!" Sid threw a stick towards the house. Billy waddled after it. They all laughed but Barbara wasn't thrown off course.

"Don't go changing the subject, Sid. You should go, it's the right thing."

As Cliff expected, Barbara got her way. He would be fascinated by this power for a long time to come. Sid insisted on waiting a week, long enough for his bruises to start healing. Barbara thought this was coun-terproductive, but it's the only way Sid agreed to go. They all piled into her T-bird, leaving Billy at home with Grandpa.

"You're finally showing some sense, Sid," Mr. H. said before they pulled out of the driveway.

"Don't blame me, blame your daughter. She's the one making me go."

"Yes, she has a way of doing that." Mr. H. said affectionately, giving Barbara a look before he kissed her goodbye.

"Goodbye, Daddy," she said. "Bye kid, be good," she said to Billy as Grandpa held him up to kiss Mommy. As they pulled out, Mr. H. was squatted down behind Billy, helping him wave.

"He's a cute kid," Sid said from his solo position in the back seat.

"Only until you get to know him. Then he can be a brat just like his Father."

Her comment made both Sid and Cliff uneasy. All Cliff could gather from Mr. H. was that Barbara and her husband were separated. He felt the rest was none of his business.

Sid took a pair of cheap sunglasses out of his pocket and put them on to cover his black eye, now the worst-looking one of his bruises. "That's better." Then, just to add the proper perspective to the situation, he decided to elucidate upon the etymology of the appropriate term, 'cop'. "There are those that hold to the theory that we get the term 'cop' from a shortened version of copper, the slang for policemen in the earlier half of our century. At that time, the regulation police uniform was constituted in part by a long coat adorned with a series of large copper buttons. Still others hold to another theory, that being it is nothing more than an acronym for Chief of Police. Personally, I subscribe to the most likely explanation, that it is an acronym, but rather for Constable on Patrol…" And so it went until they arrived at the township building annex.

As they entered, a skeptical Sid saw a promising sign in the form of a poster hanging in the lobby. It depicted a horrifying scene of an old car wrapped around a utility pole. An ambulance was pulling away while a policeman carried a six pack out of what was left of the car. Underneath, a caption read; 'Don't Drink and Drive, Think and Thrive'.

"I've never seen so many cops in my life. The place is crawling with them." It was a sarcastic pun on Sid's part. There wasn't anybody around. Three empty hallways led from the lobby with a sign above each, indicating what offices could be found where. "They're not very helpful. I don't see a Complaint Department." A lone policeman came walking down one of the hallways towards them.

"It's a raid!" Cliff whispered to Sid.

"Shh!" Barbara said aside to him. "Excuse me, sir. My friends and I were recently in an auto accident and we're having trouble collecting payment from the man who hit us. Can you please direct us to someone who might help us?"

"I'm just building security, ma'am. I don't have that information. There's an office just around this corner, maybe they can help you." Barbara politely thanked him and led the trio down the hallway.

"These guys must be good. They need a security department to protect their own building," Sid said, straight faced.

"Sid! We're trying to help you here." She didn't want to encourage him by smiling. Besides, she was used to disciplining Billy, and this wasn't so different.

In the office, a uniformed secretary led them passed several rooms and into a large, particularly crowded office. The secretary caught the attention of a man in a suit, one of the few people in the office out of uniform. She briefly explained the situation, as told to her by Barbara, then left them there.

"Let's step into my office. It's quieter in there." The man held the door open into a private adjoining office without introducing himself. The name on the door read 'Det. I. Dodge'. He followed them in, hiked up his blue trousers and sat himself down behind the desk like a little boy behind the wheel of a real racecar. An overly long slab of his straight blonde hair, combed to the side, fell into his face. With a practiced groom of his hand, he pushed it back into position where it lay practically ear to ear, covering his bald spot. "So, you're having trouble with an auto accident, is that right?" He addressed all three of them.

"Yes, that's correct, Detective Dodge," Barbara answered, sitting straight up on the edge of her chair.

Cliff sat next to Barbara and Sid had pulled up a chair on the end. He'd readily agreed earlier to let Barbara do all the talking. The detective didn't have anything to say that Sid wanted to hear, anyway. Bored already, he looked over all the plaques and awards on the walls as well as the autographed photo of the mayor on the esteemed detective's desk. "His Honor gave that to me personally," the detective paused to boast when he noticed the man with the sunglasses looking at it.

"The man who hit our car agreed on the scene to make restitution for our damages. So far he hasn't made an effort to do so." Barbara decided this choice of words was appropriate. This was a detective. She wanted to show some respect.

"Yes, the accident. How long ago did it occur, Miss?" he asked.

"Oh, um," she looked back at Sid who remained quiet. "Almost three weeks ago, sir."

"That's part of your problem. The gentleman who allegedly hit you is granted a period of one month in which to respond," the detective recited a line verbatim from the legal codes.

"One whole month? Why?"

"If he doesn't respond within that time, you may exercise your right to press charges against him."

"What do you mean, if he doesn't respond?"

Another man in a suit opened the door and stepped half way in.

"Just a minute, Ira," Detective Dodge said. The man grumbled and backed out of the office. Sid was distractedly looking at a clock on the wall with a plaque underneath. 'Presented to Det. I. Dodge for twenty years meritorious service'.

"Normally, they show up at the court proceedings," Dodge continued.

"Wait a minute." Barbara was quickly becoming exasperated. "We don't want to take anybody to court, we just want to be reimbursed for the repairs to the car. Won't you go after him?"

"Did you say you already had the car repaired?"

"Of course we did."

"Oh, that's too bad." The detective shook his head and his hair fell down into his eyes.

"What do you mean, that's too bad?" She was beginning to boil.

"Do you have any pictures of the car after the accident?" he asked, straightening one of the awards on the desk.

"Pictures? What do we need pictures for?"

"No pictures, huh? How about a copy of the repair bill? Can you get someone who worked on the car to verify the extent of the damages?"

"What are you talking about? We got hit by an uninsured drunk! It was his fault. We weren't even in the car at the time."

"So you didn't actually see the accident," the detective surmised.

"It's all in the accident report."

"Let me see that report." Dodge held out his hand.

"We didn't bring it with us."

The detective tried to give Barbara a disciplinary stare, but it was blocked by a handful of hair that fell again from his bald spot. "How about the repair bill?"

Barbara turned to Sid. He showed her two empty hands.

"You've got to understand. I need your help before I can help you. You didn't tell me the other driver was drunk or underinsured. Of course, I only have your word on that."

"Are you calling us liars?" Cliff asked plainly. Before the detective could answer, Ira showed up again at the door.

"Ira, please, just a minute."

Grumble grumble, close door.

"As I was saying, I'm trying to help you, but you've got to understand that the criminal has rights, too."

"We just want to be reimbursed. We haven't done anything wrong," Barbara argued.

"We get all kinds of people in here trying to pull one over on us with phony charges and accusations. Last year, I had a guy in here with the same problem as you. His repairs cost him three hundred dollars and he tried to get us to endorse damages in excess of three thousand dollars. He lied to us! We're the police, for Christ's sake."

"What are you going to do for us?" Barbara said slowly, carefully, hardly able to look at the detective without becoming enraged.

"If the offender doesn't respond within the next week…"

Ira came back.

"Ira, please."

"Hey Alex, I don't like getting kicked out of my own office, you know that?" Ira said as he walked all the way in this time. "Excuse me, folks."

"Ira, please, don't do, I, we have people here," the detective stuttered.

"And get out of my chair," Detective Ira Dodge barked.

"Who the hell are you?" Barbara got out of her own chair and backed the bogus detective into a corner.

"You're doing it again, aren't you, Alex? And you wonder why I don't like letting you use my office," Detective Dodge said as he rifled through his drawer. He looked up once and met Sid's guarded eyes. "Hi," Dodge said, unaffected, and continued to root through the drawer. Cliff kept an eye on the action in the corner.

"I said who are you? I want your name."

Dodge spoke up. With an outstretched arm like a circus ringleader, he announced, "Ladies and gentlemen, may I introduce one of our county's finest, Detective Alex Chicane."

"Well, Detective Chicane, I ought to give you a piece of my mind, but I don't think you'd know what to do with it! You've got some nerve." Barbara scowled at Chicane's bald spot as his head was cowered to avoid the brunt of her onslaught. He flustered a few words of mercy before Barbara finished chewing him out. She then led Sid and Cliff out of the office with a promise never to return. Through the open door behind them, Sid and Cliff walked just slow enough to hear the ensuing argument along with everyone else in the outer office. Undoubtedly, they'd heard it before.

"Thanks a lot, Ira, thank a whole hell of a lot."

"I'm getting fed up to here with your bullshit, you know that, Alex?"

"You think you're so almighty important. I've got just as many awards as you do. I've got two autographed pictures of the mayor, but I don't have my own office to hang them up in, do I? You got the only private office left because of your seniority. I joined the force two months after you. Two lousy months! What does that count for when you're talking about twenty years?"

"Shut up, Alex. I've already heard this sob story before."

"It's not easy, Ira. No one knows who I am."

"No one wants to know, Alex."

"How am I supposed to convey my sense of authority to these people when I don't even have a place to hang my Legion of Honor awards? Damnit, the chief said we could share!"

"That's right, he said share, not impersonate. You know impersonating an officer of the law is an offense even if you're an officer to begin with? You remember that much, don't you Alex?"

"Nerd!"

Sid and Cliff caught up to Barbara in the lobby. She and Cliff spouted on about how asinine the episode had been. Sid was silent until they reached the car. He straightened his collar like he was walking back into a bar after an easy fight outside.

"Now," Sid announced, "we do it my way."

9

Sid's way involved patience, and lots of it. So as he sat back and slowly schemed, life went on around him as usual.

For Barbara, when she wasn't busy at her job as a business secretary, life came to her in the form of a letter from her runaway husband. It was plastered with Mexican postage stamps. As it turned out, the man who went out for a pack of cigarettes and never came back was in trouble with the law, as well as some people on the other side of the law, down in Ciudad Juarez, just south of the Texas border. He was being held on various charges, some valid, some not, and was turning to Barbara for help. "I finally know where he's going to be every night," was her sole comment on the situation.

For Sid, all life wasn't passing him by. While reconstruction was continuing on his house, his sidewalk and streetlamp were completed. Now they'd have a good place to hang out during the oncoming summer nights.

For Cliff, yet another semester was finished. Walking out of his final in the Hungarian bear's class, he stopped to tell him to give him a call if his car ever broke down again. The last thing Cliff and everyone else down the hallway heard of Dr. Staff was his raucous laughter. Professor Gatlin's class had dwindled down to seventy students, two of whom Cliff stopped to talk to about what he alone thought was an easy test.

Strolling through the courtyard with its crisscrossed paths, he went to the cafeteria to pick up an orange soda and a fruit pie then retired to the old bench at the open end of the courtyard. A student rode by on a bicycle wearing cutoff jeans and a muscle shirt. Although these early May mornings were still a bit chilly, the hot days of summer were coming. Cliff relaxed on his bench and casually filled his mouth with soda. He liked to swish it through his teeth once or twice to get the fizz out before he swallowed.

With both arms draped across the back of the bench, he crossed his legs. His jeans covered the tops of his tight leather boots. Sid had bought them for him weeks ago. When he mentioned the fit, Sid had said, "They're supposed to be that way. They'll break in. We'll take 'em." The damn things were still too tight, but Cliff didn't mind. He sat back and looked at Blakely and Baker Halls to his left, Mattlander, Spice and Corbett to the right. The student union building faced him across the courtyard.

Riding mowers would soon be cutting the grass and little sprouts were appearing in the unkempt flower beds. The trees around campus were already covered with small green leaves, soon to be ready for a summer's worth of shading. The only other person Cliff could see was a maintenance man working on a fountain in which the pipes had frozen and busted over the winter. As he watched the man work, it seemed as if all the finals let out at once as lots of people were beginning to appear. More were coming in from the parking areas. Cliff tried to look at every one of them but no matter how hard he tried, no one looked back at him. Even when he ignored them, no one noticed him. It took ten minutes or so for the courtyard to empty out a bit. Cliff realized a situation that once terrified him had now become an obsession. With time, the novelty would wear off and he'd become indifferent to it like everyone else, but for the time being he was fascinated that people didn't scare him like they used to.

He finished his fruit pie and got up to leave. He went the long way, passed the student union building to say hello to the returning ducks at the pond. A dozen or so of the web-footed friends came gliding across the water to meet him. They were quite tame and considered the appearance of a human synonymous with feeding time. While it was true the ducks got more than their fair share of food from the students and the townspeople, Cliff still felt bad because he didn't have anything for them. They were all coming over now and Cliff recalled one of the nature programs he'd watched with Sid on public TV. He remembered a shot from an underwater camera showing duck feet paddling furiously while the scene above, as Cliff saw now, was one of grace and ease. He tried to imagine the flurry of flippers as each duck seemed to part the water before it on its way to the nearby bank.

He decided to go back to the cafeteria to find something suitable for duck stomachs. When he turned around, he found himself facing that wall he'd seen months ago. It was the brick wall that once bore the phrase 'Fuck a Duck' in white spray paint. Since then, it had been almost completely scrubbed off. Stubbornly, predictably, it had been rescrawled, this time in black. It traced along the same route as the white shadow which glowed faintly behind the thinner lines of the restored letters.

Cliff stopped to examine the phrase for the second time in five months. The first time he'd looked at it, he cursed all the vandals and their defacing deeds, but this memory was not now first and foremost in his mind. He studied it intently. "Fuck a Duck," he said out loud.

Just a jingle, a short rhyme with a ribald twist. He did like the way the words sounded. It was as if they went together for more of a reason than just because they rhymed. Slowly, a new curriculum slithered its way out from a dormant place in Cliff's prodded imagination. Right there on the spot, he invented a new course of study called Contemporary Bestiality. He concocted some of the required courses; Duck Fucking, Bovine Boinking, Camel Humping I and II, Mucket Fucking, Getting Your Goat and a credited seminar called Going Down on the Farm.

Cliff, what's happening to you? You, the kid who showed up at kindergarten with a set of colored pencils, each already sharpened, each bearing your name in gold print. You, who never even heard a dirty word until the fourth grade, the same year you stopped using those colored pencils. You, who never spoke unless spoken to, who knew the correct way to arrange the silverware in a place setting, (yes, the soup spoon goes on the right), you, who always rolled the toothpaste tube up from the bottom for best results, why are you thinking such improper thoughts? Beware, Clifford Dinsdale, the argyle gargoyles are acomin' ta getcha.

10

As surely as man was made for woman, darkness for light, hate for love, the hole for something to put in the middle of a donut, June was made for picnics.

With Billy's help, Barbara prepared some of the standard items; cold fried chicken, pickles, fruit and cake. Cliff baked a second cake and added French bread, cheese, white grapes and black olives. Sid, decked out in cutoffs and a tie dye tee shirt, stopped at Thiesmann's Burgers on the way and picked up five deluxe jumbo Thieburgers, six large fries and only two milkshakes because he also brought the beer that would be prohibited at Tammerlane Park.

They each had a reason to celebrate. Barbara finally knew where her husband was and she reveled every time she thought about his predicament. Sid had his new curb and streetlamp with the official christening ceremony to take place that evening. He would also commence his revenge, Sid-style, against Spruance soon. Billy was always celebrating the fact he was a little boy, too dumb to handle hassles and responsibilities but smart enough to enjoy himself while he could.

Four people, two dogs and lots of baskets and bags poured out of Sid's Mustang under a tall, shady tree marking the entrance of a nature trail. Billy ran around in circles with Bump and Grind all over him. Sid took a blanket out of the trunk and spread it out over the lush, green grass. It sank down like depressions in a lumpy pillow where Barbara set lots of foodstuffs down on it. Sid helped her while Cliff wandered off, peeking around the trees and into the sunny open field beyond.

"That's all right, Cliff, we'll set everything up," Sid called after him.

"Okay, thanks," Cliff answered mindlessly.

Barbara smiled and said to Sid, "Some friend you've got there."

"Yeah yeah," Sid responded, throwing a sidelong glance after Cliff. "Hey, I think one of us better call off either the dogs or the kiddo." Barbara turned to see the three of them tumbling down the nature trail amid barks and giggles. "Billy, stop that barking!" Sid said in a voice of fatherly reproach, complete with hands on hips then a wagging finger. "Bump, Grind, I told you guys to pick on someone your own size. Oh, Billy is about their size, isn't he?" Sid said aside to Barbara. "C'mon, guys, enough of this two-on-one stuff." Sid pulled out a bunless burger and flung it like a Frisbee over his car nearby. The Setters took off after it, one going around the Mustang and the other trying to go over it. Billy followed them from far behind.

"No, Billy, not you!" Barbara laughed.

"See, I told you so," Sid said, licking the grease from his fingers. Billy came back, tingling with toddler power. "Come here you dirtball!" Sid taunted him with outstretched arms.

"No!" Billy pulled the most used word out of his infantile vocabulary.

"No? No? Then I'm gonna get you, Arrr!"

Cliff watched Sid's monster pursuit after Billy's zig-zag, screaming escape. He returned to help Barbara unpack the rest of the food.

"Ah, you came back."

"I can't let you people eat all this good food without me, can I?" Cliff pulled out the two cakes.

"Hey, those are for dessert."

"Let's leave mine for dessert. You look good enough to eat right now." Whoa, a textbook slip of the tongue, definitely of the Freudian variety.

"Excuse me?" Barbara started to laugh at him.

"Whoops, ah, Jeez, I meant your cake, Barbara. Yours looks really good, better than mine, I meant to say. Aw come on, you know what I meant. Here, try some of this." He broke off a hunk of French bread and smeared some spicy cheese spread on it.

"Mm, that's delicious." She spotted a small glass jar in one of the baskets. "They wouldn't happen to be kalamata olives in there, would they?"

"Sure are. You like them?"

"I love them. I eat them right out of the jar."

"Oh well. Competition." Cliff handed them to her.

"You can have them, we have enough other stuff here to last us all summer, you know."

"I was only kidding. Go ahead, try one." Barbara dunked and came up with two vinegary fingers with an olive in between them. She popped it into her mouth as they both watched Sid twirl Billy around on his shoulders in the open field beyond the car.

"Those two sure get along," Cliff mused.

"Yes, they do. I'm glad to see it, too." Barbara wondered if Sid knew that she admired, and only admired, men who weren't afraid of the fact she was a single parent. "I feel so guilty sometimes, not giving Billy a real Father."

Cliff really wished she wouldn't talk about this. It made him feel awkward, and he still wasn't sure if he'd gotten that cake comment passed her yet. "Why don't you just hire a team of mercenaries to go down there and bust him out?" He broke off some more bread and intently looked for the grapes.

"Are you kidding? The world is a safer place with him behind bars." They were both distracted when one of the dogs knocked Sid down and Billy joined in piling on him. "It's really good for him," Barbara smiled approvingly.

"For who, Billy or Sid?" Cliff downed two olives at once.

Barbara thought a moment. "Both, I suppose, now that you mention it. Hey, stop hogging all the olives."

"I tell you, it's been a real experience, living in the same house with him these past few weeks."

"I'll bet it has. I don't know what that girl was doing on the side of your house that day, but you two bachelors sure seem to be having a good time."

"Oh, that. Well, y'know, that was just, something…"

"Uh huh. I've got to say, though, that's a far cry from watching him play with Billy. Every guy I've known has been on too much of a macho kick for that."

"Well I don't go around counting the hairs on my chest." Cliff acted hurt.

"You mean both of them?" Barbara poked at him. "Oh, here." She dropped a dripping olive into Cliff's mouth. He tried to stare her down as he bit it in two with his front teeth. He swallowed the pieces whole with his nose in the air.

"Oh, you brute!"

They kept on eating some more in a silence that lasted only a minute or two while they watched the kids playing. Sid had Billy in a fireman's carry, slung over his one shoulder, feet forward. He bounced giggles out of the little buckaroo as he danced back to the picnic.

"Say, have you guys seen Billy?" Sid gasped, long out of wind.

"Here, I'm here!" Billy called out, dangling from behind.

"Where?" Sid spun around and around, pretending to look.

"Mommy!" Billy waved.

"Look at you!" Cliff said.

"I better go look for him." Sid started off again into the sunny open spaces. Once they were back out there, Sid dropped to one knee, then two, then he fell forward, spilling Billy to the side. Sid lay still on the ground. The dogs still wanted to play.

"Up up up up up!" Billy repeated as he patted on Sid's back. He lay motionless. His tumble was convincing enough to attract attention. Cliff smiled. Barbara wondered what had gone wrong. "Up!" Billy screamed in a high-pitched squeal.

Barbara got up and had taken two steps forward when Sid rolled over and said,"Okay", tackling Billy. She let out a trapped breath and sank back down on the blanket.

"I think you worry too much," Cliff told her through a bite of bread, wondering how Barbara could have been fooled by Sid's little stunt.

"I know I worry too much. I have to, I'm a Mother. I want Billy to grow up right, that's all. It's not easy being a single parent, or a single child. I know."

"Stop trying so hard." Cliff even surprised himself by saying that. It just came out.

"I said it's not easy," Barbara said harshly, defensively.

Cliff suddenly felt very small. "I'm sorry, I guess I just don't understand, that's all." They were both silent again.

"I didn't mean to jump down your throat, Cliff. I'm sorry." Cliff, not in the habit of looking for apologies, didn't think one was necessary. "I told you it wasn't easy. It makes me nasty sometimes for no reason. Here, have an orange, it's on me."

Cliff wished it really was on her, like balanced on her naked stomach, peeled and open, dripping juices as she laid back so he could eat it off her. 'I've got to stop thinking like this'. He had to change the subject.

"So, what happened to your Mother?" Cliff asked, taking a chance with what could be a delicate subject. He hoped it wasn't.

"I still remember her. She died so long ago. It was senseless. There's not much to say about it. She slipped off a stepladder in the kitchen. What gets me is, the last thing she probably saw was a stack of cups or dishes on a shelf."

"She hit her head?"

"No, she broke her neck. Daddy doesn't like to talk about it. He still thinks he should have been there."

"That's terrible." Cliff hoped he sounded sincere, which he was, because he also thought it was terrible that all he could think of was a joke about navel oranges.

The playmates came back. "So *pant pant* we turn our backs for *pant* a few minutes and *pant* you guys eat up all the *pant* food." Sid's breathing almost sounded like that of the dogs with their peculiar metabolism by which they sweat through their mouths, prompting Sid to say on several occasions in the past that that's why their breath always smells so bad.

"Here Billy, try one of these." Cliff offered him a black olive. He gave it a curious squint and popped it in his mouth. Cliff didn't realize it would take up so much room in the little mouth. Billy chewed on it contentedly to Barbara's surprise.

"He never touches those things when I give them to him," she remarked. "Chew with your mouth closed, honey."

Cliff offered a second one, but Billy opted for Sid's cold French fries instead. The two were still playing around with each other. Billy reached across the blanket for an apple. It wasn't big at all but it took both his hands to hold it. As soon as he got a grip on it, Sid knocked it out of his hands and balanced it on top of his own head.

"Gimme!" Billy cried, fiercely annoyed.

"Come and get it," Sid teased. In a scene Cliff thought had overtures of William Tell, Billy had to stand on Sid's crossed legs to reach the apple. When Billy had his hands up over his own and Sid's head, Sid brought out the tickle brigade and reduced the little one to squirms and giggles.

"I think you've got a friend for life there, Sid," Cliff said.

"Oh, I hope so."

Most of what they didn't finish went to the dogs. Cliff took care of cleaning up while the rest of them played Frisbee. While Cliff was loading the car, he noticed the keys were turned forward in the ignition, draining power directly off the battery to play the music on the radio they had been listening to. It stopped momentarily as he switched the keys back to the accessory position.

"Hey, what're you doing?" Sid shouted.

"I had to set your keys forward. You were sucking juice right out of the battery. I hope it starts," Cliff replied with the volume turned down to make himself heard.

"Aw, crank it back up, Cliff, you worry too much," Sid said.

They all played for a little while longer and then left. They stopped at the state store on the way home for Sid to pick up a bottle of champagne for the christening. Mr. H. waved to them from the sidewalk as Sid pulled his car up to the curb. "Did you have a good time?" he asked as they piled out.

"Oh yeah," Barbara said, trying to kiss her father without bumping him with the thermos and basket she was carrying.

"So you're breaking it in already, huh?" Sid said to Mr. H..

"Just inspecting it, really," he said. "They did a good job, I suppose."

"Uh huh."

The streetlamp was fitted with an electric eye that turned it on automatically when it got dark enough. Whatever time that turned out to be, Sid decided that would be when the ceremony would take place. With Cliff's help, he draped a string over the lowest branch of the oak tree. He tied the champagne bottle to the dangling end, leaving enough slack so it would swing close to the ground. Later, as the sky darkened and the sun set, they all gathered on the sidewalk and waited.

"I don't know if I get this." Cliff was the first puzzled one to speak. "Why is a sidewalk so special to you, because no one else around here has one?"

"Yeah, I suppose that's part of it."

"I'm with Cliff. What's the big deal?" Barbara chimed in.

"Maybe I am making a big production out of this, but what's wrong with that? Listen, when I was a kid, this was where we used to hang out, in the street. We'd sit on the curb under the light, talking and being eaten alive by mosquitoes. I just kind of missed it, that's all."

"I know what he's talking about." Mr. H. expelled a few puffs. "When I was young we had even less to do than you all did. We practically lived out on the curb. Sometimes we'd just watch the cars go by. That was 'hanging out'. I missed it too, for a while."

Sid continued. "When you grow up, you're not supposed to do these things anymore. When was the last time you saw a man in a suit sitting on a curb? No, you're supposed to be successful and sit in your plush living room with your scotch and soda, watch the news and go to bed early. Well screw that, I say." Sid made his point, he thought. Cliff and Barbara were still confused, although they didn't see it as a bad idea.

When Sid finished, a crackling blue flicker snapped in the streetlamp as if on cue. The glow slowly got brighter before their eyes.

"All right." Sid prepared them as if the sky itself was opening up for business, giving free rides through the trapo, strato, meso and ionospheres. He stood on the far side of the tree with the hanging bottle in his hands. "I'd just like to say a few words as a dedication of this sidewalk. May we have nothing but good times out here, may the mosquitoes not bite us too much, and, uh," while he was trying to think of something else to add, Mr. H. stopped to relight his pipe. "And may our pipes never need relighting."

With that said, Sid cast the bottle out with a mighty swinging arc over the road. It came back swiftly, silently, and dove hard. It touched down on the dirt strip between the curb and the sidewalk which it skittered across with what momentum was left after the crash landing. It clattered and clinked before it came to rest, still intact.

Barbara busted out laughing. Mr. H. nodded his head to Cliff, who smiled. Sid smacked his own forehead and joined in with Barbara.

"How anticlimactic can you get?" he sighed. "Come over here, Billy, it's your turn." Sid helped Billy swing the bottle out again. This time it smacked squarely into the curb, which wasn't so bad even if they were aiming for the sidewalk.

"Yayhayhay!" Billy cheered. They all clapped as the champagne fizzed into the street. Billy helped Sid inspect the curb.

"I told you they did a good job," Mr. H. said. "The bottle broke and the curb didn't."

"Be careful, Billy. That glass is sharp," Barbara warned.

Cliff joined them at the curb. It was like looking for the stick of dynamite after the boom. The jagged bottle neck remained tied in place. "Sure beats popping the cork." Fragments of green glass lay scattered in the street. Bubbles danced on a puddle of champagne which scented the air and darkened the new, white cement as it soaked in.

"What a mess. Who's going to clean that up?" Barbara asked.

"I didn't think of that," Sid wondered for her benefit, not really concerned. "When they christen a ship, I guess all the broken glass just falls in the water."

"You forgot to give it a name," Mr. H. reminded Sid.

"What?"

"Whenever you christen something, you have to give it a name. That's the whole point."

"That's right, isn't it?"

"It doesn't need a name. It's a sidewalk," Cliff stated the obvious. "To me it's nice the way it is."

"Well, that's the tradition, anyhow."

"Aw, the heck with the tradition. Cliff's right. Let's leave it as it is," Sid concluded.

"Does that mean you're not going to break anymore bottles?" Barbara asked.

"Afraid so."

"Good."

"Killjoy," he teased.

Barbara had only stayed late enough to join in the christening at Sid's insistence. She started gathering up her things.

"What are you doing?" Sid asked her.

"It's getting late, Sid." Billy was starting to doze in his Grandpa's arms. "I have to put Billy to bed. Then I have some things to do before I put myself to bed. I have to go to work in the morning." They made their goodbyes, leaving Sid, Cliff and Mr. H. standing there as if it was a forgotten bus stop.

"Well, I'm going to be heading inside, too. It's getting dark," Cliff said.

"It's not getting dark. The streetlamp is on," Sid said, shocked at Cliff's concession to normalcy.

"But it's dark everywhere else." Cliff obviously wasn't about to stay. "You coming?"

"Of course not!"

"Okay, I'll see you when you get in."

The evening wasn't working out like Sid had planned. He sat himself down on the curb and turned to Mr. H. "I suppose you're going in, too?"

"No, no, not yet."

"I don't think they understand," Sid said, facing the river.

"Sid," Mr. H. began in that same tone he had used in his first conversation with his new neighbor, "let me tell you something.

God, this curb is awfully low." He grunted as he crunched his old body into a sitting position next to Sid. "You can't expect everyone to think the same way as you. Not everybody is as excited about this curb as you are."

The tobacco and champagne mixed to create a unique aroma. "But how do they know? They didn't even give it a try. They're probably just humoring me."

"Those people are your friends, Sid. Remember that. I've never seen my Barbara take to someone as quickly as she's taken to you. For crying out loud, Billy probably thinks you're his real Father." That raised a smile. "Then there's Cliff. I lived two doors away from him for nearly a year without a word between us. You show up and soon you're introducing me to someone who I should've been introducing you to."

"That was a little awkward, wasn't it?" Sid remembered.

"You've got to understand, Sid, we get along together but we all lead different lives. Cliff goes to school. Barbara takes care of Billy. I just sit around and rot nowadays when I'm not showing those clowns the right way to put your house back together. And you know something? I'm perfectly content just rotting away. If Cliff or Barbara aren't happy with their lives, you can try all you want but it's still their problem." Sid didn't agree. "I'm sorry if that's a hard line to swallow but it's true. If you want to make them happy then go ahead, knock yourself out. But if they don't respond to what you have for them, don't blame them."

"There's nothing wrong with trying to make people happy, Frank."

"You're choosing a difficult life if you're putting yourself in charge of other people's happiness, Sid."

"I think you're getting a little hard in your old age."

"I got to my old age because I got hard a long time ago. I would've never gone so far with my business, or my life for that matter, if I didn't watch out for number one. Think about that, Sid."

Sid wondered just how far Mr. H. had gotten as he sat in the progressing night, alone under the streetlamp. He just didn't know what a good time would cost him. He could still smell the champagne as he picked with a stick through the glass.

> *Ashes to ashes, dust to dust*
> *We does what we does 'cause we does what we must*
> *It doesn't have to be this way*
> *Why can't you just shut up and say*
> *I guess if you like it*
> *I guess I like it too*
>
> -Composer unknown

11

"Say Cliff, can I borrow your car?"

"What's the matter with yours?"

"Nothing, I just need yours."

"Why do you need my car?"

"Because I do, that's why. Just for tonight. And maybe tomorrow night, too. That's it. My car will be here if you need it."

"I don't like to loan my car out."

"Well hey, you'll be driving my car too, you know."

"I will not!"

"I just finished telling you it'll be here when you need it."

"Who says I'll need your car?"

"That's not the point. The point is I need your car, remember?"

"Sid, what do you need my car for?"

"I'll tell you why I need your car if you'll tell me why you need mine."

"But I don't need your car for anything!"

"There you go again. Cliff, just let me borrow your car for tonight."

Cliff gave Sid a mistrustful glance and his keys. "Don't forget to put some gas in it."

"Gee, thanks Dad." If Cliff had any idea Sid was going to use his car to tail Spruance's Gran Torino, he would never have consented. Sid couldn't take the Mustang because it looked like rain and his ragtop leaked, plus there was the possibility of it being recognized by the goons.

Cliff's night ended at two AM when he fell asleep on the living room couch with the light still on. Sid found the scene amusing when he got in just before five. Although he'd finished his business with Spruance for the time being, Sid conned Cliff's car out of him again the next evening to go to Tammerlane Park to steal a bench. He snuck in after dark and had it dismantled in no time. It was made of five long boards which fit into slots in two cement uprights, one on either end. It was too bulky and heavy to carry assembled and still required four trips to Cliff's Volvo, parked on a side road, one of the isolated perimeters of the park.

"You did what?" Cliff was seeing red when Sid asked him to come out at eleven o'clock to help him set it up.

"Come on, I've got to get it up tonight. I don't think Mr. H. will appreciate it if he sees where it came from."

"And what makes you think I appreciate you using my car to steal a park bench?"

"Take it easy, Cliff. Nobody saw me or your car. Even if they did, you could always tell the truth and say you were here all night. If I had taken my car and somebody saw me, I'd have to lie. You wouldn't want that to happen, would you?"

"I don't believe you stole a fucking park bench."

"They'll never miss it, there's dozens of them in that place. I took this one from the woods on the north side. The only people who go there are teenagers looking for a place to screw."

"How do you know that?"

"Because if I was a teenager, that's where I'd go. Besides, they won't miss it. Have you ever tried to screw on a park bench? It's a ball, ha, pardon the pun. Even if you do get something going, somebody always gets a splinter in the middle…"

Cliff helped him set it up anyway. Just as they were starting, a pair of headlights appeared around the bend coming towards them. Cliff grabbed a board and hid with it behind a tree.

"Sid, hide, they'll see you!" The car went by without so much as slowing down.

Sid laughed. "What are you supposed to be doing?"

"This is a stolen bench. If anybody sees us…"

"Cliff, Cliff, if you drove past someone at eleven o'clock at night setting up a bench on the only lighted portion of an otherwise pitch black stretch of road, would you stop to see what they were doing?"

"Well, no, but if…"

"If you get over here and help me, we can go back inside where it's safe that much sooner," Sid placated him.

Sid bolted the first piece back in place while Cliff balanced the uprights. "So that's how they put these things together," he said of the simple operation.

"This is an easy one," Sid said offhandedly, giving Cliff the impression this wasn't his first pilfered park bench. Cliff didn't want to hear about it. He handed Sid the next board. "No, save that one, it's going on the bottom." Sid turned it up so Cliff could read the engraved letters. 'Donated to Tammerlane Park by Ladies Auxiliary #709'.

"I hope you're satisfied. You just ripped off a bunch of grandmothers."

"Aw, they're probably all dead now anyway." He put the piece in last, facing downward so no one could read it.

They were still asleep the next morning as the crew came by, ready to work on the house. The crew itself was smaller now as most of them had to start work on another job they'd bid on before Sid's accident. It would be weeks before an entire crew would be working on Sid's house, but the ones still there made enough noise to awaken the bench heister and his accomplice. It was a routine they could both do without.

Cliff came downstairs and found Sid peering out the front window. "Cliff, check this out." Mr. H. was sitting on the bench, still as he could be, facing the river.

"I think he likes it," Cliff said as he rubbed his eyes and stumbled into the kitchen.

"Ah, Mr. H. has already put in his time. He can afford to sit back and relax. But you and me, we're on a mission."

"I don't care what we're on, we're not using my car."

So Sid drove them to Karina's Aquarium. The neon sign blinked like a sign in an old taproom. It sat on top of a green building spotted with white where the stucco had peeled, cracked and fallen. Inside, the air was almost pourable. Heat and humidity fed into it constantly from the dozens of tanks displaying all different types of fish. Cliff couldn't tell if he was breaking out in a sweat or if the drippy air was condensing on his skin.

"Can I help you gentlemen?" a salesman said as he approached them. He was a short, slight man with a seedy little black mustache and greased hair. His loud jacket hid most of his old wide tie which was fastened with a huge Windsor knot tied loosely around his collar. Cliff wondered how the salesman could dress like that yet not have so much as a glistening of sweat on his forehead.

"No thanks. Just looking."

Cliff followed Sid around for a few minutes. Then they parted ways at a huge fish tank filled with a countless number of goldfish, where Sid went on about the ramifications of bringing in a deck of cards and playing Go Fish. Cliff looked at the swordtails and angelfish, the cardinals and plecostomi. A woman was staring closely at a tank that was empty save for two dark, ugly Oscars.

"Hey Oscar!"

"What, Oscar?"

"Check out the blonde."

"Which one?"

"The one with her nose pressed up against our tank, fool!"

"Oh, her. She looks like a newt."

"Are you kidding, Oscar? She's beautiful!" The woman walked away. "Nice ass, too," he added, trying to nod his head for emphasis before he recalled he had no neck. "You just can't appreciate beauty, Oscar."

"I don't understand why you find these humans so fascinating. I think they're dull. They can't stay underwater for a minute without coming up for air. Wimps, all of them. You know, I heard once that they only give birth to one offspring at a time! Can you believe that?"

"Who told you that?"

"Oscar did."

"You mean the one they sold to that fat little kid yesterday for his birthday?"

"Yeah, that's the one. Now he was cute."

"Yech, Oscar! Are you some sort of queer?"

"You didn't think he was cute? God, what a set of gills. I wouldn't kick him out of my tank."

"Oscar!"

"He could spread his sperm over my eggs anytime."

"Oscar?"

"What, Oscar?"

"You're not a boy fish, are you?"

"You couldn't tell?"

"Of course not, how am I supposed to tell? I mean, your name's Oscar…"

"Wait a minute, you mean you're not a girl fish?"

"Of course not. Would I have made that comment about the blonde if I was?"

"I don't know, I just thought you were into doing it with humans. That's why I never took a good look at you. I assumed you were kinky, that's all."

"Hey, you don't suppose that's why they put us alone in this tank, do you?"

Cliff tried unsuccessfully to get a look at the two ugly fish alone in the tank. They were swimming modestly to the back corner behind some plastic weeds.

"Cliff, over here."

Cliff joined Sid at another near empty tank. It contained two goldfish, each almost two inches long. It also contained a darker fish as long as five of the goldfish. The label on the tank read 'Electric Catfish'. Cliff soon noticed the path it swam duplicated that of one of the goldfish, which was always a second ahead. As the catfish swam, its long mustache-like whiskers trailed on either side of its wide mouth.

"What I think is going to happen isn't going to happen, is it?" Cliff asked. The catfish kept stalking with no apparent effort. Its chase wasn't relentless, it was almost casual, as if it knew it was in a rectangular tank and its prey couldn't get away. It did seem to have trouble negotiating some of the turns of its nimble bounty. Occasionally, it switched from one goldfish to the other to one's relief and the other's dismay.

Sid and Cliff watched silently for a few minutes with no change in the pattern but with no loss of interest, either. As the catfish lazily switched its aim, an imperceptible thrust of its tail did the trick. It was facing the back of the tank when it slowly turned with not so much as a gold tail hung out of its bloated mouth. Where the goldfish had been, a glittery sparkle of silver and orange scales hung suspended like shards of broken glass. By the time most of the pinpoints of light settled to rest on the gravely bottom, the catfish was tailing the second goldfish.

"Did you hear it?"

"What, hear what?" Cliff stole a glance around the room. He noticed they weren't the only ones watching the show.

"In there, in the tank. When it gets the next one, listen." Cliff was confused as always but watched as intently as the three boys in baseball caps behind them.

The goldfish was shitting enough bricks to build a castle under the sea. On what seemed to be one near miss, the predator's tail sprayed over the spot of his first victim's demise, kicking up a few scales like gold dust. It followed with the same ease and confidence as before. This time Cliff was ready. He still couldn't see the tail flick but he did hear the click, the tiny, audible crackle that coincided with the disappearance of the goldfish into the catfish's mouth. Sid would later explain it was the sound made when the catfish releases an electrical charge to stun its prey. In his head, Cliff could still hear the quick, malicious snap, like the devil breaking a toothpick on his incisors after lunch.

"Did you hear it that time?" Sid asked Cliff over the cheers of the three young boys.

"Yeah," Cliff answered, somewhat awed and somewhat grossed out. Sparkles were still falling when the salesman approached.

"A fascinating creature, the electric catfish. It utilizes a unique method to stun…"

"We'll take it," Sid said.

"You'll what?"

"I said, we'll take it. Will you take a charge? Ha, just kidding, make that cash. We'll also need a tank about this size and one a little smaller, and pumps and filters and all that stuff for each. We'll need some red gravel, too."

The salesman didn't know what to do first. He was so used to people walking away halfway through his sales pitch. Sid might have done so if he hadn't walked in the door with his mind already made up.

"Are ya really gonna buy him, Mister?" one of the little leaguers asked Sid when the frenzied salesman left for the stock room.

"I sure am."

"Oh." All three little boys looked like they'd just lost the big game.

"What's the matter with that?" Sid asked.

"Nobody ever buys him," one of them answered. "We come here every Saturday and watch them feed him. We've been doing it since last Christmas. That's when I was supposed to get him but my Mom and Dad didn't buy him for me. He was only this big then." The boy held up two fingers mere inches apart. "Rodger hasn't missed a day yet." Rodger nodded enthusiastically, his visor alternately hiding and exposing his young face.

"I see," Sid said. He was at a crossroads. He needed the catfish for his plan, but he wasn't the type to spoil the fun of three little boys.

"Yo, Harry, come back here." It was Cliff, calling to the salesman who was coming out of the stock room with some boxes. Sid didn't even notice he was wearing a nametag.

"Yes sir?"

"Is this the only electric catfish you have here in this store?"

"Why, yes it is, sir. Is it not to your liking?" Harry asked as if it was Cliff's dinner.

"It's fine, just fine. Only we were thinking of buying two."

Harry jumped at the opportunity. "I believe our store in New Jersey has one in stock, sir. In fact, I'm sure they have one."

"And the Delaware is full of them too, Harry, but that doesn't do me any good, either. I don't like to go over the river unless I absolutely have to."

"I'm sure it would be no problem to have it transferred here, sir."

"Why don't you check on that, Harry?"

"Oh, yes sir, of course, sir." Harry shuffled off to the phone in his own cringingly servile way.

"Poor guy, this is probably the biggest sale of his year."

"I see, I get it," Sid chanted in light of the revelation of Cliff's scheme. The boys looked confused.

"You see, if this fish has been here since last Christmas, they must be dying to get rid of it. Otherwise, that bozo over there wouldn't be making such a big deal out of it." The boys smiled with amusement which would soon turn into comprehension as Cliff explained. "If we buy this one, you'll never see another one in here again. They lose more money feeding it than it's worth. You've got to see it from a business point of view. Anyway, since I told him we wanted another one, he'll have one brought in just to dump it on us. It's dead stock, it's taking up space they'd rather use for more profitable fish. We'll buy this one and just tell him we've changed our minds when the new one comes in."

"I get it!" Rodger said.

"You wait and see, it'll probably be this big," Cliff said with his fingers mere inches apart. "You'll get to watch one grow all over again. Now keep it down, here he comes."

"I just spoke with our people in Passaic. They have an electric catfish in stock which I can have transferred here a week from Monday," Harry said with a satisfied smile.

"Hm, I don't know," Cliff hesitated to the salesman's dismay. "Sid, when are we leaving for Switzerland?" Harry's eyes bugged out.

"I'm sure we're leaving this Friday." Sid immediately caught on that the fish had to be in the store by Saturday to preserve Rodger's marathon record.

"I'm afraid that just won't do, Harry. I would love so much to see it for a day or so before I leave. I won't be back for weeks."

"Not to worry, sir. I'll have it brought in by special courier." Which meant, of course, in the back of his station wagon on the way to work. "Shall we call you when it arrives?"

"No, that won't be necessary, thank you. I'll have my driver stop by on Thursday. I have the utmost confidence in you. I just couldn't postpone Switzerland. Business, you know."

"We couldn't have that, sir."

"Tell me just one thing, Harry."

"Sir?"

"This one, it's a bit on the large side, don't you think? The one coming from, from…"

"Passaic."

"Yes, yes, is it any smaller?"

"I'm sure it's much smaller, sir. Would you like me to locate a third, smaller one for you?"

"This will do, I suppose. Just don't make the other one too small, though. We can't have them eating each other, can we, eh? Ha, ha ha ha!"

"Oh yes, ha, very good, sir, ha ha!"

Sid went with the salesman to collect the other goods. "There you go, guys," Cliff said.

"Gee, thanks Mister," Rodger said.

"We'll write ya in Swizzerland and tell ya how big it is!" one of the other boys said. Cliff was amused and for the moment wondered what it would be like to be that happy, that easily amused, that blissfully ignorant again.

Despite Sid's clothing and Cliff's young age, the salesman either really wanted to get rid of those catfish or truly believed they were international businessmen and tried to sell them half the store. When he finally gave up, he gave them the final instructions about their purchase. "Make sure that each catfish gets two goldfish per week. By the way, if you need any more, we're having a sale on goldfish next week, only…"

"Okay, Harry," Sid cut him off. They enlisted the aid of the three ballplayers to carry everything out to Sid's car.

"Say hi to the new fish for us, guys," Sid said as he started the engine.

"All right. Thanks a lot again, Mister," Rodger said to Cliff.

"You're welcome, Rodger."

They said one more good bye to the catfish in its water-filled bag. "See ya, Gilgamesh."

"What's that? Gilgamesh?"

"Rodger named him that a long time ago."

"I like that name a lot, Rodger. I think we'll keep it." Sid drove off and they waved to each other until they were out of sight.

"That was spectacular, Cliff. Stupendous, even. You made their day."

"Aw heck, it was nothing." Cliff patted himself on the back.

"I thought Harry was going to take Gilgamesh into the back room and carve him with a knife when you said it was too big."

They set up the tanks in the living room. The larger tank was for Gilgamesh and the smaller tank for the goldfish. Cliff found it difficult to become attached to them, knowing full well none of them would be around for long. It became easier once Sid came up with the idea of naming them all 'Harry'.

"Let's hurry and get these tanks set up. I'm hungry."

By the time they were finished, Sid was more than ready for a Thieburger. He loved going to Thiesmann's. It was owned and operated by Ray Thiesmann, it being his one and only location, just off Rt. 70 near St. Elmo's Hospital. It was a mark of devastation for the big time operators of the nearby fast food joints. Ray's Thieburgers made the Big Mac and the Whopper turn tail and head for cover in the hills of corporate enterprise.

Going into Ray's place was like going home again. Wherever he was, Ray himself would often shout out 'Hi there!', more often than not calling you by name. His condiments (a word that upset a certain graffiti artist, for he could almost but not quite do something with it) need not be squeezed out of little foil pouches, for each table had its very own ketchup and mustard bottles as well as a selection of relishes and other toppings. An old woman who in one way or another looked like everybody's mother monitored all the dining room tables to make sure everyone ate all they ordered. A Thieburger, Thieshake and Thiefries you could buy with three dollars and actually get change back.

Then, like a thick, drippy fog oozing in off a stagnant lake, the day came; Ray Thiesmann died. All the fries cried. Shakes shook with grief. The condiments packed their bottles and skipped town. Burgers crawled into their buns and refused to budge. And the competition partied their socks off.

McDonalds cut all their prices in half, nationwide for a day, locally for a week. Burger King put out six hundred and thirty nine varieties of specialty sandwiches on a 'Try Me Free' basis.

Burgermaniac was a converted hot dog stand located behind an abandoned used car lot and a miniature golf course on Granada Boulevard. It was so obscure, only toddler golfers knew about it, only to grow up and forget it. Even those ex-weenie peddlers wanted to get in on the action. It was a forgotten cog on the wheel, owned by a monster megacorporation. The board of directors, acting on behalf of the millionaire owner who had mysteriously disappeared some years earlier after taking a three hour boat cruise with his wife, decided to turn a profit. They hired one hundred and fifty extra employees and bought thirty two spanking new trucks. Adorned in their colorful new Burgermaniac uniforms, they scoured the surrounding neighborhoods, altering the institution of take-out fast food to the progressive new level of take-in service. They drove the trucks from house to house, pushing their burgers harder than Jehovah's Witnesses pushing their church by knocking on your door on Mother's Day.

Sid answered the knock at the door to see a short, pimple-faced girl smiling at him through her terminal acne and announce, "Hi, I'm Patty from Burgermaniac. Can I take your order?" She waited with pad and pen poised with that smile stuck to her face like a blob of mashed potatoes on a high school cafeteria ceiling. Congenially, the driver waved from the truck out front, parked behind Sid's Mustang. Sid just stared at the Styrofoam burger, a scaled-down version of a Rose Bowl reject, which sat on top of the truck.

"What is this?" Sid had never seen anything like it.

"It's our new take-in service."

"Well, I don't think I like it." Sid acknowledged the waving driver just to make him stop. "As a matter of fact, we were just on our way to Thiesmann's."

Patty successfully hid a laugh. "But no one is going there now. All the fast food restaurants are drawing people in with special offers to celebrate the end of that Thiesmann place."

"The end? What are you talking about?"

"You mean you haven't heard? Thiesmann's is finally closing down. Unfortunately, it took old Mr. Thiesmann's passing on to do it," she said with feigned sincerity.

"Ray Thiesmann is dead?" Sid couldn't believe it.

"It happened last week during a dinner rush. I heard he keeled over in the walk-in freezer while looking for French fries. Everybody has heard about it. So, what'll it be, sir?"

Sid was appalled at her lack of dignity and said righteously, "I don't want your hamburger, Patty," and closed the door. "Come on, Cliff. We're leaving."

"For Thiesmann's?"

"You've got to root for the underdog, Cliff."

The normally busy parking lot was as empty as a mass murderer's gun after the fact. Sid entered a little anxious, Cliff a little curious. Sid removed his cowboy hat.

"Where is everybody?" Sid asked solemnly of the young man behind the counter. His attention distracted by sobs, Cliff quietly peered around the corner into the dining room. Mom was crying at one of the empty tables. Tear-soaked napkins lay scattered before her as she picked up a fresh one and loudly blew her nose before she went on weeping.

"Where did everybody go?" Sid asked again of the young man staring numbly into space.

A few more seconds passed before he spoke. "All gone." His eyes did not meet Sid's. "Everybody's gone. They've gone somewhere else for a better deal. The thrill is gone." He finally focused his gaze on Sid. "You know how guys will talk about what part of a girl's body turns them on the most?"

He waited for a sign of comprehension from Sid. The question caught him off guard but he answered nonetheless. "Uh, I'm an ass man myself," he admitted sympathetically.

"Yeah, yeah, that's it. Well, Mr. Thiesmann was like that, too." Sid was shocked. He couldn't imagine kindly old Ray Thiesmann being a beer-guzzling ass man like himself. "Whenever the subject came up," the young man continued, "he'd say, 'Me, I'm a Thighs-man'. It was the only joke he knew." Sid shared in the fond memory brought on by the grieving process by joining him in what he thought was a chuckle, until he realized it was a melancholy chortle and soon to be a bitter crying jag. Mom, who had been listening, broke out in a severe fit of wailing.

"You're not out of business. You could bring this place back, you could put it on its feet again. There's no reason to let those other places push you around. It'll be easy. I know all about this sort of thing. You were on top once. You can be there again. Mr. Thiesmann would have wanted it that way," Cliff said. No one shared his enthusiasm. The young man was staring again and Mom was still crying.

"I don't think it's that simple, Cliff. They want people to come in here because of the atmosphere, not the price list. If anybody came in here for a special offer, it'd hurt too much to know that was the only reason they'd walked in, that they'd just as soon go next door if the deal was any better. Like he said, the thrill is gone."

"But that can be fixed, can't it?"

"I don't think so." Sid turned to the counter and slapped down a twenty. "I want two dozen deluxe Thieburgers, and two plain with no buns." The request sparked the young man to life.

"Bless you, bless you both." Mom smiled at them from the dining room.

They gave most of the burgers to the construction crew but still had too many left over as they sat on the bench trying to finish them all. The afternoon was spent with burgers, beer and silence, save for the occasional belch.

Cliff had lost all track of time until he went inside to use the bathroom and to get some more beers. When he came back out, the streetlamp had come on. Under the blue-white light, Sid started to get philosophical through the suds. Some people were happy drunks, others rowdy drunks, but Sid was a thinking drunk. He felt his ideas getting clearer as his speech and vision deteriorated. Cliff normally fed him more beer at this point in hopes that Sid would either pass out or just shut up and drink.

"Whadaya 'spose hell is like?" Sid held the question up for grabs, spurred on no doubt by the ominous theme of the day. Cliff took one sip from the bottle he'd just opened for himself and handed it to Sid. "I'll tell ya what I think itz, it is."

"I thought you would," Cliff mumbled in despair.

"I think it's like bein' a character in a old, old comic strip."

Such a notion was just enough to grab Cliff's here-we-go-again attention. "All right, I'm listening. Shoot."

"Wha was I sayin'? Oh yeah oh yeah, comic trip, strip." Sid paused, cleared his throat and sat up straight. "You know those old, those dumb old those..." Sid closed his eyes and shook himself. Cliff thought this was going to be the first time he would ever see Sid throw up. Instead, he opened his eyes and started again. "It's like those dumb old comic strips that are still, are still in the paper, the ones that started, y'know, like back around the World War or somethin'. Those are the ones I was talkin' about here. They mighta been okay at first, but now, like they're just plain old dumb and they're still around only 'cause they're so old, man." He was speaking with a strained concentration. He wavered a little from side to side. "I can't think of any right now, see, but it's like one a the ones that're so stinkin' old, the artist who created it died and somebody else's taken over. Talk 'bout morbid, Jeez..." He stopped. Cliff thought he was finished. "I mean, you like only look at it, what, once a week? Just to see if it still isn't funny, and sure enough, it still isn't, and the artwork is just a little bit different and the artist isn't sign-ing his name anymore, but the chararac, characters go on day after day after day, bein' stupider and stupider and stupider, everybody's just ignorin' them. They got no control over what they're doin'. It's weird, weird. Man…"

Sid trailed off with his words, then suddenly pitched both bottles in his hands across the road and onto the thicket-covered slope that led down to the river.

"That's colorful but it's bullshit." Cliff noticed Sid was now silent and assumed he was listening. "I mean it's bullshit for me, not you. The way I've got it figured," Cliff started, maybe more interested in the subject than he'd like to admit, "when you die, you go to wherever you believed in life heaven or hell to be. I think there probably is a purgatory, but the only people you're going to find there are a bunch of bored Catholics because they are the only ones who ever believed in such a place. It wouldn't be fair to be sent anywhere, good or bad, that you never believed existed. All the good Buddhists will reach nirvana, the bad Christians will go to the lake of fire, the good Norse who died in battle are living it up in Valhalla, and you might even end up in Nancy and Sluggo. If you believe in nothing, you ain't goin' nowhere."

And with this discussion, full of whatever it was full of, Sid's sidewalk was finally truly christened. It was now becoming the kind of place he'd intended it to be. He felt sure of this when they stayed out there until dawn the following Tuesday night listening to Mickey's radio show.

Mr. H. and Barbara joined them frequently, so much in fact that Cliff almost couldn't talk Sid out of stealing another bench. By day they'd sit on the ground and watch the house go back up, which was doing fine after two straight months of work, and at night, if it wasn't raining, they'd sit on the bench or the curb under the streetlamp, just hanging out.

"Your car is going to get hit some night sitting out here so close to the road." Barbara had joined them this night. She was staying at her father's house for the night. Mr. H. had taken Billy in to bed almost an hour ago and hadn't returned yet.

Sid sipped his beer and suggested Barbara do the same. But she opted to sip on her own beer and in the momentary silence, sad trumpet music could barely be heard coming from Mr. H.'s house.

"He sure likes his blues. We can hear it out here some nights," Sid said.

"Tell me about it. I used to like it, too."

"I think it's beautiful."

"So did I until I heard it too much. The novelty wears off after a while."

"Maybe I'll lend him some of my records for a change of pace."

"Yeah, I'm sure he never heard that ukulele guy before."

"Oh, those aren't records, you guys. That's him."

"You mean he's playing that himself right now?" Cliff said, taking a renewed interest in the music he'd grown so accustomed to hearing.

"You mean you couldn't tell? He used to be very good. I just hope he doesn't wake up Billy. Dad says it's a sort of lullaby."

"I think he's still very good. Man, we always assumed it was a recording."

"No way, he's been playing the trumpet for years." They were all quiet as they listened for a while.

"Incredible. And he never said a word."

"Then I suppose he's never told you about his big break, huh? About the time he played with Glenn Miller's band?"

"Get outta town! No way!"

"I'll take that as a No. I can't believe you haven't heard it yet. He tells it to everybody at least twice." Of course, she was prodded into telling it now, at least once.

"A long time ago, Daddy and some of his buddies put an ensemble together and played some music."

"No kidding!"

"Really. They must've been pretty good at it because sometimes they even got paid." She was trying to use the same phrases and practiced grace her father would use when telling the story. "Anyway, somebody heard them play, somebody who knew somebody who was related to somebody else who had something to do with managing one of the big bands. Three guys, including Daddy, got to try out for some openings. The other two got in somewhere. Daddy didn't get a permanent spot, but he was listed as a substitute with another band."

"Glenn Miller's?" Cliff asked.

"Right. But understand, this was after Glenn Miller was killed. They kept his name for the band, and they were still pretty big."

"Oh. Yeah, but still, that's the big time," Sid nodded to Cliff.

"Anyway, the man felt sorry for my Dad because he thought he was better than the others. They both got jobs with no-name bands and Daddy got an opportunity to play where the real action was, thanks to that agent. I forget his name, but Daddy could tell you."

"He toured with the band at his own expense for nearly two months without ever playing a note. Right around Christmas, one of the trumpeters came down with strep throat. Daddy finally got a horn in the door, as he likes to say."

"He played four shows at the Glen Island Casino. After that, the regular guy came back. He says he didn't mind, that he knew the spot was only temporary, but I don't know."

"So what did he do after that?" Sid asked.

"He quit. He found he had done what he wanted to do and that was enough for him. He went looking for another thing he wanted to do, so he got into the construction business and married Mom. The rest is me and Billy and history."

"And that rascal never told us," Cliff said.

"Don't let on that I said anything and he'll get around to telling you. It's a much better story when he tells it."

More drinks went down and more stories came out, this time about themselves.

"I remember this girl I used to go to school with." It was Cliff who started. He'd already had enough to drink and he had another bottle in his hand. "Her name was Tina Carpenter. She went to Carbleson for a couple of months. They used to say she was built, which she was then, but I suppose people will laugh at anything that even sounds dirty when they're sixteen and they find all those hormones. But I didn't really know her then. I knew her in Mrs. Applebaum's third grade class. I sat in the desk behind her. I remember I used to carry her books for her."

"That's sweet. My biggest letdown in school was that I never had a boy carry my books for me."

"My biggest letdown was never being able to find an apple with a worm in it to give to my teacher."

"Every day at recess, we'd walk around the perimeter of the play-ground and talk. I got on the good side of the cool crowd because they always came up to me after recess and asked me about her. They thought I actually had something to say! Anything between a girl and a boy was a hot item. We'd see them in the higher grades going out on dates and the more progressive third graders really tried to imitate them. It was so silly. Everybody was trying to grow up so fast."

"So why did you hang out with her?"

"I just helped her with her schoolwork. That's all we talked about, really. Of course, I would've been happy talking about anything at all. I was enjoying myself and everybody else thought Tina and I had some playground romance going."

"You mean you didn't?" Sid asked.

"No, I told you, nothing at all. We just talked about school. The only time the subject changed was when the low life crowd would tease me. They used to chant 'Cliff likes girls, Cliff likes girls' until the old lady monitors would make them stop. I didn't care, but Tina did. I remember, whenever she would get pissed off at them she'd wave her arm like this and say, 'Let them eat cake', just like Marie Antoinette. It used to confuse the hell out of them. Me, too. I liked cake. I bet Tina was the only one in that whole school who knew who Marie Antoinette was. She had class. I still think of her every time I smell Elmer's glue."

"Okay, and why do you think of Tina every time you sniff, uh, smell glue?"

"Not just any glue. Elmer's glue. The whole school smelled like Elmer's glue. The art room stank of the stuff. All of the decorations in the hallways were student projects held together with nothing but Elmer's glue. Any time anything broke, that's what they always used to fix it. One spring, Elmer the janitor, who we all thought for years invented the stuff, patched up something in the air ducts with it. The following fall when I was in third grade, they turned on the heat which melted the glue. They had to close school early that day because of the fumes. Whenever I smell it now I think of Tina because that day was the first time I carried her books home for her."

"That's a nice story, Cliff," Barbara said.

"That's nothing," Sid said. He was reclining on his windshield with his hands behind his head. He sat up and swung his legs over the fender to face them. "Did I ever tell you how I met Mai?"

Now this was a story Cliff had been dying to hear ever since he had first seen the drawing. If he ever did meet her, he was sure he would recognize her even with her clothes on.

"I met Mai a long time ago. I was working in a medical clinic in a Delaware hospital, studying to be a chiropractor."

Barbara had to laugh. "You? A chiropractor?"

"Yeah, I still don't know why, either. There were two of us, me and Larry, and we shared one examination room. We were considered interns and we worked on real patients. I had a lot of free time on my hands because chiropractic medicine isn't that popular now and it was even less popular back then. Since I shared with Larry, I only worked on every other patient. All we got each week was a load of old men and women whose spine was the least of their health problems and they made sure you knew that by the end of the session. But once, it was my turn and Mai walked into the clinic. She said she'd hurt her back while helping a friend move into a new apartment. She didn't have an appointment, so Larry complained it was against the rules to take her. I tilted the table in front of him, spilled his game of solitaire and took Mai into the examination room while Larry whined and picked up his cards."

"Yeah, I can see you doing that." Cliff said.

"We had this old examination table. I helped her up on it. She laid down on her stomach and I checked her out. Then I looked at her spine. I still remember it to this day. Two sublimations in the lumbar region, the third and fourth vertebrae. I cracked her back the way this Indian showed me after a fight a few years earlier. It had nothing to do with the training I was getting in the hospital. If I'd used their methods, Mai probably wouldn't be walking today."

"Mai said it felt better and thanked me, a lot. I told her I wanted to schedule her for a follow-up examination soon, just to make sure. I went nuts thinking about her all that week while I worked on all those old folks. I even got hot over this one old lady who had the same color eyes as Mai's. Mai showed up with those brown eyes the next week wearing nothing but sandals, cutoffs and a big football jersey, cut around the waist so it only came down to here. Larry was almost as excited as me. You see, it was his turn. Mai was walking down the hall looking straight at me. Larry said she was looking straight at him. He was standing right next to me so I said, 'No wonder she's looking at you, you've got a coffee stain on your jacket', and I pointed to the front of his silly white lab coat like the ones we all had to wear. 'Where?' he asked, so I told him, 'Right there'. 'I don't see any coffee stain' he said, so I picked up his coffee and spilled it all down his front."

"Either I didn't realize just how hot it was or Larry was over-reacting, but it worked because he took off like a shot for the men's lockers. I just smiled at Mai and held the door open for her. She smiled back at me and got right up on the table. I tried to casually scrape a chair across the floor so I could prop it up against the door because there was no lock on it. I asked her how she'd been feeling and she said she was still in some pain and wanted me to take another look. I thanked her for wearing such thin clothing because it was easier for me to examine her spine through it. She said that was why she'd worn it."

"She was on her stomach, so I couldn't see her face as she spoke. I checked out her vertebrae again, working my way down to where her skin was exposed between her jersey and her cutoffs. I slowed down as I got to the end of her tan. She wiggled her ass and the cutoffs slid down a little. I kept telling her about her spine. 'This is the fifth vertebrae of the lumbar region, no problem here'. She wiggled again and again her cutoffs slid down further. I swore I heard her moan once, so I just kept on counting and helped her wiggle out of more of her shorts. I said, 'These are your sacral vertebrae, and these are your coccygeal vertebrae, and this is the sweetest ass I've ever seen.'. She rolled over and lifted her jersey and right then and there I thanked God for making me a chiropractor."

"Don't you know it, I had just unbuttoned my pants, my lab jacket was wide open, and in comes Larry with Dr. Melrose, the Chief of the whole fucking Staff. The guy is busy all day running a hospital but he's not too busy to come down to the clinic to catch me with my soon-to-be-lost credentials showing."

"He opened the door but he got hung up for a second on the chair. He said, 'Is that you in there, Lasvistas? What's going on here, you know you're supposed to share the pa...' He saw what was going on and kind of figured out why I didn't want to share this patient when he got a good look at me and Mai jumping off the table. It was a wonderful way to end a career and a wonderful way to end a day when I met Mai that night at her friend's apartment. On the way home, I stopped by Larry's apartment and hung Mai's bra on his door knocker."

"So now you think of her every time you smell that industrial clean smell of a hospital, right?"

"Not even close, Cliff."

"I like Cliff's story better," Barbara said.

"You're such a girl," Sid answered that one.

"Yeah, so?" she laughed.

"Like you never did anything like that with a guy."

"Well, I didn't say that."

"So tell us about it," Sid prodded her.

"Oh no you don't." Barbara just smiled into her beer. She wasn't about to start trading fuckbuddy stories with these guys. She was already beginning to feel like she was standing outside of a men's locker room. She knew it was still unfortunately the case that men who get laid are studs and women who get laid are sluts. It wasn't fair, but she had never heard of anyone who could make it sound any different. She wasn't going to tell them about how she seduced her husband the first time, how she secretly cuffed him to the couch while they were watching TV and making out in her old apartment. How she surprised him by dancing around while taking her clothes off and dancing in her bra and panties, just out of his reach with the handcuffs keeping him locked to the couch. How she danced around some more in less than her bra and panties, just watching his pants get tight as she touched herself while he struggled with the shackles. How she teased him and got too close sooner than she wanted to, how he reached out with his free hand and caught her ankle, how she got free again and danced some more before she let herself get caught and they started breeding in captivity.

She had told that story to her girlfriends before, as surely as her husband, well, boyfriend at the time, had told his friends about it. That's not where Billy came from, that was another story from after they were married. She'd be too embarrassed to tell these guys about it. Besides, she thought it would drive Cliff wild, and she would have been right. She wasn't interested in doing that.

"Well?" Sid waited for her to start talking.

"Never you mind," she answered, and that's all she was going to say.

"Chicken," he taunted her. It's a shame, he thought. He really would have been interested, too.

12

Through some cosmic rationalization he'd developed some time ago, Sid counterbalanced any wrongdoings he planned to commit by accomplishing various acts of kindness beforehand. The number of acts depended on the severity of the wrongdoing.

He drove around all morning but could only find one stranded motorist to help. When he had no luck finding any stray pets listed in the lost and found column, he went to the Franklin Mall to help old ladies carry their packages to their cars and to give pennies to the little children so they could make wishes and throw them into the fountains while their parents ignored them. He mailed off an anonymous charitable contribution to the United Way before stopping at Tammerlane Park to pick up the garbage, apparently left on the ground by blind people who couldn't find even one of the gazillion trash cans found everywhere, when he noticed all the ducks coming up to him for food. He went home to pick up some popcorn. Cliff made the return trip with him.

They sat on a bench that had not been stolen from the perimeter of a pond that was not big enough to be called a lake but was anyway. The ducks stormed out of Tammerlane Lake towards them, catching the popped kernels pelting them from above as Sid threw handfuls in the air. The geese also came over and soon outnumbered the ducks which Cliff specifically tried to feed, but were often bullied away by the bigger birds.

"Okay, I'm going to have to borrow your car again," Sid began.

"I hope this is the last time for that."

"It will be," Sid assured. "Spruance went to some bar on Roosevelt Boulevard last Friday when I tailed him. I'll follow him again tonight. If I lose him, at least I'll know where to look. I've got to keep him at wherever he goes, so I'll probably let the air out of his tires or something."

"Why don't you take his distributor cap? I saw that in a movie once."

"Because this isn't a movie, Cliff. It's real. I can be much less conspicuous letting air out of his tires than I can with my head under his hood."

"Then I'll come back to the house and call Spruance's place. I've got a plan to get them out of their house that I'll tell you about later. You and I will wait a few minutes, grab Gilgamesh and go."

"You really think you're going to pull this off, don't you?" Cliff said with no real interest in any of it. "Hey you, get away from him," he said, trying to scare some of the geese away from the mallard he was trying to feed.

"I don't need you to come along with me if you've got that kind of attitude." Sid was serious. He looked Cliff in the eyes as a goose pecked at a handful of corn from his open palm.

"Okay, okay, I didn't say a thing."

"Cliff, what we're doing is as bad as what Spruance's friends did to me. It's probably worse, it's premeditated. You don't have to be a part of it. I can do it myself."

"You'll need someone to drive the car, won't you?" Now Cliff was getting serious about it, too.

"Okay, that's fine," Sid agreed.

Cliff finally got a duck to come up and eat out of his hand. It was too difficult to tell who was more upset when they ran out of corn, them or the ducks. They discussed the possibility of installing a pond in their front yards so they wouldn't have to leave home to feed the ducks. On the way home, Sid stopped to pick up some more beer for the construction crew. He left the case in the car when he saw that Ben was there.

Ben took them through the house and showed them the work they had done. The toasted aroma that formerly filled the house was replaced by the scent of freshly cut wood. The staircase and surrounding walls were completely replaced except for the door to the closet under the steps. Upstairs, the hallway was done and the studs were replaced in the room where the fire had begun. The ceiling was exposed all the way up to the underside of the roof. The sheet rock and floorboards would be laid down soon.

"After we finish this room we have some more work to do downstairs," Ben said. "That room below took a lot of water damage. I'd say you'll be back in here in a little over a month, though."

Cliff was dubious, uncertain of what would happen when Sid moved back into his own house. He wouldn't mind having his house to himself again. He wouldn't mind if Sid stuck around, either. He figured he was just stuck in a comfortable little rut. Besides, it wouldn't be like Sid was going away. He would only be moving next door.

At seven o'clock that evening, Cliff handed his keys over to Sid. After he left, Cliff did as Sid had instructed and put Gilgamesh in a special white plastic bucket which remained submerged in the tank, confining him but making him transportable while staying in the fresh water as long as possible.

Next, he took the remaining goldfish out of the smaller tank below and put them in the big tank with Gilgamesh. There were eight of them left, half as many as the number of days since the catfish's last feeding. Certainly the fish was hungry by now, and Sid figured that would taunt Gilgamesh, keeping his dinner just out of reach. When he first got the idea, it reminded him of the stunt that Mai used to do to him, leaving him tied to the bed while she hovered above, teasing him until he couldn't stand it anymore, then teasing him some more.

Cliff sat in the living room, illuminated solely by the bulb over the large tank. If anyone had seen him staring, they might have mistaken his expression for one of deep concentration, but all he was doing was looking at the tank at the far side of the room. At times he couldn't even make out Gilgamesh's shadow on the inside of the translucent basket, and twice he was tempted towards a closer inspection until a dark flash assured him it didn't starve to death. Cliff just kept staring until Sid came in the door shortly after ten o'clock.

"Why is it so dark in here?" He turned on a light and Cliff stirred. After pausing to glance at the fish, he turned towards Cliff. It was evident Sid had a bit of a scare or at least some trouble. "He went to the same bar I followed him to the other night."

Bump and Grind trotted over from another room to say hello to their master who was already busy in the kitchen getting some stuff together. Cliff joined him, squinting his eyes from the bright lights. Sid needed some background noise. He ran back out to the living room and put some vinyl on the turntable. "Now Cliff, when I dial Spruance's number, I'll tell you to start the record. Okay?"

"I know, you told me. Go ahead."

Sid dialed Spruance's number as he read it directly off the accident report. Before he punched the last number, he signaled Cliff, who brought the stylus down. Just some background noise, piano and horns to start. That was the sound he was looking for.

"Uh, hello." Sid made a face. Someone had answered before the music started. He got his confidence back when the song began. "Put Jake on, will ya?" Sid had to raise his voice to be heard over the music. Cliff was next to him, clinking glasses together. "Yeah, is this Jake? Listen, you know a guy named Steve?" He opened the refrigerator, shook the door and closed it again. Cliff was holding a dripping, shaken beer over the sink. As he turned on the faucet, one of the dogs let out a sharp bark. Somebody's remake of a Chuck Berry tune came out of the speakers, not a slow song at all. Cliff rushed the dogs into the living room and turned on the TV. "I'm calling for him. He gave me this number and told me to ask for you. What? Oh, this is La Cantina Mosca." Sid fumbled the name, saying it really fast, hopefully so Jake couldn't really catch it. "Your friend is in a little trouble here." Sid smiled at Cliff for his idea of turning on the TV. How he'd found a rugby match he never could tell, but the effect was real, at least on the other end of the phone. Sid had to cover one ear to hear Jake better.

"I didn't see it happen but this Steve got beat up pretty bad here. These three guys did a number on him. Hang on." Sid pulled the phone away from his ear and covered the mouthpiece. "Give me a break, will ya?" he said to an imaginary Spruance at the end of the imaginary bar.

He returned with a confident look at Cliff, who was making all sorts of little noises.

"Look, he pissed somebody off, that's all I know." He shook the fridge door again. "Hey, look pal, I really don't care if you believe me or not. Listen, he wants you to come down here and get him. What's that? Yeah, he's at the bar. What? Look, he asked me to call, so I'm calling. Sure, you got it." Sid covered the mouthpiece again. "Get over here, he wants to talk to you." Jake had told Sid he wanted to talk to Spruance. Sid just held the phone away from his ear for a couple of seconds. Then a couple more seconds. Then he got back on. "Listen up, Jack, your friend's all fucked up here. He won't come to the phone. He's got a trashed Gran Torino in my parking lot, he's pissing off my customers and I ain't nobody's baby sitter. Wait a minute." Sid covered the phone and waited. "Never mind, he's leaving." Sid hoped this whole thing was working. "I said never mind, he's leaving. Huh? No way, pal, I don't want him in here anyway. You come down here and stop him. Speak up, will ya already? No, I told you, La Cantina Mosca," Sid fumbled the name again. "Look it up in the book," he said and hung up.

"Yeah? So?" Cliff asked.

"Don't ever start a cult!" Sid joked. So far so good, he hoped. All they needed was to get them out of the house for a while. Now they had to go find out if it worked.

They grabbed Gilgamesh, hopped into Cliff's car and took off. There was no La Cantina Mosca, if Jake had understood what Sid told him anyway, so hopefully the house would be empty as they were all looking somewhere, anywhere for Spruance.

When they got to Spruance's street, Sid told Cliff to pull up to the curb next door. He told Cliff to take off if anything went wrong and he couldn't get back to the car. He got out and walked up to the house. No cars were in the driveway, and at least the house was dark. He knocked on the front door and quickly ran away to the neighbor's side yard and hid, just like he and his friends used to do when they were little pranksters. He waited, but no one came to answer the door. He went back to the car for Gilgamesh and a crowbar.

"Okay, it looks good. I should be back in a minute." With that, Sid disappeared behind the house, leaving Cliff with his hand on the keys in the ignition.

The curtains were drawn, so Sid wasn't positive the place was empty. He tapped on the back window with the crowbar, ready to run if anybody moved the curtains. Nothing happened, so he went to the dark, covered patio, careful to not trip over any of the tons of crap stowed away back there. He set Gilgamesh down on an old gas grill. The back door into the house gave way with a surprisingly slight pry of the crowbar. He was soon through the kitchen and in the living room, guided by the faint glow of the fish tank, the only light in the house. He headed towards the tank. The banner with their crest on it was rolled up and tossed on the floor. A black velvet painting of a ship hung on the wall in its place, and what looked like one of their robes was draped over the back of the couch.

Sid figured he'd interrupted their service, but it doubled his nervousness to think at least some of them were probably there less than thirty minutes ago. This was not his most favorite place in the hemisphere to be, but the thought of them racing down a road somewhere, fighting amongst themselves about where to look for the imaginary bar, calmed him down. He'd broken into houses before, crawling through open windows, fooling with his friends, but never into a stranger's house. He felt justified, though, after what these wack jobs did to him. Standard violence just wouldn't do. He still didn't understand just what all this stupid fish worshipping was all about, but he didn't really need to know. It was enough that it was important to them.

Just the same, he was shitting bricks like a goldfish. It'd be bad enough to get caught by the cops, let alone by the goons who lived here. Aside from the punishment, if the incident made the papers he'd be sunk. There were things about him that might come to the surface, things he didn't want anyone to know about. He tried not to think about it much, but with each passing day he believed it might all work out for the best after all.

He lifted the hood of the tank. Against the red gravel, the mollies appeared as slippery, dark purple shadows, scattering as if to swim around the beams of florescent light. He took the lid off the bucket. A dark Gilgamesh stood out against the white plastic, barely moving. He hoisted up the container and partially submerged it into the tank. Before releasing Gilgamesh, he stopped. The tank had to be five feet long, and the mollies were spread out over the whole length. They swam independently, not in schools. Anywhere Gilgamesh went, he would find dinner. Of the three dozen or so mollies, the biggest Sid could see was barely half the size of the goldfish Gilgamesh was used to. Used to on a regularly fed stomach, that is. Like a Roman raising the gate into the arena, Sid tilted the basket and within a short time the score was lions one, Christians nothing.

Sid took a step back, astonished at the episode he had just unleashed. He knew he had to go, and as he stepped into the kitchen he heard that faint crackle and turned to see the score at two to zero. He laughed softly, celebrating his success, closing the back door behind him as a little girl with dirty brown hair watched from the pitch black front hallway.

He walked back to the car with a smooth, easy stride. He tossed the bucket and crowbar onto the back seat and almost casually hopped into the car. "Piece of cake," he said, to which Cliff responded by gunning the engine and taking off.

"Take it easy, Cliff. Everything worked out just like we planned." In a way, Cliff's job was more difficult than Sid's, who at least knew what was happening the whole time. Out in the car, Cliff had vividly imagined dozens of things going wrong. Twice while he was waiting, headlights had appeared at the end of the street. He had crouched down in the front seat, holding his breath until they passed, hoping it wasn't the goons coming back to catch them and make human sacrifices of them. An imagination will run wildest when it doesn't know what's really going on.

Sid's smile was widest when they pulled the car back into their own driveway. Cliff scurried out of the car and hurried into the house, followed much more slowly by Sid.

They collapsed in the living room which was faintly filled with soft music and light. Sid lit a homeroll. Cliff's heart was still pounding, and some of his beer went down the wrong pipe, choking him. He went into the bathroom and gagged quietly, not so much from the beer but from nerves. He pretended to go to the bathroom, not wanting Sid to know how shaken he really was. When he came back, Sid calmed him down and reassured him about how smoothly it all went.

The next few days were eerie ones for Cliff. He was too quiet, too introverted. He didn't join anybody out front at the bench until the following Tuesday night. That was the marathon night when they all would try to stay up just as late as Sid and listen to Mickey's radio show. Sid and Barbara would see who could name the old songs first, and she held her own against Sid's expertise. It was all out of Cliff's league and he normally just listened, keeping score. But this particular Tuesday, Barbara wasn't around, leaving Sid and Cliff alone with the radio.

"Hey, welcome back." Sid had been getting lonely out on the bench, smoking and listening to the music.

"Is it safe?" Cliff tried not to sound concerned, making fun of his own paranoia. He hugged his beer.

"What are you so edgy about?"

"I'm edgy about getting caught, that's what."

"Cliff, it's been days now. If we were going to get caught, it would've happened by now." He was annoyed at Cliff, who was doing nothing to settle his own nerves. "Carrie Ann, The Hollies, nineteen sixty, some-thing," he announced when the next song started, as if Barbara was around.

"Where is Barbara, anyway?" Cliff asked. Sid was glad for the change of subject.

"Mr. H. told me Billy's got a cold. She's staying home with him. Poor kid, all this beautiful weather and he's got the sniffles."

"He'll be okay, kids are tough."

"Yeah, you're right."

"You're sure we're not going to get caught?"

"Cliff!" Sid's face was twisted, pissed.

"Okay okay, just asking." He was unsteady, unsure of how to act around Sid when he was annoyed. It happened so rarely. The music played on.

Cliff could tell it was nearing two o'clock. The traffic on their road always picked up then as the bars were letting out, and it was also time for Mickey's news break.

According to their broadcasting license, WBJB had to have so many minutes of news within a specified time. Mickey grudgingly zipped through the world and national news and normally tacked on some trivial items he'd picked up somewhere as news features.

"Tabanus the Tiny, noted soothsayer to the stars, whose most recent fabrication added to the downfall of actress Margo Schrillrer when he convinced the failing superstar her dead uncle told him to tell her to invest all her assets into what he predicted to be the biggest boom in sod farming history, has been exposed as a swindler and a fraud! Yes, it's true, folks. The three foot five inch midget fortune teller and possibly the shortest celebrity on the west coast swindled nearly eight hundred thousand dollars from distraught suckers with floundering careers whom he met at posh Hollywood parties. He has left the country to elude the law and is reported to have gone underground somewhere in his native Bolivia. But the victimized Beautiful People aren't taking it sitting down. At least five of Tabanus' former clients whose names have not yet been released but sources say include an actress, a former Olympic pole vaulter, a cosmetics magnate, an author and someone from Greenland's Bureau of Tourism have banded together and hired an army of private investigators, mercenaries, bounty hunters and whatnots to retrieve the little scoundrel and bring him to justice. Police in Nevada have already questioned and released Tabanus' personal body guard, one Myron Perelle…"

"Corky," Sid muttered under his breath.

"...but would comment no further on the investigation. Tabanus the Tiny has been exposed as a rip-off artist, and we here at WBJB feel that is a great injustice, not to mention bad publicity for all you real live genuine psychotics, uh, psychics out there. So we're not going to just sit back, either. We're going to do something about it. All you witches and mystics, break out your crystal balls and tarot cards, incense and wolf's bane, tongue of newt, eye of frog, clavicle of rhinoceri, patella of octopi, whatever you're into, because WBJB is sponsoring the first and hopefully last 'Small Medium at Large' contest. Here's all you do."

"Using whatever means you see fit, predict what day and at what time, within one half hour, that the best soldiers of fortune Beverly Hills has to offer bring Tabanus the Tiny back into the country. The only restriction that applies is that the use of sacrifices, animal or human, will void your prediction. That means no blood, no guts, please. Dried entrails may be used sparingly. Family members and friends of the search party are excluded, void where prohibited by law or anywhere else that might get us into trouble."

"Dim the lights, draw your curtains and start soothing and saying. Write your predictions down on a postcard and be sure to indicate 'Small Medium at Large' on the front and mail it care of this station. We just thought of this thing tonight so we don't have any prizes lined up for the winner yet, but our budget is kind of skimpy this year so don't get your hopes too high."

"I don't believe it." Sid thought to himself and smiled.

"Where are you going, to catch Tabanus yourself?" Cliff asked. Sid had gotten up and hopped into the passenger side of his Mustang. With the door open, Cliff watched him get the peanut butter money jar out of the glove compartment. He unscrewed the lid and stuffed in a few loose bills he'd pulled out of various pockets.

"Well, gotta go now," he said, smiling, holding the jar up for Cliff to see it was full.

"What are you talking about?" Cliff asked from the bench. "It's two o'clock in the morning."

"You're right. I'd better turn on my headlights."

"Sid, what are you doing?"

"The jar is full. I have to get going."

"Where do you possibly have to go that can't wait until tomorrow? If you're going after Tabanus, let him wait. He's been on the run and he needs his sleep. Besides, you'll fall asleep at the wheel and some poor schmuck will have to go into work early just to clean you off a guard rail."

"You know, you're right again. I'm not properly prepared." Sid obediently replaced the jar and got out of his car. "I'll sleep first, then I'll go."

"You're so weird," Cliff told him.

"Thank you. Now I'm going to bed."

"Oh sure, the one night I feel like staying up late and all you can think about is going to bed early. Thanks a lot, pal."

"Sorry, Cliffer, I'm on a mission."

"Oh Christ, another one already."

"Good night." Sid waved an arm and the rest of his body followed in the general direction of Cliff's front door, leaving Cliff to ride out the night alone. The next afternoon when he woke up, Sid was long gone for Nevada.

Cliff slept through the building racket of the crew. He ate while watching from the usual spot. He enjoyed the way Mr. H. chewed them out and how they didn't listen, and how Mr. H. didn't mind as he showed them a better way to do everything from driving nails to laying shingles on the roof.

He sat there alone, unnoticed but for a wave from Mr. H. when he paused out front to repack his pipe. Three hours rolled by until Cliff went back inside and prepared a quick meal that by standards of time might be called dinner but felt more like lunch. He reread his new Super Sloth, something he hid even from Sid. He enjoyed it more this time because he knew to expect those three words at the bottom of the last page, To Be Continued. He hated to get so far into the story only to be cut off at, pardon the expression, the cliffhanger scene with a whole month to go to catch up on the action.

He piddled around, watched the goldfish for a while, watched some TV, listened to some music and laid off the beer for a night. He was content. Time flew by and he was happy in the fact he didn't feel he had to do anything in particular to keep himself occupied. As a matter of fact, he felt best when he just sat there and did nothing, which faded into a night's sleep when he pulled off his tight boots and fell asleep on the couch.

He awoke the next morning with one of the dogs licking his socked foot. Cliff realized he'd forgotten to feed them the night before. Bump and Grind devoured an excellent breakfast of dry food and canned food with an egg mixed in. Sid did that once in a while as a treat, and also because it was supposed to be good for them. Cliff cooked his eggs and fried up some extra bacon for the dogs. Goddamnit had gotten into their food and eaten some of it before Cliff could get around to feeding her.

He cleaned up and sat back down to decide what to do with the day. It was still before noon, so he went back to sleep. He woke up two hours later and took two jumpy Irish Setters to the park, hoping the girl in the pink jogging suit would still be running her laps. She wasn't, of course. But the dogs had fun and were even so kind as to do their big doggie dump there, one less mess for Cliff to clean up, although he vaguely remembered it was supposed to be Sid's responsibility. Taking them home, he drove past the boarded up building that was once Thiesmann's Burger Place. He stopped at a deli nearby and picked up two hoagies, a large for himself and a small for Bump and Grind to split. Sid also did that once in a while as a treat, not that it was very healthy for them but it did make their tails wag at a tremendous clip.

He lured them out to the back porch and threw half of the hoagie one way and the other half the other way like Sid always did so the dogs wouldn't slobber each other to death over one piece. He finished his own hoagie non-stop, pausing only to come up for air. On a full stomach, he drew the curtains to block out the afternoon sunlight. He locked the front door and stretched out on the couch. There was still enough light to see the drawing of Maivina, and he contemplated doing what he had only done once before in Sid's absence. But self abuse always left him both satisfied and guilty, which ultimately led to feeling unsatisfied, so he just watched some more TV. An old movie came on, and after that another one. When they were over, he wondered where Sid was. He really hadn't expected to hear from him, so he wasn't surprised when he didn't. He just laid around all day, and by the light of the eleven o'clock news he decided to feel guilty but satisfied. Then he went to bed and fell asleep before the unsatisfied part came upon him.

With no one around for the next several days and with nothing needing to be done, Cliff realized that this sitting around stuff was actually just boredom in disguise after all. He wasn't as good at passing time as he thought he was. He killed two whole days replaying out Sid's old chess game with Polia. Some of the letters were missing, so he had to fake a few moves, but when he was done Sid was still losing just like before the firemen knocked the game over.

He started to go to bed earlier each night because there was nothing to do. The dissatisfied feeling that had started nights ago wouldn't go away. He was fast asleep on the living room couch at just past one o'clock when two cars, one a black Gran Torino, pulled up in front of Sid's house. Betrayed by the light of the streetlamp, but with no one watching anyway, one of the dozen robed individuals silently shot it out with two arrows from a crossbow. The main body stormed the house, Twenty River Road according to the accident report. While the one with the crossbow drove a long stake into the front yard, the others threw three Molotov cocktails through Sid's front windows. In less than a minute, Sid's house was on fire, again.

Cliff awoke, jolted by the sound of tires squealing outside his door. He got up and peered through the slit in the curtains. He immediately noticed the lack of the blue-white light of the streetlamp. He ran out front in his underwear, and from this vantage point he could see that familiar yellow fire glow coming from inside Sid's house.

He deja-vued back inside, called the fire department, threw some clothes on, and this time he grabbed the fire extinguisher he'd thought to purchase after the last incident. Still groggy, he ran next door. Sid's house was not yet engulfed, but the fire was spreading quickly, just like it had the first time. Apparently due to a faulty cocktail, only two rooms were on fire. One was just flickering, but the other room, the one upstairs where the first fire had started, was blazing, fueled by the new wood used in the reconstruction. Grabbing Sid's house key out of his pocket, he stopped when he saw the stake driven into the ground. It was positive evidence from the perpetrators, whom he knew would catch them eventually. He had found the stake Spruance and company had left behind. Gilgamesh, gutted, was impaled on the pointed tip of the shaft. He couldn't just leave it there, so he pried it out of the ground. The fish smell was stronger than the smoke as he ran between the houses and pitched it into his own backyard.

He unlocked the front door and went to work with his fire extinguisher. It was one of those tiny household models, and it was barely enough to put a dent in the flickering room. He had emptied it completely but there were still some flames left. The firemen and also the police arrived quickly. Cliff was scared. He had only called the fire department. Many of the men there were the same ones who'd been there the last time. Mr. H. came out amidst the sirens and flashing lights, dumbfounded. He didn't realize Sid was still out of town and got frazzled when he couldn't see him in the crowd.

"He's gone away, Mr. H.," Cliff shouted to him.

"What? Sid's gone?" Mr. H. asked, panicking.

"He's out of town. He's still not home."

"You mean he's not in the house? That's good. Oh, thank God. So what in the hell happened this time?"

"I don't know," Cliff lied. It was the same lie he repeated to the police a few minutes later. Sid would have been proud to hear the way Cliff acted so dumb. He was too scared for himself and Sid to do anything else. He even surprised himself with how convincing he sounded.

"Are you sure nothing else happened that you know about, Mr. Dinsdale?" The policeman inquired of him.

"Of course not. Nothing else I know happened that I know."

The fire was contained almost at once. Luckily, it hadn't even come close to reaching the severity of the first blaze. Cliff and Mr. H. looked on with a couple of neighbors.

"What happened? Whose house is that, anyway?"

"I hope they're all right."

"This house, on fire again?"

"Is it your house?"

"No, it's not. It's my neighbor's." Cliff answered the curious house-wife who wore curlers to bed.

"Is he all right?"

"Yes, he's fine."

"Well where is he?"

"Where's Mr. Lasvistas?" The fire captain addressed Cliff and Mr. H.. Cliff was startled that the captain had remembered Sid's name.

"He's out of town."

"When is he coming back?" The fire captain shot the question at Cliff, who of course didn't know a thing. He was of no help to anyone and he didn't want to be. He'd been through this before and knew there was nothing to be done. He eventually went home and tried to lie down after the fire and excitement died down. That's where Sid found him.

"Yo Cliff! What the fuck is going on here?" Sid came barging into the living room followed by a huge, hairy, tree-trunk of an individual. "My house has been torched again!"

Cliff, wishing he had gotten back into the habit of sleeping in his bedroom again, promptly flipped off the couch and onto the floor at the outburst. He had just fallen asleep. He knocked his head on the coffee table on the way down. "I know, Sid, I know!" Cliff yelled, holding his head.

"What do you mean, you know? Who the hell…" Sid stopped himself, as if Cliff's I-told-you-so glance alone couldn't stop him.

"They sliced Gilgamesh open and stuck him on a stake in the front yard. Christ, this hurts," Cliff said, rubbing his head.

"Those assholes did what?"

"What did you expect?" Cliff got up. "It's in the back yard. You'd better trash it before somebody finds it or the dogs eat it. Oh yeah, they blew out the streetlamp, too."

Sid sped out the door and his quiet friend followed him. Cliff stubbed his toe while rubbing his head and trying to pull his jeans back on. He was still cursing when he stepped outside and saw an old van, dull matte maroon with brush marks and rust, leaning in the driveway behind his Volvo. Sid was out at the bench, looking up at the broken streetlamp, and the stranger was nowhere to be seen. Cliff went to join Sid, but he started coming up the sidewalk to the house when that familiar voice called from Sid's front door.

"So!"

There he was in all his fleshy finery and splendor. It was none other than Deputy Fire Marshal Marshall Marshmallow. "I thought I'd come out and inspect this case personally. How have you been, Mr. Lasvistas?" the puffed man asked.

"That's Schrieber," Sid said, taking brisk strides up to Marshmallow and his two assistants.

"Ah, still the witty one, are we?" Marshmallow jiggled as he laughed. Crennley and the new aide easily hid behind him, shuffling through clipboarded papers as always.

"Why Marshalmallow, I do believe you've been promoted!" Sid said in mock admiration as everyone met at the door.

"Very perceptive, Lasvistas. That is correct. I am now Chief Fire Marshal Marshall Marshmallow."

"Yeah, I could tell," Sid continued, revolted by the obese blob of a man in white pressed overalls before him. "They even stenciled your name on your hard hat. Isn't that nice, Cliff?" Marshmallow ignored the comment.

"So what is it this time, Lasvistas? Playing with matches?"

"Don't start on me, you stuffed bag of shit."

"Now now, Lasvistas. Temper temper."

"He wasn't even home this time, Marshmallow. Nobody was in the house," Cliff said.

Marshmallow glanced at him like he was an unwelcome outsider, then turned to Crennley. "I suppose we can rule out smoking in bed."

Sid was obviously startled at the comment, wondering if Marshmallow knew something he shouldn't. "What's that again?" Sid asked, trying to get Marshmallow's attention.

"I don't miss much, Lasvistas. That's why I've been promoted."

"We're going inside," Sid said, assured Marshmallow was still relatively harmless.

"Not this time. Boys?" Marshmallow signaled Crennley and the other man to block the doorway.

Sid just smiled. He'd been waiting for this. "Oh, Boy?" he mimicked the fat fire fighter, directing his shout to the van in Cliff's driveway.

The side door of the van slid open and Sid's friend stepped out. "Yes, boss?" he answered.

"Could you please stop what you're doing for a moment and join us over here?"

"What's the matter?" Sid's friend asked, coming across Cliff's lawn. Everyone just watched silently as the behemoth of a man approached.

"These gentlemen seem to be in our way," Sid informed him as he arrived at the group. With no further instructions, he deftly removed the two assistants, one in each hand, by lifting them into the air and setting them down in the bushes by the door. Then he got in Marshmallow's face.

"Can we go in now, Chief?" Sid was in no particular hurry. Marshmallow was too flustered to speak, let alone breathe. Sid's friend had eaten two Italian hoagies with extra onions for breakfast on the road. Sid and Cliff walked in, leaving him to watch Marshmallow melt.

"Is that guy who I think he is?" Cliff waited until they got inside to ask.

"That, Cliff, is Myron Perelle, alias Corky, ex-bodyguard of Tabanus the Tiny. Me and Corker go back a long way. We used to be in different professions together. You'll get to meet him later when he doesn't have to act so mean. He's really a pussycat. Goddamnit, what are you doing in here?" Sid reached out and the sooty, soggy cat jumped into his grasp. "You're going to use up those nine lives real quick if you keep this up."

"I was wondering where she was. She's been gone for two days."

"You must have been keeping an eye on other things," Sid said as he dropped the cat and they went upstairs. None of the damage was too serious. They met up with some field inspectors in the first room who were looking at some broken glass.

"Here's some more from the bottle," one said.

"Molotov cocktail?" Sid asked.

"Who are you?" the other inspector protested.

"I live here. You're in my house. Does it look like a Molotov cocktail?"

"We haven't determined that yet," the inspector lied.

"Here's another one," a third inspector called from another room. He stepped out into the hallway. "Hey, who the hell are you? We're conducting an investigation here."

"Boy, I get my house burned down and you guys think you own the place," Sid said as he brushed passed the inspector who looked at Cliff, who shrugged his shoulders and brushed passed, too.

The first room was burnt, but not so badly as the first time, thanks to the lack of clothing, magazines and boxes. The second room, the one Cliff had worked on, was scorched but there wasn't too much irreparable damage. The third room was fine except for the broken window through which the bottle had been thrown. The flaming rag had come out somewhere along the way, leaving behind only broken glass and long gone fumes. The fire was put out much faster this time, so there was much less water damage.

"What are the chances of fire striking twice?" Cliff mused.

"I don't know. I thought it was safe," Sid said. "Twice. Man…" he muttered. He kicked a hole in some new, water-weakened sheet rock. "Looks like I'm going to have to impose on you for longer than I had expected."

"Don't worry, I'm getting used to it," Cliff answered what wasn't even a question as he led their way back out.

Corky had Marshmallow backed into the bushes while the other two clowns stood by, not knowing what to do. "Corky, come." Corky growled once more before he followed behind Sid and Cliff. "When you finish that inspection, Chief, be sure and send me the report. I don't recall ever getting a copy of the last one."

Sid made the introductions on the way back over to Cliff's house. "Corky, I'd like you to meet a very good friend of mine. Corky, Cliff. Cliff, Corky."

"How's it going, Cliffer?" Corky held out a paw like a St. Bernard. For once, Cliff didn't mind the handshake ritual.

"So I suppose I have to be a nice guy and set up a room for the fugitive here, too."

Sid just smiled. "No, Cliff," he said, "you don't have to worry about that."

"Why 'Corky'?" Cliff asked, trying to figure out the nickname.

Sid answered. "Would you have the nerve to call someone who looks like this 'Myron'?"

A day or two later, after the streetlamp was fixed, there was an extra person out at the curb. Corky and Barbara got along quickly, but Billy was still shy and scared. It didn't help when Corky leered at him. Corky insisted little kids never liked him and he stopped trying to get them to do so a long time ago. True, he had the massive, stumpy body of a keg carrier at a polka party and a face that made Charles Bronson handsome by comparison, but he was one of the good guys. He spoke with ease, his gruff voice uncomplimentary of the crude sort of sensitivity that showed through even when he leered at Billy.

"Do you remember the first time I found you, Cork?" Sid asked. Corky let out a laugh, almost a deep throated giggle. "I left my car at home and went hitch hiking for a while. I really don't remember why." Sid addressed himself directly towards Cliff and Barbara while Corky smiled and drummed his fingers. "I was hiking along this four lane highway when up ahead I saw this guy walking down the middle of the road on the double yellow line. There wasn't much traffic coming my way, but both lanes were jammed coming towards him on the far side of the highway. Being the stupid type, I caught up to him, waited for a few cars to pass and went out and joined him." Corky started to laugh again.

"These cars were flying by on either side of us just a few feet away, and none of them were slowing down. They'd just blow their horns and maybe swerve away from us. It actually made me feel like I had some sort of power over them, like I could will them to veer away from us sometimes."

"It was great, man."

"Okay, I was lying. Don't listen to him, it was scary as hell. He probably didn't even know he was doing it. Elvis died with less shit in him than Corky was on that day."

Corky stood up. He handed his bottle to Sid and walked out to the middle of the road. "You don't know what it's like to be out here with the cars zipping by and then they're gone and you're still here." He was spinning around in a stunted pirouette. Sid, of course, joined him.

"Ha! Hahaha!" Sid stood behind Corky, who was now standing still on the asphalt, facing south, looking for headlights.

"I definitely think these guys are crazy," Cliff leaned over and whispered to Barbara.

"You're not kidding."

"This is the smart way to do it. If I stand behind him, the car will hit Corker first. I figure that gives me a sporting chance."

"There is no smart way to do what you guys are doing," Cliff said. He wasn't really worried until he saw Corky's beady eyes light up to high beam.

A car was coming around the bend, about a hundred and fifty yards away. When he spotted it, Sid quickly switched positions as it was coming from the opposite direction than he'd anticipated. With Corky in front of him again, he was braver.

"Come on, Cliff!" Sid shouted.

"Guys, this isn't funny." Barbara was getting closer to a sudden panic.

"Sid, Corky, get out of the road now," Cliff begged calmly. He was so anxious only because he knew they wouldn't listen. The only one amused by the whole ordeal was Billy. Even Sid and Corky got scared when the car got so close it started blowing its horn in short bursts. Barbara was holding Billy tight, worrying above all else that Cliff might try to go out there to pull them to the curb. Cliff was about to do no such thing. He'd come to understand there were things which Sid decided he was going to do, things which aren't even considered by sane people who are able to reckon with their sensibilities and weigh the consequences before they happen. He knew if he tried to stop them, they would probably sandwich him in between them and keep him out there against his will.

The car did not slow down. There was ample room for it to pass as Corky and Sid held their positions on the yellow line. The driver hit the horn and held it down, scarcely swerving an inch out of its path. Barbara looked down and away. Billy was having trouble breathing in her tight grasp.

The car turned out to be a Monte Carlo. It whizzed past, all light and sound. The high pitch of the horn peaked as it reached a frozen Corky and Sid and wound down into a deeper pitch as it stung passed and drove off, the condition named after the Austrian physicist C. J. Doppler having taken effect.

"Christ I hate Monte Carlos!" Sid screamed into the wind, moving nothing but his mouth for a second. Corky was the first to stagger slowly back to the curb.

"You were right, Sid. It is scarier when you know what's going on." Sid shuffled off behind him, trying to go into an anxiously exhausted explanation of the Doppler Effect for everyone's benefit. Cliff held back a smile, not wanting to encourage him.

"You're all nuts," he said.

"You could've been killed." Barbara was more flamboyant in her judgment. She was as scared for them being hit as she was for herself and Billy at seeing it happen. Corky and Sid remained silent for the moment. "Did you hear me? You ought to be locked up, both of you."

With that, Corky busted out laughing. Over his uproar, Sid said to Barbara, "What are you so worried about? It was us out there, not you. You'd have cause to be scared if you were out there with us. You'd have cause, but no reason as far as I'm concerned, but that's another point of view." Sid was acting braver than he actually felt. It wasn't sinking in. "What better way is there to appreciate the life you have than to come this close to losing it?" Sid held up two fingers, the distance between them about the size of a goldfish. Barbara was thinking Sid's brain would fit in there quite nicely.

"How about by spending more time living and less time trying to kill yourself?" she retorted. Cliff didn't participate. He just watched the scene unfold.

"Hey Barb, take it easy. We didn't mean to scare you," Corky said with his inane sense of compassion. It silenced her voice but not her emotions. She asked herself what the hell she was doing there, something Cliff rarely felt the need to do anymore. Sid's way of thinking sometimes had a way of rubbing off on him.

"That's right, Barb." Sid imitated Corky, the only one of them to ever call Barbara 'Barb'. "There's nothing wrong with what we do, at least not with us. It feels good. We do it. I might not agree with everything you do, but I don't try to stop you. Give me the same courtesy, huh?" Sid took a sip from Corky's bottle, still meeting her eyes.

"But that was pretty irresponsible of you guys," she said, calming down a degree. "No, it was stupid. It was damn stupid."

Sid took a deep breath. "And it was pretty irresponsible of you to marry that guy who gave you a child and then walked out on you."

"How dare you," she pouted out slowly, not believing Sid could say such a thing. "That's not fair at all, I…"

Sid cut her off. "And it's not fair of you to tell me what's irresponsible or not, either." Sid was just trying to make a point, but Cliff thought he could have chosen a better example. Corky thought so, too. There was no need for the conversation to go on any longer. The same sentiments would just be rehashed, perhaps in even harsher words.

"Well, I'm going to bed," Cliff broke the silence. He and Sid would sleep in their respective rooms and Corky, as he had been doing for the past couple of nights, would sleep out in his van. He declined Cliff's offer of a pillow.

"Okay, then I'm going in." He rounded up the empty bottles.

"Good night," Sid and Corky said, but Barbara remained silent on the bench with Billy, who was beginning to fall asleep in her lap.

"Good night, Barbara."

"Oh, 'night Cliff."

Cliff clinked to the front door, trying not to drop any of the many bottles.

"Hey Barbara, sorry I played so rough," Sid apologized.

"Yeah," Corky agreed.

"Just let me be mad for a while, okay?" Sid and Corky looked at each other. They sat in silence for a while, just listening to the river go by, until a set of headlights appeared from up around the bend. "You both just sit there and stay there!" Barbara blurted out suddenly, waking up Billy who started to cry.

13

Barbara cooled off for the next few days, over which time some adjustments were made. Corky's van took up residence by Sid's Mustang at the curb, when he wasn't running off for two or three days at a time. "I think he's part gypsy, he likes to travel a lot," Sid explained of him. Cliff registered for his fall classes. Work on Sid's house was suspended briefly until new plans on how to proceed could be devised. Ben was dumbfounded at how the place could get hit by fire again. At least this time they knew what the cause was. Sid would have them believe it was a random sort of vandalization. Unlike the first fire, this one made the newspapers as a brief entry in the county police records. This upset Sid. There were standard inquiries and investigations, but luckily nothing became of them. Corky was the only one they'd told about the attack on Spruance, although Barbara had her suspicions. Corky was impressed with both the story and Sid's car. "It looks good all red."

So as unsatisfied fire inspectors, laughing fish worshippers and dumbfounded construction workers went about their business, Cliff received a phone call.

"Hello, Clifford. How are you, baby?"

"Mother!" Cliff had truly forgotten about her, as much as anyone can forget about the one who gave them birth. "What are you doing, uh, with yourself?" Cliff stumbled over his words and intentions. He hadn't heard from her in months. Nor had she heard from him.

"Well that's no way to greet your Mother," she said with a well-meaning chuckle. "Of course, I might just as easily ask the same thing. We haven't heard from you in months, dear."

Cliff stalled. He knew she wouldn't believe him if he told her he'd been busy. "I've been very busy, I suppose I should've called to say hello just the same."

"That is precisely what I'm calling about, Clifford. I've got wonderful news."

"What is it, Mother?"

"It's much too good to tell over the telephone. I'll be coming down this afternoon to tell you in person."

"Oh great. We can go out to dinner. There's this new restaurant in town, I can meet you there…"

"Don't be silly, darling," Sheila interrupted. "We have so much to talk about. A stuffy old restaurant just won't do."

"But this is a beautiful restaurant. You'd like it. It's very, very unstuffy. There aren't even any stuffed items on the menu. No stuffed shrimp, no stuffed cabbage, stuffed artichokes, stuffed shells. I think they do have turkey and stuffing, but they even refer to that as turkey and filler…"

"Clifford, Clifford darling." Sheila stopped her son's nervous banter. "I can only come to see you this afternoon. I can't stay for dinner. We'll have a lovely chat. Oh, I can't wait to tell you the news."

"When can I expect you?" Cliff asked, defeated.

"Three-ish, I should think. That is, if I can remember how to get there."

"Father's not coming?"

"No dear, he's sorry he can't come, he has some arrangements to make about the, oh, but I'll tell you all about it when I see you."

Cliff gave her brief directions for the hour drive, somewhat tempted to send her the long way, or better yet the wrong way. The conversation ended with the usual wet, smacking kiss and Cliff hung it up.

He checked his watch. Ten twenty five. Four hours and thirty five-ish minutes left.

"You guys have to get out of here now. I'll take care of the house," Cliff ran out front to tell Corky and Sid, up early for some reason and tossing a Frisbee on the lawn in the August sunshine. He jumped back inside, followed nonchalantly by Sid and one of the dogs. He joined Cliff in the living room, which didn't look like it did several months ago.

"Cliff, slow down. What are you doing?" Cliff was taking down the drawing of Mai.

"My Mother is coming over," he said, rattling the frame as he was having trouble getting it down.

"Hey, be careful with that!" Sid helped him. "So your Mother is coming over. Great, I'd love to meet her."

"No you definitely would not!" Cliff set the drawing on the floor, propped up against the stereo. "I never told my family you moved in here with me."

"Why not? Anyway, what's the difference? It's your house."

Cliff stopped long enough to face Sid. "Do you have any idea what my Mother would do if she came in here and found a drawing of a naked woman, an old van and a Mustang out front, crumbs under the cushions, dog hair in the air, water rings on the coffee table and, and underclothes on the lamp shade?" Cliff ripped one of his socks off the lamp.

"No."

"Neither do I, and I don't intend to find out."

"The place looks like it always has to me," Sid reasoned.

"That's the problem." Cliff sniffed the air and asked a serious question. "Do you smell onions? I think I smell onions. I definitely smell onions..." He went into the kitchen. Sid got the point. He went to explain it to Corky who was still out front, trying to teach the other dog to play Frisbee.

"Hey Sid, this is never going to work. He can catch all right, but he can't throw for beans and he keeps getting dog spit all over the damn thing."

"We've got to help Cliff clean up this place and then we've got to get out of here," Sid said, disappointed, not looking forward to explaining this to Corky.

"Okay," he answered, flinging the Frisbee so hard and straight it almost reached the river before the dog stopped chasing it halfway down the front lawn. "What's the matter?"

"You see, Cliff never told his parents that I moved in with him. His Mother's coming over this afternoon. I guess we have to get out along with my stuff. It's got to look like I was never here."

"Why in the hell doesn't Cliff just tell her you moved in while they work on your house?"

"You can't blame Cliff, man. It's his folks. I've never met them but from what I can gather they're a couple of royal assholes. I think they supply Cliff with most of his money. So come on, let's help him clean up and get out of here. We were going to leave next week anyway for your arraignment. What do you say we leave a few days early and see what happens?"

"This is bullshit. Why can't Cliff just tell her? Is he afraid of her or something? If he's worried about the cash, hell, you could take care of him until he gets himself started."

"You know Cliff doesn't know that about me and it's going to stay that way. I don't want him to know anything. He's a good guy and he's got enough hassles as it is."

Sid went back into the house and found Cliff still in the kitchen, whipping up a box mix cake. "Mother likes stuff like tea and cake in the afternoon." Cliff said it like a shy apology.

"Hey, that's cool. Listen, Corky's going to do your lawn and I'm going to start moving my stuff back over to my house. Then you can get rid of me and those crumbs and watermarks, okay?"

"Hey, yeah, that would be great, thanks." Cliff paid close attention to the milk as he poured it into the mix and said, "You know, Sid, it's not like I'm ashamed of you or anything. I want you to know that. You just don't know my Mother. I've had a lot of fun in the past few months."

"Yeah, it has been fun, but now I'm going to get that dirty picture out of your living room, okay?"

"All right, Sid."

The place was spotless by one o'clock. They started carrying Sid's things back over to his house. To save time, they stashed everything they could, except the stereo, in Sid's room behind a locked door. Cliff was getting too anxious.

"Okay, we'll be taking off now. We'll be gone until at least next week. Somebody got into trouble and now we've got to go back and straighten things out. Isn't that right, Mr. Perelle?"

Corky came out of the kitchen licking his fingers. "Hey, I didn't do anything. Tabanus ripped everybody off, not me. I just hope I don't get into too much trouble. The man in the robe released me on my own recognizance and told me not to leave the state."

"We stopped at the border and looked for somebody to tell but there wasn't anybody there," Sid added.

"You'll have to mention that to the judge," Cliff said. His attitude towards the pending events showed in his voice.

"Don't worry, Cliff. You have nothing to fear but Mother herself," Sid said.

"Thanks, thanks a lot. For helping me, I mean." Sid had his arm around Cliff's shoulders shaking him vigorously, manly, sternly, encouragingly, stupidly, nearly breaking his back.

"Yeah, hang tough, kiddo. Remember that kidney punch I showed you, it might come in handy," Corky advised.

"Lead on, Your Corkness," Sid said. With that, they hopped into Corky's van. Sid's Mustang would remain in his driveway next door.

Cliff waited at the doorway and waved to them as they drove past with Sid hanging out the window yelling, "Give 'er hell, Cliffer!"

Cliff certainly felt he was in for a confrontation. Whether it would be with his mother or himself remained to be seen. All he could do now was sit and wait. He hated the way his house felt, so still, so dead. No Sid playing his records too loud, none of the already familiar/already missed sputtering of Corky's van, no Bump and Grind looting around, sniffing, stealing socks and underwear to hide under the couch. They were in Mr. H.'s backyard. He took them in with no questions asked.

All that was left was Cliff in his clean living room, trying to remember how to make time pass while still enjoying it at the same, uh, time. He noticed the gurgling of the fish tank. He listened to it drag on and on until he recalled what his mother said. What was the surprise she had spoken about? Was there something amiss at home, or away from home? Was he being disinherited? What?

His train of thought was eventually derailed by the shatter of the shrill door bell. Cliff was surprised he'd been so engrossed he didn't hear his mother pull up. It turned out he still remembered how to make time pass, only he'd forgotten how to enjoy it.

"Clifford darling, hello!" Sheila gave him an affectionate embrace. He wondered if she ever got tired of calling everyone 'Darling'.

"Hello, Mother. Come in." He walked her to the living room.

"My, I see I taught you to keep house quite well," she said, inspecting the room just the same. Cliff tried to remember seeing his mother with a feather duster in her hand, ever. "Oh, I didn't know you had an aquarium." She hurried over to see it. Cliff had decided to leave it up rather than go through the hassle of dismantling it. "They're, goldfish." Her efforts to be kind were transparent. Her eagerness to please upset Cliff. He was suspicious. "They're really very lovely, dear. And what's this?" Sheila pointed to the stereo next to the tank. "Are you listening to music now? I hope it's not that dreadful opera music your Father is always listening to. Pavaroni or something like that, I believe."

Cliff resisted the temptation to say something like, 'Yeah, I like Pavaroni on my pizza'. He was cut off before he could have said anything, anyway. Sheila was rambling on non-stop.

"Where did you get this stereo, dear? It's all scratched on the side." Cliff didn't even notice the damage on the side and front of the receiver anymore. They were put there in transit to his house on the night of the first fire. He cursed himself for deciding to leave it in the living room.

"It's from next door, from my neighbor, Tim, Tom, well his name's Tim Thompson but we call him Tim." It was Cliff's turn to babble.

'Why didn't I move this thing?' he thought. "His house caught on fire and it's being rebuilt and he doesn't want to leave anything of value in the house, what with the construction workers in and out all the time, you know how they can be."

"I wondered what all the commotion was next door when I pulled up. So, he gave it to you?"

"What?"

"The stereo, Tim gave it to you to while his house is being reconstructed?"

"Yes, yes, he's a good friend of mine."

"That's very nice, Clifford," she said emphatically, so glad to hear he'd made a friend. It was possibly the one thing she worried about when she found time to do anything concerning Cliff.

"Why don't we sit in the dining room? Can I get you some coffee?" Relieved to be out of the living room, he sat his mother down at the table and went into the kitchen.

"So how is school?" She trailed the question after him.

"I'm between semesters right now but it's fine, really. I'll be going back in another few weeks, though."

"Are you enjoying your courses?"

"Uh, no, I'm not." He hadn't even mentioned this to Sid. "As a matter of fact, I'm trying something different, probably just for this semester." He tried to justify the change before he even told her about it. "I'm taking a psychology course and another in anthropology." He froze at the sink after he'd said it. The ensuing silence gnawed at him. Sheila was out of sight in the dining room, and Cliff was glad he'd decided not to tell her to her face. He was still fearful of her reaction, fearful to a point had he reached before he told her, he wouldn't have mentioned it at all. He always felt his parents expected him to make something of himself. He'd always felt he was supposed to put all that financial support to good use. He always felt he had to excel, always with the possible exception of the last few months.

"If it makes you happy, dear, that's what's important. I'm just glad to hear you're not going into this computer rage. I couldn't imagine you doing the sort of work Curtis does. It just doesn't fit you."

"Who's Curtis?"

"You met Curtis, darling. Remember? At the dinner party we gave last year? He's Priscilla's beau. That's what I'm here to talk to you about."

What was she up to? What was she doing? She didn't even seem to care about his switch in curriculum. 'If it makes you happy, dear,' who paid her to say that? And what about that Curt? Cliff fairly cringed to think of that dinner party. It seemed ten years in the past, so much had happened since then.

"Yes, you did mention something about a surprise, didn't you?" Cliff mentioned casually, lifting the lid off the cake dish as the coffee perked. The words 'Hi Mom!' were scrawled in finger-wide letters across the top of the chocolate frosting.

"Priscilla's getting married!" Sheila gushed from the dining room. Cliff hurriedly replaced the cover on the cake dish, stealing a quick second look as if the message would disappear like some warped magic trick.

"Priscilla's getting married, eh? That's great, really wonderful." Cliff had momentarily inherited his mother's sincere tones. "Who's the lucky guy?"

"Why, Curtis, of course. Clifford, are you all right? You seem beside yourself."

"I'm fine, sure. That's great news. When's the wedding?"

Sheila was pleased Cliff was showing an interest in the situation. "They announced it a while ago and we've done nothing but plan plan plan from the beginning. I'm sorry I didn't come and tell you sooner but the wedding is going to be at the end of next month. I hope that gives you enough time." Sheila twitched. Cliff couldn't think of a thing he had to do in preparation which could possibly take a month and a half, but he knew his mother was only apologizing for her lapse behavior according to the rules of etiquette. Cliff had trouble dealing with a bunch of Emily Post clones who ate pizza with a fork. A month and a half was plenty of time for him. But his mother was actually more concerned about him getting a date.

Not knowing what else to do with the cake, Cliff simply brought out the coffee. When he turned into the dining room, a cup in each hand, Sheila held a long, copper colored hair up to her eyes to examine it. "Clifford?"

"Oh, that. That must be from Tom. Or his dog maybe. Well, his dog isn't named Maybe, it's, it's Duchess. We gave Duchess a trim, too. That's probably where that's from. I mean we gave him, her a bath…"

"Is that a rag I see stuffed under the hutch?" Sheila got up and pulled out one of Sid's old socks. Cliff knew he had been sabotaged, first by Corky and now by Bump and Grind. "Clifford, what exactly is going on here? You're acting very peculiar and I know I raised you better than to keep your dirty laundry in the dining room."

So this was the confrontation Cliff had felt coming on. He was now painfully aware of his ineptitude at fabrication. He also knew he couldn't lie very well. Sheila, one hand on her hip, the other cautiously holding the malodorous evidence, waited for answers.

After going through the right front brake assembly in Nevada, not one but both radiator hoses, one rebuilt carburetor with a faulty choke mechanism in Oklahoma and one flat tire caused by accidentally running over a little kid's lemonade stand (abandoned), Corky and Sid returned home with disgusted attitudes and an over-heated radiator.

"Hey guys," Cliff greeted them, laid back, stretched out on the couch with his hands behind his head, slowly sipping on a beer, an old movie on the tube. He'd apparently reached nirvana, or so it appeared to the weary travelers in contrast to their own sullen moods. Cliff was the picture of contentedness, like an ever petted cat.

"So how'd it go with your Mother?" Sid asked while Corky disappeared for a beer.

"Fine, just fine," Cliff teased and added with a smile, "She's looking forward to meeting you."

"What?"

"You're invited to the wedding, too, if you can talk yourself into putting on a suit."

"Wait a minute, you told your Mother about me?"

"It wasn't exactly my idea, but…"

"Hey Cork, did you hear that? He told her!"

"And thanks for the cake decoration, Corky. Mother loved it."

Corky came out with two beers and a piece of that very cake, the piece with the '!' on it. "Way to go, Cliffer."

"You should have seen it." Cliff's eyes went into retrospect.

"Sounds like you had a good time."

"Yes, I did, once I told her the truth. I was so worried about what she was going to think, and it was all for nothing. I wasn't even going to tell her but I got trapped by a dog hair and one of your old socks. We had such a good time once we started acting like ourselves. It feels good to have that stuff off my chest. I've been walking around for days just being happy about it."

"Feels good, huh?"

"Damn good. Hey, how did you guys make out, anyway?"

"Corky got fined for violating probation, but when they found out he didn't know anything about Tabanus, they decided not to do anything about it if he promised to stay out of Nevada for a while." Corky smiled when Sid said that.

"Did they find Tabanus yet?"

"Nope, not yet."

Corky asked Cliff for a bucket so he could carry some water out to his beleaguered radiator. "It waited until we got all the way back before it blew. What a trooper."

"You mean you guys drove the whole way? Why didn't you just hop on a plane?"

Sid waited until Corky was outside. "Because he's afraid of flying." Cliff couldn't imagine someone like Corky being afraid of anything.

Corky came back in for a refill, his arms loaded with clothes and souvenirs. "Here's something for you." Corky tossed a magazine on Cliff's chest. It was the new issue of Orifice.

"Page twenty three," Sid said and followed Corky into the kitchen.

On page twenty three, the pictorial with Suzi started. It was titled 'Pumpin' Muffin'. Most of the shots were of Suzi in a bakery kitchen. The cover shot showed her wearing only a baker's hat and a full length apron, her eyes on the rolling pin in her hand. Cliff rifled through the pages of pictures, ignoring the captions about her making your dough rise and silly stuff like that. The first three pages were just of Suzi in the bakery doing things he'd never seen done before with egg beaters and mixing bowls. Then there were two shots he immediately recognized as those which were taken in his spare room. She looked just like he had remembered her. Of all the dozens of shots they'd taken, they only used two, but Cliff thought they were good ones. On the facing page was a great shot of her with the construction crew. It looked like some sort of a dream. It was so strange to see their houses in a nationally circulated, albeit underground magazine. He laughed to himself as he rescanned over the bakery shots, wondering what Iggy might say. He had never imagined a girl could look so good all covered with flour.

He managed to get his eyes back into their sockets and turned the page. The next photograph he saw caught his attention immediately. It was Suzi, referred to as Muffin in the layout, singing on some club stage. It was the part of the pictorial where they liked to demonstrate that the model had more going for her than just a killer ass. But what seized Cliff's attention was the fact Sid could be clearly seen in the foreground, facing the camera, shit-faced as could be, eyes like two pissholes in the snow, as the saying goes.

"Hey Sid, it's you! You're in the magazine!" Cliff jumped up off the couch, running to show it to him, like he hadn't already seen it.

"Yeah, I know."

"What's the matter? I think it's wild."

"Let's just say I don't like having my picture taken."

"Are you pissed, I mean peed because they're not paying us for the use of our houses, or your face? I know I don't mind." Cliff buried himself in the picture again.

"Cliff, I'm going to ask you not to do something and I'm not going to tell you why not and I'm not going to say another word about it, so

I insist you trust me the first time around. Don't tell anybody it's me in the picture. I don't want anybody to know."

"You look pretty happy in it. Didn't you know they took it?"

"Where's the wedding? For that matter, who's getting married?"

"No no no," Cliff corrected. "You're not very good at changing the subject. I've noticed that about you. See, first you have to break the conversation away from the main subject by candidly including the subject you wish to divert into. Then you simply exclude the old subject in favor of the new one. Then it appears as if you're only picking one of the two separate subjects to talk about."

Sid played along. "No, I didn't know they took my picture because I was drunk, but not as drunk as I like to get at weddings, which is what you were about to fill me in on."

"Much better. See, now was that so hard? That was the surprise my Mother had to tell me in person. My sister, well, really she's my half-sister, Priscilla, you know, the one we used to call 'Prissyilla'? She's marrying some army or navy guy and you're invited. Me too."

"Sounds great. This is almost like taking me home to meet the folks. How romantic. I hope I catch the bouquet."

"I really don't think it's going to be as much fun as you imagine. We'll be surrounded by a bunch of stuffed shirts and flowers and jewelry. If there's one thing rich people like to do, it's to wear lots of jewelry." Sid self consciously twisted the ring on his finger a few times. "I don't know if Corky can come, though," Cliff continued, stopping Corky in his tracks through the living room with another bucket of water for his van.

"How about it, Cork. We're going to a formal wedding with suits and ties, y'know, clean clothes. You want to come?" Sid asked.

"Fuck that."

"Good old Corky," Sid cracked, "you can't dress him up and you can't take him anywhere."

14

"I don't know why we didn't just take my car," Sid said from the passenger side of Cliff's Volvo.

"If we pulled up in your heap they'd make us drive around to the servant's entrance, that's why. Hey, did anybody ever tell you look sexy in a suit?"

"You always get me horny when you know we can't do anything." They were starting to sound like a couple of not so newlyweds. "So how are the new classes going?" Sid had enrolled in a glass blowing class himself and was curious to see how Cliff was taking his own new curriculum. He was more than pleased to see him trying to get away from the business courses for a while.

"It's more interesting than I thought it would be."

"Did they tell you about Phineas Gage yet?"

"You mean the guy that had a metal shaft blown through his head and lived?"

"Some things never change. I think anyone who has ever had to take a psych course learns about old Phineas. Personally, I thought it was neat but irrelevant."

"It sets the scene for lobotomies. Phineas Gage's behavior was altered..."

"Lobotomies are like making a man a eunuch to make him forget about sex," Sid interrupted, loosening his tie which was performing its own type of lobotomy, cutting off little things like blood and oxygen to his brain.

"Hey, I forgot to tell you, my Mother had our family tree traced."

"Oh yeah? What did they come up with?"

"I'm nearly related to royalty."

"Really?"

"It turns out we're descended somehow from a General Dinsdale who fought in the American Revolution. He married the daughter of a wealthy English nobleman after the war. Isn't that something?"

"Sure is."

When they arrived at the church, Cliff got a chance to briefly introduce Sid to his parents. "Mother, Father, I'd like you to meet my friend, Sid Lasvistas."

"Mr. Lasvistas, it's so very nice to meet you at last," Sheila said with a practiced charm and grace she was using to greet the plethora of friends, relatives and associates who were flocking to the church in automobiles of conservative color, chrome and shine.

"It's my pleasure to meet you, Mrs. Dinsdale, and greetings to you, sir," Sid said, meeting Arthur's handshake.

"Mr. Lasvistas," was all Arthur mumbled.

"I understand you had a bit of a mishap at your house," Sheila addressed Sid.

"Yes, it was unfortunate, but Clifford has been a great friend to me, what with taking me into his house and all. I hope the situation doesn't upset you," he added with a glance to the silent Dinsdale. "I do so appreciate Clifford's assistance. You've got a son to be proud of here."

"Oh, we are, aren't we, Arthur?"

Cliff sat up front with the family while Sid remained in the midst of the friends of the bride. Cliff had invited him to join them up front but Sid declined. Even he would feel ill at ease there, and this way Cliff would be free to reacquaint himself with his family whom he hadn't seen in many months. Sid spotted a man in uniform. From what he could discern, it was Loudon, Cliff's half-brother, the technical writer. Next to him and his wife, he could see what he believed to be the top of Elliot's head, then Cliff. Sheila sat in the next pew up with an empty spot reserved for Arthur after he gave away the bride.

Sid sat alone also, the nearest people being an older couple at the other end of the pew, nearest the center aisle of the church. He hoped no one would be seated by squeezing by them and into their pew. They both looked so decrepit they might break if someone bumped them too hard. The woman wore an aqua print gown which hung limply on her frail frame. Her wrists were weighed down with the diamond and gold bracelets that kept falling off, once requiring her a full minute to replace to their original position. Her husband did not assist. Sid could only see a profile of the back of his bald head as he sat on the far side of his wife, who was bent over and leaning forward slightly, no doubt from the combined weight of her corsage and hefty jade necklace which dwarfed her small frame.

Sid opted to watch Cliff up front, catching glimpses of him through the many shifting heads. He regretted not taking Cliff up on his offer when a family of eight was led into his pew from his side in order to avoid trampling the old folks. He balanced himself at an awkward angle while they seated themselves, insisting they not trouble him to slide over but to stay right where he was. The fattest little son stepped on his foot.

Sid knew he wasn't cut out for this sort of occasion but felt confident he could fake his way through it. All the same, he still wanted to stand up and scream, mess up his hair and run out the door, but not before taking off his tie and strangling the blob of a boy next to him. Sid got angry with himself when, while trying to ignore him, he caught himself breathing with the same depth and tempo. He'd spent four hours in a jail in a foreign country, he was on the tram car that goes under Niagara Falls the time it stalled out in the middle for half an hour, he'd even had lunch once in Runnemede, New Jersey, but he would've gladly traded in his present situation for a repeat of all of them, with the possible exception of that lunch.

At least he was able to avoid making conversation, as all the boy did was wheeze and the only adults near by were behind and in front of him, speaking in their own quiet circles, like in a hospital. Soon enough, the music started and all heads turned to see Priscilla, escorted by Arthur, make her veiled way to the altar. Arthur was as straight as a board, unlike his mustache, which Sid noticed was slightly askew. He wouldn't have that problem if he shaved with a straight blade razor, he thought, fingering the border lines of his own goatee and sideburns, well cropped for the occasion. Ah, what a marvelous device.

Priscilla parted with her father as he gave her away to join her uni-formed fiancé to begin the ceremony, a custom that Sid didn't like to admit fascinated him. He still tried to avoid it on principle, as the idea of matrimony for himself never settled quite right. He couldn't get past thinking of it as nothing more than legalized babies and holiness in the eyes of others, not the eyes of God under which they never failed to mention they were performing the act. To him, it was more beautiful to live the way he and Mai had, which was actually close to three years of glorious sin before she got sick of supporting him and left. If they'd been married, they would've had to go through yet another absurd institution, divorce court. It was much less complex their way, more personal, too. They didn't try to prove to everybody how much they loved each other by seeing how much money they could blow on a fancy wedding. They proved to each other how much one loved the other every day, when it really counted. So when they had nothing left to prove, they split up rather than tie each other down. Of course, they were apt to do that on occasion, also. Sid smiled, recalling the first time they reinvented the Mai Tai. Where the traditional one makes use of rum, lemon and pineapple juice, their version of the Mai Tie used ropes, knots and bedposts. Sid never even realized the drink's name came from the Tahitian phrase for 'the very best', which it very much was.

Sid was engrossed in imagining what might have happened if he and Maivina had done what Curt and Prissyilla were doing now. The best aspect he could come up with was perhaps Mai might still be with him today. She had more respect for these sorts of things than he ever did. They probably wouldn't be happy with each other after so much time, but he missed Mai so badly now he'd settle for whatever he could get.

He realized he'd daydreamed through the entire ceremony when the sniffles and song cut loose. Now that it was over, he wanted to watch it. He had to settle for the sight of Mr. and Mrs. Curtis Thloem walking down the aisle. The ushers started releasing people from the front rows first. It would be a while before Sid's row was excused so he waited silently, Cliff being the only person to notice him. He waved to Sid with a lowered hand and walked out with the rest of his family. The people slowly poured out into the aisle, and Sid was glad to see Cliff waiting for him near the doorway. The progress was slow as he followed

Pudgo to the reception line where everybody was congratulating the happy couple. Cliff made the introductions. "Priscilla, Curt, this is my friend, Sid Lasvistas."

"Hello, it's nice to meet you."

"Nice to meet you, and congratulations, to both of you."

"Thank you, Mr. Lasvistas."

"Well, see you at the reception." Cliff waved as he and Sid broke off from the crowd and headed for the Volvo.

"How'd you like it?"

"I need a drink."

That's exactly what Sid got at the reception. The open bar certainly was, so he grabbed a beer with two other men while Cliff found their seats. The hall was done in pink and white with circular tables staggered around the dance floor in such a way you had to look closely before you realized they were set up in a pattern. There were eight clusters of four huge tables each with alternating pink and white tablecloths. A bouquet of carnations, red or white for contrast, adorned each table. The dance floor contained not a speck of the oft-repeated colors. Sid finished his beer and cut across it to join Cliff.

"I don't recognize any other names at our table."

"That would make two of us," Sid said, sitting down. "Hey, wait, aren't you sitting with your family or something?"

"Nope. I asked Mother to seat us together. Besides, they'll be sitting right over there, and Loudon will get stuck with Elliot for a change."

They were soon joined by the remaining members of their table, one of whom turned out to be a gentleman Sid had shared his beer with at the bar, and his wife. A staff of hosts was going around from table to table, filling the champagne glasses for the toast as the wedding party, parents of the bride and groom and finally the couple themselves were introduced and ushered in amid music and applause. After a toast by the best man, the hosts returned to take orders as small talk dominated the room. 'Isn't her gown lovely?' 'What a handsome young man.' 'I'm sure they'll be happy together.'

"I think the carnations are fake," Sid whispered loud enough for Cliff to hear. Upon a discreet closer inspection, Cliff said, "They're not fake, they're silk."

"I hope your folks didn't sink too much into this gig," Sid said while looking around the hall for the old couple from the church but instead finding Kid Blimp. He started breathing hard and decided he needed another drink. His new drinking buddy, Peter Sampson, accepted the invitation to join him. Cliff stayed behind, fielding questions from the rest of the table. They were all surprised to discover they were sitting with the bride's brother, well, half-brother he explained. No one knew how to ask why all the family wasn't sitting together. It didn't bother Cliff. He knew they weren't a close family. In fact, he felt it was better this way, certainly better than putting on a show by acting like they were all intimately connected. The feeling he had experienced during his mother's visit was short lived. But he was happy for Priscilla. After all, it was her wedding day.

He figured they'd eat and then he'd circulate and say good bye to his parents and brothers and wish Curt and Priscilla well one more time, maybe sneak in a dance or two if he really had to, then he and Sid would be on their way. He could see Sid was only mingling with Mr. Sampson and the bartender and was probably not having a good time, anyway.

Dinner was served just as Sid and Sampson returned to the table. Mrs. Sampson shot her husband a you're-drinking-too-much-again stare while Sid sat down and happily dug into his stuffed capon. What little conversation of any note there was during the meal existed mostly between Sid, Sampson and occasionally Cliff. The other members of the table joined in when Sheila arrived, making the rounds as the bride and groom should have been doing. She greeted everyone while standing at Cliff's side, giving him a hug or a touch as much out of affection as for something to do with her hands. Even she was frazzled, trying to keep up appearances for this long. Sid complimented her on her dress and she welcomed the chance to comment on it rather than come up with any more of the ad lib pleasantries she was spreading everywhere else.

After dinner, Cliff momentarily parted company with Sid to make his final good byes.

"You mean you're not going to stay here and hold my hand?"

"You're a big boy now, Sid. You can hold your own hand. I'm going to say good bye to everybody."

"You don't have to do that, do you?"

"It's expected," Cliff said in a regal tone.

"What say we mingle at the bar, Lasvistas?" Sampson said with a chuckle in his voice and an empty scotch and soda in his hand, so suave he almost made Sid sick. But it was a good idea.

"What say we do," he agreed.

"Be right back, hon," Sampson assured his wife who pouted but didn't want to make a scene.

It was three deep at the tiny bar, but the bartender spotted his steadiest customers and slipped a scotch and a beer back to them.

"You're pretty friendly with Clifford, aren't you?" Sampson said, sticking a finger under his collar to give himself room to breathe. Sid already had his tie off and inside the hidden pocket he'd found inside his new suit.

"Yeah, he's a good guy." Both men's eyes were looking around the room as they talked.

"Now that's odd. Everyone always thought he was a bit of a chump."

Sid liked Sampson. Like himself, anyone who drank and talked like that didn't belong here, either.

"He's not a chump," Sid said just the same, turning his eyes on Sampson who was swimming at the bottom of his scotch.

"All right, no offense," Sampson conceded. "It's just that you're a strange pair, that's all I meant."

"I suppose opposites attract," was all Sid said, not wanting to waste any wisdom on this guy.

Mrs. Sampson approached in the middle of the third scotch and insisted on dancing.

"But darling, there's no music. Oh yes, there it is," Sampson corrected himself, realizing the buzzing in his ears came from the twelve piece band dragging Tie a Yellow Ribbon through melodic mud. "Hold this." He handed his drink to Sid as his wife led him to the dance floor. Sid felt sorry for her. She seemed like such a nice young woman, certainly more deserving of a man better than Sampson, whom Sid did not expect to see again.

The beer had shaved the uneasiness off his own mood a while ago. He tried to find a hip looking-group, but no one appeared to fit that description. He found a conversation had begun around him as several men at the bar, who undoubtedly had dumped their wives like Sampson, started getting acquainted.

"I love an open bar," said the man standing right next to Sid.

"I used to have shares in a distilling company but I got out. The market was getting too tight for me," said another.

"You ought to look into real estate. That's solid investing. People will always be buying property."

"It's a shame they got married. They could have saved thousands if they just lived together." This was meant as a joke, and it did elicit a few laughs, but not from Sid.

"I've got a ton wrapped up in pharmaceutical engineering. I guess you could say I'm into drugs." Well, that was just about the funniest thing they had heard all day. Then Sid joined in.

"I just opened my own office. I'm a gynecologist, I'm into puss…"

"Sid! There you are. I might have known you'd be here when I couldn't find you at the table. I wanted you to get another chance to meet my sister," Cliff surprised Sid from behind.

"Hello, Mr. Lasvistas," Priscilla said.

"Oh, please, it's Sid." He was caught totally off guard. "Would you like to dance?" He didn't know what else to say.

"Yes, I'd love to." Neither did she.

"Excuse us," Sid said, smiling at Cliff who wanted to dance with his sister, well, half-sister you know, after the introduction. It was now Cliff's turn to stand at the bar. People kept asking him, 'Aren't you the bride's brother?'. He answered only 'Yes' a dozen times and left because everyone insisted on buying him a drink. From an open bar, even. He was more interested in watching Sid dancing so smoothly with his pleasantly surprised sister. People recognized the bride, of course, but no one knew who the debonair fellow was, gliding with her across the dance floor. Other couples were wafting out of their way and almost yielded the floor to them before the song ended. They actually drew applause. Cliff was stunned. Sid was really a magnificent dancer.

There were too many others who wanted to dance with the bride, so they parted ways after many thanks and an innocent kiss on the cheek. Before Sid could even make it back to the bar, Sheila had intercepted him and sure enough, Sid was right back out on the floor with her. Cliff couldn't believe his eyes. Sampson came by and got them both a drink.

"Looks like your buddy has become the life of the party," he said, gulping down his drink.

"Yeah. Here, hold this." Cliff handed him back the drink.

"Of course," Sampson said as Cliff made his long way back to the table, stopping to acknowledge anyone who recognized him. Before the band finished playing the song, someone had cut in and Sid was now dancing with a girl Cliff didn't even know. He reached his table, empty save for Mrs. Sampson.

"Please, call me Carrie," she said when Cliff addressed her.

"Looks like we've both been stood up, eh?" Cliff tried to be light hearted.

"Yes," she managed a grin. "Mr. Lasvistas is quite a dancer." Cliff couldn't help but notice as her eyes wandered over towards the bar.

"Can I get you a drink?" he asked, almost making Carrie cry. Cliff realized his mistake too late and apologized. They spoke a little while the band destroyed 'Feelings', 'New York, New York' and 'The Way We Were'. The next song began and Sid actually had to fight off three women to get back to the table. It made for quite a scene. Cliff was anxious to talk to him.

"May I have this dance?" He came up behind Carrie and touched her lightly on the shoulder. Nothing could compare with the excited, grateful expression on her face as Sid led her to the dance floor while so many other women just watched. They danced that song as well as the next three, all slow dances, but Sid had to excuse himself when the band tried 'The Pennsylvania Polka'.

"I don't do polkas," he apologized to Carrie.

"That's okay, neither do I," she laughed.

"Do I have to dance with you too, if I want to talk to you?" Cliff asked him.

"We could, but people would talk. Besides, who would lead?"

"Where did you learn to dance like that?"

"I don't know, but the only part of high school I ever went to regularly was the dances."

Carrie was thrilled with Sid and even asked Cliff to go get her that drink just to be alone with him. Here, Cliff brings Sid along as his guest, and he's playing waiter while Sid makes a big splash with everyone. Cliff almost hit a woman who complimented him on his friend's ballroom expertise.

When they finally left, Sid said good bye to more people than Cliff did, with a special farewell to Carrie. He hated like hell to leave her, especially with the likes of Sampson, but he knew it would be foolish to entertain any of the other notions floating around in his head.

Back home, there was no mirrored ball or dance floor, just the streetlamp and the bench. Sid and Cliff sprawled out, looking like a couple of well dressed bums. Sid was distracted. He even turned down a beer Cliff offered him, forcing Cliff to drink from both bottles. Sid smoked a homeroll and toyed with his tie which he'd pulled out of his pocket. Actually it was Cliff's tie, as he'd forgotten to buy one when he'd picked up the suit last week. The silence might have gone on all night if Corky hadn't pulled up in his van.

"Jeez, I didn't know this was a formal affair. I'll go put on some socks."

"You don't even own any socks," Sid said as Corky approached Cliff and said "Thanks." Cliff gave him one of his beers. He remained standing, clamped the bottle between his forearm and stomach and started to rummage through a small brown paper bag he was holding. He decided to set the beer down before he dropped it.

"Anybody got a match?" Sid asked. He'd been chain smoking his homerolls and had put the last one out before he remembered he had one more left. He'd started rolling his own cigarettes so he wouldn't smoke so much, having to roll each and every one he wanted. Now it was becoming a pain in the ass because he had to set aside some time each day, his own Twenty Minute Workout he called it, to roll a day's worth of smokes ahead of time.

Corky shuffled through the totally empty pockets of his ragged camouflage army jacket as Cliff pulled out a pack he'd taken from the wedding. 'Joined this day in holy matrimony, September twenty third, nineteen hundred and eighty two, Priscilla and Curtis' it read. Cliff lit Sid's last cigarette for him and Sid laid back again in thought. Corky began to pull jelly beans out of the bag one by one and tossed each into the air. The first one came down and missed his open mouth. In fact, it barely brushed his bearded, upturned face.

"What's up, Sidney?" Corky asked. No response. "He must be all shook up. He hates being called Sidney," he said in a moment of candor to Cliff. He tossed another jelly bean. His mouth was still empty.

"I think he just had too much to drink," Cliff said as if Sid wasn't even in their presence, which in a way he wasn't. Cliff wanted to say something, anything to snap him out of his uncharacteristic trance.

"Sid, your beard's on fire."

"It's a goatee," was all he got out of him.

"Aha, he is awake." Corky tossed some more jelly beans. Not even a near miss.

"Sid, what's the matter?" Again, silence.

"Oh my, I know what's wrong," Corky said in almost a playful tone, suddenly realizing the trouble from the look on his friend's face.

"Oh my Mai," Sid said, taking a deep drag on his cigarette. He stood up, crushed his butt and walked wordlessly towards the house. Cliff stayed behind and watched Corky miss all those jelly beans.

"You're not very good at that, are you?"

"Shh, I'm practicing."

Cliff finished his beer and watched Corky practice, the only thing in his mouth after each throw being a curse.

"Are you going to drink that?" Cliff pointed to Corky's beer on the curb.

"Naw, go ahead."

Cliff bent down and grabbed the beer, noticing at the same time there wasn't a single stray jelly bean in the street at Corky's feet. He looked up mistrustfully. Corky just smiled.

"I think I'll go in now." Cliff backed away. He hoped Sid would be more talkative now.

"He won't talk to anyone right now. But here, take these." He handed the bag to Cliff. "He likes the black ones the best."

"You sure you don't want to practice anymore?"

"Naw, they say practice makes perfect, but who wants to be perfect?"

Cliff went in and Corky sat down on the bench. He stole a few sidelong glances and checked once more to be sure Cliff was inside. Impishly, he reached into his breast pocket, which had been hanging limply open the whole time, and started eating jelly beans.

15

The men who worked on Sid's house would remember this particular job for a long time to come. After more than five months of steady work, usually with a skeleton crew, not one but two fires, countless drunken afternoons on free beer and one certain afternoon spent posing with a naked girl, it was no longer summer but early October. On an unseasonably warm afternoon, Sid and Corky started moving Sid's things back into his house. Cliff came home around noon from his classes, which he'd been attending regularly, to help with the heavier stuff. He thought he'd take a shot and ask Sid if he would consider leaving Maivina behind, not expecting a positive response. He did not get one. Sid did promise to draw him something someday as winter always used to be his favorite time of year to sketch.

There wasn't much to move. They might've had some trouble with the bed and frame if Corky hadn't been there to help. Mr. H. was also on hand, but they made him do more supervising than even he cared to do.

"Just because I'm an old man doesn't mean I'm totally useless, you know."

"Just be quiet and tell us where to put this, will you?" Sid said as he stole Mr. H.'s cap.

"Is this guy giving you a hard time, Frank?" It was Ben, stopping by to see if the work was to Sid's liking.

"No more than usual, Ben, no more than usual," he said, packing his pipe.

"How's it look, Sid?" Ben asked. He hadn't gotten the chance to talk to Sid since the job was completed earlier in the week.

"Hey, it's great, Ben. It was great the first time you rebuilt it and this time it's even better."

"You never did tell me what happened with that first fire," Ben hinted.

Sid made up a lie about fire inspector's reports and faulty wiring. He didn't expect Ben to believe it, which he didn't.

"I suppose," Ben declined. He knew he wasn't going to get anything out of Sid but he felt like trying anyway. He really didn't have too much cause to be suspicious. The house was done, Sid's checks had all cleared the bank and everything was in perfect order. "Guys, this is getting heavy," Corky said, waiting just inside the front door with one end of a massive headboard balanced in his hands.

They packed it back in with the rest of Sid's things. While Bump and Grind romped around their old home (Goddamnit the Cat was missing as usual), Sid pulled down the pictures from Orifice which the workers had taped and pinned up everywhere.

That night was spent not out at the curb but in Sid's living room. Barbara wasn't around and Mr. H. turned in early, so they missed Cliff's dinner. He had thrown a mess of stuffed cabbages in a crock pot that morning and now they went down just fine. After the late dinner, Sid showed Cliff how to roll a cigarette and got him started on smoking. It would take a while to grow on him after the novelty wore off, but just like beer, he would develop a craving for it.

Corky, who was still spending his nights in his van despite the dropping temperatures, went to bed an hour before Mickey came on. This left Cliff and Sid alone in the living room, passing time. By the time Mickey came on, Cliff wasn't listening to the music so much as he was trying to roll another good cigarette. His first one was good, but it appeared to be an accident he couldn't repeat. Sid had taught him to roll by placing the paper in a dollar bill. He tried rolling a couple without the dollar with no luck at all. He switched back to using the bills, a ten to be exact, and even Alexander Hamilton smiled when it came out perfect.

"Sid, look, you just have to use bigger bills," he said, tamping the stray ribbons of tobacco that hung out the ends like Sid had showed him. The apprentice roller held up his work to show his teacher, but Sid just grunted and shifted in his chair, fast asleep.

Cliff was confused. He lit his homeroll with one of Sid's stick matches, the strike-anywhere kind, ignorant of how raw his tongue was from smoking for three straight hours. He even inhaled once or twice. He realized for the first time that he wasn't home. He took a few puffs and thought about it. This was not his own home but Sid's, and although he knew he was welcome, he still felt uncomfortable somehow. As easy as it was for Sid to move into Cliff's house, it seemed just as easy to move back out again. He couldn't recall Sid ever even saying thank you, but that didn't really matter much. He just didn't understand why he felt so much like he was alone in a stranger's house, the same feeling an intruder might get before he's absolutely sure there's nobody home once he's inside. He choked back a cough, anxious about not waking Sid. He didn't want to have to explain why he was going home. He left an empty bottle sitting in Sid's lap and turned off the lights, but not before saying good night to Maivina, once again hanging in her old spot on the wall.

Things went smoothly in the weeks that followed, the only major change aside from Sid's change of address being that he dropped out of his glass blowing class. He finally convinced Corky, when he was there, to spend his nights indoors as the weather was turning colder. Bump and Grind spent their days eating, sleeping and playing in the piles of dead leaves Cliff had so carefully raked, and burying bones to be dug up next spring. Cliff spent most of his time studying his school work, often with Sid's help. He felt he had a right to some extra help because he wasn't cutting any classes and he was handing in all his work on time. His work load, as light as it was, still weighed him down, so when an early snowstorm dumped eighteen inches on them one day in November, he cut loose. School was closed for a day and a half due to impassable roads, so he took the whole week off. At Barbara's suggestion, they all went to Tammerlane Park for a picnic. Just as people can yearn for a snowball fight in July, so did they want beach balls and barbecues in the snow. And that's exactly what they got.

Sid dug out a hibachi which was hardly ever used, along with some charcoal and a near empty can of lighter fluid. For some unknown reason, Corky did have a beach ball in his van. No one thought anything of it. Sid even brought along some sand. It was in a little glass jar labeled 'Regis Harbor, New Jersey, USA', part of an international soil collection he'd started and abandoned all in the same year. He had eight such bottles of dirt, five of them from foreign countries, and would've had more had certain customs officials with raised eyebrows not taken them. They invariably pegged Sid as the suspicious type and searched his bags, confiscating the dirt on the pretense it might spread non-indigenous soil microbes. Sid looked into the situation to find past incidents of accidental transport of such things, but his research only turned up information about Japanese beetles reaching this continent on infested cherry trees, English sparrows escaping from their cages en route to a zoo in Michigan and armadillos from South America falling off a circus wagon as the convoy moved from town to town where the poor little critters were part of the freak show. All interesting tidbits to Sid, but no dope on his dirt. So he resolved to sneak it in, sometimes in his shoes, his pockets, even once inside a camera. He clandestinely became the sole successful dirt smuggler in the world. Methods have been devised to sniff out drugs and metals with various instruments, but the detector hasn't been made that could stop Sid from smuggling anywhere from half an ounce to a full half pound once, brought in from Germany, disguised as dried mud on and in his boots.

As usual, the reasons why were vague, but the sand from Jersey had been an easy job and it did lend to the atmosphere. Sid let Billy carry it on the way to the park and he almost dropped it out of the Mustang when he pointed to a half-built house in yet another new development. Its construction had been halted by the early snowfall.

"Sid house, see?" Billy said with a voice and intuition that only a preschooler can possess. Everyone cracked up. They were frozen when they arrived because Sid insisted it was summertime and kept the top down, open to a sky so bright it was hard to see with the glare off the snow. Corky and Cliff unloaded the trunk while Barbara poured some hot chocolate as Sid straightened his sunglasses and undid another button on his Hawaiian shirt.

"You must be freezing," Barbara had to say. Sid stood stupidly in boots, jeans with thermal underwear and his shirt with parrots and palm trees all over it. He waved his arms and kept hopping around to stay warm.

"It's summertime, I'm roasting!"

"I think you're losin' it, man," Corky said, removing his gloves to make a better snowball. It hit Sid in the shoulder. He had to jump around even more to shake out the crystal bits that had splintered off and fallen down his shirt.

"Wait a minute, this is summertime, where did all this snow come from?" He eyed each flake suspiciously. "You! What are you doing here?" He pointed to any one of the millions of flakes on the ground and assumed its voice, a cooperative, weak-willed whine. "Well, I was a drop in this biology project, see, and like um, I, the Kid was in summer school and I was like a dispersing medium for his amoeba until he spilled me. I didn't even evaporate until three days later. I just floated around in the atmosphere for weeks and weeks. I didn't do nothing, honest. It started to get colder and colder so I ducked into this cloud and the next thing I know I'm crystallized and falling to the ground. I crashed here with everyone else and there's talk we're going to melt and I'm scared!"

No one paid any attention to Sid, so he joined Corky at the trunk and pulled out his surprise, a volleyball net. He and Corky set it up while Barbara fired up the hibachi. A ranger stopped by in his official forest ranger car and before he could say anything, Sid called out, "It's okay, we have our day passes from The Home right here," at which

Corky laughed and Barbara explained that they'd let Sid out for the day to get some fresh air. The good-natured ranger humored them with only a hint of disbelief. Sid added that they would save him a hot dog.

Cliff thought it was terrible they had to justify themselves. So what if they were acting a little off center? What was it to him? He wouldn't have approached them if they had been building a snowman.

"You'd probably be boring too if you were a park ranger," Sid responded to Cliff's ideas.

"Maybe he's just jealous because he can't have fun like us because he's working," Barbara suggested.

"That might be it," Sid agreed, not wanting to pursue the point.

"Anyway, I'm glad you invited him back for a hot dog, Sid," Barbara said.

"Speaking of food," Corky said as he grabbed a roll and attacked the grill.

"Just save us some, Corker," Sid advised. Corky handed the first hot dog to Barbara.

"For the cook." He handed it to her with all the pomp of a king bestowing a title on a knight.

"Why thank you sir." Barbara faked a curtsy.

"Now me." Corky, buns in hand, snagged three hot dogs, two for himself and one for Billy.

"Thank Corky, Billy," Barbara instructed her son.

"Thank you, UnCorky," Billy's fragmented vocabulary squeaked.

"Oh no, what's this? Uncle Corky?" Sid started to tease.

"Aw, be quiet. I like it." Corky smiled as Billy tried to fit the whole end of the hot dog between his little lips.

Cliff opted for a hamburger, as did Sid. More meat had to be slung up on the fire. They never before appreciated the fact that hot dogs and hamburgers were hot. Steam rose from the cooked meat as Sid reached out for Barbara's hot dog.

"Just wanted to warm my hands on your buns. Oh, ah," he moaned.

"Get away, you pervert!" Barbara snatched her sandwich back.

"So soft, yet firm," Sid sighed like a paperback romance.

"This is great. Whose idea was it, anyway?" Cliff asked.

"Mine," Barbara smiled.

"Your Dad should be here."

"No, you kids go on ahead," Sid imitated Mr. H.'s response when they invited him along.

Corky bounced the volleyball on Billy's head, walking around him in circles as Billy laughed and chewed on his first hot dog, Corky his third. He then started tossing the ball over from the far side of the net, rushing underneath to help Billy hit it back over. On the last pass, Corky got snagged in the net and brought the whole thing down. Billy laughed and pointed at him, figuring that was the way volleyball was supposed to be played.

"Hey, this isn't a proper snowbecue without one thing," Sid realized.

"What's that?"

"Snow burgers, of course!" Sid picked up a handful of the white stuff and made a flat patty from it. Billy, when he realized he wasn't going to get hit with a snowball, climbed through a belly high drift to get a closer look. He watched curiously as Sid laid two snow burgers on the grill. Barbara picked him up so he could see the dripping chunks fall through the grate, snuffing out half the fire.

"All gone." Billy reached out to touch the hibachi. Barbara pulled him away.

"Let's do it again!" Sid picked up some more snow.

"Yo pal, you already killed half the fire. You have to save some to cook that hot dog you promised to your ranger friend here," Cliff said, referring to the ranger's car as he drove past without stopping. Sid slapped up some more hot dogs and tried to wave him down.

"I guess he doesn't get as hungry as I thought he might, driving around in his car all day." Sid stared after him as Cliff rolled the hot dogs to the hot side of the fire. Corky and Billy resumed their volleyball game without a net. Cliff grabbed Sid's keys and popped a tape into the tape deck. "How can people be so senseless as to not know when to have a good time?"

"Sid, he's working, this is his job. He's probably a very nice person. Stop picking on him," Barbara said.

"Or he doesn't like hot dogs," Cliff added as a possibility.

"If he is such a nice person, you wouldn't know it to meet him, if you could meet him."

"Give the guy a break, Sid. He's only doing what he's supposed to do," Barbara argued. Sid never bought that line.

"I'm with Sid," Corky said, taking a break at the grill. "Even if you're only doing what you're supposed to do, you should still let people know where you're coming from." He swallowed half a hot dog whole, wiped his mouth on his coat sleeve and returned to play with Billy.

"I think I like this music," Cliff said, sitting in the front seat of the car, shielding himself from the breeze to roll a cigarette.

"I just don't get it." Sid was sincerely troubled. "It's as if people like to be unhappy." Cliff rolled his cigarette and his eyes.

"What makes you think the park ranger isn't happy?"

"He'd be happy if he was over here eating hot dogs with us."

"That's your idea of happiness at this particular moment, Sid, not his. His ideal afternoon might be spent riding around this park, watching the snow and avoiding some lunatics who are pretending it's Labor Day weekend."

"Are you trying to tell me he'd be driving around in circles through a park which probably bores him to tears by now if he didn't need the money they're paying him to do it?" Sid asked incredulously.

"Maybe. Maybe he's willing to put up with it instead of doing something else for a living."

"Sure," Sid said, trying to end the discussion.

"His solution is the World Become One theory. You know, everybody gets what they need, no more haves and have-nots, all that impossible crap. Whoa, sorry, Barb." Corky knew Barbara didn't appreciate him saying 'crap' in front of Billy. "Then again," he continued, "I've never seen him in a soup kitchen ladling minestrone out to homeless people."

"It's not impossible." Sid was going off again. "Just improbable. Too many people oppose it. They'd rather have their possessions and hoard them from anyone else who really needs them. That's the real reason why the park ranger is here. He's not looking at the snow, he's an authority figure. He's here to stop people from using the park in ways that have been deemed 'inappropriate'. They don't let people do what they want, so now they have to protect themselves from people who want to fight back. The ranger makes sure nobody brings beer into the park, that nobody sets off a pipe bomb in the rest rooms…"

Cliff wasn't impressed. He couldn't get over how corny it was starting to sound. He could see Barbara was warming up to the subject, and even Corky had something to say. They were all listening to a man who, among other things, stole a bench from the very park they were now picnicking in.

"…oh, I don't know, I just get so damn disgusted. Sometimes I'd like to just live barefoot down on the farm if I didn't have to worry about someone stealing my carrots or kicking me off to build condos or putting me on TV as a human interest story. I just want to be happy, is that such a crime? Aw heck, are there any more hamburgers left?"

"Nope, just hot dogs."

"Story of my life," Sid gave in.

"If you really want to be happy," Cliff was going to have his say, "look over there." He pointed a cautious finger across the field to the wooded border. A buck and three does were alternately chewing bark off the trees and sniffing through the snow which covered their food.

"I read somewhere once that woodland creatures just love hot dogs," Sid said, transfixed in his spot.

"You did not, you're making it up." Barbara watched the deer like everyone else, even Billy.

Sid almost burned his bare hand reaching for a weenie on the hot grill, his eyes never leaving the gentle deer a hundred yards away.

"Come on," he whispered. He was a sight to see, leading them across the field ever so slowly, his hot dog leading the way. The deer were now standing silent and still, staring with their big, dark eyes. With a gleam in his own eyes, brighter than Billy's, Sid plodded ahead, making more noise by telling everyone to be quiet than they were making in the first place. They hadn't made it but thirty feet or so when the deer bolted for the cover of the woods. With a yell, Sid led a frantic, futile chase after them. Billy was far behind, falling down in the deep snow, his mother losing herself and running on ahead. Each time he fell, he'd get back up and laugh so hard at the grown ups who were acting his age.

Cliff, who had stayed behind in the car, took a straight-faced drag from his homeroll and watched through the smoke as he exhaled slowly.

16

All the way home, Cliff wanted to roll another cigarette. The wind was too strong for him with the top down. He seized the opportunity when Sid pulled into a convenience store for provisions. Corky went in with him.

"You should have helped us chase the deer, Cliff. Did you see Sid pointing with that stupid hot dog?" Barbara laughed. Cliff pulled out a rolling paper and laid it across a ten dollar bill on his thigh.

"I knew the deer would outrun you guys. They have more legs," he answered, distracted by the scene in the store. Sid was poring over a magazine. Corky was looking over Sid's shoulder with equal concern. It caught Cliff's attention only because they seemed so still, so engrossed in whatever it was they were reading. He watched as he dug out some tobacco, Sid's tobacco, and the clerk told Sid to buy it or leave it. Corky turned to him and must have said something intimidating, because the clerk backed off and stood next to his register.

"What are they doing in there?" Barbara had been watching also.

"I don't know." Cliff returned his attention to his cigarette, seeming to have forgotten how to roll. He was still trying when they came out. Corky held the magazine, not paid for, rolled up in his hand. He shuffled next to Sid with his head bowed, kicking at the cement like a soon to be losing pitcher kicking at the mound before the last pitch is thrown.

Sid looked at Barbara and Billy, then at Cliff as he stood directly in front of the car. His arms hung limp at his sides.

Corky walked around Sid and towards the car without looking at anybody. He was in before Sid even made a move to follow. He carefully stepped off the curb and leaned with both arms on the outside of the door Corky had left opened for him. His face was turned away, trying to gather up words as if they were written somewhere on a billboard within view. Of course they weren't, so Sid dove behind the wheel, gunned the engine and took off. Cliff looked back at Corky, evasive as ever, then gave a questioning gaze to Barbara, who returned it. They were well down the road before anyone spoke.

"Well?" Cliff drew the syllable out into a sentence, expectantly, as if one word could pull an answer out of them. But the answer was in the magazine Corky wasn't about to let go of. He hastily pulled it away from Billy's playful reach.

"Give me a minute, will you? I've got to think," was Sid's response. That minute turned into however many minutes it took to get home. It was a quiet ride, aside from the wind blowing over them, making it difficult to be heard anyway.

When they pulled into Sid's driveway, they found a middle aged man in a black leather jacket, dress shirt and tie peeking into the house through the front window. He quickly regained his composure and directed a second man with a large leather carrying case and two cameras around his neck to start taking pictures. The man approached them as a car salesman does the minute you pull into the lot. He was the first of many to come.

"Hello sir, I'm Harry Cretz, I'm with an independent..." He stopped when Corky literally jumped out of the back seat. A single right cross brought the man down. He made the mistake of trying to get back up. Corky put him down for good.

Sid also jumped out and chased the photographer across the front lawn and brought him down with a well executed tackle. He started ripping rolls of film out of the cameras and canisters, pinning the man face down in the snow with a knee in the small of his back.

Corky went to help him, leaving Harry bloody and moaning beside the car. Cliff leaned over to look at him, curled up in a fetal position in the snow, blood issuing forth between the fingers covering his bludgeoned face. Barbara noticed the crumpled magazine Corky had left on the seat.

"Who sent you? How did you know where to find me?"

"Talk, shitbreath."

As Sid and Corky interrogated the photographer, Cliff sat there transfixed, but Barbara had something even more interesting.

"Cliff, look at this," she said slowly, peeling open the pages so he could see it all. It was the December issue of Licks and Riffs. The title of the article read, 'The Kid's Allright'.

Below that in smaller letter it read, 'Discovered in Jersey bar' with an arrow pointing to the next page. It contained some text, but most of the page was plastered over by two nearly identical photographs. They were prominently labeled 'Courtesy of Orifice Publications, Inc.'. Both were copies of the photo of Sid in the bar where Suzi was performing. The first one was untouched, but the second one had his goatee shaded in, giving it the appearance of a full beard. He looked like he did when Cliff first met him. Barbara turned the page to reveal more photos of the same bearded one on a concert stage, colored lights against a dark background, guitar in hand, singing into a microphone with sweat flooding his eyes and matting his hair to his forehead.

Cliff didn't need to read the text, there would be time for that. He looked up at Sid, now making careful strides back to the car. He looked frightened and ran his hand back through his hair. Corky was stomping what was left of the photographer and his equipment. Sid looked at his friends in the Mustang. He haphazardly brushed the snow off his pants then suddenly appeared as if he was going to cry.

"Hey, listen up, guys. Ha, I bet you're sort of wondering like, what this is all about." His breathing was spastic and he started looking around again, not wanting to meet their eyes. "I didn't mean to, I didn't want to lie, I'm, just, I'm all fucked up here, sorry…"

Sid turned his back to them and they both got out of the car. Barbara hugged him from behind, almost making him totally break down. He turned and collapsed in her embrace.

"What's this all about, Sid?" Cliff was leaning on the car, standing next to a mangled Harry. Sid couldn't answer yet. Cliff felt all alone, and he also felt betrayed. There was so much about himself that Sid chose to hide. That bothered him. He'd told more about himself to Sid than to anyone else, ever, he'd felt more comfortable being around Sid, he even shared his house with the man, and now he finds out all the while Sid was doing nothing more than hiding out. "What did you think we'd do, tell on you? You must trust us a whole hell of a lot, pal."

"Cliff," Sid started to say.

"I mean, where the hell are you coming from? That's one of your phrases, isn't it? We don't know anything about you. What gives you the right to come in here and treat us like this?"

"Cliff, please. I, I…"

"I don't want to hear it. I've never been made out to be such a horse's ass in my life. You come waltzing in, turn my whole fucking world inside out with your little games without taking anybody else into consideration. Well how about the rest of us? How do you think I feel, huh? How about it, Kid? You think I like being used, being lied to? You Goddamned bastard, you…"

"Cliff!" Barbara shouted at him and he was silenced. Sid was beyond words. He felt too guilty already to realize Cliff was being more than a little too rough on him. Cliff cut across the snow to his own house. Corky approached him.

"And you fuck off." He pushed Corky's chest and lived to tell about it.

Inside, his house was dark. He locked the door. Tracking snow on the carpet, he laid down on the couch and wiped cold sweat off his forehead. He stood back up, ripped his coat off and fired it through the room, knocking over a lamp. The flash from the bursting bulb jolted him. He ran over as if he had time to catch it. He poked mindlessly at the crumpled shade for a few minutes before he decided it was beyond repair and tossed it back down.

He was glad to at least be alone now. He desperately wanted to know how to feel, and more importantly to figure it out for himself. He knew he had really let Sid have it. He wondered if he overreacted, maybe because of the way Sid's little speech at the park sort of set the mood for the way he was feeling towards him when he saw the magazine. This was just a possibility now, although he would realize later it was probably true. It didn't seem to serve as much of an explanation for his actions right now, though. He could have just as easily been sympathetic towards the situation. Barbara certainly was. But no, he was genuinely pissed off. Omitting the truth about his past was exactly the same as lying. Cliff had always believed they were closer than that. The worst he ever did was to hide a stupid comic book from him. Part of him wanted to go right back over there, not to fight, not to apologize, but just to find out what was happening, or more correctly what had happened, in the past, with Sid. A musician? Sid didn't even hum to himself, let alone sing. Maybe he wasn't a very good musician. But Licks and Riffs thought he was. Then again, they also did an article on that rooster guy. And hey, there was that article in an older issue of that same magazine about someone named Kid! Shit, it was right there, he remembered, he did, in his own two hands.

So maybe Sid was a musician, used to be a musician, whatever. It did explain a few things. Maybe that's why he never seemed to be short of cash. But hell, by that logic, Cliff could appear to be a former successful musician, astronaut, brain surgeon, bank robber, anything at all, too. He wondered if it might not be a bad idea to be a former successful friend of Sid's. He had to think about that.

Twice there was a knock at the door and twice he ignored it. He heard a shouting match taking place somewhere out front and he refused to check it out. There was a time and place for sulking in this world, and by God, this was the time and the place. He could use a homeroll, though.

"He had no right to talk to you that way," Barbara said. She and Sid sat in his living room while Corky fed the dogs.

"No, he's right. I've treated you all pretty shitty, shittily, aw, you know what I mean."

"Don't worry about me, Sid. I didn't even know who The Kid was until I saw that article."

"Yeah, I wasn't too well known, I suppose."

"But why did you run away? And what are you doing here, of all places? Didn't you like what you were doing? Why did you become a musician? Is that where you got all your money? You're in trouble with the police, aren't you?"

"Yo, hey, Barbara, slow down. The game is called Twenty Questions, but you're not supposed to hit me with them all at once."

Before Sid got the chance to answer Question Number One, there was a knock at the door. Sid jumped up and peeked out from behind the curtain. "Here we go," he mumbled. "I think the scene earlier today plus the one you're about to see might make the game Nineteen Questions. Hey, Cork!"

Corky appeared with a forty pound bag of dog food slung over his shoulder. "Yes Boss?"

"Stop eating for a second and dispose of the gentleman at the front door, would you?" Barbara was pleased to see Sid hadn't lost his sense of humor.

"I would be delighted, sir." Corky opened the door. The man outside pretended not to notice the bag on his shoulder.

"Excuse me, my name is Barney Saxon. Is this Twenty River Road?"

"Why yes, it is."

"Great, I'm looking for The Kid. I was told he…"

Corky always did have a certain style about him. Saxon was cut short and knocked flat when Corky swung the bag across his chest. It burst open and buried the toppled Saxon with crunchy nuggets that form their own gravy when water is added that dogs just love.

"Thank you, Cork."

"Anytime, Boss."

"Oh Barbara, forgive me, I'm so sorry."

"It's okay, Sid. Really, it is."

"No, no, I forgot. I'd like you to meet Myron Perelle, my drummer."

"Your what? You're kidding, right?"

"He was the only other steady member of my band. They insisted I used set musicians, but nobody can…"

Barbara had to cut him off. "Now before you get started, you have to assume I know nothing about music, unless it's trumpet music. And even then…"

"Okay, I got it. Set musicians are the guys who play for anybody and everybody in the studio. They're very talented, they play well, they always have work and the best of them can charge whatever they want, but they're just not Corky. I had one rough time convincing my producers to let me use him on the album."

"Do you have a copy of it around here?" Barbara was excited about this side of Sid she'd just discovered. She felt like his very own personal groupie, only she didn't know squat about his music. The same was true of many people who had yet to show up.

"Well, sort of. You remember where it is, don't you, Myron?"

"Sure, Sidney." Corky started shuffling through Sid's records.

"I don't have the record sleeve but I think there's a picture of it in that article." Sid was trying to remain subdued, to not get worked up over what finally really did happen. Hiding out in suburban America sounded like such a good idea, too. Now that his secret was out, he wanted to talk about it. It wasn't easy for him to keep quiet all this time, and he sensed that Barbara understood that. He wished he could say the same for the guy sulking next door.

Barbara remembered seeing a tiny photo of the album cover somewhere in the mangled magazine. Sid's album was called 'Smoking in Bed'. This was written across the bottom border, 'The Kid' across the top. In between was a scene of a couple mixing it up under silk sheets. Smoke billowed out from under the covers, fogging the edges. Barbara thought it was clever. Sid thought it was stupid.

Corky pulled out a copy of John Prine's 'Bruised Orange'. Sid's album was stashed inside.

"Why is it in there?"

"Paranoia, I guess. I figured nobody would look for it in there. What better place is there to hide a record than in another record jacket?"

Barbara looked at the Smoking in Bed cover again. The caption underneath said it was The Kid's only album to date, reaching sales of over two hundred and twenty thousand since its release in October '78.

"You were really worried about all this, weren't you?"

"You don't know the half of it. Of course, you will be hearing about it."

"From who?"

"Hey, I'm a hot music news story now," Sid said sarcastically. "Who do you think these guys are who are knocking on my door and looking in my windows, Jehovah's Witnesses? If they know where I am, soon everyone is going to know." Sid was suddenly quiet, as if he'd just told himself the news for the first time. "Listen, I've got a feeling this place is going to become a bunker inside of the next few days."

"A bunker? Come on, Sid. This isn't a war."

"Oh yes it is, as far as I'm concerned, anyway. Barbara, you don't know what it was like. Too many people knew who I was, and I wasn't all that popular. They'd break into my house, hide in my closets, once two guys broke into my bathroom while I was taking a crap!"

"Ah, the good old days," Corky reminisced. He opened the front door, poured a bucketful of hot water over the mess on the stoop and let the dogs eat their dinner.

"Can I ask you to go out to the store for me and pick up some provisions?" Sid asked Barbara.

"Why don't you just find a motel and hide out until you can come up with a plan?"

"Because this whole thing proves I'm no good as the fugitive type."

"You know, I was wondering why you thought you could remain undiscovered in a big house in a populated residential district like this. I mean, they could've traced anything, your mortgage, your driver's license…"

"But they didn't." Sid smiled in defense of his almost perfect plan of hiding in plain sight. Besides, his attempt to relocate to Germany didn't work out like he had planned. "It took some clown to recognize me in that photograph before they caught up to me."

"I suppose you're right," Barbara conceded.

"Listen, on your way back, try to talk Cliff into coming over. I've tried calling him but he's not answering his phone."

"Okay Sid, I'll try again." Sid slipped her some money and a verbal list of necessities, like double fudge cookies, cheese curls, frozen pizza…

"Dog food," Corky added.

"…dog food, two cases of beer, canned peaches, some TV dinners, plus anything else you can think of," he told her.

"All right, I'll go, but only if you promise to let me hear some of this when I get back," she said, checking out Sid's album. 'Farmer in the Deli', 'Necrophilia Makes Me Stiff', 'Argyle Gargoyles', 'Oh My Mai', and that was only the first side.

Sid was happy she wasn't so gaga over his music to insist on hearing it then and there. He had the sinking feeling he'd be seeing plenty of people like that soon enough. In preparation, while Barbara was gone, he and Corky went all over the house covering windows and bracing doors with the scrap wood left behind from the reconstruction. They were nailing shut an upstairs window, a window which faced Cliff's house.

"I sure hope Barbara can talk him into coming over," Sid said, staring at the house, missing the nail by a few inches, his thumb by less.

"Don't worry, he'll come around." Corky never understood what Sid saw in Cliff.

"Just come over for a little while," Barbara pleaded with Cliff. "He really wants to see you."

"Do you realize that was the first time I ever yelled at him? I lived in the same house with him for five months. I put up with him drinking milk straight from the bottle, I even kept quiet when I found a sock in the dishwasher. I never said a word until now."

"So come over and make it the last time you yell at him."

"What do you think this is, a fairy tale? It's really striking me as odd that you're taking this so casually. Tell him I'm still pissed off, tell him anything. I'll be over tomorrow."

"He thinks that might be difficult. A couple more reporters have already been there. Soon, anybody who wants to know will find out where he is. He's boarding up the windows right now."

"Preparing the ship for battle, eh?" Cliff smiled at the far fetched asininity of it all. "God," he reflected. "I can't believe he did this to us. Did you know he can't even tell his dogs apart?"

"Look Cliff, you can just drop that 'us' crap," Barbara snapped. "What kind of friend are you, anyway? You're the only one who's upset about this. You've forgotten everything Sid ever was to you because your precious pride was hurt. When you put your ego back together, you know where we are."

"I'll be over tomorrow," Cliff mumbled, not looking up at Barbara until she walked out, slamming the door behind her.

He slept straight through the night, not hearing any of the commotion next door at three AM when yet another reporter was forcibly evicted from the premises. When he pulled out of his driveway the next morning, eight teenagers were milling about on Sid's front yard which was literally trampled with footprints in the snow. It was in stark contrast to his own lawn, white and untouched but for a deep path in the snow between Sid's house and his own front door.

Cliff drove to the mall to check out the record shop there. They had just opened up and the place was mobbed with people Cliff's age and younger searching for a copy of Smoking in Bed. Unfortunately, that was obviously why Cliff was there. He tried a few more shops. The crowds were getting smaller and smaller as the few available copies soon sold out.

Similar scenes were not taking place all over. As a matter of fact, although sales did increase slightly nationwide, the only places that were deluged with customers were the nearby shops. Sid was truly a cult figure. He had no wide spread popularity. His fans were far fewer in number than those of superstars, but more focused and intense. The situation had a local flair and people were getting caught up in the excitement of a story in a nationally distributed magazine like Licks and Riffs going down in their own backyard.

Cliff got back before noon empty handed. The group in front of Sid's house had doubled. They hung out in groups of three or four, nonchalantly, as if waiting in the lobby of a movie theater for the lights to flicker. Not knowing how to do it inconspicuously, Cliff simply walked through them all unnoticed until he went up to the front door and knocked.

Some of them laughed when they saw what Cliff was doing. One said, "Hey man, they won't let you in. There's a big guy in there, he'll take your..." Corky opened the door, first just a crack, then wide enough to admit Cliff.

"Hey, he got in!" A bushy haired young man led the dash to the door. At the last second, Corky stepped out and crossed his arms. Those in the front of the pack stopped immediately, if not sooner. Those in the back stumbled ahead, pushing the crowd from behind until the bushy one was shoved into Corky who didn't even budge.

"Oh God, please, I'm sorry, I don't want to die!" He cowered and crawled away from the staring stature of Corky, who just turned and went inside again. The young coward did his best to act tough and yelled at the others for pushing him.

"I'm glad you came." Sid walked over to Cliff.

"Yeah," Cliff responded. He looked over at Barbara.

"Billy's next door with my Dad," she said.

"Yeah, Barbara filled him in on it. Would you believe he called me to ask if I needed a trumpeter in the band?"

Cliff sat down and petted one of the dogs. He didn't know what to say, so he didn't say anything. "You want some pizza?" In seconds, Sid grabbed a piece from his own plate and offered it to Cliff.

"Sure." Cliff took it. "Thanks."

"Look Cliff, I'm sorry, I shouldn't…"

"Shut up." Cliff startled everyone with a voice which sounded convincingly annoyed. They all sat there watching, waiting to see what would happen next. "So what's it like to be a rock and roll star?"

"I am not a rock and roll star." Sid sighed and Barbara laughed. Sid stole his pizza back from Cliff and took a bite.

"You're right, you're not, you're just an asshole," Cliff said as he grabbed it back.

"Okay, so I'm an asshole. I've learned to live with it and so have you, only you haven't realized it until now."

"Corky, put the record on, please?" Barbara asked. She was anxious to hear Cliff's reaction to it. While Corky was setting it up, she showed Cliff the photo of the cover in Licks and Riffs. She didn't know he'd seen it in the car the day before. This time he was amused by it.

Then there was music, beautiful music, sweet, sweet music.

"That's you?" Cliff asked ready to believe any answer he got.

"Yes."

It was an acoustic piece, a song about a girl named Mai. The chorus was announced by a little finger roll on the guitar which was heard nowhere else in the song.

> In a room full of losers
> Beggars and choosers
> What were we doing there
> You and I
> Oh my Mai, Oh my Mai
>
> -Composer now known

"Isn't that incredible?" Barbara gushed.

Cliff wasn't quite that impressed, but he didn't want to hurt Sid's feelings. "You're still an asshole."

"Cliff, try and understand me. I had to do what I did. I was tired of the run-around, I needed to get away. Maybe I didn't do it the right way, and that's my fault, but what's going on out front right now is only part of what was beginning to happen all the time."

"So what are you doing here now? How could you think for a minute that they wouldn't find you? Did you want to get caught? Why didn't you leave the country or something, start a new life somewhere? You seem to have enough money to do that, don't you?"

"He likes his questions one at a time, Cliff," Barbara told him.

"The idea of being swamped by a mob of kids doesn't particularly appeal to me, Cliff. Somebody recognized me in that picture and somebody else told where I was. It'd have to be John or Suzi. Anyway, they're out there and I'm in here and it's going to stay that way until I can figure something out."

They heard several more cars pull up, followed by someone screaming, 'We love you, Kid!'. The group was becoming a crowd, there was more pounding at the door and some people were unfurling a sign to stretch across a row of cars parked along the curb. It didn't show much imagination and it was already tiresomely repetitive. 'We Love You, Kid!' was spray painted over the patchwork sheets that made up the twenty foot long banner.

"Go away." Sid turned away from the noise and went into the kitchen for another beer. Cliff looked at the crowd through the cracks between the two by fours Corky had nailed over the front windows. He was just starting to get the picture.

"Don't you think we ought to call the cops?"

"They'll be here soon enough," Corky said.

The music changed. The beat was like a drunken band playing the Song of the Volga Boatmen. It was 'Necrophilia Makes Me Stiff'.

"What's necrophilia?" Cliff had to ask.

Corky laughed. "Erotic stimulation derived from corpses."

"Oh."

"Hey look, now we're all going to be famous." Out front, Barbara saw that a TV news van had scarcely stopped at the curb when people started to jump out of it with cameras and lights and sound equipment.

"Great, we should just make the end of the twelve o'clock news," Sid said, surveying the situation with a fresh beer in his hand.

They turned the TV on and watched. It took the crew a while to set up, what with fans jumping in front of the camera and shouting over each other to be heard through the microphone, neither of which was even turned on yet. Finally, a familiar scene appeared on the screen and the words 'Mobilcam Live' were printed below. Local reporter Tom Dauffer set the story.

"We're here outside the home of Sid Lasvistas, better known to his fans as The Kid. Until recently a rising star in the pop music industry, his disappearance two years ago was never solved and this exclusive report will no doubt shed much light on that investigation." On the screen, they flashed the two photos from L+R.

"Bob Macallum, whom we'll be speaking with later, is a resident of Newark, Delaware, and also the man who recognized his idol in this photograph which originally ran in Orifice magazine. The one on your left is a copy of how it actually appeared, and on the right is the retouched version, shading in The Kid's beard, showing him as he looked during his career." They showed some stills of Sid's concert footage with the retouched photo in the upper corner so you, the viewer, could decide.

"Gathered around me are fans from all over the area." The camera panned over them, the banner, etc. Cliff spotted his house and car in the background.

"This is strange," he whispered.

"We're going to talk to these fans, but first we're going to have a word with The Kid himself." Dauffer stepped out of frame. The camera soon caught up with him. The crowd, which had been barely less than rowdy so far, cut loose. Not only did they constantly try to get on screen and wave into the camera, they were bumping into the cameraman, evident from the helter-skelter scenery zooming across the screen. They were tripping on the tangle of cords that led back to the van and unknowingly hampering Dauffer's progress. When they found this out, they began to stand on the wires on purpose for a laugh.

Cliff looked out the window, then at the TV. It was an odd dream. What was happening on the screen was exactly what was happening in the front yard. An obvious fact, but it was right there in front of him. It was real.

"Kill the music," Sid ordered Corky, who abruptly obeyed.

"They won't let you in," a voice called out. "Look out for the big guy," said another. "I claim The Kid as my personal savior," one girl managed to grab the microphone and blurt into it. Disturbed to say the least, Dauffer finally reached the door and, crushing stray bits of dog food with his Italian loafers, knocked.

"Hello, Mr. Kid, are you in there? This is Tom Dauffer from WSBR news. Could we have a word with you?" The camera steadied and the crowd quieted down for a moment, watching the door like a rocket that failed to leave the launch pad. Sid cranked up the volume on his TV and opened the window.

"Over here, Dauffer," he shouted just as dozens of fans saw him and started screaming. But neither Sid nor the crowd made it over the airwaves. The raised volume on Sid's TV upset the sound relay with feedback, creating much the same effect as when someone gets on a call-in radio talk show and forgets to turn his radio down. All sound that was picked up by Dauffer's microphone was transmitted back to the station, broadcast to the TV sets, specifically Sid's, which was again picked up by the microphone, turning it into little more than deafening squeals and crackles. Bump and Grind, with their sensitive auditory equipment, went berserk. The crowd went wild, not knowing what was going on but liking it just the same. Inside the house, they had to cover their ears to block out the painful noise. The sound man ripped his headphones off and waved his arms around as if fighting off a swarm of bees, and the cameraman fell down while trying to catch the camera being pulled from his grip. Dauffer spazzed out. He knew Sid's actions were intentional. He was yelling about technical difficulties as if someone could hear him. This went on for some twenty seconds before his feed was finally cut off and the picture went back to the station.

"We appear to have had, uh, some problems with the sound there, in that report, I mean from Tom," the anchorman paused, "but we'll have more on that exciting story later. In other news, noted soothsayer..."

Sid turned the set off. Through the ringing in their ears they could hear Dauffer, who thought he was still on the air.

"This is Tom Dauffer reporting from the home of The Kid, live on the Mobilcam on WSBR. Cut! Get the hell away from me, all of you, you're sick! Dan, Sam, Phil, get me out of here." He turned towards the house. "I know what you did, Lasvistas. I'll get you for it, I swear, you prick!"

Uh oh, bad move. You don't cut up a man when you're surrounded by legions of his devoted fans. To make a short story even shorter, Dauffer left while hanging onto the outside of the news van without his coat, suit jacket, half his tie, microphone, glasses, wallet, watch and one ounce of blood. The van had to stop once during the getaway because Dauffer fell off under a barrage of snowballs.

"So what's it like to be a rock and roll star?" Cliff asked again soberly as the news van quickly disappeared.

"Privacy was only one of the things I was denied." They all sat in Sid's dining room that evening. The crowd had turned into a restless mob and the dining room was the quietest place in the house. The police arrived shortly after the news report and cordoned off the area. Freedom of peaceable assembly prevented any arrests, although the definition of 'peaceable' was being closely scrutinized as they spoke.

"There was always somebody who wanted something from me. An autograph, a piece of my hair, a new recording contract, always something. I made a couple bucks off the record sales even though I got ripped off in my first contract because I didn't know what I was signing."

"That's where you got all your money." Cliff realized.

"Yeah, some of it." Sid avoided telling them all about reneging on his contract, signing letters of intent with other labels, eager to add The Kid to their roster, and collecting advances against future rights and royalties. There were a number of record companies that had once dangled a check under his nose who were very interested to hear of his sudden reappearance.

"You should've gotten an agent," Barbara said.

"You would think that was a good idea, wouldn't you? I had one once. He convinced me to let him represent me because although he'd be taking a cut, he guaranteed it would be a cut from an amount bigger than anything I could get on my own, so I stood to make more money in the long run. We spent a lot of time going over the record contract he got for me, but not so much time going over my contract with him. He ended up with the bigger cut, not me." Sid looked at Cliff and Barbara, envious of what he thought was their simple lives. "See, people don't realize what goes into doing what I did. I was always coming up with lyrics and melodies. That was the only part that ever came naturally to me. Most of them stunk. The trick was, I had to take the good stuff from both sides and try to match them together. The words and the music don't always jive with each other, at least not for me. Then, as if that wasn't hard enough, I had to work in accompanying parts, instrumental and vocal. That meant changing it around, normally a lot. Sometimes when I'd finished a piece, I'd look at the words and melodies I started with, then at the finished product. I wouldn't be able to figure out how I got from one end to the other, and I wrote the thing, for crying out loud. So when I finally finished one, all that was left to do was sing it twenty times a day until I was as close to satisfied as I was going to get." Corky gave a knowing smile. "Then we'd all go into the studio and lay down our track of it, after only a million or so 'let's try it this way's and 'I want to do it again's."

"I left the mixing and engineering up to the guys in the booth. By that time, I never wanted to hear the song again. I knew that was only one song and I had to come up with at least nine for the album, preferably ten, and I had walked into the project with only three complete songs. I was so sorry I'd convinced them I had three done and three more almost finished."

"None of my friends could believe it. I couldn't believe it. I thought I was their Golden Boy. Or maybe they were just jerking me off, I don't know."

There was no stopping Sid. He'd kept it pent up for too long. "We stopped at seven songs because yours truly was going bonkers. We filled in the time by making 'Gargoyles' a longer instrumental than we'd originally planned. Now that was something." Sid paused for a moment. "If I'd had my way, the whole album would have been Argyle Gargoyles. That one I can play forever. Not a word in it. It didn't need any. It didn't happen often, but sometimes I would write some lyrics that were so damn good they just had to stand alone. I never set them to music. That would only distract from them. Gargoyles was the only time I ever wrote a melody that made me feel the same way, made me feel it needed nothing more than what it already had."

"Can I see some of your lyrics?" Barbara asked cautiously.

"They got torched in the fire. I don't think I remember any of them completely, just bits and pieces." He spoke about them like they were a lucky pair of socks he'd long since lost.

"How do you write the music?" Cliff asked. The music was what fascinated him. He'd heard Sid talk about things and assumed the lyrics were the same thing, maybe a bit more memorable, and in rhymes. He didn't know what Sid was capable of.

"How do I explain something that comes naturally to me? It's like tying your shoes. It's almost impossible to describe it correctly, but it is second nature. For Gargoyles, I remember the initial thrust hit me when, well, let's just say I had taken a mood enhancer and leave it at that, shall we?" Sid felt uncomfortable talking about drugs with these people. Sure, they were illegal, but they still made him smile. He had been off them for a while now, more or less, and nobody there, except for Corky, had much experience with them. At least none that they ever cared to talk about. "I saw all these little monsters running around on the floor, behind the chairs, under the table, everywhere. They weren't even paying attention to me. When I closed my eyes, they were still there, only nothing else was. I mean, it was as if they were still running around things because sometimes they'd disappear from my view right around where I knew the couch or chair was, then reappear on the other side. But the furniture wasn't there, I mean it was there, but I couldn't see it, I had my eyes closed. The whole background was black, just black. I got dizzy when I watched them with my eyes open, but with my eyes shut it was okay, they kind of glowed, y'know? And then they kind of disappeared, even with my eyes closed. Only they didn't completely disappear, I could still see just their feet running around with no bodies attached. And they were all wearing these tiny argyle socks. It was so funny, I guess that's why I remembered it. When I came back down I had these little melodies running around in my head, just like those gargoyles with their argyles. I tried to put them together and after a few weeks of playing with it, leaving it and playing with it some more, I ended up with Argyle Gargoyles."

Corky was smiling. Cliff was just saying 'uh huh' to himself.

"So, you got to the top because of some imaginary monsters. Uh, with funny socks," Barbara tried to ask.

"The top? Where I was didn't look like the top of anything to me. Besides, everybody else saw the song for exactly what they thought it was, a poorly constructed tune for which I couldn't come up with any words but used as a filler on the album anyway. The Company frowns on songs without lyrics because they rarely go anywhere on the charts.

It was almost seven minutes long the way I played it for them, and they all said it was done after three. What do they know?"

"Excuse me, but who are They?"

"They are the producer, the promoters, the record company, the businessmen, the people who aren't creative enough to play with themselves but have figured out a way to turn a profit from other people's attempts at expression. They're the ones I'm talking about when I say nobody knows what goes into making a record. I was interested in putting out a quality item, a real piece of work. They were interested in constructing a well built pile of shit with low overhead costs. About halfway through, they came to me with 'By Night, By Train' and asked me if I wanted to do it. Now when I say asked, it's like having the Mafia ask you if you want to launder some money for them. They so much as said they'd pull out their backing if I didn't do it, and do it good. I was stupid enough to think they had so much invested in me that I could call the shots, that they were the ones with something to lose. I told them I'd do it only if they'd let me use Corky on the rest of the songs. I found out you don't just tell the bossman how it's going to be. He tells you. There was a big fight and the whole thing almost collapsed. But somebody up there admired spunk, I guess, so I wound up doing the song and I got to use Corky in four songs plus on tour."

"What's the matter with them asking you to do one of your own songs?"

"I didn't write it."

"But it credits you right here," Cliff said, holding the album.

"I don't care what it says, I didn't write it. It's nothing but a hokey piece of trash on an acoustic guitar. I figured afterwards they had noticed I was running out of material that they liked. I'm sure I'm not the first one they made this sort of deal with. They said they wanted to show I was versatile. That song was as close to country and western as I ever want to get. Mind you, there's nothing wrong with country and western, some of it's pretty good, but that's not my sound. I like to make some noise sometimes, mellow out other times, but this song just wasn't what I wanted to do. They credited me with writing it, stressing the importance of a singer having original material. It might've bothered me that they probably ripped off the original composer to give it to me if it was at least a good song."

"When all the recording was done, over a year's worth of work, they took the tapes and decided in what order the songs would appear. They chose which song to release as a single, they picked the cover concept and the photography, they even gave me this silly name. But I was nobody. I had no pull at all, so what could I do, say no? When they said I could tour, they made up my playsheets, they decided who I was going to open for..."

"You didn't have anything to do with that cover? I swore that was your little tush sticking up from under those sheets," Barbara said.

"Sorry, ma'am, you've mistaken my ass for somebody else's," Sid continued. "I mean, of all the songs to release as a single, they picked Smoking in Bed. I think it turned out to be one of the weakest, clichéest songs on the album. You can't even hear some of the instruments in parts where my vocals cover them up. I would've been happier with Necro or Don't Fear the Reefer." Sid wrote that song in just a few nights after watching Reefer Madness on a public TV station. It started out like a nice fairy tale with xylophones and chimes, innocent like the characters in the beginning of the movie. Sid's vocals sounded like a meek minister practicing a stirring sermon. But just as the young people are dragged in by the evil 'weed with roots in hell', the song kicks off into a wildly spastic guitar blitz sharply executed by The Kid. They got the whole solo down in one lightning take.

"The single got good reviews and it did help sales, but people forgot I worked just as hard on the other songs, even that one they made me do. That album represents a whole year of my life. While everybody was telling me how sensational the single was, I simply wanted somebody to listen to the rest of the album and tell me what they thought of it."

Outside, one of the fans broke loose in a mad dash for the house. "Kid, please, help me, I need you!" It was a young man's voice. The police were already dragging him away by the time Sid got to the window. There he stood, hands in his pockets, slumped.

"Does that kid actually think I can help him with his problems? I don't even know who he is. Did I say anything in my songs about being a Goddamn savior?"

"You didn't have to, they like you. That's enough," Cliff said from the other room.

"Huh?" Sid spun around.

"It must really bother you, to see it come to this," Barbara said.

"Not really, not now. I knew it was coming. They aimed my stuff right at the eighteen to twenty six year old demographic. It seems they aimed a little high, that's all. I'm not even as popular as they're making me out to be. The media is blowing it out of proportion as usual. I never had any big rock parties, exotic drugs, no hoards, make that no big enough hoards of women, none of that stuff."

"You've got to do something, Sid, You can't just sit there and hope it will go away."

"Well, I hope at least the cops don't go away. I'd never be able to hold them off without their help. Who'd have thought I'd ever be thankful for cops?" Corky shook his head and rubbed his shoulder, bruised in a meeting with three guys the night before who were trying to get up on the roof.

"There's nothing I can do. I'll just have to wait until the excitement dies down. It will, you'll see." Normally the resourceful type, Sid had imagined this day coming for a while but he could never think of a single way to cope with it. 'What did I do?' he thought. 'I wrote a few songs, I cut an album so I could make some money, I never wanted all this.'

"It won't just dry up and blow away, Sid," Barbara said. Sometimes Sid really hated having those kinds of comments hanging around.

"Yes it will," he reasoned. "You know, if I wanted it to end sooner I should've stayed at it. People liked my first album, so they expected more. I could've gone ahead and done another one the way I wanted to do it, changed my style, done something different. They would have dropped me without a second thought." Sid was alone in the living room, pacing the floor. The others were listening to him talk to himself from the other room. They could grasp the ideas, but none of them, not even Corky, knew enough about what Sid was saying to really feel it. "You see, that's the one thing I learned when I finally brought myself to take a close look at my 'small but ever growing audience' (a quote from L+R). If you do something they like, they want more of it. Whether you're able to do it again or not doesn't matter, you always have to thrill them one more time. If you do, you're probably listening more to them than yourself. All that because they went out and bought your crummy album."

"And that's why you quit?"

"And that's why I quit."

"I remember that night," Corky said into his beer. "He didn't even tell me he was going to do it."

"I didn't tell anyone I was going to do it," Sid corrected. He knew it bothered Corky, but he had apologized a thousand times for it already. Barbara and Cliff looked at him expectantly, so he went on with it. "Okay, okay, I was playing this place called the Caterpillar Trap. My album had been released, so enough people knew who I was and some of them even knew the words to my songs. But one album does not a concert make. I had some more of my own stuff that I hadn't recorded, and I announced before each one that it was my song like the promoters told me to. But I still had to do some other stuff to fill out the sets, so I dug out some trusty Prine. My manager didn't like for me to cover other people's songs but he knew it was better than shortening the show. I did 'He Was In Heaven Before He Died' for the first time anywhere other than my car. It's really beautiful." Sid did a verse for them a cappella. They had heard his voice on the record, but to hear him live, well, they'd never even heard him sing along with the radio. So he really could sing after all.

"They hated it," he pronounced, forcing a smile, "they hated it. They wanted to hear what great things I had to throw at them. Never mind what a great song it was."

"I was supposed to do Necro next, according to my playsheet. But that never did sound good live, you lose the echoes and everything, so I figured screw 'em, I'm going to do what I wanted to do. Everybody got set up for Necro, but I kept my Martin in my lap and played the intro to 'Fish and Whistle'. Okay, so it was another Prine song, so sue me," Sid laughed. "Nobody knew what to do. Corky was the only one to pick up on it. He gave me a backbeat while everyone else just stood there holding their instruments. And then the guys in the lighting booth, they went ahead as scheduled and hit the program that was meant for Necro. I was sitting there, rolling no more than three chords off my acoustic and there's all these green and blue and red lights flashing and pulsing. I mean, it was actually pretty funny! Cork, where is that album?"

"Oh no, you go on with the story."

"Yeah, well, most of them just got quiet after that, except for a couple of jokers in the back who started to boo me. I hadn't been booed in a long time and it pissed me off. The heckling spread, nobody knew the song and I don't think they wanted to know me, either. At that point I'd had enough. My manager was in the wings waving like an idiot and telling me to go back to the playsheets like I was supposed to. So I gave it to them, I gave them my masterpiece, the long version of Don't Fear the Reefer."

"You should have seen it, guys. You did, didn't you, Cork? It was like giving a bottle to a crying baby. All of the sudden they liked me again. I went through the song by rote and gave them a sloppy guitar solo which they loved anyway. It ends with a long, slow fade with keyboards and drums. I told Corky and the keyboard man to just keep playing. I grabbed my Martin and stepped out of the light and towards the rear of the stage where I slipped off. I told my road manager I had to go to the bathroom. I was working with some real dumb shits. He believed me. I could have told him my guitar had to go to the bathroom and he wouldn't have questioned me. I grabbed my stuff and snuck out to the back lot where my car was parked. They never even gave me transportation. I always brought my car along, but it's the principle of the thing, you know?"

"Wait a minute, nobody saw you leave?" Barbara couldn't believe the way Sid made it sound so easy.

"The Caterpillar Trap was no Caesar's Palace, Barbara. Backstage meant exactly that. Anything that didn't have another place to be stored got shoved back there. I almost killed myself climbing over the risers, rolled up carpets, scaffolds, folding chairs, lumber, props, you name it. Most of the lights didn't work anyway. The engineers and the lighting crew were in their own booths up above and the sound crew was busy making sure we didn't blow the amps or anything because they knew how old the equipment was. Everyone else was either counting the money or watching the show. Like I said, there were no backstage parties. Within two minutes I was on the road and gone. I was about five blocks away and I'm thinking 'I sure pulled one over on those clowns, here I am behind the wheel of my car, cruising down Franklin Street, and they all think I'm going to reappear on stage for some big finale. I'd love to see their faces', so I pulled off into a parking lot and walked back to the theater. I wore an old jacket somebody had left in my car and a hat, an old knit cap my Grandma made for me. I didn't care if I got caught, I just had to see their faces. Everyone was already coming out by the time I got back. They were all stomping and bitching about what a rotten way it was to end a show. I found out later they just dropped the curtains and turned on the house lights while the band was still playing. I bet they crucified my road manager. I could just hear him. 'It's okay guys, he's just taking a leak!'. But I was out front, out there with my adoring audience, my fans. They were all so stoned or drunk they didn't even know they were outside yet. Those who were coherent enough made remarks about what a lousy show it was, how they wished The Kid would do more of his own material instead of covering songs that nobody ever heard of. I just kept walking through them all. Man, it was like being invisible! I couldn't believe nobody recognized me. I found myself walking behind this old couple, and I mean old. The husband was this tall guy, all bent over, with a head full of long, white hair tied in a pony tail. I remember he was wearing a leather jacket over a paisley shirt. His wife was this butterball of a lady, leather vest, hip boots, I mean, it was Grandma and Grandpa gone funky, y'know? Everybody walked passed them, they were moving so slow, so I came up behind them and said, 'Shitty show, huh?'. So they wife, she turns her head around to face me, and just like the grandmother she probably was, she scolds me. 'That's not a very nice thing to say'. I tell you, I just had to keep walking behind them. The husband said, 'Say, I liked the one about that there fella dying and going to Heaven. I could have stayed up late and listened to that one forever. What was it called again, Ethel?'. I stopped and watched them hobble away, fighting over the title to the song. I wanted to follow them but I had to go. I doubled back passed the entrance where they were still coming out. I didn't want to see anymore, I wanted to remember how good the old folks made me feel. I lowered my head and went back to my car. I pulled out with the people who had just been to my concert. I can't tell you what a head rush it was to be out there, unknown to any of them. I got a little cocky and took off my hat and even put the top down so that anyone who looked could see my guitar. I drove up and down those streets until all of them were gone."

Sid was cut short by another outburst from the crowd. Such events were becoming so frequent they'd stopped bothering to check them out.

"We can't keep this up forever, Sid," Barbara said. "I forgot the dog food and there's only half a case of beer left."

Corky belched. "'Scuse me."

"You forgot the dog food? Oh, I've got to think of something."

They spent that night sprawled out all over Sid's living room. They were awakened early the next morning when an enterprising young woman pulled up in a lunch truck and sold hot coffee, cocoa, donuts and sandwiches. There were easily over a hundred and fifty fans to feed. Cliff wondered where the Burgermaniac truck was. Since the incident the day before, not one reporter tried to get into the house. The police did, though, and Sid spoke with them twice before noon. They insisted Sid take some kind of action to resolve the situation, and if he didn't, they would. Sid found it easier to procrastinate rather than speak to the crowd, his fans, the people he'd been running away from for all this time. They all sat out front, some of them who really knew who he was singing his songs, other waving banners, eating overpriced ham and cheese sandwiches and wondering where they were going to go to the bathroom. Sid wondered what the cops might do to the gang of pubescents in jeans and camouflage pants, flannel shirts and funny hats, head bands, long hair and muddled expectations. He'd also been told by the police there were some representatives from several law firms out there who had some business to conduct with him.

In the midst of the stalemate, a little Mexican mailman pulled up as close as he could to Sid's house, forty car lengths away. With a stuffed mailbag slung over his shoulder, he worked his way through the crowd. They let him pass until he got to the cordon where the police checked his ID, pinned to his lapel, matching his picture to his reddening face as the mailman puffed and wheezed under his heavy load. "Neither rain nor snow nor crowd of boys and girls can stop me from making appointed rounds." His revised rendition of the mail carrier's credo sounded cute under his thick accent. Barbara was the first to spot him dragging across the snowy lawn while fans shouted messages to him to be delivered to their hero. 'Tell him to come out to us!', 'We want him back!'.

"Corky, quick, get the door." Corky waited while the mailman trudged through the snow with his huge bag. When he was close enough, Corky stepped out and took the load off his back. A cheer went up when they saw him, hoping he would be followed by their Kid. Corky invited the mailman inside. As graciously as possible, he accepted.

"Hello, everyone!" he said, straining with each syllable in his attempt to perfect the English language. Barbara handed him somebody's beer. "Thank you, thank you so much." He took a long draught and had to catch his breath again when the bottle left his lips. "Oh, you are very famous, Mr. Lasvistas. All of these mail, it is for you."

"We've only been here for two days," Sid said, speaking to the mailbag.

"Yes, and many people know now who you are. Here, I also have these for you." He handed Sid another copy of Licks and Riffs as well as the past two day's newspapers. "Hello, Mr. Dinsdale! I did not know you are here also too. I would bring your mail. Your new Sports Illsistrat, Sport Illis," he was hung up on phonetics, "your new sport magazine has arrived."

"Super, thank you," Cliff answered reasonably, imagining he'd find the pages wrinkled as usual. But it didn't bother him. He never read them anyway.

The mailman stood there, not knowing what to do, having already done all that mailmen are supposed to do. He remembered the beer in his hand and quickly chugged down what was left.

"Well, thank you," Sid checked his ID badge, "thank you, N. Velopez. It was very nice of you to go to all this trouble. I really appreciate it."

"Yes, Mr. Lasvistas. You know, I don't want for you to be offended by what I will say, but before all these crazy things they happen, I do not know who The Kid is." Sid smiled slightly, knowingly. "But my son, he is a very big fan and he ask his Father can I get for him, from you, what is the word…"

"An autograph?"

"Yes! yes, this is it! A auto graph. That is what he say to me." He already had a pen out and a blank piece of paper in his hand. "This is so nice." Of course he knew the word 'autograph'. But he also knew how to tactfully use his disadvantages to his advantage to fool others into thinking something else. Lots of people did that.

"Who do I make it out to? What is your son's name?"

"Ah." Velopez was being trapped. "Yes, his name. He is Nigel."

"I see. Nigel, huh?" Sid said. This was certainly different, he thought. "To my dear friend Nigel," he spoke as he wrote, "the bearer of good news. Best wishes to you and all your family. The Kid."

"Oh," Velopez gasped. He was visibly moved by Sid's simple sentiments. "This is so beautiful, Mr. Kid. I will, I am sure my Nigel will be very please."

"El gusto es mio," Sid said.

"Ho ho!" Velopez startled everyone with his outburst. "El gusto es mio!" He repeated Sid's words expertly as if they were part of a magical incantation. "Thank you so much, thank you everybody." He thank-youed himself out the front door and strutted tall and proud through the crowd, ignoring their questions. It was his finest hour.

Corky was already into the letters. "Come on, I'm going to need some help with these." Barbara and Cliff dug into the pile he had spilled onto the floor.

"Dear Kid," Corky read the first one out loud. "I'm so glad they found you, exclamation point. I was so worried about you, another exclamation point. I don't have anything else to say other than I love your music and I'm glad you're back. Love, two exclamation points, Sara Vaugh."

"Here's a good one." Cliff held one written in big block letters on yellow paper with extra large lines. "Dear Kid, my Daddy was glad to see you in Ricks and Riffs magazine. He likes you very much but he's sick right now so I am writing this letter for him. Love, Mindy."

"So I don't have such a literate following." Sid was still pleased. He was thinking he could get used to this sort of treatment when he noticed Barbara shoving her letter back into its envelope.

"Hey, what was that?" he asked her.

"Nothing," she said, trying to hide it.

"Come on, let's see it."

"No, it's nothing."

"All right, don't tell me, I'll guess." It didn't take a genius to figure it out from the look on Barbara's face. "Dear Kid, I'm going to kill you and rape your wife and children and burn down your house, again."

Barbara slowly handed the letter to Sid. She didn't want to open any more.

"And the winner is," Sid pulled it back out and read it, "me. Ha, I knew it." Corky looked over his shoulder, smiling also. "Dear Kid, I hate you."

"Exclamation point," Corky added.

"I'm going to kill you if it's the last thing I do." Sid started laughing. "Signed, unsigned," he commented on the lack of a signature. "It's not even original." He folded it into a paper airplane.

"How can you make fun of that? Someone just threatened your life!"

"Exclamation point," Corky added.

"Barbara, half of these letters are probably threats. If I were to take them all seriously, the Happy Wagon would be too busy chasing me instead of picking up the wack jobs that wrote them." He sailed the threat across the room.

"Oh, Savior?" Cliff said.

"Yes, my son?"

"I've got a good one for you here. Dear Kid, I am a thirty three year old divorced man. I can't afford to make this month's alimony payment. The transmission fell off my car on Porter Street. The repair bill was so high because I couldn't find all the parts. Some rolled into the sewer, I think. The IRS is refusing to accept my three hundred and fifty dollar tax credit from the new insulation I had put into my house before my wife kicked me out. I owe the three fifty, plus interest, plus auditing fees. Last week I had my first date since my divorce. She came over for dinner, I burned the spaghetti and she left after I sneezed on her. But my real problem is my feet. They're killing me. It happened in the war. I'm a veteran. They gave me the wrong size shoes. I was too scared to ask for new ones. My superiors were always picking on me."

"I think my feet are permanently damaged. I'm sending you a pair of my socks," Cliff held up the surprise he was hiding. "If you could just pray over them I'm sure my feet would feel much better."

"Is that what I smelled?" Barbara backed away. She screamed when Cliff threw them at her.

"Wait, there's more. I really liked your record. I got it a little wet when I was singing with it in the shower, though, and now it doesn't play so good. I promise to go out and buy a new one real soon. Please help me with my feet, and if you want to say anything about the other things, that's okay, too. Thank you, Cyril Womp. P.S. Some people say I look like you."

"Oh, Cyril, some people say my feet smell like yours, too, but I still can't help you."

"Hey, let's wash the socks and send them back and say Sid prayed the evil out of them," Cliff suggested.

"I say we burn the suckers," Corky proposed.

"I've got a better idea," Barbara said. "Let's nail them to the front door. That ought to keep everyone away."

The foursome was laughing and carrying on so over Cyril's socks they missed the episode out front. Two people distracted the police while four others broke through the barrier and ran for Sid's front door. While Cyril's socks might have slowed them down, it would have taken more than a couple cops to stop them. These guys were big.

The pounding at the door alerted Corky like a faithful watch dog. Sid, Bump and Grind were the back-ups. Corky opened the door a crack and the first guy busted it open the rest of the way. He rushed in at Sid as Corky clotheslined him, catching the front of the man's throat with a swinging forearm. The second one, with Corky's help, stumbled in over the first one and never even saw Sid's foot as he planted his boot right in the middle of his face. For the brief moment that he saw him, though, Sid thought the guy looked familiar. Corky was in the process of making it three in a row when number four in the rear spoke up.

"My name's Spruance."

Corky was on a roll. He couldn't stop himself from taking out number three with a right cross and a kidney punch. He would have gone for Spruance had Sid not intervened.

"Yo, down Corky," he ordered. Sid was reluctant, but it was a surprise to meet Spruance. If he was going to pull anything, he would have to do it without the aid of his little army, now sprawled on the ground.

"We have to talk," Spruance said. The cops were closing in from behind.

"In here," Sid agreed, keeping an eye on him. Corky grabbed him with both hands by the front of his coat and pulled him in. In two lightning moves that blended into one, Spruance swung both arms up under Corky's and broke the hold, then brought a slicing chop down on both sides of Corky's neck. He immediately slumped to his knees, bowing before Spruance.

"I owed him that, he took out three of my men," Spruance reasoned calmly. Sid was horrified. He'd seen Corky take on eight guys at once without dropping his sandwich. He made a guy who allegedly used to be a Hell's Angel eat a sprocket chain. He once caught someone messing with his van and put him in a phone booth then mangled it so badly the guy couldn't get back out. Well, okay, he'd only heard about that one, he didn't actually see it, but Corky was a mean guy when he had to be. Now he was kneeling in front of a reasonable but hulking, hovering Spruance. The cops joined them and grabbed Spruance, who didn't budge.

"It's okay, let him go." Sid was trusting his instincts.

"I'm not going to put up with this much longer, Lasvistas," warned the officer in charge. "You make a decision, you got that? Mobs of kids, beatings, singing. I just won't stand for it!"

The cops tried to revive two of Spruance's people. "Wait out there," he told the third. The crowd booed when they took the show inside.

"Did ya see it? He brought down the big guy!" Sid heard someone say before he closed the door.

"He's good," Spruance said of Corky. "That normally renders a man unconscious. He held on. I like that."

"He did better than your guys." Sid couldn't resist the insult. "Okay, so what do you want?" Sid wanted to know why the man who was responsible for wrecking his car, rearranging his face and trying to burn his house down had come to see him with his gorillas in tow. Sid's own gorilla was sitting on the floor in front of Barbara while she rubbed his neck.

Spruance took off his coat, revealing a lean but muscular body which was not as big as his coat made it seem. "I, we, owe you an apology."

"An apology? Well, I really appreciate that, Spruance, you're a real pal. Which one of the things you did to me would you like to apologize for? Trashing my car? How about the time you tried to fry me in the middle of the night? I might've been killed if I was home that night. You want to apologize for that?" Sid was pissed off enough to take on a dozen Spruances.

"There's no need to get condescending, Lasvistas."

"Oh, condescending. That's a mighty big word to come out of somebody who prays to fish."

"Now you listen to me. I'm here to help you, you stupid fuck!" Spruance snapped, but just as suddenly regained his composure. An uncharacteristically meek tone overcame his speech. "We didn't know who you were when we did those things to you. We're sorry. We want to make it up to you."

"Let me get this straight. You want to help me?"

"That's what he said, Sid," Barbara clarified it for him.

"You're having trouble with the cops and you're having trouble with the crowds and the media, right?"

"Yeah, and lawyers, too. But why do you want to help me?" Sid thought he knew, but he wanted to hear it from Spruance himself.

"We like your music. We all do. Personally, I like Don't Fear the Reefer the best." He fell out of character and smiled a little before he caught himself. "Besides, I believe we owe it to you."

"You mean you're not all a bunch of scum sucking, demonic, fanatical fish following, violent, vengeful opportunists?"

"No, I didn't say that. We're all of those things and then some, so don't push your luck."

"Oh, okay."

"First thing we've got to do is get a restraining order and clear the munchkins out of here. That shouldn't be a problem. They probably have it all drawn up and waiting for your signature on the dotted line."

Sid and Spruance, once unseen enemies, now orchestrated the plans to remove the fans and the media from the premises. Spruance had a unique sort of respect for Sid. He not only admired him for his music, but also for the fact he found a way to make his music real. Spruance had inclinations towards a career in music at one time, and could still play jazz sax and clarinet. But he could never find the time, incentive, drive, energy, ambition, whatever, to make what he played in private, accompanying old, scratched records, into something more public, something shared, something he felt would be more worthwhile and enriching. He envied Sid his ability to hone his craft into something more than just a closet activity. And Spruance knew all about closets, being a homosexual ex-Marine. He didn't feel comfortable about coming out now, but hey, maybe someday, y'know?

But he somehow ended up in an offbeat sect of fish followers and working as a stone mason, hardly a replacement for what he really wanted to do, but certainly proof that you never know just what's going to happen each day when you get out of bed.

He found satisfaction in helping Sid. With the restraining order, the fine for trespassing was three hundred dollars for the first offense, then mandatory sentencing. Over twenty five teenagers made the enforced monetary donation to the county and several less spent a few hours each in a detention center as a scare tactic until the rest figured maybe it was best to stay away. While this worked with the thrill seekers, it did precious little to deter the more brazen ones who thought they couldn't get caught. Had the situation been left up to the cops alone, they might've been right. But this is where Spruance and his people came into play.

Most of the time the cops didn't even know they were lurking in the trees and bushes around the house. After the first few round ups, the only surveillance the cops provided anyway was passing in a patrol car three or four times a day and less at night. Sid would wave to them from the bench when they drove by. Spruance and his friends caught three prowlers in the first five days. Some claimed to be reporters, one in particular from Licks and Riffs. None of them got the story. There were already enough articles appearing about The Kid, his short career and his recent exposure. Lawyers and old managers were trying to contact him through the mail, as well as a certain Russian-born chess player, but their letters were lost in the stacks of fan mail Nigel Velopez delivered regularly. Large packages were inspected carefully by Spruance's makeshift bomb squad, which proved to be an unwarranted precaution. Sid spent his time secretly hoping some radio station would play one of his songs. He was getting some air time again, but all he ever caught while flipping up and down the dial was the end of Smoking in Bed on a college radio station. Aside from the letters that kept pouring in and the recent formation of The Kid Fan Club and the dozen or so kids keeping constant vigil with binoculars on the far bank across the Delaware River, things were starting to calm down. That is, until one night when Mai showed up.

She'd learned of Sid's whereabouts from the scores of articles on his recent 'capture' as one reporter had put it. They spent two hours alone, consisting mainly of Sid gazing into his returned Mai's eyes. It was nearly eleven at night when Cliff got home from a visit with his parents, saw the dark green MG in Sid's driveway and decided to call when there was no answer to his knock on the front door.

Cliff told him his mother said hello, about how everyone at school was still talking about The Kid and how Sid probably didn't want to hear it, then invited him and Corky over to watch Reefer Madness on TV.

"Corky took off this afternoon on one of his excursions, Cliff," Sid said in the slow, enchanted voice of an airport Moonie, "and I'm about to go off on one of my own," he added.

"What are you talking about?"

"Cliff, Mai came back to me."

"Oh." Cliff's thoughts stalled in his head. He hadn't expected to hear that, and in the oddest way he suddenly felt replaced. This scene had been played many times over in the lives of other people, friends losing touch after one of them gets involved or married, but it had never happened to Cliff before. "That's great, Sid."

"Here, you want to talk to her?" He was already handing the phone to Mai.

"Hello, Cliff." She sounded just as he thought she would. She sounded like she wasn't wearing anything at all.

"Mai, hi." He tried to sound casual but felt stupid at his unintentional rhyme. Apparently she'd heard it before as she glazed right over it.

"So you're the Cliff Sid's been telling me about."

"Afraid so. And you're the Maivina I've heard some about and seen even more of." He tried to keep it light, not wanting her to take that seriously. He was worried he'd just embarrassed her.

Mai giggled and Cliff imagined her blushing, all over. "Sid can do wonderful things in pen and ink." Cliff was glad she took the comment in stride.

"So what brings you back here?" Cliff asked the silly question, running out of things to say already. Mai didn't mind.

"Well, you see, Sid's an old habit of mine. I guess I can't shake him." She was cut off by her own laughter as, unknown to Cliff, Sid ran his tongue across the back of her naked thigh.

"Old habits die hard," Cliff finally said, confused, not knowing what else to say. On the other end, there was silence for a second which Mai broke with deep, sardonic laughter. She never recovered from the fit and had to hand to phone back to Sid.

"Hey buddy, something good might come out of this yet, huh?"

Cliff could tell Sid was smiling. "Yeah, maybe."

"Hey, we'll see you, all right?"

"Okay, Sid. Bye."

Watching Reefer Madness alone wasn't Cliff's idea of a good time. It did put him in the mood to roll a cigarette, watching the movie and listening to Don't Fear the Reefer. He set his tobacco down on his autographed copy of Smoking in Bed that Sid had given to him, more as a joke than anything else. Its novelty was wearing off.

He went through four poor excuses for homerolls, thinking about what was going to happen now. The fifth one finally came out right. He smoked that one, too, and fell asleep on the couch just as Sid's front door opened up and a girl with dark, wispy hair that fell well beyond her shoulders stepped out. She walked lightly but firmly over the lawn which was covered with melted slush by day but by ice at night. She got into her sports car and cleanly, calmly, methodically drove off into the dark bend of the road.

Cliff awoke on the couch the next morning, soon to realize he had slept through his classes. A half smoked cigarette was clenched between his fingers. There used to be a constricting pang in his chest when he became aware of doing things like that. No more. He showered and dressed, grabbed the three hoagies he had bought on his way home last night and went next door to meet Maivina in person. He tried to think ahead of what to say to her. He was anxious to see Sid.

After waving at one of Spruance's friends hiding in the back yard, he knocked a few times but got no answer. He tried the doorknob anyway

408 Argyle Gargoyles; A Darkly Humorous Novel

which was surprisingly unlocked. He went in and closed the door behind himself, calling out. He might have realized it wasn't any use had he closed the door by the inner knob, which was both dry and sticky with a dark paste.

"Yo, lunch is here, you two. Screwing makes you hungry." No answer. "That's what I've heard, anyway," he said, not loud enough for anyone but himself to hear.

He went to the kitchen and unrolled his hoagie out of its white paper. He'd gotten Sid his usual, roast beef and cheese with extra mayo. "I hope you like ham and cheese, Maivina," he called upstairs, citing Corky's favorite. He was careful to use her full name, to not sound too familiar, although he knew Sid wouldn't mind. He stuck his head into the living room to glimpse at her drawing.

"Hey, come on you guys, your hoagies are getting cold," he tried to joke at the silence that was beginning to unnerve him. He realized then about the car he had seen in the driveway last night, that it was probably Maivina's and they were both out somewhere. He started getting that feeling of being alone in a stranger's house again and figured he'd better leave. But the door was unlocked, and that was odd, especially nowadays. He went to the kitchen window and looked out back to see the familiar sight of Bump and Grind playing in the yard.

Holding his hoagie like a flashlight, he went to the bottom of the steps. Since the reconstruction, Sid had moved his bedroom to the room at the top of the stairs where the fires had broken out.

"Hey, look, if you don't like hoagies I'll get something else." As he'd expected, no answer. He started to run up the steps, following his lunch's lead. He looked curiously similar to a man who had once chased deer into the forest with a hot dog. He stopped in the open stairwell when his eyesight was level with the second floor. He was still five steps away from the top but he could see Sid's room, the door only slightly ajar. The hallway was well lit by the window that opened into it, an innovation of the contractors. Cliff stood there for several minutes.

"Wake up you two?" Still trying to convince himself they were in there, he was reluctant to approach. He looked very silly and a little scared as he followed his hoagie up the remaining steps and soon found his feet taking him up to the door. He knocked loudly, ready to say something, when he realized he was knocking the door open even farther. He grabbed it and pulled it back. He didn't notice the absence of snoring, which Sid did for each of the five months he stayed with Cliff, as he was overcome with a nasty, gagging odor clearly coming from Sid's room. He had never smelled anything like that before, sure he would have remembered if he did. He backed up and set his hoagie down on the floor before returning his attention to the door.

"Hey, what've you guys got in there, anyway?"

Cliff, finally reckoning with the fact something had happened, boldly stepped into Sid's bedroom. He first averted his eyes, not wanting to embarrass Sid or Maivina if they were in some awkward position. When his entrance got no response and he could no longer hold his breath against the horrid odor, he looked straight ahead.

Sid was the only one in any position as he was the only one on the bed. Spread eagle, on his back, his wrists were tied to the massive headboard with leather thongs. Cliff's first fear, first of many, was that the piled, bloodied sheets near Sid's side was really part of his guts that had spilled out from the gaping slash across his belly. There were long, dripping streaks all over his body, including a shallow one across his face. The once white sheets were more than soaked with Sid's blood which was actually turning to a rust color where it lay thin on his skin, drying for hours. The thicker clots were red, as blood should be. Cliff would later be thankful that at least his eyes were closed. On the corner of his bed, next to his one unbloodied foot, was Sid's straight blade razor. No light gleamed off the clean metal, and only a trace of red stained the ivory handle. The one image Cliff would have the most trouble forgetting, though, had something to do with an old adage coming true. It was revolting, sickening, but old habits do die hard.

Maivina was caught only five miles away in an all night service station. She didn't pull up to the pumps, she just pulled in to get off the road. After twenty minutes, when the solitary attendant came out to see if he could help her, he noticed the blood on her neck and hands and immediately called an ambulance, thinking she was hurt. She stayed behind the wheel shaking, the only other sign of life she showed aside from fighting off the attendant. The engine was still running even when the ambulance arrived. At the sight of the flashing red lights, she lurched the car forward a few feet and into a retaining wall. The paramedics finally got her out and she started screaming. "…The bastard, the bastard!". They soon discovered she hadn't been hurt herself, rather she'd hurt someone else, and called the police.

The investigations and reports, as well as the many psychiatric evaluations which ensued, would reveal that Sid had lived with her as the last in a string of girlfriends before his career took off. Like the others before her, she brought all the money into the relationship. He rarely held down a job for very long, preferring to sink deeply into his music, promising to share his fame and fortune with her, just as he had done with all the others. After two and a half years of supporting him, she finally had enough and walked out on him. Shortly thereafter, when he hit it big and made all that money, or so she assumed, Mai felt cheated, she felt like he owed her something. She was never impressed by the sentiments in Oh My Mai. She only saw it as him using her to write a song to make money, none of which she would ever see.

She never heard from Sid. The truth was, he intended to find the time to look for her but was too wrapped up in the recording studio, and after that with his road shows. He did try to contact her once or twice during that time, but people who walk out on a relationship rarely leave a forwarding address. When he went underground, he couldn't afford to look for her for fear of attracting attention to himself. It was enough of a risk scooping Corky out of Nevada. His music had pulled him into a vicious circle. When he was ultimately discovered, one of the reasons he decided to stick it out was because he secretly hoped Mai would come looking for him. She did, of course, but not for the reasons Sid had in mind.

Sid's body was cremated and his ashes spread over the ocean. Memorial services were held by thousands of fans, and even more articles came out about the tragic story of the 'Erstwhile troubadour of American pop culture'. Plans were made to re-release his album, this time with rare studio versions and a bonus track of a previously unreleased song, plus a ten page retrospective published by The Kid Fan Club.

Corky, who undoubtedly heard all about it while out on the road again, never came back. In the days following Sid's death, Cliff locked himself up in his house. The only person he saw was Barbara, spending an evening with her, just talking all night about everything that had happened. The remainder of those days he spent alone. He only cried once, when there was a knock at the door. 'Hello, Mr. Dinsdale? I'm Fred Winget, I'm with Licks and Riffs music magazine. Can I ask you a few questions, please? Hello, Mr. Dinsdale, are you in there…'.

Cliff would remember the day in the beginning of December when he emerged, clean shaven, hair combed, clean clothes, smoking a homeroll. The cold air stung his lungs. For the first time in over two weeks, he went next door to Sid's house. A police officer guarded the front door of the house where nothing had yet been removed. They were waiting for word from any family Sid might have had. So far, seventy men claimed to be long lost uncles or brothers and forty four women said they were sisters or cousins. Some even claimed to be his grandmother.

Cliff was disappointed to see only a patrol car in the driveway. He walked across the lawn, a spare set of keys in his pocket given to him by his friend long ago. The cop stopped him as he went to check the garage.

"I'm sorry, sir, you'll have to leave the premises." He said it in such an official manner that Cliff started to laugh, recalling the episode in the same spot with a certain fire marshal. "You have to leave, sir," he repeated.

"I know, I'll only be a minute." The officer stepped forward and forcibly restrained Cliff from going any further. From the bench out front, Mr. H. stood up and faced them. Cliff didn't even notice him out there until he lifted two fingers to his lips and let out a shrill whistle. He smiled and casually sat back down as Spruance and five other men came out of nowhere, rushed the policeman, and somehow gagged him and handcuffed him to a tree on the side yard. They didn't even hurt the man, that was never the intent. There would be repercussions for sure, but that would have to wait for a later time. Spruance also broke in the front door for Cliff, all without saying a word. Cliff just shrugged his shoulders, looked over to see that the policeman was okay, considering he was hugging a tree, and went in.

He found the Mustang in the garage where he'd hoped it would be. He opened the big, swinging doors, started up and backed down the driveway into the street, pulling up in front of the bench.

"They're helping me guard the house," Mr. H. said. Bump and Grind were resting obediently at the ends of leashes. Cliff wondered who Mr. H. was talking about, the dogs or Spruance's men. "Almost lost them, you know. Good thing he never registered them." The dogs had none of their usual pep. One of them was lying on its side, panting.

"You going to miss him, Mr. H.?"

He took the pipe out of his mouth. "Me? Naw," Mr. H. muttered gruffly through a week's worth of soft gray stubble covering his cheeks.

"Me neither." Cliff drove away slowly, watching the three of them in the rear view mirror.

It was another overcast day. The snow had all melted away a week ago and it was nearly cold enough to snow again, maybe. Cliff put another homeroll between his lips and reached for the cigarette lighter. In the empty hole where it should have been, he found loose stick matches. He smiled. He struck one on the dashboard, lit up and pushed in the tape that was sticking halfway out of the tape deck. He took off.

It was the end of another John Prine song, one Cliff couldn't recall ever hearing before. But he liked it.

Today I walked down a street I used to wander
Yeah, shook my head, and I made myself a bet
There was all these things that I don't think I remember
Hey, how lucky can one man get
Hey, how lucky can one man get
Hey, how lucky can
one
man
get.

Made in the USA
Charleston, SC
03 April 2013